THE CURE

A novel

BY

Bradlee Frazer

Diversion Books

A Division of Diversion Publishing Corp.
80 Fifth Avenue, Suite 1101
New York, New York 10011

www.DiversionBooks.com

First Diversion Books edition June 2012.

ISBN: 978-1-938120-32-9

CHAPTER 1

Craig Marcus did not enjoy watching people die. The Driver, on the other hand, enjoyed it very much. Marcus mused over this fact as he stared at the surrounding sea of cactus and sand that blistered in the Arizona sun, mesmerized by the dull thrum of the tires and the sameness of the landscape flowing past his window. His head bobbed, his chin dropped to his chest and his hand twitched, jostling the Coke can in the cup holder.

"How old is she?" the Driver asked.

Marcus' head snapped up and his gut tightened. He looked at the man driving the car, studied his cold gunmetal eyes and then noticed for the first time that he still wore a "Hello My Name is Walter" sticker on the lapel of his matte black jacket, no doubt a vestige of some social event to which he had driven Phillip Porter, and then Porter had made him accompany him inside. "Thirty-one," Marcus said. The Driver did not respond, but Marcus looked at him and watched his face as the corners of his mouth twitched upward, not quite forming a smile. Marcus grimaced at the display.

"Nice," the Driver said.

Marcus opened his mouth in protest, a finger extended toward the Driver's head. "Look Walter," he said, "you —"

The Driver glared, cutting him off. "Only Mr. Porter can call me that," he said. "Please don't forget."

Marcus inhaled as if to speak, then withdrew his finger and wilted. He turned away to continue watching the parade of desert flora.

The Mercedes pulled into a long cobblestone driveway, and Marcus saw the stately facades and sun-bleached columns of The Complex's red brick buildings. Like a college campus, Marcus thought, except for the hundred miles of lifeless desert surrounding the place. The Driver nosed the Benz into a space labeled "Dr. Craig Marcus," and they got out of the car. Marcus felt the sun's heat burning his scalp, and he stole an envious glance at the Driver's thick, short-cropped hair.

The security guard at the entrance scanned their lapel badges and said, "Hello, Dr. Marcus," before looking back down to his computer screen. He did not acknowledge the Driver. Marcus stepped through the metal detector into the lobby and offered silent thanks for air conditioning, then headed toward the elevator, the Driver on his heels.

Marcus stabbed the call button twice, then stepped back and looked around. "Where is everyone?" he said. The Driver shrugged. Marcus inhaled and enjoyed the medicinal tang of Mentholatum and rubbing alcohol, the smell of childhood visits to the doctor's office. His reverie was interrupted when the elevator doors popped open and the Driver grabbed his elbow to pull him into the car.

Music was playing, tinny and flat, from a speaker hidden in the elevator's roof. Marcus heard mumbling and looked over at the Driver, who was, despite the elevator's subdued lighting, sliding on a pair of sunglasses, snake-like and cool. Marcus noticed that the Driver's lips were moving: " . . . long and lovely, the girl from Ipanema goes walking . . . ." The Driver was singing along with the Muzak.

The elevator doors opened, exposing the third floor lobby, and they stepped out into an empty foyer where the hospital smell was stronger and the air was cold. Marcus shuddered and looked around, aware of the security cameras trained on him. He saw no nurses' station, only a lone sign indicating that rooms 312-320 were down a hallway to the left. It was quiet, except for the occasional murmuring of conversation coming from the rooms. Marcus tried to make out the words, but they were muffled and distant, like they were coming from yesterday. "What was the room number again?" he said, his voice bouncing down the cinderblock corridor.

The Driver motioned Marcus to walk in front of him. "Three-one-eight," he said, singsong, "The Girl from Ipanema" still coloring his intonation. Marcus hesitated, then sucked in a breath and headed down the hall.

Marcus walked with determination and focus, aware of the Driver right behind him, their heels clicking in cadence on the polished tile floor, the kind the janitors were always buffing in grade school. He looked left and right into the rooms as they walked. *Click, click, click.* He could see big chrome hospital beds with crisp white linens enclosing thin, pale patients. Most of them were alone. Some were reading. Others watched television. Almost all of them had no hair. *Click, click, click.* Marcus kept walking and forced himself to keep his eyes straight ahead.

"Three-one-eight," the Driver said, pointing.

Marcus glanced at the nameplate on the door: "Katrine Waters," he said. He peeked inside and saw a woman lying in bed with various plastic bags hooked on poles beside her, potions dripping into her veins. She was reed thin and pale, her skin translucent against her bones. "She looks bad," he whispered to the Driver.

"Yep," the Driver said as he clapped Marcus on the back. "Good job." A man and a little girl were with the woman, and the Driver pointed at them, his left eyebrow raised. "Husband and daughter," Marcus said.

The Driver made a face.

Marcus forced a smile and stepped forward, the Driver at his side. He listened, a doctor's instinct, for the EKG's beeping as he entered the room, but the woman's labored breathing eclipsed the monitor's sounds.

The little girl sat on the bed next to her mom while the husband stood nearby, the family talking and laughing, a folded-up cot and sleeping bag against the wall behind him, a picture of displaced domesticity. The conversation stopped when Marcus and the Driver entered the room.

"Hello, Dr. Marcus," Katrine wheezed. She tried to smile. Her husband did not. Marcus moved to the bed and took the woman's hand in his as Katrine brushed a wisp of hair out of her face and said, "You don't have a bottle of Rogaine on you by any chance, do you?"

Marcus laughed. "Oh, come on," he said. "You look great. Besides, your hair will grow back when we finish the treatments. How are you feeling?" The Driver had retreated to a corner of the room and now watched from the shadows, sunglasses glowing alien-like with reflected light.

"I'm O.K., I guess—except for the nausea." Katrine inhaled, and then coughed a deep hollow cough that shook her entire frame.

"You know what they say," Marcus said. "'They have to kill you to save you.'" The Driver snickered once, and then the room fell silent as the failed attempt at humor hung in the air, an elephant in the corner of the room. Marcus cleared his throat and turned to the child. "And how are you, Amy?" he said.

The little girl scooted up toward the pillow and placed her hand on her mother's shoulder. Katrine responded and reached out to stroke her daughter's hair. "Thanks, sweetie," Katrine said. Amy smiled, but her eyes glistened.

"Amy," Marcus said, "do you like stickers?" The little girl nodded, and Marcus pulled a package of dinosaur stickers from his jacket pocket. He handed them to Amy, who grinned and held them up to show her mom. Katrine smiled and said, "Thanks."

The husband caught Marcus' attention and motioned him to the foot of the bed. Marcus moved to join him and saw the Driver scowl, so Marcus placed his hand on the man's shoulder and turned him away from the caustic expression. The husband paused for a moment before speaking, his hand on his forehead. "The drugs you're giving her are killing her," he finally said in a rasp, his eyes rimmed with red, his chin covered with three-day's growth of beard.

Marcus tightened his grip on the man's shoulder. "I appreciate your concern, Mike, but the trial won't be done for another two wee—"

"She'll be *dead* in two weeks," Mike said, cutting Marcus off, his voice rising. "You and I both know you're just guessing at this since this disease is new and no one really knows what it is or how to treat it. I mean, look what it's doing to her!"

Marcus looked at the Driver, his scowl now ugly and coarse, and moved Mike farther from the bed. "Look, you've got to calm down," Marcus said, his voice low. "It's not a good idea to let Katrine see you get upset. Your attitude is a big part of her recovery."

Mike took a deep breath and looked at the floor, and Marcus threw a reassuring nod to the Driver, who still glowered at the pair. "Besides," Marcus continued, "we have all the facilities here to monitor—"

"Daddy!"

Marcus stopped mid-sentence, interrupted by Amy's scream. Mike shoved Marcus out of the way and ran to the side of the bed, where Katrine sat bolt upright, the color gone from her cheeks, her eyes staring dully ahead. Mike held her shoulders and searched her face for recognition. "Honey?" he said. "Baby?"

Suddenly, as if to answer, Katrine began to cough. Not polite coughs, but rasping barks that shook her body again and again, her breathing now reduced to wheezing gasps, the EKG racing with arrhythmia. Amy moved back away from her mom and huddled at the foot of the bed, her knees to her chest. Mike held Katrine's face in his hands. "Calm down, baby," he begged, but the convulsions threw her head back and forth, and she clawed at his arms. He turned to Marcus. "Do something!" he shouted.

Marcus rushed forward with a start and grabbed the phone on the nightstand, punched numbers on the keypad and held the receiver to his ear. "Answer!" he shouted. He threw the phone to the floor and turned to run into the hallway, but stopped short of the door, listening: the coughing had stopped. He looked at Katrine. She was no longer convulsing, and her head now rested against Mike's chest. Mike was stroking her hair and whispering, "It's O.K. It's O.K."

Marcus ran to Katrine, but Mike had enveloped her. "Let go!" Marcus shouted as he forced his hands between their bodies and pulled them apart, pushing Katrine back onto the mattress. "Take Amy," he commanded. Mike grabbed the little girl, now silent, too frightened to cry, and held her. Father and daughter stood by the side of the bed, watching Marcus depress Katrine's sternum. "Come on, Katrine," he said through clenched teeth. "One, two, three, four, five—breathe," he recited, trying to remember the rhythm. Marcus stopped pushing, put his mouth around Katrine's cold lips, and exhaled. He felt the disease resist him, and listened to his breath rattle and bubble as it came back out her fluid-filled lungs. He again put his hands on her chest. "One, two, three, four, five."

Mike held Amy tight, her face against his chest, but she slipped from his embrace and moved to the corner of the room, where she crumpled into a ball, her arms over her head. In the other corner, the Driver watched, his face still and cold.

Marcus heard a noise in the hallway and looked up to see two nurses and an orderly barrel into the room. He backed away from Katrine as the team descended on her and affixed tubes to her throat and stuck needles in her arms, and kept moving back until he bumped into the wall, where he stood, pale and sweating, watching Katrine stiffen and jump in response to the paddles they placed on her chest, again and again.

The Driver looked over at Marcus, and then sidled up next to him and put his arm around his shoulder. "Pretty brave," the Driver said, his voice low. "Wrapping your mouth around her mouth like that. Never know what you might catch. Yeah, brave," he said, "but still, it didn't help, did it?" The Driver leaned closer, placed his lips next to Marcus' ear and whispered, "Way to go, Killer."

THE CURE

—

The specialist's office was located in the wooded hills near the University of California San Francisco Medical Center. The receptionist ushered the Holloways into a conference room lined with diplomas and certificates and dark walnut paneling. "Dr. Marcus will be with you in just a minute," she said.

The three sat in silence while the little girl played with a Mighty Morphin' Power Rangers doll until the door opened and a man with thinning hair and wire-rimmed glasses came into the room. He wore a blue pinstripe suit, black wingtips, and a red silk tie. Carmen looked up and managed a slight smile, but Tom remained impassive, his face unchanged. Tom extended a calloused hand, and the man clasped it within long slender fingers finished by well-groomed nails. "I'm Craig Marcus," the man said.

"Tom Holloway, and this is my wife Carmen."

They shook hands, and Dr. Marcus joined the Holloways at the table. He looked at the little girl and smiled. "You must be Jennifer," he said.

The girl looked up, wary, her eyes and face carrying worry and pain. She twisted Red Ranger's arms until they were almost pulled from the sockets. "Jenny," she said.

Marcus smiled. "Jenny. Got it." He reached out and touched Red Ranger. "Is this your doll?" he said.

Jenny rolled her green eyes. "Action figure," she said.

He nodded. "Ah. Sorry. Do you like stickers?"

Jenny smiled. Marcus pulled a package of stickers from his jacket pocket and laid them on the table. Jenny examined the gift, and her smile vanished. "Barney's for babies," she said.

"Strike three," Marcus said.

Carmen grabbed the stickers and placed them in her purse. She scolded Jenny with a frown, and then looked at Marcus. "Sorry," she said, "she's tired."

"Not a problem," he said, smiling a little, his eyes still on Jenny. "I hear you don't feel very good."

"Uh-uh," she said.

"Why don't you tell me what happened?"

Jenny looked up at Carmen for support, and Carmen nodded. "Well," Jenny said, with the practiced recitation of a doctor's office veteran, "my friend Ben and me were playin' with Hoover and —"

"Who's Hoover?" Marcus said.

Jenny grinned. "Hoover's my dog. He's a Jack Daniels terrier."

"Russell," Carmen corrected her. "Jack Russell terrier."

"Oh," Marcus said. "I like terriers."

"So anyway, we were throwin' a ball for Hoover and I fell and broke my leg." Jenny pointed at her cast. "When I went to the doctor to get it fixed, they found that my bones were all messed up inside me."

Carmen exhaled, her shoulders slumped. "The fall shattered her femur," she said. "They operated to insert some metal pins and screws, and they couldn't do much with what they found. So they sent us here."

Marcus nodded, and then opened a folder on the table. "I spoke to Jenny's doctor," he said, looking down at his notes. "No specific diagnosis," he said. "That's odd. Most juvenile illnesses are well defined. But we've been hearing more and more about this new idiopathic—"

"Huh?" Tom said.

"Sorry. Means 'of unknown origin.' New idiopathic disease that has symptoms like this."

Carmen opened her own folder and pulled out a well-worn piece of lined notebook paper. "Tom and I have been over it and over it, and we can't afford to pay you very much—here's our budget, so you can see for yourself." She slid the paper across the table. "But we'll do whatever we can, as long as you can help Jenny."

Marcus looked up from his notes, then reached out and slid the paper back toward Carmen. "I'm not worried about money right now. Let's worry about Jenny first. Yes?"

Tom relaxed at Marcus' words. He adjusted his baseball cap, and then put the paper into his pocket. "Sounds good to me," he said.

"Good," Marcus said. "Now. How's she been feeling?"

Carmen's bottom lip began to quiver. She grabbed the arms of her chair and took a series of labored breaths, fighting tears as Tom watched, his face red. Finally, Carmen's breathing eased and she loosened her grip on the chair. "It's been really hard," she said. "We're afraid she's going to hurt herself."

"They said her bones are all brittle now, like an old lady's," Tom said. "We keep thinking she's going to break—like a china doll."

Marcus looked at Jenny and reached out to pat her hand. "It's probably doing Jenny more harm than good for you to be overly cautious," he said. "When you're stressed, Jenny gets stressed, and that's not conducive to her getting better."

Tom shifted in his chair but didn't speak, and Carmen made an obvious effort not to look in his direction. "We'll work on it," she said.

Marcus looked back at his notes. "I understand Jenny's doctor couldn't offer you many different treatment options."

Carmen sat up with purpose, animated now, tears gone. "Yes," she said, "yes, that's right. We've done a lot of research on our own on the Internet, and this bone thing is really weird, but there seem to be more and more cases like Jenny's around the country. Like a new strain of flu or something. Her pediatrician said you were the best diagnostician around, and that all these new cases were coming to you," Carmen said. Tom grunted an affirmation.

"Thank you," Marcus said. "I admit that I am intrigued by this, as I've also seen several new patients presenting with similar symptoms."

Tom blanched and swallowed hard, then spoke up. "The leg," he said. He looked at Jenny, who was moving Red Ranger through a series of high kicks worthy of the Rockettes. "Can we save it?"

Jenny looked up, her face pale. "My leg? Cut off my leg?"

Tom picked Jenny up and moved her to the couch on the other side of the room. "No, honey, everything's gonna be fine.

You play over here, O.K.?" he said. Jenny, suspicious and not mollified, watched the adults out of the corner of her eye. Tom returned to the desk and whispered, "The leg?"

Marcus cleared his throat. "It depends on how damaged the femur is, and her other bones and surrounding tissues. From what I have seen, this thing, this new disease, whatever it is, spreads quickly."

"Metastasizes," Carmen interrupted.

Marcus nodded. "'Metastasize' is a cancer word, but yeah, that's a good analogy. It seems to start in the lungs and then move to the bones."

Carmen nodded, her jaw clenched to preempt more quivering.

"So there's probably not much we can do with surgery at this point," Marcus said.

Tom nodded. "So there's no reason to take the leg."

Marcus shook his head.

"Thank heavens," Carmen said. She turned and gave Jenny a thumbs-up, and Jenny beamed. "So," Carmen said, turning back to Marcus, "what next?"

"We need to figure out what this is, run some more tests," he said.

Tom and Carmen sat, staring at Marcus, until Tom began to stir. "That's it?" he said. "'Tests?' We're not just going to let her die while you run more tests! We need to do something now!"

Marcus shifted in his seat. "Of course you're not going to let her die, Mr. Holloway," he said. "What I'm telling you is that it is pointless for me or any doctor to try something to help Jenny until we know what's wrong with her." Marcus glanced up at Tom's "Kreizenbeck Construction" baseball cap. "You don't use a cement mixer to hammer a nail," he said.

Tom stood and pointed his finger at Marcus. "I've had just about enough of you doctors!" he yelled. Carmen motioned to Jenny, who slid onto her mother's lap and put her head on her shoulder. Carmen put her arms around the girl and smoothed

Jenny's strawberry blonde curls against her chest as the two hunkered down together, seasoned veterans, to wait out the approaching storm. "I may look stupid just because I work for a living and my hands are rough, not like yours," Tom said, "but I am not stupid, and I am tired of you getting our hopes up and then telling us all we can do is more tests. If that's the best you can do, well then, no thanks."

Marcus extended his hand and gestured toward the chair. "Sit down, Tom," he said. "Please."

Tom's face was still red as he stood and stared down at Marcus, breathing hard. Finally, he turned and sat.

Marcus cleared his throat. "We are fortunate that I have access to some very sophisticated tests in a very sophisticated setting, tests that Jenny's pediatrician did not have, so that we can figure out what this is and find something that will help her," he said.

Tom looked hard at him through squinted eyes. "I'm listening," he said.

—

The sun had long since disappeared into the Pacific and was now only a rose-colored glow from beyond the edge of the western horizon. Marcus sat at his desk and looked out at the Bay through a large window, the spires of the Golden Gate Bridge just visible to his left. He turned on a reading lamp, its light casting him in stark shadow against the beige office walls. His computer monitor displayed a web site containing search results on news stories about a mystery virus, and Jenny's file lay open on the desk next to a half-empty bottle of Dewar's and a shot glass. Marcus sighed. "Damn," he said. "Damn the disease, and damn Phillip Porter." He picked up the telephone handset and punched a series of numbers, then refilled the tumbler. He tossed back the whiskey and swallowed, appreciating the burn and hoping the spirits would dull his comprehension. "Mr. Porter?" he said through clenched teeth, "this is Craig Marcus."

He closed his eyes and rubbed the bridge of his nose, the Scotch not working. "I've got a promising new candidate for The Complex."

CHAPTER 2

–

JASON

The face in the mirror was not handsome, but it clearly suggested good humor and a love of the outdoors—a bit leathery, offset by laugh lines. At the moment, the face was covered with shaving cream. Jason Kramer yawned and stared at the reflection, taking his usual Monday morning inventory. "Yuck," he said. "Need juice." He studied his bulbous nose, then pushed it up and out of the way of the razor.

"Jason, breakfast!"

"Coming!" Jason yelled back. He finished shaving, toweled his wavy brown hair, pulled on a T-shirt and boxers, then dropped to the floor beside the bed and knocked out fifty push-ups. He bounced to his feet and trotted downstairs to the living room, where he leaned down and eyed the two goldfish swimming slow circles in the aquarium. "Mornin' boys," Jason said, sprinkling a pinch of food into the tank before moving into the kitchen.

Linda Kramer, her blond hair drawn back in a French braid, a navy blue suit and black pumps her uniform of the day, stood at the sink eating cold cereal and scanning the front page of the *San Francisco Chronicle*, her Droid and iPad waiting by the door. Jason watched, amused, as she groped around the countertop for the sugar dispenser and counted to himself "one one thousand, two one thousand . . ." as she dumped the white crystals into her bowl for a full five seconds. "You're late," she said without turning around, eyes glued to the paper, dispenser in hand. "I made you breakfast."

Two pieces of nominally toasted white bread, limp with butter, sat on a plate by the refrigerator. "Yum," Jason said, holding up one slice by a soggy corner.

Linda's face remained stony. "I'm thinking of a two-word phrase," she said. "The first word is 'smart' and the second word starts with an 'a'."

Jason grinned at her riposte. "Nice talk for so early in the morning," he said. He watched Linda and admired her slender lines and graceful neck, the muscles in her calves enhanced by the nude hose she wore. "You look nice today," he said.

Linda managed a weak smile, milk and cereal in the corners of her mouth, the open Cap'n Crunch box at her elbow.

Jason moved to the other counter, removed a blender from the cupboard above his head, and plugged it in. "Might as well just eat sugar cubes," he said.

Linda turned and watched him fiddle with the appliance. "Maybe," she said, "but it's better than that health crap you eat."

Jason sliced carrots, broccoli, and beets into the blender, then pulled a bottle of tomato juice from the refrigerator and poured a liberal shot on top of the vegetables. "Not crap. Antioxidants. Make you strong, like *bull,*" he said, doing his best Russian weightlifter accent.

Jason measured out two heaping tablespoons of protein powder and dumped them into the concoction. Linda made a gagging noise, then said, "I can't take this. I'm outta here." She turned to grab her computer, but stopped at the sink and poured a glass of water. Jason watched her for a moment, then sneaked up behind her, put his arms around her waist, and nuzzled her neck with his cheek.

"Hey!" Linda yelled as she jerked away, the tumbler crashing to the floor and shattering, glass shards littering the linoleum. Linda wiped her ear, then turned to Jason and thrust her hand out to him, shaving cream dollops dotted with blood covering her fingertips.

"Oh, man," he said, rubbing his cheek. "Guess I missed some. Sorry."

Linda grabbed a dishtowel and wiped her hand and the side of her face, the white cloth now tan with removed foundation. "You're always sorry," she said, still rubbing. "You better not have gotten blood on my jacket! I have a client meeting first thing." She looked at the floor in disgust. "And clean up this mess," she said. She started to turn toward the door, then paused and said over her shoulder, "Remember, don't be late tonight."

"I won't," he said, taking a gulp from the blender. "I didn't get to run this morning, so I want to get to the track before it gets crowded." Silence descended on the kitchen, and Jason felt Linda staring at him—*that* stare, the baby-blue stare that condescended and emasculated at the same time.

"You've forgotten, haven't you?" she said.

Jason looked away, out the kitchen window. He saw his neighbor, a single man in his early twenties, getting into his car. Another neighbor, an elderly woman, was walking her dog. She looked up at Jason, then smiled and waved. Jason smiled back. "I, . . ." he muttered.

"This is important to me, Jason," Linda said. "I try to remember things that are important to you."

Jason looked back, but Linda was gone, halfway to the parking garage, her heels smartly striking the cement sidewalk. He made a move to follow her, but pulled up short and cried out in pain, a glass shard protruding from his left heel. He grabbed his injured foot and hopped around the kitchen, blood dripping onto the floor, red connect-the-dots on the white linoleum. He limped to the door, opened it, and shouted, "Linda, wait!" but she was gone.

—

"You're late," Scott Durrant said.

Jason jumped. "I hate it when you do that."

"That's why I do it," Scott said.

"Just because the cubicle walls are six feet tall and you're six-four doesn't give you the right to scare the wits out of people by sticking your head over the top and blabbering down at them."

"But you can see me coming," Scott said, wounded.

"Yeah, if you consider a mop of blond hair bobbing along the top of the partitions as fair warning," Jason said.

Scott took a sip from his "I'm a Programmer–Byte Me" coffee mug. "Missed you this morning. You know how I hate to run alone."

Jason sighed. "Sorry. I got up late. How was it?"

"Great, except I hit the wall at five miles. Must have been all that pizza last night."

"Not to mention the beers," Jason corrected. "That stuff is gonna kill you."

"Yeah, but what a way to go. I'd rather die young from pizza than live to be a hundred eating that brownish-green goo you do." Scott grinned at his unintentional rhyme, and then came around the cubicle wall into Jason's work area where three piles of spreadsheets sat on his desk, each stack held down by a small sign. The first sign read, "Jason Kramer–Financial Analyst." The second read, "Pressure Makes Diamonds," and the third sign read, "Work Hard–Play Hard." On a shelf above his computer were a framed picture of Linda and a golf trophy inscribed with the words, "JASON KRAMER–FIRST PLACE."

Scott looked around for a chair. "Where's a guy supposed to sit?" he said as he shoved a stack of papers off a bookcase and parked himself. He looked up at Linda's picture. "So how was W-Cubed this morning?" he said, his grin exposing white, horsey teeth.

"I don't know what your beef with her is," Jason said. "And she's *not* the Wicked Witch of the West."

"You're right. She's a babe, and you're whipped," he said. Scott's smile then faded into deadpan seriousness. "I'm a psychic," he said, "and I can foresee that she will be subjecting you to unbearable torture in exactly . . ." Scott glanced at his watch ". . . 10 hours and 20 minutes."

Jason stared back without comprehension until Scott pointed at Jason's desk calendar. There it was, in red letters with a little box around it: "Lawrences– 7:00–Provençal." Jason shook his head, and then looked up at Scott. "Yikes. Keith and Mary Lawrence," he said. "I forgot."

Scott grinned. "I bet W-Cubed was pissed that you spaced it."

Jason kicked off his loafer and massaged his heel where the glass shard had punctured him. "Don't call her W-Cubed," he said, "and yeah, she was." Jason dug into his pocket, pulled out a five-dollar bill, and wagged it at Scott. "Here's a fin if you'll go in my place."

Scott slurped coffee from the mug and stood up to leave the cubicle. "Not on your life, sucker," he said.

"Dude! You know what this dinner will turn in to. Three-on-one against Jason the Loser for not being 'all he can be,' as my dad, the ex-Marine, was fond of saying."

"Um, that's an Army thing, the 'Be All You Can Be.' Marines is 'Semper Fi.'"

"Whatever," Jason said. "Remember how he almost got us to enlist after high school?"

Scott nodded. "Thank heavens I read that programmers in the private sector start out making $80,000 a year or I might be working on a computer in the middle of the desert right now."

"Yeah, he was thrilled that I was able to get someone like Linda to marry me. His last words to me were, literally, like 'Take care of Linda, son.' So when they all start bashing me tonight for not making more money or whatever the condescension *du jour* is, I am sure I will see his crew cut and stern face floating over the table staring down at me at . . ." Jason glanced at his calendar ". . . Provençal."

Scott laughed. "If you start hallucinating like that at least you'll have an excuse to leave the dinner. Have a ball, dude!"

—

In an overpriced French restaurant in the Embarcadero, Jason was trying hard to stay focused, but Provençal's Vichyssoise made him queasy, and Keith's high, whiny voice made his head hurt. He caught his reflection, pale and gaunt, in the back of his spoon, and sweat beaded his forehead. Jason waved at the waiter and pointed at his empty water glass.

"My Lord it was hot, though," Keith said.

"Small price to pay for two weeks in Barbados," Linda said.

"The beaches were magnificent," Mary said. "Pure white sand, and you could see the bottom of the ocean out to about thirty feet." Linda placed her hands together and sighed.

"You and Jason really should come with us sometime," Mary continued. "The four of us always have such fun together." She looked at Jason. "Isn't that right, Jason?"

Jason smiled blandly and nodded, then smoothed his tie against his shirt.

"You've been quiet tonight, Jace," Keith said. "Anything wrong?"

Jason felt his cheeks go hot. "It's Jason," he said under his breath.

Keith leaned forward. "Excuse me?"

"No, I'm fine," Jason said. "My stomach's just a little on edge."

"Oh, I'm sorry," Keith said. "French food *is* pretty rich if you're not accustomed to it." Keith winked at Linda and took a sip of wine. "For a minute there, I thought we were boring you."

Jason smiled, the corners of his mouth arching up a bit too high. "Like they say, when you've seen one Caribbean island—"

"He's never been there," Linda said, cutting him off. "We can't afford to go."

Keith looked up, his eyes darting between Jason and Linda. "Right," he said. "You know, I've been thinking," he said. "You're still working for Anderson Kaplan, aren't you?"

"Yes," Jason said. "For five years now." Jason held his water glass up to the waiter, who refilled it.

"Five *long* years," Linda said.

"Have you given any consideration to a career change?" Keith asked as he glanced at Linda, who gave a slight nod in response.

"Keith, please don't start," Jason said. "I think I have some good advancement opportunities at A.K." He felt Linda kick him under the table, her stiletto heel leaving a mark.

"Oh, come on," Keith said, "you and I both know you need an Ivy League MBA to move up into management there, an Ivy League MBA you do not have. At Rockport, an aggressive first-year salesman can make sixty thousand—eighty his second year. First, we'll get you a policy, and then we'll get you a job. What d'ya say?"

Jason did not respond, and the three of them stared at him. He took a gulp of water and adjusted the fork on his plate as the guy in black tails at the baby grand played *Fur Elise*. He felt hot and angry and confused. Jason looked at Linda, and, finding no support in her demeaning gaze, at Keith. He just smiled at Jason, the cold dead smile of a salesman trying to close a deal. "I don't need any life insurance," Jason said, "and I think I'll take my chances at A.K."

Linda's face fell and Keith opened his mouth to respond, but the waiter appeared with steaming plates and sat one down in front of Keith, who rubbed his hands together and inhaled the fumes rising from the platters, his sales pitch interrupted. "Escargot," he said, grinning, and then added with a hint of superiority, "they're snails."

Jason looked at the shells and their occupants lying in garlic butter, and his stomach twisted. "Right," he said. "I know. They eat the lettuce in my garden." He broke into a cold sweat and mopped his forehead and nose with his napkin, hand shaking. Keith grabbed the pliers and picked up a snail, fragrant sauce dripping, then twirled it in front of Jason's face. "Big ones," Keith said. Jason watched the mollusk floating at the tip of his nose, then turned his head away and put his hand to his mouth. "Excuse me," he said through closed fingers. "I'll be right back." Jason stood and began to walk—then jog—toward the men's room.

Keith turned to Mary and said, "Go with him, hon. Make sure he's all right." Mary stood and followed Jason while Keith watched, waiting for her to be out of earshot. He leaned close to Linda and whispered, "Now what?"

Linda picked up her wine glass and took a swallow. Bright red lipstick prints remained on the rim. "Don't worry," she said. "I'll take care of it."

—

The apartment complex was quiet and dark as Jason descended the stairs to the street.

"Hey!"

Jason looked to his right and saw Scott coming toward him, waving. He wore gray sweats with a hole in the knee and had an orange bandanna tied around his head. Only his shoes were high tech, with the latest shocks and gel inserts, but even they were lime green. "Pick it up," Scott yelled. Jason broke into a trot, and they jogged together toward the park.

"Didn't know if you were gonna make it," Scott said.

"I almost didn't," Jason said. "I had a rough night last night."

"Oh, that's right," Scott said, remembering. "The pity dinner with Mr. and Mrs. Sunburn. How was it?"

"I got sick during the appetizers."

"Lovely," Scott said. "Did you have to hear about Bermuda?"

"Barbados," Jason corrected, "and yes I did, in excruciating detail. Did you know Barbados is less than one-tenth the size of Rhode Island?"

Scott laughed. "Fascinating," he said, doing his best Mr. Spock imitation. "We really must go there sometime."

"That's what Linda said."

The sun was up now, shining warm in their faces, and Scott began to run faster. They jogged in silence, Jason working on his form and struggling to match Scott, stride for lanky stride. Jason blinked into the rising sun, sweat stinging his eyes and trickling down his back, his breathing labored and his gut knotted, the taste of escargot and garlic still in his nose and mouth. His legs ached, and his punctured heel still hurt.

"So how was Linda?" Scott asked.

"We actually got along pretty well," Jason said.

Scott looked disappointed. "What'd you do, win the lottery?"

Jason laughed. "I think it was a set up. Three on one, as predicted. Keith tried to sell me some insurance again."

Scott made a gurgling noise. "Oh, man, what were you drinking?"

"I didn't say I bought any," Jason said. "It was Linda. She started batting those eyelashes at me."

Scott winced in commiseration. "Fell prey to the baby blues again, huh?"

"Yeah."

"She totally controls you," Scott said. "I remember at your bachelor party, I said, 'Dude, it's not too late. Let's drive to Oakland, hop in my plane, fly to Tahoe and hide out.' . . ." He looked over at Jason. "Hey man, you O.K.?" he asked. "You look kind of pale."

"Yeah, I'm fine," Jason said. He took a deep breath and shook his head, trying to clear away the fog and pain and nausea.

"So, you going to go through with it?" Scott asked.

"What, buy insurance from Keith? No way!" Jason said. "I just played along to make points with Linda."

"And so you got lucky when you got home, right?"

"Luck had nothing to do with it," Jason said, slugging Scott in the arm.

Scott slugged him back. "It's just like that old nursery rhyme—'there once was a girl that was very, very good, but when she was bad she was awful.' You get slapped around 95 percent of the time just so you can have the rush the other five percent. You're a junkie."

"It's not that bad," Jason said.

"Oh, yeah right," Scott said. "You are the poster boy for the 'When Momma Ain't Happy, Ain't Nobody Happy' club. You only agreed to humor Keith so you could stay out of the doghouse. You probably even told him you'd get a physical."

Jason pulled up short and stopped running, then walked off the jogging path onto the grass, hands behind his head, fingers interlocked. He stood, taking deep inhalations, wheezing. Scott ran on for several more yards, then slowed to a walk and turned around. "Hey, I'm sorry," he yelled. "Come on."

Jason waved him on, then turned and began walking back up the path toward home, his breathing still labored. He heard Scott approaching behind him. Jason walked off the path and stopped, then leaned over and put his hands on his knees. He couldn't catch his breath, a sharp pain in his side interfering with each inhalation. Then the nausea came again and hit him hard, dropping him to his knees. He began to vomit, not stopping until the dry heaves had passed. Jason sat down in the damp grass and tried to stop shaking, but he was cold, and his nose and throat burned.

"Are you still with me, bro?"

Jason looked up at Scott through bleary eyes. "That was brutal," he said.

"Looked like it. *Sounded* like it." Scott stood two yards back, watching Jason and shifting his weight from foot to foot. "I'm sorry I said that about the physical. I mean, you're in good shape, right?"

Jason nodded. "Yeah."

"No reason to fear a physical, right?"

Jason squinted up at him. "That's enough, Scott."

Scott moved closer and bent down to tie his shoe. "So," he said, "that must have been some pretty noxious dinner you had last night. Food poisoning?"

Jason shook his head. "It was Keith's appetizer. Snails."

"Nasty little creatures, those. Appropriate though, for a slug like him." Scott extended a hand. "Come on. I'll walk home with you."

Jason spat into the grass and wiped his mouth on the back of his arm. "No, I'm all right. You can finish."

"Why? You ruined my chances with any of the babes out here. I can hear it now: 'Hey, aren't you the guy whose friend just hurled?' I mean, the next time you have to call Ralph on the big white telephone, could you please do it in private?"

Jason climbed to his feet, holding his side. "I'll be more considerate in the future," he said. He pressed his fingers into his abdomen, trying to ease the pain that now radiated from his stomach and into his lower back.

Scott moved closer and put his arm around Jason's shoulder, a maniacal grin on his face. He leaned in toward Jason and said, "What do you say we stop for a nice gooey cheese danish on the way home?"

—

Jason could hear water running when he entered the apartment. He walked to the bathroom door and peeked in at Linda in the shower. Mmmm, he thought. Nice.

He toyed with the idea of joining her, but the ache in his gut dissuaded him. Jason went to the kitchen and drank a glass of water, his hand still pressed into his side, then limped into the front room and collapsed on the couch. He had just closed his eyes when Linda came into the room, wearing a short robe and toweling her shoulder-length blond hair. Jason turned and groaned in greeting.

Linda gasped and jumped back. "You scared me!"

"Sorry. Hit the wall at two miles."

"What happened?"

Jason rolled onto his side. "Snail's revenge."

"It's all that health food. Your system can't handle a real meal."

He leaned up on one elbow and looked at Linda. The short robe flattered her legs.

"Are you going to see about the physical today?" she said.

"Oh, man, you're not really serious about that insurance thing, are you?"

Linda's stopped toweling her hair. "Hell yes, I'm serious! What was that last night? Just pillow talk? Besides," she said, "let's not forget about your dad."

Jason rolled onto his back and covered his eyes with his arm. "Thanks for bringing *that* up," he said.

Linda walked to the couch and knelt by Jason, and he inhaled her soapy-clean scent. "I just don't want to lose you," she said. She leaned in and kissed Jason's cheek. "Call Keith—he can help you find a good doctor. Will you do that for me?"

Jason stared into Linda's eyes for a moment then turned away, his face in the cushions. "I'll think about it," he said.

"Don't just think about it," she said. "Do it." She glanced at the wall clock then bounced to her feet. "I'm late," she said as she marched off to the bedroom.

CHAPTER 3

—

TRIPS LITE

"What the hell is this thing?"

Dr. Ruth Wilson stared at the electron microscope's stark black and white image of several coiled balls of cells clumped together. "It took forever to isolate it and take its picture from those tissue samples. Its morphology looks like it comes from the *Orthomyxoviridae* family," she said, "but it doesn't act like the flu at all. Respiratory effects actually seem secondary to the bone disease, but no known viruses cause bone disease."

Dr. Vincent Samuels consulted a web page in front of him. "What about Paget's disease and *Paramyxoviridae?*"

"Yeah, I thought about that," Ruth said, "but Paget's is secondary to the primary viral infection, like measles, caused by paramyxovirus, and even then usually only in people with a genetic predisposition."

Both doctors jumped when the reminder alarms on their computers chimed in unison. "Staff meeting," Ruth said. "What have you got?"

Vincent sighed. "I got nothin'. Let's go see what the other teams came up with. It's odd that we've not been permitted to work with any of them yet."

Ruth and Vincent, thick notebooks and coffee mugs in hand, made their way to a secure wing on the fourth floor of the Centers for Disease Control headquarters in Atlanta. They scanned their badges and entered the conference room, taking seats at a compact round table. Only ten other chairs, Ruth noted to herself, looking around. Pretty select group.

Vincent opened his notebook and placed several web page printouts on the table in front of him. "I thought you didn't have anything," Ruth whispered.

"I don't," Vincent said, *sotto voce*, "but I can at least try and look the part."

The heavy door clicked and opened, and a tall African-American man with a shaved head came into the room. Ruth noted the American flag lapel pin he wore on his crisp gray suit, and how the pin matched his blue tie. She waited for others to come in behind him, but none did. She recognized the man as John Cornwall, the newly appointed director of the CDC's National Center for Emerging and Zoonotic Infectious Diseases. It was not lost on her that both the "Division of Bioterrorism Preparedness and Response" and the "Division of Emerging Infections and Surveillance Services" were also within Cornwall's jurisdiction. She stood and extended her hand.

"Dr. Cornwall," she said. "I'm Ruth Wilson, and this is Dr. Vincent Samuels." Vincent stood and shook hands with Cornwall.

"Thanks," Cornwall said. "I know you both by reputation already, of course." Vincent smiled at this, and Ruth blushed. "Shall we get started?" Cornwall said.

Ruth looked around. "Is it just us?"

"For now," Cornwall said, "yes. You, Dr. Wilson, were selected to be on this team because of your specialized post-doc work in virology at Stanford, and you, Dr. Samuels, because of your research on communicable disease propagation at DOD and here at CDC." He handed each of them a sealed folder marked "Confidential. Eyes Only." "Page one, please," he said, tearing open the seal.

Ruth watched Vincent fumble with the paper clasp as she opened her own folio. At the top of page one she read, "Unknown Virulent Pathogen Identification, Sequestration, and Immunization Project."

"Ten days ago," Cornwall said, "you were both provided with biological specimens taken from persons recently deceased due to unknown causes. You were told only that the samples were an unidentified, communicable and fatal pathogen, most likely a viral agent of some kind. You were both asked to employ your considerable skills to identify that agent, and to date, I am told neither of you has succeeded. Is that correct?"

Ruth swallowed and said, "Yes," and Vincent nodded.

"Normally," Cornwall continued, "given the urgency of this situation your lack of progress would be grounds for your termination so somebody presumably smarter than you could give it a try, but your experience here at CDC is not, unfortunately, uncommon. We've had similarly situated teams at other labs around the country doing the exact same thing, and thus far, the pathogen that we feel is responsible for the deaths remains unidentified."

Vincent cleared his throat. "Excuse me, Dr. Cornwall," he said, "but why weren't we told of the other teams so that we could share our data?"

"Because," Cornwall said, "it is imperative that word of this pathogen not be made public, and the odds of an unwanted disclosure become more likely if you had any idea of the magnitude of the problem, an inference at which each of you would have likely arrived had there been cross-pollination between the teams."

"Magnitude?" Ruth said. "We were told that there had been a few isolated cases, mostly in rural areas. No more than twenty or thirty deaths."

"You were lied to," Cornwall said. "You are big boys and girls and you know that's how things work here sometimes. Also, we find that worrying tends to cloud a researcher's focus, so we elected to obfuscate and employ redundancy among isolated research teams. In truth, there have been over five thousand deaths from this thing in the three months since we first became aware of it; probably hundreds or thousands more before that. But that number is growing exponentially. We've been able to explain it away as the flu thus far, and we've managed to keep a lid on news reports tying the deaths together, but as more and more ineffective vaccine is disseminated, vaccine which would work fine against, say, H1N1, we will have questions that we cannot answer and a breeding ground for both a nationwide panic and an epidemic. People are already starting to blog about it." Cornwall swore under his breath. "You ever try to find and stop a blogger?"

"Any cases outside the U.S.?" Vincent said.

"There have been the usual reports of deaths from diseases, but their news reports, like ours, attribute them to the flu or SARS some other identified pathogen, so who knows?"

Ruth reached into her pocket and removed a flash drive. "Dr. Cornwall, with all due respect, it's true that we've not been able to identify it—yet—but we did manage to take its picture. In fact, we were just studying its morphology for clues before we came to this meeting." Ruth placed the drive into the laptop computer on the table and manipulated the mouse until a picture of the scanning electronic microscope image was displayed on the monitor. Cornwall put on his reading glasses and peered at the screen.

"So there it is," he said. "No other team has been able to isolate it yet from the samples, let alone capture an image. Well done. I've not seen anything quite like it before." Cornwall watched the image, and then turned to the pair. "Based on your work," he said, "we should be able to develop an ELISA test for the antigen to this bug, so we can diagnose it correctly."

Vincent coughed, then said, "So are we thinking that this is like the Andromeda Strain—you know, a germ from space, or something like that?"

Cornwall laughed. "No. This is not a precursor to an extraterrestrial invasion. This looks more like Captain Trips."

"Sorry?" Vincent said.

"Captain Trips," Ruth said. "The fictional superflu in Stephen King's novel '*The Stand.*' Killed almost everyone on earth. No vaccine, and the only survivors were those with immunity."

"So is everyone worried that this bug will become a Captain Trips? An E.L.E.—Extinction Level Event?" Vincent said.

"Not yet. Captain Trips was a true global pandemic—and was a fictional creation," Cornwall said. "Everyone died except those with immunity, and it spread extremely rapidly. If current projections hold, this thing will only kill maybe one out of every 100 people in infected populations, more akin to the current cancer death rate."

"'Only'? Um, that's still over three million people in the U.S. alone," Vincent said.

"Yes, assuming the contagion rate stays the same—and assuming, more importantly, that it does not mutate into a more virulent strain."

"So, sort of a 'lite' version of Captain Trips," Ruth said, making air quotes.

Cornwall laughed. "Sure. For now. But let's not forget that this thing *will* kill people who are infected, we do not have a vaccine, we don't know for sure what it is, how you catch it, how or when it will mutate or how bad it will be if it does mutate—and it certainly will." Cornwall sighed. "So, keep your doors and windows locked."

"What if it mutates into a *more* virulent strain?" Vincent said.

Cornwall shook his head. "Who knows? Might be game over if we can't find a vaccine."

Vincent and Ruth stared at each other, the impact of Cornwall's statement hitting them. Then Vincent said, "There is one upside, here. Since you found the bug, Ruth, you get to name it."

Cornwall nodded. "That is the protocol."

Ruth thought for a moment, and then made a sweeping hand gesture toward the computer screen. “Gentlemen,” she said, “I give you *Triptovirus L,* Trips Lite.”

CHAPTER 4

Phillip Porter sucked on his cigarette and then spoke, smoke issuing from his nose and mouth. "I received your message regarding the new referral to The Complex," he said. "Sounds interesting. We've not yet had someone quite this young. A real find!"

Marcus looked at the floor. "Her name is Jenny," he said.

Porter did not acknowledge the comment. "I also understand from Walter that things went well with Katrine Waters," he said. The Driver, arms folded, stood behind Porter's chair. He did not react to Porter's using his given name.

"As well as can be expected," Marcus said, "given that the woman died in front of her husband and daughter." He glanced at the Driver and watched a grin bounce on his face, then disappear.

"Death does not discriminate, Dr. Marcus," Porter said. "You of all people should know that."

Marcus cleared his throat. "Yeah," he said. "I should." He paused for a moment before looking Porter straight in the eye. "Katrine Waters did not respond to Batch 919."

Porter flicked an inch of ash into the tray on his mahogany desk. "So the trial was a success then?" he said.

Marcus did not respond immediately. He stood and walked to the window of Porter's corner office, resplendent with crystal brandy decanters and original oils by respected artists, and looked out at the view. The evening sun, now just an orange ball resting on the Pacific, was warm on Marcus' face. Porter Pharmaceuticals' headquarters, surrounded by the lush vegetation that was characteristic of Marin County, California, stretched out below him. He could see the roof of the large white building that housed the manufacturing division where tractor trailers parked at cargo bays were being loaded with box after box labeled "Porter Pharmaceuticals." He watched a fully laden truck rumble away through the main gate. "Yes," Marcus said, "the trial was a success."

"Good," Porter said. He stubbed out his cigarette and lit another, then turned his attention back to the paperwork on his desk. "Send me your report."

Porter's tone suggested the conversation was over, but Marcus did not leave. He remained at the window, hands in his pockets, looking south toward the Golden Gate. He could just make out the usual flock of sailboats and catamarans—small white triangles zipping across the Bay. The Driver moved toward Marcus and grabbed his arm, but Porter looked up and cleared his throat. "Walter," he said, shaking his head. The Driver released Marcus and resumed his position behind Porter's chair. "Something bothering you, Dr. Marcus?" Porter asked.

"No, everything's fine," Marcus said, rubbing his arm, his voice tired and strained. There was silence, and Marcus could feel Porter staring at him.

"So you got your hands a little dirty on this one, did you?" Porter asked. Marcus turned and looked at him, a well-preserved man of fifty-four, his silver hair still thick, designer suit accenting his broad shoulders. There was just a suggestion of crow's feet beginning at the corners of his eyes, only evidencing themselves when he squinted, as he was doing now. Marcus felt the weight of Porter's stare, but did not respond. The room was silent, fingers of sunlight streaming through the cigarette smoke that hung in the air. He could still hear the roar of the departing trucks outside.

Porter stood and walked to the window, then put his arm around Marcus' shoulder. "You've been isolated from things here in your ivory tower for a long time, and you've apparently forgotten what it feels like to see death—real death—up close. Cancer has given us a good run, sure, but it's been too long since you were up close and personal with the actual suffering part. But now, now a new opportunity has come to us, and we must not look a gift horse in the mouth—even if that means you have to smudge your brow a bit." Porter paused, then said, "And you and I both know you've gone much too far down the road to start feeling conflicted now. Right?"

Marcus' eyes dropped to the floor and watched the way the carpet massaged Porter's Italian loafers as he shifted his weight from foot to foot, like a boxer, the remaining sunlight bouncing off the shiny leather. "Right," Marcus finally said. "Too far down the road." He turned and began to walk from the room.

He was at the door when Porter called after him: "I'll need your written report on 919 as soon as the autopsy on, um . . . ."

"Katrine Waters," Marcus said.

"Right, Waters, as soon as the autopsy is completed."

Marcus continued walking. He did not answer and did not look up. "Do you have a problem with that?" Porter said.

Marcus spun around and faced the desk, turning directly into Porter's stare, then glanced down and noticed Walter's hands, knotted into tight fists. He opened his mouth to respond, then muttered, "No. No problem at all."

"What about the husband?"

"He signed all the releases."

Porter waited several seconds before smiling, porcelain veneers gleaming. "Good," he said. "Very good." Marcus turned and left the room.

Porter stared at the door for a moment before returning to his desk. He sat down in the high-back leather chair and swung around, checking his hair in the brass-framed mirror on the wall behind him. "That was pathetic," he said. "Absolutely pathetic." The Driver, anticipating Porter's next request, had already moved to the bookcase and lifted a decanter, waiting.

"Walter," Porter said as he grabbed a cigarette, "bring me a drink."

—

Marcus' office at Porter Pharmaceuticals was tiny compared to the CEO's, and not as richly appointed. The desk was standard company issue: industrial-strength brown with a plastic wood-grain laminate top.

Marcus took a file folder labeled "Katrine Waters–Notes and Labs" from his briefcase and threw it on the desk, then removed his jacket and wrestled the tie from around his neck. "Bastard Porter," he said, tossing the tie across the room. He picked up a remote control and pointed it at the iPod on the credenza. *La Grange* by ZZ Top boomed from the speakers in the corners of the office. Marcus sat down at the computer, sifted through the folder, and began to type:

> Katrine Marie Waters, Case Number 000286, age 31. Patient diagnosed 2 October with idiopathic lung and bone infections characteristic of unknown viral pathogen. Rapid degradation of condition observed, typical of disease progression observed in other patients. ELISA enzyme immunoassay test performed to confirm presence of viral agent.
>
> Rimantidine and azidothymidine antiviral and linezolid antibiotic regimens prescribed with only nominal slowing of disease progression. Patient last seen on outpatient basis 15 November.

Marcus leaned back in his chair and placed his hands, fingers laced, behind his head. "They got a lotta nice girlz-zuh," growled Billy Gibbons from the speakers. "Ah how, how, how," Marcus sang along. He started typing again:

> Admitted 6 January to Porter Pharmaceuticals' facility, Arizona Complex, for evaluation and treatment. Disease progression escalated, primarily manifesting as chronic obstructive pulmonary disorder. Batch 919 administered intravenously beginning 8 January. Facility records indicate patient's initial response to 919 produced slowing of disease progression and symptoms.

Marcus paused and looked out the window. The sun had now set, and he could see the lights twinkling across the bay in San Francisco, the luminous points representing people in restaurants, people in cars, people safe at home. He continued typing:

> Rapid degradation of patient's condition noted beginning week five following initial administration of 919. Consultation ordered, and patient examined at Complex 18 May. Patient suffered cardiac arrest during examination. Resuscitation attempts were unsuccessful and were suspended 09:42 a.m. Autopsy pending.

Marcus scrolled to the top of the report and read what he had written. When he got to the bottom he hesitated, fingers drumming on the keyboard. "Screw him," he said. The keys began clicking again:

> *Specific autopsy inquiry requested* as to whether cardiac arrest caused by cytotoxic effects of Batch 919 or systemic organ failure due to viral pathogen prior to administration.

He read the sentence again and again, pulse racing, knowing full well the consequences of his question. He password-protected the file and saved it to a flash drive, then locked the drive inside his desk drawer. Marcus inhaled and sighed. I should just kill Porter now, he thought. "Ah how, how, how, how," sang Billy.

CHAPTER 5

"Mr. Kramer?"

Jason turned and looked at the smiling young nurse who had called his name. "Right this way," she said.

Jason put down his magazine and followed the nurse into an examination room. "Nice sweater," Jason said. The nurse looked down at her blue cardigan. "Thanks," she said. "I knitted it myself." She handed him a plastic cup. "I'll need you to fill this," she said. Jason blushed, and the nurse smiled and left the room.

It was only a minute or two after Jason had filled the cup and returned to the exam room that the doctor came in. He was a big man, with a bald head and a tidy mustache. He wore thick glasses and was stuffed into a shirt that was too small, his collar a starched cotton garrote, his neck extruding up and over the top. The doctor extended a beefy hand. "Gerald Montweiler," he said.

Montweiler's paw engulfed Jason's hand. "Jason Kramer," he said, grateful when the doctor finally let go. "Keith Lawrence sent me," he said, lowering his voice.

The doctor smiled. "This is not a speakeasy, Mr. Kramer."

Jason tensed, embarrassed. "Of course not," he said. "I only wanted to make sure you knew this was an insurance physical."

"As a matter of fact, Keith Lawrence did call to tell me you were coming."

Jason's eyebrows shot up. "He did?" Jason asked. "What did he say?"

"Only that we should take very good care of you."

Jason smiled and peeled off his regulation Anderson Kaplan white shirt and tie and tossed them over a chair. Dr. Montweiler began probing Jason's chest and back with a stethoscope. "You look like you're in pretty good shape for a bean counter," Dr. Montweiler said. "Are you a runner?"

The stethoscope was cold, and it tickled. "Financial analyst, and yeah," Jason said, trying not to squirm. "I go about five miles every morning."

"Mmm hmm," Dr. Montweiler said, listening to Jason's heartbeat. He removed the stethoscope and hung it around his neck. "Any current health problems?"

"No," Jason said.

"Any family history of illness I should know about?" he asked.

Jason thought for a moment, his eyes locked on the doctor's, then looked down. "Nope," he said.

"Mom and dad still alive?"

"Um, yep," Jason said.

The doctor picked up a clipboard. "Do you use alcohol or tobacco?" he said, making notes.

"Tobacco, no." Jason said. "Alcohol, an occasional social drink."

Montweiler jotted more lines, and Jason relaxed a bit. "Can I get dressed now?" he asked.

Montweiler kept writing. "Sure," he said, "but leave a sleeve rolled up. Wendy will be in to take some blood." Montweiler handed the clipboard to Jason and pointed to the bottom of the form. "Sign here," he said.

Jason scratched his name on the paper and returned the clipboard. "Is that it?" he asked.

"Depending on the lab results, I would say yes, that's it."

"How long does it take to get the lab work back?"

"Couple of weeks, usually."

"And then the policy is issued?"

Dr. Montweiler laughed. "That's up to the company, not me. And of course, it depends on the test results, too."

Jason nodded. "Of course," he said.

Montweiler again extended his hand and Jason shook it. "Good luck at Rockport," the doctor said.

Jason swallowed. "Thanks," he said. He watched Montweiler gather up his things and leave the room. As the door closed, Jason exhaled and realized he was covered with sweat. He wiped his face and began to flap his arms to cool off, but just then the pretty nurse with the blue cardigan came into the room carrying a syringe and three corked test tubes. Jason looked up and blushed, his arms frozen in mid-air, elbows up and out. "You must be Wendy," he said, grinning and lowering his arms.

"Wendy Ross," the nurse said, grinning. "No relation to Betsy. And you must be The Famous Chicken."

Jason laughed. "No. It's just a little warm in here," he said. "So, you're also a blood sucker, huh?"

"Phlebotomist, thank you," she said. She knotted a length of surgical tubing around Jason's arm and watched the veins distend while Jason looked at the wall.

"Squeamish?" Wendy asked. Jason nodded, his face pale. Wendy inserted a needle into a vein in Jason's arm and filled the three vials with blood. "Do you know your blood type?"

"Um," Jason said, "B-positive."

"Me too! I can always remember that because my mom, who was a nurse, always told me to 'Be Positive!' She thought that was so funny," Wendy said, as she applied a bandage to Jason's arm.

"That wasn't so bad," he said.

"Just wait 'til you see the bruise you have tomorrow," Wendy said.

Jason probed the bandage Wendy had applied, checking for soreness. "I heal quickly," he said. "I gave blood last week at work and didn't even get a bruise."

Wendy nodded. "I see. I'd better make a notation in your records about the donation. Sometimes they get weird results when you're down a pint." She put a rubber band around the vials of blood and put them into a manila envelope.

"What do they check for?" Jason asked, indicating toward the vials.

"Oh, the usual, hepatitis, influenza, HIV."

He took a deep breath and stood up from the examination table, wobbling, reaching behind himself for support.

Wendy watched, her brow furrowed, and then placed her hand on Jason's shoulder to steady him. "How are you feeling?" she asked. "Between the blood donation last week at work and this today, you might be a little lightheaded."

Jason recovered, pulling his head up and straightening his back. He smiled. "I'm great," he said. "Thanks. Kind of a pain, though, just for some insurance."

"Oh," Wendy said, tugging the cardigan around herself, the animation gone from her voice and face. "You're one of the Rockport guys."

Jason's smile faded. "Yes. Is that a bad thing?"

Wendy took a step back and examined Jason. "Bad?" she said. "Not necessarily. Disappointing?" Her eyes narrowed. "Definitely" she said, as she turned and left the room.

—

Jason stood in front of the bathroom mirror and probed his bruised arm. "What are you doing in there?" Linda asked through the door, toothbrush in hand.

"I'll be right out," he answered. He heard Linda sigh and march off to the living room, where she turned on the TV and started flipping through the channels.

He replaced the bandage, straightened the baggy shorts and tank top that doubled as pajamas, and went out to join Linda.

"It's about time," she said when he entered the family room. Her toothbrush was parked on the coffee table next to the remote control.

Jason grinned and sat down next to her on the couch. "That's why we need a second bathroom." He grabbed the clicker and changed the channel.

"Tell me about it." She grabbed at the remote, but Jason stuffed it down into the crack between the cushions. "Hey!" Linda protested, retrieving the device and changing the channel back. "We need another TV, too."

Jason looked at her, incredulous. "Just so we don't fight over the clicker? I don't think so."

"No, not that," she said. "Most people have two TV's, one in the bedroom and one in the family room. Then we could watch TV in bed." Linda inched closer to Jason as she said it.

"Oh," Jason said. He watched Linda slide toward him.

"So the physical went well?"

Jason slid away, toward the end of the couch. "No, actually, it sucked. It was invasive, and the doctor was creepy. I can't believe I let you talk me in to it."

"But you did it, and you get the policy, right?"

Jason stared at her. "Wait, don't you mean, 'Oh, honey, I'm glad you went in to get a physical so we'll know you're in good health?'"

Jason felt Linda's warm soft toes working their way up the back of his foot. "Of course that's what I meant," she said. "You always twist my words." She was now right next to Jason, the green silk of her Victoria's Secret nightgown slick and cool on Jason's leg. "You know," she said, "once you get the policy, you should think about going to work for Rockport, too."

Jason tried backing away some more, but he was up against the armrest. "Aw, babe, not again. We've been through this. I don't want to sell insurance. I like what I do at A.K., and I'm good at it."

Linda turned to Jason, her soft hair tickling his arm. "Who said anything about selling insurance? I was talking to Keith—"

"Oh, great."

"—and he said you could get into management after selling for only a year. Maybe a vice presidency after five years, if you work hard and with his help. Think of it Jason—a vice presidency at Rockport! We could move closer to San Francisco, go on a real vacation . . ." she put her arms around Jason's neck ". . . maybe even start a family."

Jason stared at the TV screen, but he could feel Linda's breath on his ear.

"And you know what? Keith said if you didn't like it after the first year, you could quit and they'd give you six months' severance. To help with expenses while you find a new job."

Jason was silent for a moment before responding. "I couldn't get back on at A.K.," he said.

"Oh, baby, that was a dead-end job anyway. You know Keith was right about your not having any real advancement opportunities there, not without a good MBA, anyway."

Jason scratched the carpet with his free toes, while the others were engaged in serious footsies with Linda. "Well, yeah," he said.

"The annual starting salary, even without commissions, is more than what you're making at A.K. now," she said. "Once commissions kick in, we're in fat city."

Jason folded his arms and tried to move away from Linda, but she put her arms around him and held him fast. "You've got this all figured out, don't you?" he said.

Linda kissed his neck. "I just want us to be happy, honey. Give A.K. notice. Do it tomorrow. You've got so many talents, you shouldn't be wasting them."

Jason allowed Linda to nuzzle his neck for several more minutes. "That thing you said about starting a family," Jason said, his eyes closed. "Were you serious?"

"Mmm hmm," Linda breathed in his ear.

Jason turned his head to Linda and kissed her, then pushed her back down on the couch. "You know I've always wanted kids," he said.

"You'd be a good dad," Linda said, as she pulled Jason's tank top up and off, then kissed his chest. "So, you'll give them notice?" she said.

Jason took a deep breath, then exhaled. "I'll think about it," he said.

Linda continued kissing his chest. "I love you," she said.

CHAPTER 6

Marcus stared out the car window at The Complex's manicured lawns, which, he thought, were too green. He squinted up into the blue sky, where no clouds obscured the oppressive Arizona sun. Marcus felt the air conditioning on his forehead and realized he was sweating. He took his handkerchief from his pocket and wiped his brow, then looked at the Driver. Walter was not perspiring at all. Marcus muttered in annoyance and shifted in his seat, sweat running down the small of his back.

The Driver parked the Mercedes, and its occupants emerged. Tom Holloway whistled and looked up at the red brick structures before them. "Nice buildings," he said. "Big. But why did they build this place out here in the middle of nowhere? That strip we landed on must be a hundred miles from here."

"Hundred and nine," the Driver said.

Marcus pulled a wheelchair from the trunk, and then helped Carmen fasten Jenny into place and elevate her leg. "We need an isolated environment," Marcus said, "with a consistent climate so we can be sure the results of the drug studies are caused by the drugs and not some outside factor."

Tom looked at Carmen, who nodded. "Oh," Tom said. He moved to help the Driver unload the bags from the trunk of the car. Marcus stood and began to push Jenny toward the entrance as Carmen, Tom, and the Driver followed. A brass sign next to the front door proclaimed "Westchester Oncology Clinic" in pretentious script.

"Sure is peaceful here, with all the trees and flowers and things," Carmen said. "Why do they call it The Complex?"

Marcus thought for a moment. "I'm not sure," he said. He glanced at the Driver, but Walter kept staring straight ahead. "They've been calling it that since before I started with Porter," Marcus continued. "Porter built Westchester in the early nineties to conduct clinical trials on cancer drugs. We've added more buildings over the years, and now the whole thing is called The Complex."

They walked in silence, and then Tom said, "But Jenny doesn't have cancer."

"Right," Marcus said, "but we have state-of-the-art facilities here for all types of tests and diseases now, not just cancer."

Tom continued, "But how can Porter afford to do this if they don't charge anyone to come here?"

The Driver increased his pace until he was even with Marcus, then turned and stared at him. Marcus could feel the heat of the steel-blue glare, even obscured as it was behind the sunglasses. "Some people do pay," Marcus said, "but most people are like yourselves. They agree to accept treatment with drugs that are still being tested. Insurance companies won't cover experimental therapies, so Porter underwrites the cost. We can then write it off as research and development."

"And then Porter gets paid back when it finds a good drug."

Marcus looked at Carmen and nodded. "That's right," he said.

The Driver moved forward and pulled the door open. "Thank you," Jenny said to the Driver as Marcus wheeled her past him into the lobby, the Driver managing a thin smile in return. They pulled up to the front desk and could see behind the receptionist through tall glass windows into a large open-air courtyard.

"Sure is nice and cool in here," Tom said.

"Nothing but the best," Marcus said. "Now, we just need to get Jenny settled in her room, and then I'll show you folks to the guest quarters."

Jenny squirmed in her wheelchair and managed to turn around enough to look up at Marcus and ask, "Do they have ice cream here?"

Marcus knelt next to the chair. "Yep. And it's homemade, too." Jenny beamed and settled back down into her seat.

—

The conference room at The Complex was cramped and stuffy. Marcus and the Driver sat at a round table, a speakerphone in front of them. The Driver punched in a series of numbers and then sat back in his chair, his calm, unnerving countenance unchanged. Marcus avoided looking at him, concentrating on the telephone instead.

"Hello?" The voice boomed from the speaker on the table.

The Driver nudged Marcus with his foot, and he jumped. "Ah, hello Mr. Porter. It's Craig Marcus."

"Marcus! Where are you?"

"At The Complex. I wanted to talk to you before we left for home."

There was a brief silence, which Porter interrupted. His voice now carried an edge of irritation. "Well?" he said.

"We've got Jenny Holloway settled into her room."

"Good. She's the new viral patient, right? What about the parents?"

"No problem. The guest quarters are nicer than their house."

"So then I'll see you back here," Porter said.

"Uh, Mr. Porter? There's just one problem. I prescribed a regimen of Batch 920 to begin tomorrow morning and the Dri—, uh, Walter, tells me you want to start her on 919."

Silence. Then: "And? . . ."

"We don't have Katrine Waters' autopsy back yet."

"So what?"

Marcus looked at the Driver, who stared back at him. "Excuse me?" Marcus said to the phone.

Porter sighed. "You told me Katrine Waters probably lived three weeks longer than she would have without 919."

"That's probably right."

"So what's the problem? Run an ELISA test on the new girl to make sure it's the virus and then start her on 919—"

"With all due respect, Mr. Porter," Marcus said, interrupting, "the only reason I recommended Jenny to The Complex was because of her age. We've not seen the virus in someone so young yet, and I thought it would be nice if we could send someone *home* from The Complex for a change. It would be a good first trial for 920."

"Look, I want to know how 919 affects Jenny Holloway. I can't go to the Board with a recommendation to proceed to market unless I know its effect on a broad demographic. Plus, if she's as good a prospect for a cure as you say she is, let's not waste her on the first clinical trial of 920."

Marcus took a deep breath and steeled himself. "I feel very strongly that we should wait at least until the Katrine Waters autopsy is done."

"I don't give a damn what you think or what the autopsy says! You're the only one who sees those things. FDA just relies on your summaries of the animal trials."

"But it may be bad news. It may show that 919 killed her."

"If it had *cured* her we'd all be out of a job right now, wouldn't we," Porter said. "Ever since this thing came along, this 'Trip the Light Fantastic' or whatever they're calling it —"

"Trips Lite. TL, short for *Triptovirus L.* Somebody at CDC thought they were clever, I guess," Marcus said. "I wonder if Stephen King is getting a royalty."

"Whatever. Ever since it came along and ever since you perfected the enzyme immunoassay test for it so it could be diagnosed, Porter has been the leader on this thing. Everybody is working around the clock to try and crack the code on this bug and get a vaccine, and I want the market to be convinced that Porter will be the source for the *vaccine*, not just the source for the ELISA test, and not Pfizer or Merck. We know that 919 stopped TL's progression in Katrine Waters, we need one more trial for 919, and Jenny Holloway is it." The line went dead, the speaker emitting an angry buzzing sound.

The Driver reached forward and depressed a button on the speakerphone, then lifted the handset and dialed a four-digit number. Marcus watched him dial. He recognized the number as the nursing station for Jenny Holloway's wing. The Driver handed the phone to Marcus.

Marcus was pale, and his voice quivered. "Hi, this is Dr. Marcus," he said. "I need to change my dispensing order for Room 411, Jenny Holloway . . . start her on Batch 919." Marcus kept the phone pressed to his ear for several seconds before the Driver reached up and took the handset away from him.

"Good boy," Walter said.

—

Jenny Holloway looked very small and frightened, lying in the exact center of the big hospital bed, swallowed by the sheets and metal railings surrounding her. She was staring glassy eyed at the TV, Tom and Carmen sitting beside her. They were holding hands.

"We're leaving now."

Tom and Carmen started, and then looked up at Marcus standing in the doorway. "Where are you going?" Tom said.

"Back to San Francisco."

"When will you be back?" Carmen asked.

"I'll fly out in a week," Marcus said. "Until then, you're in very good hands. The staff here is excellent."

Tom stood and walked to Marcus, his hand extended. "I want to thank you for everything you've done for Jenny."

Marcus took Tom's hand and shook it limply, not meeting Tom's eyes. "You're welcome," he said.

"Goodbye Mr. Driver." Jenny had spotted the Driver standing behind Marcus, and she was now waving at him, her tiny hand flapping. The Driver held up a hand in acknowledgment, but then a smile formed and he wagged his fingers a bit toward Jenny. Jenny grinned, showing missing teeth.

Marcus released Tom's hand and turned to leave. "I'll be in touch," he said without looking back. As he moved through the door, a nurse carrying a plastic IV bag came into the room. Marcus glanced at the bag and the writing on the label, where black numbers spelled out "919." He paused to watch as the nurse moved to the side of Jenny's bed and hung the bag on a metal frame, then inserted a needle into a vein in Jenny's thin arm.

"Ow!" Jenny cried out, "that hurts!"

"It's O.K., honey," Carmen said. "This is the special medicine that Dr. Marcus said will make you all better. Right, Dr. Marcus?" Carmen turned and looked toward the door, but Marcus was gone.

—

Marcus trudged back to his office at Porter Pharmaceuticals' Marin County headquarters, his head bent in thought, passing several white-coated technicians without returning their greetings. He paused before entering the room and looked at the sign on the door: "Craig Marcus, M.D. Director of Research." What a joke, he thought. He shook his head and went in.

He loosened his tie and shook off his jacket, then sat down at the desk and sighed. His in-box was piled high, and Marcus began sorting the contents into categories. "Medical journal," he mumbled, "junk mail, journal, letter, junk—" He stopped and lifted the next package, a manila mailer, for closer inspection. It was from the autopsy lab in Cupertino, and the "RECEIVED" stamp on the outside had today's date on it—June 9. "Finally!" Marcus said.

He ripped open the package and removed a five-page form. Bold letters at the top spelled out "KATRINE MARIE WATERS." He was suddenly hot, perspiration building on his forehead and cheeks. "Here we go," he said. He placed the document on the desk and wiped his palms on his trousers, then grabbed the papers and held them up, squinting, scrutinizing each line. "Where is it?" he muttered, pulse racing. "Come on, come on," he said, turning to the last page. "Date of death, time of death, age . . . ." Marcus held his breath and looked at an underlined sentence in the last paragraph. "Cause of death," he said, his voice muted. "Death was caused by cytotoxic effect of antiviral agent resulting in renal failure and eventual cardiac arrest."

He held the paper for another moment, then dropped it on the desk, his hand frozen in mid-air. "It killed her," he said. He turned his chair and looked out the window at the Bay. It was sunny, and no fog was threatening. He watched the sailboats play on the waves for several minutes. "It killed her," he said again, this time in a whisper.

Marcus spun his chair back around to the desk and turned on his computer, then summoned up the Katrine Waters memo he had written last May. He sat, eyes glued to the screen, reading: "*Specific autopsy inquiry requested* as to whether cardiac arrest caused by cytotoxic effects of Batch 919 or systemic organ failure due to viral pathogen prior to administration." He put his fingers on the keyboard and typed: Autopsy confirmed cause of death as kidney failure and cardiac arrest induced by Batch 919. He saved the report, then e-mailed it to Porter and to his personal Gmail account, password protected. He printed off a hard copy for himself and turned off the computer.

Marcus got up from his chair and went down the hall to the copy machine. He glanced around, and then made one copy each of the autopsy and the memo. He went back to his office and typed out a mailing label, then affixed the label to an envelope and put the copies inside. He looked at his watch—five o'clock. Marcus put his jacket back on and straightened his tie, then gathered his things and hurried to the mailroom, where he buried the envelope deep in a pile of outgoing mail.

CHAPTER 7

Jason's termination package was waiting for him when he got back from lunch. Wow, he thought, they don't waste any time. He sat down, opened the envelope, and removed a half-inch thick pile of papers and forms. "Anderson-Kaplan Confidentiality Agreement," Jason read out loud as he flipped through the documents, "Waiver of Severance Pay, Surrender of Parking Privileges—"

"I hear you sold out to W-Cubed."

Jason didn't look up. "I'm married to her, Scott. I'm trying to make that marriage work."

"So off you go to sell insurance."

"Yeah. You need some?"

"Insurance is for married guys," Scott said. He ambled into the cubicle and started reading over Jason's shoulder. "They must be afraid you're going to sue them," he said.

"I guess," Jason said. "Look at this one." He handed Scott a piece of paper.

"Acknowledgment of Gender-Neutral Treatment," Scott read out loud. "Thank you, Clarence Thomas."

They sat in silence until Jason said, "So. How ya been?"

Scott reached down and picked up one of the forms Jason had already reviewed. He kept his eyes focused on the paper. "Good. But I was beginning to think the smell of my sneakers had offended you or something."

"That's true," Jason said, "but besides that I just haven't felt much like running lately." He looked at Scott. "Sorry."

Scott nodded, smiling. "No problem. At least the girls at the track have started talking to me again after that barfing episode." Scott read to himself for a moment, then said, "Your gut still bad?"

Jason studied the fine print at the bottom of legal-size piece of paper titled, "Release of Liability for Non-Disclosed Workplace Injuries," holding the paper up close to his eyes. "Yeah," he said.

"Getting worse?"

Jason put down the paper and nodded, his mouth open, jaw slack.

Scott stared at Jason, his eyes moving from feature to feature, from forehead to chin. "It's your face, man," he said. "You look like you've lost ten pounds. You could cut yourself on those cheekbones."

"It's just indigestion from the stress," Jason said.

Scott smirked. "Just wait. You want to talk about stress? Can you say 'commissioned insurance salesman?'"

Jason tensed, but didn't respond. "I passed the physical," he said.

"You got the results back?"

"No, not yet. But everything went fine."

"You *hope*. You won't know for sure until the tests are back, right?"

Jason remained silent.

"Right?"

Still nothing.

"Look, we've been friends a long time, man, and somebody needs to say this, and it sure as shootin' won't be Linda." Scott bent over and put his face in Jason's. "What do you think you're doing?"

Jason kept reading the form in front of him.

"You're quitting your job to go sell insurance, you don't even know if you passed the physical, you have to work with Keith—" he made a face as he said it "—and all because Linda's got you on a short leash. It's more than a little crazy, man. I mean, what are you gonna do if this doesn't work out? You know A.K. can't hire you back since that hiring freeze went on. You and that pretty wife can't make it to Barbados on welfare."

Jason turned to Scott, his jaw clenched. "Look, ever since my dad died you've assumed this big brother role that I never asked for. This is my life, Scott." He turned back to the form he was working on, his head bent.

"Big brother? Oh man . . . ." Scott took a step back, his face red. "Ever since Linda came along you and I have danced around this conflict, this tension between your old loyalties to me and Linda's obsession with money and power and status and your need to kiss her ass and feed her mania. Tell you what—let's not dance anymore, all right? You know where I stand." Scott took two big steps toward the exit, and then stopped. "By the way," he said, not turning around, "don't be late getting home tonight."

Jason didn't look up. "Why?" he said.

"You're the genius with all the answers," Scott said. "You figure it out."

—

"Hey buddy," the delivery man said, holding five large flat boxes, "do you know where 313 Oak Hill Terrace is?"

Jason stood speechless, knowing the address sounded familiar. Then it dawned on him. "Uh, yeah," he said. "That's where I live."

"Cool," the pizza dude said. "Lead on, Macduff."

Jason headed up the stairs from the parking garage with his pony-tailed, box-laden charge close behind. "Who ordered pizza?" Jason asked over his shoulder.

The pizza guy consulted a receipt Scotch-taped to one of the boxes. "Linda Kramer," he said. "She sounded like a babe."

Jason smiled. Linda's voice had always matched her general level of hotness. "She ordered *five*?" he said.

Pizza Dude nodded. They stopped in front of apartment 313. Jason tried the doorknob. Locked. He put his key in and opened the door. It was dark inside, and Jason pushed the door wide to let the delivery man through and followed him in. The lights flashed on, and bodies sprang from behind couches and from under tables.

"Surprise!"

Jason staggered back from the concussion of the greeting. The room was suddenly awash with people wearing party hats and holding glasses half-full of colorful liquids. He looked around at the sea of smiling faces, finally finding Linda standing next to Scott under a banner that read "Congratulations Jason." Several of the party-goers descended on Jason, taking his briefcase and handing him drinks. He recognized many of them only vaguely—people he had met at Linda's office or her health club. He recovered a bit and smiled bravely, taking a long gulp from a glass handed to him and accepting congratulations from these strangers. "Thank you," he said, again and again, as hands were thrust toward him for shaking. He moved against the tide, making his way toward Linda and Scott. He tried to glance at tags affixed to guests' chests, but instead of the usual "HELLO My Name Is . . .", the phrase "Can I Interest You In Some Life Insurance?" was written. He heard a noise to his left and turned to look. The TV was on, and several guests were gathered around watching an old black and white movie.

"*Double Indemnity,*" he heard Scott say behind him. "That was Linda's idea."

"Cute," Jason said, turning and shaking Scott's hand. "Name tags too, I bet."

"Uh, no, that was mine."

"Figures."

Scott tried to pull his hand away, but Jason retained his grip. "About this afternoon, . . ." he said.

Scott looked at the floor. "Forget it, man," he said. His eyes came up, and he smiled. "Hard to be rational when you're married to *that.*" He nodded toward Linda. Jason looked over at her and watched as she haggled with the pizza dude. "Pity the fool," Scott said in his best Mr. T impression. Linda continued to browbeat the young man until he finally slammed the receipts down on the table and shoved his way through the crowd to the door. Linda picked up the receipts and tore them into pieces. She noticed Jason and

Scott watching her, and then smiled sweetly before moving to join them.

"He was trying to overcharge me," Linda said. She paused a moment to compose herself, took a breath, then looked at Jason and smiled. "Surprise," she said.

Jason grinned. "What's all this for?"

"I'm just proud of you, that's all." She put her arm through Jason's. "Did you see the cake?" She led Jason toward the kitchen, leaving Scott behind. They stopped in front of a long table covered with food. The centerpiece was a huge rectangular cake covered with white frosting. Big blue letters across the top spelled out "POLICY," with lines of blue squiggles beneath. "It's a theme party," she said.

"I gathered."

She pointed at the squiggles. "That's the fine print," she said, grinning. "But we have to wait until Keith gets here to cut it," she continued. "He made me promise."

"Keith's coming?"

Linda nodded.

"Does Scott know?"

Linda shook her head. "I thought it best not to tell him."

"Good idea."

"He wouldn't have come otherwise."

"I know. Remember the Christmas party?"

Linda's jaw tightened. "How could I forget?"

Jason smiled as he remembered Scott's introduction to the Lawrences at the Kramers' last Christmas party. Keith had made an unkind remark about Scott's jacket and tie not matching, and in turn, Scott had furtively dipped the bottom of Keith's blazer into the eggnog. Scott apologized again and again as the thick yellowish goo dripped onto Keith's shoes while winking at Jason behind Keith's back.

"It took a month to get the eggnog out of the carpet," Linda said. A buzzer sounded from the kitchen, and her smile returned as she turned and moved for the door. "Stuffed mushrooms," she said.

Jason grabbed a carrot stick from a platter on the table and started gnawing on one end. He felt a hand on his shoulder and looked around. "Hi Keith," he said, his mouth full. "When did you get here?"

"Just now."

"Where's Mary?"

"She's waiting in the car."

Jason stared at Keith's stiff expression and swallowed hard. "Oh, oh," Jason said. "You don't look happy."

"Look, this'll just take a second," Keith said. "Is there someplace private we can talk?"

"Uh, yeah. The bedroom." Jason could see Scott approaching from behind, a wicked grin on his face, a brimming cup of punch in his hand. "Down there," Jason said, pointing down the hallway and stepping between Scott and his intended victim. Jason shot him daggers and stuck a finger in his chest. Scott pulled up short, eyes wide. Jason and Keith moved toward the back bedroom and went inside.

Keith closed the door. "Nice party," he said. He stood in front of a chest of drawers, not looking at Jason, picking up and examining the cologne bottles and assorted wristwatches scattered on top of the dresser. Jason stood behind him, staring at his back, listening to the music and conversation and laughter coming from the front room. After several seconds, Jason said, "What's up?"

Keith turned to face Jason and placed his hand inside his jacket, then pulled out a long white envelope and handed it to him. "I got your test results back," he said.

Jason removed a three-page computer printout from the envelope and sat down on the edge of the bed, staring at the figures on the form, not understanding. Keith pointed down at a small box in the corner of one of the pages. "Right there," he said.

Jason squinted and held the paper closer, still not understanding. "What?" he said, looking up at Keith.

Keith turned back to the cologne bottles. "You tested positive for TL. You're going to need some more tests."

Jason's hand, still holding the papers, fell to his lap. "TL? But I feel fine. It must be a false positive. I read that they only very recently even came up with a test for TL!"

"Look, you need to make another appointment with Montweiler for a blood test or whatever."

Jason sat, unmoving, staring at the floor. "Uh-huh . . .," he said.

"I can't hire you until this is cleared up."

Keith turned and took the printout from Jason's hand, then folded it and put it back in his pocket. The envelope, one end torn off, remained on the bed. "Look," Keith said, "I'm sure it's nothing." He moved to the door and opened it.

"Yeah," Jason said, nodding. "Nothing."

"But you should get in to see Montweiler as soon as you can—"

"Just in case," Jason said, finishing the sentence for him.

"Right," Keith said. "Just in case."

Jason heard Keith leave the room and return to the party. From the delighted squeals that accompanied each salutation, it was apparent to Jason that Keith knew more of the people in his living room than he did. Jason stood and moved to the door, his breathing strained, now acutely aware of the ache in his gut. He pressed his fingers deep into his side, probing, trying to massage away the sharp pain, but it persisted, growing instead more intense as he rubbed. He began to breathe faster, a sudden panic seizing him. Oh man, he thought, oh man, what am I gonna do now? He sank to the floor behind the closed bedroom door and put his head on his knees.

—

It was ten-fifteen when the second-to-last guest left the party, leaving Scott alone to search for and then consume the few, cold, remaining hors d'oeuvres. "These stuffed mushrooms are pretty good if you put a little sauce from the sweet and sour meatballs on them," he said to Linda as she passed him, carrying a tray laden with empty glasses.

"I'm glad you like them," she said, beaming, as she pirouetted into the kitchen, glasses making a pleasant tinkling sound as she walked.

Jason was sitting on the couch, a glass in his hand, staring at the floor. Scott came over, brimming cocktail plate in hand, and sat down next to him. He leaned in and put his mouth next to Jason's ear. "She's in a good mood," he said.

Jason drained the glass and grabbed a mushroom off Scott's plate. "Her party was a success. Keith and Mary's rich friends were here. She'll be flying for days." Jason stood up and shouted toward the kitchen: "Honey, I'm going to walk Scott to his car!"

Linda poked her head around the corner. "Already? It's not even ten-thirty."

"Yeah. He has an early day tomorrow." Scott looked up in surprise and started to protest, but Jason grabbed Scott's elbow and lifted him from the couch, sending two mushrooms toppling off the plate down into the crack between the cushions.

Scott looked down into the abyss that had swallowed the mushrooms. He sat his plate on the coffee table and started to dig for the errant appetizers, but Jason pulled him toward the door. "I'll get them later," he said.

It was quiet in the parking garage. "What gives?" Scott asked. "I don't have an early day tomorrow." Jason watched Scott fumble with his keys. "Good thing I didn't drink tonight," Scott said, finally managing to open the door to the red Karmann Ghia. He started to jam his lanky frame into the driver's seat. "I gotta get a bigger—"

"I didn't pass the physical," Jason said.

Scott lurched backward, knocking his head against the car's roof. He withdrew from the vehicle and looked at Jason. "Ex-squeeze me?"

Jason didn't smile. "They think I have TL."

Scott jumped back and covered his mouth and nose with his hand. "Dude! That crap's contagious!"

Jason did not react, and Scott exhaled, whistling. "Oh man, I'm sorry. Does Linda know?"

"I just found out tonight."

Scott thought for a moment, then, nodding, said, "Keith."

Jason nodded.

"You should have let me dump the punch on him. So when do you tell her?"

Jason sighed. "I guess right now."

Scott moved next to him and put his long skinny arm around Jason's shoulder, and they stood there, next to Scott's car. "Come on," Scott said. "I'll go back up with you."

—

"Honey, I've got some good news and some bad news."

Linda was on all fours, rinsing a rag in a plastic bowl of water, cleaning up red wine that a partygoer had spilled on the carpet. She looked up at Jason and Scott standing in the doorway. "I thought you left," she said to Scott.

Scott nudged Jason back into the apartment. "I'll call you tomorrow," he said as he turned and left.

Jason shut the door and sat down on the floor next to Linda. "Keith was here tonight."

Linda kept scrubbing. "I know. I saw him for a second. Too bad he couldn't stay."

"I got my physical results back."

"That's nice," Linda said, spraying the spot with rug cleaner. "You passed, right? You get the policy. That's the good news."

Jason placed his hand on Linda's back. He started to rub the spot between her shoulder blades, the spot that was always sore. She stopped scrubbing and looked at him. "Right?"

"They think I might have TL."

Linda's head fell forward, like a weight had been tied to her neck, and she issued a long, heavy sigh. Silence descended on the room, punctuated only by the ticking of the wall clock.

Linda stood, knocking over the basin. Rose'-colored water cascaded across the floor, turning a patch of beige carpet pink. "This is your fault! Running around with Scott, outside, with all those strangers, pretending everything was fine!"

"Me? How can you blame me? This whole insurance thing your idea—yours and Keith's! Besides, this doesn't mean anything. I have to go in for some more tests is all. It might be a false positive. I feel fine!"

"Everybody with TL feels fine at first," Linda said, jaw clenched. "You never went in for physicals, never had tests!"

"I don't have TL."

Linda walked back and forth in front of Jason, her brow furrowed in thought.

"I don't have TL!"

"Keith won't take you now, will he? That's why he left early."

Jason nodded, his eyes down.

"Can you get back on at A.K.?"

Jason shook his head. "There's a hiring freeze on."

Linda continued pacing, stammering and rubbing her forehead. Jason watched the pink water settle into the carpet. Suddenly, Linda stopped and turned, her eyes full of tears. She covered her face with her hands and began to cry, then sank to her knees in the middle of the wine stain. "What are we going to do?" she said. "What are we going to do?"

Jason felt tears in his eyes and put his arms around her. "It's O.K.," he whispered. "We're gonna be fine."

They remained there, huddled together on the mushy pink carpet, until Linda had stopped crying.

Jason stood and extended his hand to Linda. She looked up at him.

"So what's the good news?" she said.

"I don't have to go in to work tomorrow," Jason said.

—

Linda lay awake in bed and glanced at Jason every few minutes until his eyes finally closed at 1:19 a.m. She inched her way out from under the covers, tiptoed into the kitchen and closed the door behind her, then picked up the phone and dialed.

"Hello?" came the sleepy answer.

"What are you doing?" Linda's whispered voice was high and strained.

"I'm downstairs working. I must have nodded—"

"No! I mean the test results!"

"Hey, I got the results as we were getting in the car to come over to the party. What was I supposed to do?"

Linda opened a cupboard and grabbed a Snickers, snapped off the wrapper and bit the bar in half. "Why didn't you tell me?" she said, mouth full. "I had to find out from Jason."

"Linda, there was a room full of people, you were busy, Jason was right there—not exactly ideal circumstances to break the news. Plus Mary's been with me all night. She just went up to bed."

Linda swallowed and slammed the Snickers down on the counter. "You could have warned me," she said. "You've got to fix this!"

"High blood pressure I can maybe fix. Certain types of cancer I can fix. But this is TL. If I mess with this, somebody will catch it."

"You told me this would work. You said, 'We'll get him insured, then get him a job at Rockport because that doubles the face amount of the policy.'"

"I can't control lab results," Keith said. "Maybe it won't be TL. Maybe he can still get the policy. Let's at least wait for the test results before we call this off. It might be a false positive. The tests for TL are still new. Still working the kinks out. Montweiler will do some more tests—I'm sure everything will be all right. Might just be the flu. I mean, the guy lives on carrots and wheat germ, right?"

Linda slipped open the refrigerator, grabbed a can of Coke, and took a gulp. "You damn well better be right," she said, an angry quaver still in her voice.

"Look, I can hear Mary upstairs. I gotta go. Worst case scenario is that he still dies but we don't make any money off of it. We'll still be together." There was a pause, and then Keith said, "Are you all right?"

Linda breathed into the phone for several seconds before responding. "Yeah," she said. "I'm fine."

"Thata girl," Keith said. "Do me a favor? Wear a mask until we know for sure?"

"Oh yeah, that's real subtle and supportive."

"Think about it. And you know what?" Keith said.

"What?"

"I love you."

A smile appeared on Linda's chocolate-stained lips. "Me too," she said.

CHAPTER 8

Marcus smiled and said good morning to the security guard at the main entrance. He saw the Driver walking across the parking lot and honked and waved, but Walter didn't look up.

Marcus made his way to his office and found a package on his chair. He picked it up and examined it, but it had no labels or identifying marks. He sat his briefcase down on the desk, opened the envelope, and looked inside. Marcus felt the blood drain from his face.

He reached in and pulled out the manila mailer he had prepared and mailed the night before. He also removed a thick folder. A yellow sticky note with the words "Naughty, Naughty" scribbled on it was affixed to the mailer, and a big red circle was drawn around the words "FDA Compliance Division" on the address label Marcus had typed.

Marcus collapsed into his chair, and the contents of the folder spilled onto the desk. He surveyed the pile of photos and articles that splashed out, his life passing before his eyes as the materials remained in roughly chronological order as they fell. Marcus grabbed the first piece of paper and looked at it, sucking in air as memories flooded him. It was a copy of an article that had appeared in *Cancer* magazine twenty years ago. Marcus read the lead paragraph:

> In a paper presented to the faculty last month, Craig Marcus, 33, a graduate student at the University of California, San Francisco, School of Medicine, reported that he had achieved favorable results in animal trials with a type of genetically altered interferon he had developed. According to Marcus, the altered interferon reduced malignant tumor size and growth in mice that were injected with large doses of the drug. Human trials are still months away, but Marcus, who completes his graduate studies next month, is confident a sponsor in the private sector will provide funding to enable him to continue his research.

Marcus dropped the article and grabbed another from the stack, this one from the "News Briefs" section of the Journal of the American Medical Association, dated ten years ago:

> After two years in a private oncology practice, noted cancer researcher Dr. Craig Marcus has announced his affiliation with Porter Pharmaceuticals Company. Marcus will act as a consultant to Porter and will head up the company's chemotherapy research division. In a press release, Porter confirmed the appointment and acknowledged it was anxious to assist Dr. Marcus with the interferon research he had begun while a graduate student at the University of California.

Several photos of Marcus with Phillip Porter came next. Look how young I was, Marcus thought. Still had all my hair. The photos had been taken for use in an illustration accompanying a story in the Wall Street Journal. The story was paper-clipped to one of the photos. The headline read: "Porter Stock Soars on New Chemo News." Marcus kept reading:

> Porter Pharmaceuticals' common stock rose for the third straight day, closing yesterday up 1.50 to 37.75 on rumors it has successfully completed animal trials of a

> new cancer treatment. The therapy, developed by Dr. Craig Marcus, uses recombinant DNA technology to alter the structure of interferon, a naturally occurring protein with inherent cancer-fighting properties, to increase the interferon's toxicity to malignancies. Although Porter has not yet made an official announcement, the company is expected to publish its findings within the next two weeks. Porter will then likely seek FDA approval to conduct human trials, the last hurdle before the drug may be prescribed by physicians and sold domestically.

Marcus looked up, startled by a knock at the door. He straightened the pile of documents on his desk. "Come in," he said.

The door swung open and Phillip Porter walked in, a smug grin on his tanned face. He moved to the desk and rummaged through the papers, his fingers caressing the sheets. "Enjoying your trip down memory lane?" he said, continuing to sift the stack before finally removing a piece of paper from the bottom of the pile and handing it to Marcus. "This one's my favorite."

Marcus looked at the document. It was an internal memorandum from Marcus to Porter dated one month after the Wall Street Journal article. "EYES ONLY–HIGHLY CONFIDENTIAL" was typed in bold letters at the top, and next to Marcus' name were his handwritten initials, although he could tell from the smudgy black marks around the letters that the document was a photocopy. He looked up at Porter.

"The original is in a safe place," Porter said.

Marcus dropped the paper on the desk without reading it. "Go ahead," Porter said, but Marcus did not move. Porter snapped up the memo and began reading out loud: "RE: Interferon Trials. The papers are buzzing about our successes with the altered interferon, but we're not ready to go to market. The side effects in the human trials have been unusually severe." Porter paused for a moment to look at Marcus, and then kept reading. "Normal interferon produces flu-like side effects, including fever, fatigue, joint pain and loss of appetite. It can also damage the liver. But the altered interferon magnifies those effects. Two deaths have occurred in the human trials that may have been caused, or at least hastened, by the altered interferon. So despite the fact reduction in tumor size has been noted," Porter read, "I recommend we neither attempt to take the drug to market nor seek FDA approval for official human trials."

Porter stared at Marcus and said, "That's enough, I think, right?"

Marcus blinked several times, but did not respond.

Porter placed the memo back into the stack of papers on the desk, then gathered up the documents and photos and returned them to the folder. He tucked the package under his arm, then looked down and tapped his finger on the envelope Marcus had tried to mail. "Stupid," Porter said. He opened the door and left the office, leaving Marcus staring stone-faced at the floor.

CHAPTER 9

"Thanks for coming in," Dr. Montweiler said as he ushered Jason and Linda into his office. He pointed them toward a pair of chairs in front of his desk and sat down. "We have the results back," he said, "and I am sure you are curious so let's get right to it. We used what is called an enzyme immunoassay test to examine Jason's blood for presence of an antigen that is specific to the TL virus. The test is fairly new, but we ran extra safeguards this time to guard against false positives. Then we—"

"Uh, excuse me, Dr. Montweiler," Linda said, still standing, a sweet smile on her face, "I don't mean to be rude, and that's fascinating and all, but we're really anxious, and we'd just like to know the results."

Dr. Montweiler looked up at Linda, his countenance hardening. "Very well," he said. "Your husband has *Triptovirus L.*"

Linda's smile faded as she stiffened and swayed, then reached backward and grasped for the chair. Jason grabbed her arm and steadied her, lowering her into the seat.

"That can't be. That can't be, can it? He's so healthy," Linda said. "I mean, he's healthy, right? He can still get the insurance, right?"

Montweiler took off his glasses and massaged his eyebrows. "I'm sorry," he said.

The three sat in silence for a moment, Jason staring out the window, Linda, her head down, eyes fixed on the top of the desk. "So what do we do now?" Jason asked, not looking at Montweiler.

"When this thing first broke, you may remember the news reports recommending that everyone stay inside and wear face masks—they even became a fashion accessory in Paris for a time, as I recall. Anyway, since TL first broke, we've realized that while it is contagious, a person with a reasonably healthy immune system like you, Mrs. Kramer, is not necessarily at an increased risk. But because TL does remain fatal if you do get infected, we recommend that you employ reasonable safeguards in your dealing with Jason. Hand washing, good hygiene, safe sex, things like that. And of course, as soon as a vaccine becomes available, you," Montweiler said, nodding at Linda, "must get inoculated right away. This also all assumes that the virus does not mutate into a more contagious or deadly form, which it could do at any time, just like the flu mutates each year requiring a new vaccine each year." Montweiler looked into Linda's blank stare and paused, then consulted a chart in a folder in front of him, brows furrowed. "What's puzzling," he said, "is that Jason appears in all other ways to be perfectly healthy. You feel OK, right Jason?"

"Yes, other than some nausea and stomach pain, but I guess that's just stress."

Montweiler thought for a moment, and then closed the folder. "So no specific TL symptoms, like lung congestion or bone pain?"

Jason shook his head.

"That's good," Montweiler said. "Odd, but good. Maybe TL is already mutating into a *less* virulent strain. But that's no reason to relax. I'm going to send you to Craig Marcus."

"He's a specialist?" Jason asked.

"He's the guy who perfected the CDC's test to diagnose TL, so yes, he's very good. His company, Porter Pharmaceuticals, also appears to be leading the race for a vaccine, if what I read in the trade journals is any indication."

Jason nodded and rubbed his abdomen, and Linda stirred and pulled herself upright in the chair. She looked at Dr. Montweiler. "Is he going to die?"

Montweiler's mouth fell open a half inch. Jason caught the doctor's eye and offered an apologetic shrug. "Yes, eventually," Montweiler said, smiling. "But hopefully not before he can pay my bill." Jason laughed, but Linda stared dully ahead, not seeing or hearing. Montweiler's smile vanished. "I told my nurse to make an appointment for you with Dr. Marcus."

"Great, thanks," Jason said. Montweiler stood, but Jason remained seated. "Worst case scenario," he said. "How long?"

Montweiler rubbed his hand across the top of his bald head and exhaled, blowing air through pursed lips. He looked at Linda, who was still staring at Montweiler's now empty chair. "Marcus is the man to give you a prognosis."

Linda looked up at him. "Take a shot," she said.

"Based on what we know about TL's progression, and moderated by the fact Jason appears to be asymptomatic, *and* if TL doesn't mutate and he catches a more virulent strain—I'd say six months. But that's without treatment. And if I know Craig Marcus, you'll get the best treatment available."

Jason nodded. He stood and extended his hand. "Thanks, Doctor," he said. He grabbed Linda by the shoulders and pulled her to her feet, then steered her out the door.

—

The doorbell rang at 6:30 a.m. Jason, bleary eyed, stumbled to the door and looked through the peep hole. It was Scott.

"Go away!" Jason yelled at the door.

"Get dressed!"

"I'm not going this morning. I'm dying."

"Then a little run can't make you any worse."

Jason thought for a moment, but once again Scott's improbable logic had left him without a retort. He opened the door. "You have to buy breakfast," he said.

Scott pointed up at Jason's wayward brown curls. "Hair's trying to crawl off your head or something there, dude." He inhaled, then made a face and waved his hand in front of his nose. "Phew. Go brush your teeth."

Jason staggered back to the bathroom. Scott went into the kitchen and opened the refrigerator, found a pitcher of orange juice and poured a glass. He stood at the sink drinking it and noticed a piece of paper by the phone. He picked it up and read it.

"Why don't you read the mail, too, while you're at it."

Scott turned around and looked at Jason standing in the hallway, a towel around his neck. He was pulling on his sweat pants. Scott held up the piece of paper. "Xanax. Good stuff."

"Montweiler prescribed it for the anxiety."

“Linda can do that to a guy,” Scott said. He finished his orange juice, opened the fridge again and peered inside. "Do you have any fruit? What am I saying? Of course you have fruit. You are the fruit *man*!" Scott took an apple from a bin and crunched into it with gusto. Still standing at the open refrigerator, his mouth full of apple, Scott asked, "So how did it go?"

Jason pulled his sweatshirt over his head. "Not good."

Scott closed the refrigerator door and put his apple on the counter. He turned and looked at Jason. "I'm sorry, man. Is it what you thought?"

"I didn't think it was anything."

Scott looked down his nose at Jason. "C'mon, man. It's me."

Jason remained silent.

Scott nodded and picked up the apple. He took another bite. "I see. Hey, if that's the game, I can play."

Jason sat down at the kitchen table and leaned over to lace up his shoes. "It's Trips Lite."

Scott remained by the sink, chewing and looking out the window. "Damn," he said. "Capital ‘T,’ capital ‘L." Scott continued staring out the window, then turned his back to Jason and rubbed his hand across his eyes and dragged the back of his hand under his nose. "So, how are you holding up?" he said.

"Me? I'm all right," Jason said. "Not planning on buying any long term stocks, though." Jason watched Scott move to the refrigerator and put the apple core inside on top of half of an uneaten Pop-Tart. "How's Linda?" Scott said.

"She was pretty wigged out at first—lots of anger. But now she seems to be more at peace with it."

"Uh-huh," Scott said. "Maybe she'll be nice to you now." Scott looked around the apartment. "Speaking of which, where is W-Cubed?"

Jason did not rise to the bait. "She went in early to work," he said. "Said something about not being able to sleep."

Scott stood up, stretched, and pointed at the front door. "Let's go," he said.

Jason shook his head. "Why bother running?" he said. "I'll be dead in six months."

Scott jogged over to Jason and began kneading his shoulders and upper arms. "Not if I can help it. With the world famous Scott Durrant program of high-fat foods and alcohol-enhanced beverages, we'll have you all fixed up in no time."

Jason chuckled. "What a way to go. Um, by the way, why aren't you running out of here, screaming?"

Scott laughed. "I read *The Stand*, man. I am one of the chosen with immunity! That, plus I read online this morning that they don't think it's airborne, at least not yet, so just don't kiss me."

"No worries there, mate."

CHAPTER 10

SYMBIOSIS

"Are you ready?"

Linda sat in front of the mirror on her dressing table, staring at her reflection, her eyes somber and red. "I'm not sure I want to go."

Jason walked behind her, seeing himself in the mirror, and placed his hands on her shoulders. "I know it's hard for you, but I thought we agreed we'd work through this together."

"Isn't it just going to be more of the same? I mean, Montweiler told us pretty much everything we need to know, right?"

"Dr. Marcus is a specialist," Jason said, watching Linda in the mirror, her pretty face laden with worry. "We have to confront this sometime," he said. "Let's go figure out what we're dealing with." Jason grinned and bent down to kiss Linda's cheek. "Besides," he said, "we don't want our kids to grow up without a dad."

It wasn't quite a smile; it was more a softening of the lines on her forehead and around her eyes, a lessening of the frown creasing her brow. She stood and turned to face Jason, then placed her hand on his cheek. "You're right about that," she said. Linda turned back to the mirror, adjusted her hair and put on some lipstick, then picked up an envelope from her dressing table and put it in her purse.

"What's that?" Jason asked, indicating toward the envelope.

"Nothing," Linda said. "Let's go."

They sat in silence in the conference room, each staring at a different wall, the fluorescent lights buzzing overhead. Jason reached into his pocket and took out two white pills. Linda watched as he dry swallowed them, then looked at the door as Dr. Marcus came in. Jason automatically popped to his feet, but Linda remained seated.

"I'm Craig Marcus," he said, shaking hands with Linda and Jason. "Thanks for coming in." He sat at the table and opened a folder, then looked at the papers inside. "I understand Dr. Montweiler told you the test results."

Linda and Jason nodded.

"So you know that we need to start an aggressive antiviral treatment regimen," Marcus said. He took a pen from his jacket pocket.

"Mont Blanc," Linda said. Jason and Marcus looked at her. "The pen," she said. "It's a Mont Blanc."

Jason rolled his eyes, and Marcus smiled. "Yes, it is," Marcus said. He removed a form from the folder and laid it on the table. "I just need some background information." He filled in a few items on the form and then paused, his hand poised over a blank line. "Who's your health insurance with?"

Jason cleared his throat. "Uh, we're between insurance carriers at the moment."

Marcus' hand moved to the bottom of the form and placed an "X" in the box next to the words "Referral to Complex." "I see," he said. "We'll need to do some more tests to make sure we prescribe the best treatment, and typically tests have to be approved in advance by the insurance company."

"Tests?" Jason rubbed his stomach.

Marcus smiled. "Nothing too horrible, I assure you. We just need to find out exactly how far advanced the virus is."

"Once we know that, what are his treatment options?" Linda asked.

"We're lucky that Jason remains in relatively good health, despite the virus. So right now, while we continue researching this, we start him on strong antiviral medicines so that his immune system can try and catch up."

"So," Linda said, "what's the prognosis?"

Marcus took off his glasses and rubbed his eyes. "As you know TL continues to have a one hundred percent mortality rate, but based on Montweiler's notes and the test results, I'd say you've got a good chance of making it another six months."

Linda leaned forward. "How good?"

Marcus thought for a minute. "Fifty-fifty," he said.

"Otherwise?" Linda continued.

"TL can kill people who appear to be healthy overnight."

Jason exhaled and swore under his breath, and Linda chewed her bottom lip.

"I'd like to run those extra tests today if possible," Marcus said.

Linda stood up. "Sure," she said, not looking at Jason. "Let's go."

—

"Will you drive? I'm a little sore." Jason fished into his pants pocket and retrieved the car keys, then held them out to Linda. She grabbed them, and they climbed into their white 1998 Toyota Camry. "How'd it go in there?" she asked.

"It wasn't pretty. They had to look into every orifice to see how TL is affecting my lungs and bones."

"Is it?"

"They couldn't tell—or they wouldn't say, one of the two. Dr. Marcus is supposed to give me a call with the test results in a few days. Either way is bad—lungs, and you suffocate, bones, and you turn to mush."

They drove in silence for several miles, and then Linda reached between her feet and grabbed her purse, placing it on the seat between them, and removed the envelope from the purse and placed it on Jason's lap. "Open it," she said.

Jason felt the envelope, rubbing it between his fingers, gauging its weight and thickness. "Tickets to Barbados?"

Linda didn't answer, keeping her eyes glued to the road. Jason tore off one end of the envelope and dumped its contents into his lap. He opened the folded paper, looked at it and felt his gut tighten. "Summons and complaint for divorce," Jason read out loud. He looked through the documents, stopping here and there as he considered particular allegations. "Mental cruelty, mmm hmmm. Ahh, lack of support. Always a good one." He finished reading and shook the document in Linda's face, his initial anger hiding shock and dismay. "This is all B.S. and you know it!"

Linda pulled up in front of the apartment complex and brought the Camry to a stop. "Is it?" she said. "First of all, you're unemployed. My income is not enough for us to live on, but it's too much for you to qualify for welfare. You're better off without me. Second of all, you have no life insurance, so I can't count on having that income after you're gone. I'd better get myself in financial shape now while I can. Third, you won't be able to get health insurance at your new job, assuming you find one. And fourth, you're probably going to have to file bankruptcy, and there's no sense in screwing up my credit if you're going to be dead."

Jason stared at her, his mouth open. "Keith have you memorize all that?"

"You bastard. How dare you insinuate that Keith is promoting this!"

"Oh, please, Linda, I'm not stupid. Is Keith divorcing Mary, too?"

Linda reached over and slapped Jason hard, her long nails cutting three bright red stripes into his cheek. He reached up and touched his face, wincing as the salt on his fingertips burned in the wounds. "Yeah," he said, "just as I thought. Truth hurts, doesn't it?"

Linda reached across Jason's lap and pushed open the door. Jason stared at her for a moment, then relaxed and got out of the car. He slammed the door, then watched as Linda roared away, grinding hard through the gears. He squinted in sympathy with each groan from the Camry's transmission, then turned and trudged up the stairs to the apartment.

—

Keith and Mary had been busy. Linda's closet was empty, and most of her toiletries were gone. That's why she didn't mind staying for the extra tests, Jason thought.

He went into the kitchen and opened the refrigerator. At least she had left it well stocked, he thought, as he looked at the bottles of tomato juice and the piles of carrots. He stared at the vegetables for a moment, then grabbed a bunch of carrots, moved to the sink, and turned on the water full blast. He flipped the garbage disposer switch and listened to the metal teeth churn to life with an angry grinding hum, then grabbed a carrot by the green sprouted top and lowered it into the disposer. "Thanks for nothin'," Jason said. The disposer chewed, gnashing and swallowing great bites of orange carroty pulp, and when the first carrot was gone, Jason fed the grinder another, and another, until the whole bunch of 12 had disappeared down its maw.

He then looked through the cupboards, grabbing boxes of whole grain cereal and cans of salt-free, organically grown vegetable soup, and threw them to the center of the kitchen floor, the pile growing until finally, under the sink, he was rewarded. He reached in and retrieved a half-full bottle of vodka. Smiling, he returned to the refrigerator and found a carton of orange juice, then grabbed a glass and some ice and made his way into the front room. The remote control was on the floor. Jason stabbed at it with his big toe until the TV clicked on. The announcer's booming voice filled the room: "It's time for Jeopardy!"

Jason plopped down on the couch, the Stoli between his knees, the orange juice resting back on the cushions. He dropped some ice into the glass, filled it two-thirds full with vodka and splashed in some juice. He took a liberal swallow, shuddered, and smacked his lips. He turned his attention to the TV. "What is Cleveland?" he hollered, chagrined when Alex Trebek said, "Oh, no, sorry. The correct question is Cincinnati. What is Cincinnati?"

Jason drank two more screwdrivers in rapid succession and noticed that *Jeopardy* was becoming increasingly easier. "Who was Van Gogh?" he shouted to the answer about the Ottoman Empire. "What is calcium chloride?" He drained the glass and fell back on the couch.

"The Final Jeopardy answer tonight," Jason yelled at the TV, "is Jason Kramer." He stood and moved to the center of the room, Alex Trebek-like. "Let's check our contestants' questions." He pointed at the wall. "Contestant number one has 'Who is a loser?' Correct!" Jason began laughing and wobbling. "Number two? You wrote, 'Who's got Trips Lite, no job, no money and no insurance?' Right again!" Jason began to cry and sway back and forth. "Number three," he said, "what did you write?" He dropped to his knees, his body shaking, his face in his hands. "Who's gonna die?" he said. He rolled onto his back, his arm over his eyes, and sobbed.

CHAPTER 11

Irwin Memorial Blood Bank was busy. In a city with a large population at risk for HIV and thus ineligible to give blood, Irwin Memorial was always looking for donors. Irwin had a big message board in front of its main entrance on Masonic Street in San Francisco that announced the blood types for which there was currently the biggest demand. It also encouraged people to drop in and leave a pint in exchange for cookies and juice. Today the reader board proclaimed, "B-positive urgently needed," and so it was with pleasant surprise that Harold Watson, a volunteer at the bank, cataloged the blood collected from one of Irwin's recent corporate on-site collection efforts and found not one but two bags of B-positive. He put bright yellow stickers on the bags, wrote "B-pos" on the stickers with a black marker, and put the bags in a bin labeled "Urgent." He placed the bin in a segregated compartment in the freezer, knowing the blood wouldn't stay there long. Irwin Memorial was the chief blood bank for the whole Bay area, and demand was tremendous. I hope it's *good* B-pos, Harold thought, as he closed the freezer door.

—

"Here's the B-positive you ordered." The courier from Irwin Memorial smiled and handed the insulated container to a nurse behind the front desk at Berkeley General Hospital. She did not smile back. She grabbed the container and handed it to a waiting orderly, who whisked it away down the hall. "We've been waiting for that," the nurse said.

The courier shrugged. "Sorry. We've had a run on B-pos this week. That was one of only two bags we had."

"Where's the other one?"

The courier consulted a clipboard he was carrying. "Some clinic down in Fresno got it."

"Too bad. We could have used both pints."

The courier nodded. "Drive-by shooting?"

The nurse pursed her lips. "This is Berkeley, not Oakland. We need it for a surgery this afternoon."

"Oh. Right. Sorry." With an embarrassed grin, the courier turned and left.

Upstairs in a room at Berkeley General, 41-year-old Carol Davis was being prepped for surgery. A bag of whole blood hung next to her from a stand beside the table, the symbol "B+" written in black ink on a bright yellow sticker affixed to the bag. The viscous red fluid dripped down a tube into a vein in her arm.

"It'll be gone this time, honey."

Carol looked up into her husband James' face and nodded, wishing she felt some part of the hope mirrored there. She squeezed his hand.

The orderlies had finished working on Carol and were ready to wheel her into the operating room. "You'll need to wait in the lounge," one of them said to James. "I know," he said, his eyes still locked on his wife's, her hand still clasped against his chest. "The lounge and I are old friends," he said. He walked backwards beside the gurney as the orderlies pushed it out onto the hallway.

"Tell Julie I love her," Carol said.

"I will." James let go of Carol's hand and tucked it under the sheet. "We'll be in the waiting room," he said.

She smiled. "Where else would you be?"

He stood in the hallway, watching them wheel her into the operating room, and then walked to the waiting area and went inside. The teenage girl sitting in front of the TV didn't look up. "Hi Dad," she said. "How's she doing?"

James walked over and sat next to his daughter. "She says she loves you," he said, not answering her question

The girl still did not turn away from the screen, but James could see her eyes fill with tears. "She's going to be better this time, right?"

He reached out and put his arm around her, pulling her close. "You bet she is."

—

"Mr. Davis?"

James stirred from his partial slumber and looked up toward the waiting room entrance where Carol's surgeon, still wearing hospital scrubs, stood in the doorway. James nudged his daughter, who was asleep on his shoulder. "Julie. Honey, wake up."

The girl opened her eyes. "How's Mom?" she said, rubbing her face and sitting up straight, trying to focus on the garbed green form in the doorway. The surgeon walked toward the pair and joined them on the couch, then took a deep breath and exhaled. He sat for a moment, tapping his foot on the floor. "I'm sorry," he finally said. "The TL has moved into her bones."

James and his daughter sat in stunned silence, and then Julie placed her head against her father's shoulder and began to cry. The doctor looked away and stared down at the pattern in the tile on the floor.

James' hands, folded in his lap with fingers interlocked, began to tremble, the nail beds going white, the knuckles blanching. He looked at the doctor fiercely and said, "You told me that the medicine was going to work. You said that you had slowed it down."

"TL is a very new illness," the doctor said. "We had hoped that this new drug cocktail would work on Carol, but obviously . . . ." The doctor's voice trailed off.

"Obviously, you were wrong," James said, finishing the doctor's sentence. He put his arms around Julie and pulled her close to him.

"I can't take this anymore," the girl said, reaching up to wipe her eyes with the back of her hand.

The doctor stood and turned to leave. "She's in recovery," he said. "She wants to see you."

James watched the doctor walk out into the hall, and then turned to Julie. "Come on," he said. "Mom needs us."

CHAPTER 12

Jason opened his eyes, fighting the sunlight flooding his room, and looked at the clock on the bedside table. The big red glowing numbers read 11:37 a.m.—Jason groaned and pulled the pillow over his head. When he opened them again, he was still lying in a bed that hadn't been made since Linda left a week ago and was still staring at a clock which now smugly proclaimed that he was still in bed at 11:42 a.m. on a Wednesday morning when every other normal 38-year-old adult was at work. Jason sat up and looked around. The room was resplendent with the residue of a week of the Scott Durrant Therapy for Anxiety and TL—so named during a Charlie's Angels re-run at 3 a.m. last Saturday morning after several too many beers and chili dogs. Someone had thoughtfully arranged 28 beer cans into a pyramid on the dresser. Jason admired the work's aesthetic appeal before moaning and rolling out of bed. He wasn't sure what he landed on, but it left a reddish-brown stain on the side of his white cotton JC Penney briefs. The stain smelled vaguely of tomato sauce. Jason coughed and rubbed his temples, then grabbed two Alka Seltzer off the nightstand and hobbled out of the bedroom.

Jason made his way to the kitchen and threw an empty beer can at the flashing light on the answering machine. He glanced at the numeric display—16 calls. Up two from yesterday, he thought. Not bad to be so popular. Linda must be out trying to buy stuff using the credit cards he had cancelled. The thought of that gave him a wry sense of pleasure.

He opened the refrigerator and surveyed its contents: two pizza boxes, three cans of Budweiser, and a pint of orange juice. He grabbed the orange juice, dropped in the seltzer tablets and started gulping before he remembered that Scott had decided to make screwdrivers in bulk to save time. Jason spluttered and coughed, spewing the fizzing potent potable onto the cupboards. He had just about caught his breath when the doorbell rang.

He looked out the peephole and saw a kid in his late teens with spiky bleached-blond hair standing next to a bicycle. The bike had a rack over the rear tire with saddlebags attached to either side.

"I didn't order a pizza!" Jason yelled through the door, still watching through the peephole.

The kid didn't smile. He held up an envelope. "Courier. Hand delivery."

"Who's it from? Linda Kramer?"

The kid shrugged. "I just deliver `em."

Jason opened the door and waved the courier inside. The kid wrinkled his nose and made a face. "Ugh. Pretty ripe in here, man." He handed Jason a clipboard. "Sign on line 14."

Jason scrawled his signature and exchanged the clipboard for the envelope. It was plain and white with no return address—just his name typed on the front. The courier was still standing there, palm out. Jason slapped his hands on his thighs and rear where his pockets would've been if he'd been wearing pants. "Sorry. I'm tapped out."

The kid smirked and nodded. He turned to go but stopped, his eyes fixed on the stain on Jason's rear end. "Nice undies, man," he said. He went into the hallway and shut the door.

"Nice haircut, man," Jason called after him. Jason walked to the window and held the envelope up to the light, but he couldn't make out what was inside. He tore off one end and slid out a one-page letter, then sat down on the couch and read:

Dear Jason:

I've been trying to contact you by phone and e-mail, but you haven't responded. I hope this reaches you. It is very important that you call me at my office in San Francisco as soon as possible. I have some urgent news about your latest test results.

Sincerely,
Craig Marcus

Jason rubbed his left temple and threw the letter onto a pile of mail on the counter. He sat down at the kitchen table and took another draw on the orange juice carton, contents still fizzing. Jason jumped when someone started pounding on the door.

"I told you I'm tapped out!" Jason yelled over his shoulder, but the pounding persisted.

"Jason! Open up! It's me!"

Jason shuffled to the door and looked out the peephole at Scott. He flipped the deadbolt latch and made his way back to the table. "It's open."

Scott pushed the door open and walked into the front room. "You look like hell." Scott sniffed. "And you smell like hell."

Jason looked up through bloodshot eyes. "Thanks to you." Jason tried again to focus on his tall skinny friend. "What are you doing here?" he said.

"I took an early lunch to come and check on you. You had just finished the beer-amid of doom there when I left," Scott said, gesturing toward the stacked Budweiser cans in the bedroom. "That's a lot of brew, bro."

Jason belched, tasting acid in the back of his throat, and waved toward a chair at the table. Scott made his way into the kitchen but did not sit, walking instead to the counter to survey the growing stack of mail. "Just because you're going to die doesn't mean you don't have to pay your bills."

"I'm leaving `em to Linda in my will."

"Nice. No, seriously, you need to look through this stuff." Scott picked up the letter from Craig Marcus and read it. He looked at Jason. "Have you called him?"

"What, he's going to tell me I have three months instead of six?"

Scott sat down and placed the letter in front of Jason. "Look man, everybody is entitled to a little pity-party, but yours has now officially ended." Scott grabbed the phone from the counter and put it on the table. He picked up the handset and stuck it in Jason's face. "Call him."

"Why? I feel fine."

"That's what you keep saying." Scott wagged the phone in front of Jason's nose. "Put your money where your mouth is."

Jason stared at Scott, thinking. Then, with a snort, he snatched the phone and punched in Marcus' number. He held the handset to his ear, glaring defiantly.

"Dr. Marcus' office."

"Uh, hi, this is Jason Kramer and I—"

"Mr. Kramer! Thank you so much for calling! One moment, please."

Jason's mouth remained half open. Scott looked on, perplexed. "What?" he said.

"I'm on hold."

Scott got up to go to the refrigerator. He opened the door and peered inside. He was just reaching for a slice of pizza when Jason said, "Yeah, it's me."

Fifteen miles to the north in an office in the San Francisco hills, Craig Marcus was breathing hard. A file was open in front of him on his desk. "Thanks for calling, Jason," he said into the phone. "I've been worried about you."

"I know. Sorry. I just haven't felt much like talking to anyone for a while."

"I understand. Look, Jason, we need to talk about your latest test results."

Jason remained silent, watching Scott gnaw on a cold, tough piece of pepperoni and black olive pizza.

"Are you there?" Marcus said.

"Yeah."

"Do you remember when you were up here last and we took some more samples so we could monitor how fast the TL was spreading and what it was doing to your bones and lungs?"

Jason's sphincter twitched at the memory. "I remember."

"Those results came back and you are, uh, well, . . ."

Jason waited, rubbing his stomach. "Yes?"

"For lack of a better word, you're cured."

Jason sat, watching Scott chew a thick piece of crust. He watched him take another big bite and then chase it with a swig of screwdriver, wondering how Scott could eat so much junk food and stay so thin. It must be the genes, Jason thought. Genes, and all that running. He remembered at that point that he was on the phone talking to Dr. Marcus. "Excuse me," Jason said, his voice thick and garbled, his surroundings becoming surreal, like a Salvador Dali print. He watched Scott begin to rotate counterclockwise. "What did you say?" Jason said.

"The virus has disappeared."

"Uh-huh," Jason said, as he noted with amusement that Scott had now reversed rotation and was spinning to the right.

Scott stopped chewing, his mouth full of partially masticated pizza, and looked at Jason, who was now swaying in his chair. "Jason?" he said, moving toward him.

Jason, still holding the phone to his ear, tilted and fell to his right, toppling off the chair onto the floor. Scott rushed to him and knelt by his head, leaning over into Jason's field of vision. He tried to take the phone from Jason's hand, but a type of rigor mortis had set in, and Jason's stiff, unyielding fingers gripped the phone with white-knuckled fervor. Scott put his face close to Jason's. "Are you all right?"

Jason smiled, enjoying watching Scott's face twirl above him. "The pizza musta gone bad," he said before he passed out. His eyes remained half open, a faint smile on his face, his breathing deep and regular. The phone clattered to the linoleum.

"Hello? Hello?" Scott could hear the tinny voice coming from the handset. He picked up the phone. "Dr. Marcus?" he asked.

There was a moment of silence. "Yes. Who's this?"

"Scott Durrant. I'm Jason's friend. I was here when he called you. He's passed out." Scott looked up at the orange juice carton on the table. "He hasn't been eating too well lately."

"Call 911 and tell them to send an ambulance. I'll meet you at the UCSF med center emergency room," Marcus said.

"Should we come clear into San Francisco? There's a closer hospital here in the South Bay."

"No, bring him here. And hurry." Marcus hung up the handset and opened Jason's file. He grabbed a pen and began to write:

> Contacted patient 30 June. Reported test results and arranged transport to UCSF. Anticipate prescribing full battery of tests to analyze spontaneous suspension of viral activity.

Marcus put the end of the pen into his mouth and chewed on it, thinking, then picked up the phone again and dialed. "Mr. Porter?" he said. "It's Craig Marcus. We found Jason Kramer."

—

"I hate these things." Jason struggled to close the back of his hospital gown, but the fabric continued to part, revealing his nether region. "Every time I get up I moon somebody."

Scott laughed. "Humiliation is part of hospitalization. That's why doctors feel superior." Scott studied Jason's face. "How are you feeling?"

Jason looked up at a painting on the wall of his room. "Better," he said. "Bozo has stopped moving."

Scott followed Jason's gaze to the impressionistic rendering of a clown. "Wonder if that's an original Gacy?" Scott mused. "Must've been the first thing you saw when you came to. You screamed for five minutes."

"Salmonella-induced hallucination. I thought it was real. 'Coming to take me away, ha ha.'"

Scott shook his head. "Pizza didn't make *me* sick."

"Yeah, well you hadn't just been told you were cured of TL either."

"True."

Jason starting flipping through the channels on the TV. "I appreciate your staying here with me," he said. "I know you had to miss work."

"Yeah, well, I only have about three thousand vacation days to use up and what better way to spend one than sitting in a hospital room with you looking at your naked butt." Scott glanced up at the TV, and then pointed at the screen. "Hey, turn it up. It's the Mariners game."

Jason was pointing the remote at the set and obliging Scott when Craig Marcus entered the room. "Hi Jason, Scott," he said. They turned and looked at Marcus and the man and woman who were with him. Marcus gestured toward the strangers. "Let me introduce Dr. Ruth Wilson and Dr. Vincent Samuels from the CDC in Atlanta. They are actually the ones who discovered Trips Lite. I brought them in to confirm my findings."

Jason stared at Marcus, waiting for him to complete the pregnant pause. He did not. "Which were?" Jason finally said.

Marcus sighed. "In the last three hours we've done every test we can think of to look for *Triptovirus L,* short of killing you and performing an autopsy. We can't find any. It's like you never had it," he said.

Jason reached for his stomach and rubbed it with extended fingers. He looked at the three doctors, his eyes moving from face to face. "How can that be?"

"We don't know," Ruth said. "Your blood contains no traces of the virus. It's quite remarkable."

The room was quiet except for the television sportscaster's blathering. Jason felt the doctors watching him and waited for them to lick their lips. "I feel like a Thanksgiving turkey," he said. "You guys just can't wait to carve me up, can you?"

Marcus moved closer to the bed and placed his hand on Jason's arm. "We *would* like to perform a few more tests, yes."

"No!" Jason jerked his arm out from under Marcus' hand. "No. No more tests. You say I'm cured, fine. Let me out of here."

Scott stepped forward, defiant. "You can't keep him here if he doesn't want to stay. That's false arrest or imprisonment or something."

Marcus smiled. "No one is forcing him to stay. We'd like to pay him."

Jason opened his mouth to protest, but stopped, coughing out only a half-formed expletive. He looked at Scott. Scott in turn squinted at Marcus. "How much?" Scott asked.

"Are you his lawyer?" Jason and Scott turned in unison to look at Dr. Samuels. Vincent considered them through thick glasses that magnified his eyes, making them big like a bug's. His curly black hair was boyish, not at all befitting a senior cancer researcher. Vincent smiled and waited, his hands clasped behind his back.

Scott returned the smile, sarcasm evident in the lines around his eyes and mouth. "Does he need one?" Scott said.

Marcus held up his hand and shot a glance at Vincent. "No point in getting heated here, gentlemen. Jason is of course free to consult with his attorney. We have some papers here for Jason to look at—" he turned to Ruth who handed Marcus a stack of papers "—and we'll talk to him again tomorrow." He put the papers on Jason's lap, and then looked at Scott. "Good?"

Scott motioned toward Jason with his hand. "It's up to Jason."

Marcus looked at Jason. Jason thought for a moment, then nodded.

"Good," Marcus said. He motioned to Ruth and Vincent, and the three turned and moved toward the door. "In answer to your question," Marcus said, "free room and board, and $1,000 a week." He pulled the door shut behind him.

Jason whistled. "A thousand bucks a week? Just to lay here and get stuck with needles? Man, they must think that something really weird is going on inside me to offer that kind of money."

Scott sat down on the edge of the bed, lifted the cover off Jason's dinner tray, and surveyed gray meat loaf, stiff mashed potatoes and gravy, canned peas, a limp tossed salad, and a red Jell-O block. He swallowed hard and put the cover back on the tray. "Either that, or they feel they have to compensate you somehow for the free room and board."

In a conference room three doors down, Doctors Marcus, Samuels, and Wilson sat huddled over Jason's file. Computer printouts littered the table.

Ruth held up one of the printouts, scrutinizing the rows of numbers it contained. "It's the most amazing thing. Is it possible Jason's original ELISA results were a false positive?"

"No way," Marcus said. "I performed it again myself, twice, and the TL antigen was clearly present."

"But the amount of time between the procedures and today, . . ." Ruth said, thinking.

". . . is insufficient for a remission this dramatic to occur," Marcus said, finishing her sentence. He stood and began to walk around the room. "Plus, we have no idea how long he's been clean. He may have been virus-free for days before he called me." Marcus took a breath and looked at Ruth, who shrugged, while Vincent folded his arms. Marcus exhaled. "He killed it. He just killed it, that's all."

Vincent took a long drink from his coffee mug and grimaced. "Cold," he said, swallowing. He put the cup down and looked at Marcus and Ruth. "I guess all we can do is start running more tests and see if we can find out what makes this guy tick."

Ruth dropped the computer printout she was holding and rubbed her eyes. She laughed. "Maybe it was all those carrots he ate," she said.

CHAPTER 13

"Man, my butt is cold!" The words popped out of Jason's mouth the moment he awoke, verbalizing his nocturnal experience. He looked down and discovered that his hospital gown had parted company with his posterior sometime during the night, and his rear end was now poking out, exposed from beneath the covers. He adjusted the gown, and then saw the stack of papers Craig Marcus and his entourage had left for him yesterday afternoon. They were still on the nightstand, stacked where Scott had placed them.

Jason rolled onto his back and adjusted the blankets, then picked up the papers and started to read. After a few pages he sighed and dropped the stack on his stomach. Scott was right, he thought. I need a lawyer. He opened the drawer in the nightstand and pulled out a phone book. He flipped to the yellow pages, but stopped cold when he saw the thousands of entries under the heading "Attorney." He remembered that one of his high school buddies had gone to law school, so he looked up the name. There he is, Jason thought. Connor McHenry. Right here in San Francisco. He picked up the phone and dialed. He was amazed that Connor himself answered on the second ring.

"Connor! This is a voice from the past. Remember Jason Kramer?"

There was a pause. "Jason? Oh, my gosh! What's it been? Ten years?"

"At least. Since the last reunion, I think."

"So, how are you doing?"

Jason chuckled. "Things are a little weird right now, Connor, if you want to know the truth. I need your help."

"What's up?"

"I need you to look at a contract for me. And I need you to do it right away."

"Buying a house?"

"No, it's—tell you what. What's your fax number? It's easier if I just send it over."

"At least tell me what kind of contract it is."

"It all started when I got a life insurance physical. Basically, I'm in the hospital now, and the doctors want me to sign a consent form," Jason said.

"An insurance company's involved? Uh-oh. Those guys are tough. Who's your agent?"

"Um, Keith Lawrence at Rockport . . . sort of. Why?"

"You call him and tell him your lawyer wants to see your insurance application and the physical results. Have him fax them to me. Then you send me the contract."

"But the contract is between me and Porter Pharmaceuticals."

"Doesn't matter. You wouldn't be where you are if it weren't for the insurance company, and I need to see the whole playing field if I'm going to advise you."

"Sure," Jason said. "I'll call Keith right now."

"Sounds good," Connor said. "Get on it, and I'll talk to you later. And don't let that agent give you any crap. And don't sign anything."

"Right. Thanks, Connor." Jason depressed the switch hook, then dialed another number. He heard a series of rings, then a click and a voice saying, "Keith Lawrence."

Jason took a breath and paused, unable to suppress a grin. Keith is gonna freak out, he thought. "Hi Keith," he said. "It's Jason."

There was a long silence, then: "Jason! I haven't heard from you in ages. How are you? *Where* are you?"

Keith's voice oozed with its usual sham concern. Jason's grin vanished. "Listen, I need a favor."

Another silence. "Uh, you've put me in kind of an awkward spot here, Jace. You know Mary and I are helping Linda right now and—"

"It's not about the divorce," Jason said. "I need you to fax my insurance application and physical results to my lawyer."

"Lawyer, huh?" Jason could hear the wheels turning in Keith's head. "Um, Jason, how are you feeling?"

"Don't you mean, 'why aren't you dead yet?'" Jason said.

"Well, uh . . . ."

"I'm in the UCSF hospital, Keith. They want me to sign some kind of consent papers so they can keep me here and do tests." He paused for dramatic effect, then said, "I'm cured."

There was another long pause. "Excuse me?"

"Cured. Some kind of spontaneous remission," Jason said.

"Isn't that a cancer term?"

"Yeah, but I guess they don't know what else to call it with TL. I am virus free."

"What do you mean? Did they do surgery or something?" Keith said.

"Nope. It just went away. They want to pay me a thousand dollars a week to stay here so they can figure out why."

There was a low, long whistle from Keith's end of the phone. "A thousand bucks a week?"

"Yep. Plus room and board."

"Room and board, great." Jason thought he could hear muffled voices, like Keith had his hand over the phone. Keith came back on. "Look, Jace," he said, "you haven't signed anything yet, have you?"

"No. That's why I need you to fax my Rockport stuff to my lawyer, Connor McHenry. He's in the book, in San Francisco. He wants to look everything over before I sign the contract."

"You've got the contract there?"

Jason could hear more muffled talking. "Yeah," he said. "Right here."

"Understood," Keith said. "I made a note. I'll tell my secretary to fax those to Connor right away." Another pause. "Uh, wow, Jace, that's uh, great news! Cured! Kind of a miracle."

Jason grinned. "Yep," he said. "A miracle."

Across town in Keith's office, Keith disconnected Jason and put Linda through as he flapped his hand at his secretary, shooing her from the room. "Linda!"

"Keith what is it? I was in a closing, but your secretary said it was urgent."

"I want you to call your lawyer and delay the divorce hearing."

Silence. Then: "But Keith, the hearing is only—"

"Plus I need you to call the UCSF hospital. Tell them you're Jason Kramer's wife and you want them to fax you a copy of the consent form they want him to sign, except give them my fax number."

"What consent form? What are you talking about?"

Keith took a deep breath and exhaled. "It's Jason, Linda. He's cured."

There was quiet, then a sound like a phone hitting the floor.

—

"Who wrote these?" the lawyer asked, squinting at Keith over the top of a thick set of documents. The lawyer was seated in front of Keith's desk, his cordovan briefcase balanced on his knees.

"Impressive, aren't they?" Keith took a noisy slurp of coffee and settled back into his chair. "A friend of mine faxed them to me today, and now I need you to look at them for me."

The lawyer shifted in his seat. "I understand that. I want to know where your friend got them."

"That's not important," Keith said. "I just need you to review them and tell me what all the 'wherefores' and 'whereases' mean."

The lawyer laid the papers down on his briefcase. "I'm afraid it *is* important," he said. "I may have a conflict of interest if my firm has represented the other party."

Keith put his coffee cup on the desk and leaned forward, his jaw clenched. "Tell you what, sport. You do *not* have a conflict. I know who's on the other side of this and you do not represent them. Second of all, I throw about five hundred thousand dollars' worth of insurance defense work to your firm every year, and I can have you fired with one call to your senior partner. Now can you do it or not?"

The lawyer swallowed and picked up the papers again. "No, I mean, sure, there's no problem. Of course I can help you." He looked down at the stack. "Will the first of next week be all right with you?"

Keith shook his head. "No, I'm afraid not. This is sort of a rush job. So why don't you sit right there and read through them, and then we can talk about them."

The lawyer's eyes opened wide, but he didn't move. "Of course," he said. "I'll read through them here." The lawyer put the papers on Keith's desk and removed a legal pad from his briefcase. He sat the briefcase on the floor and started to page through the documents, making occasional notes.

Keith was on his third cup of coffee when the lawyer looked up, eyes bloodshot, hair disheveled. The documents were face-down in a pile on Keith's desk, the legal pad full of notes. "Hmmm," the lawyer said. "Interesting."

"Need specifics," Keith said. "What have you got?"

The lawyer started turning through the legal pad. "This is a very comprehensive and sophisticated release," he said. "Someone obviously wants to make sure that whoever signs these has very few rights left."

"What do you mean?"

"For example here on page 18, this paragraph dealing with informed consent—I assume your friend is a patient somewhere?"

Keith remained silent.

The lawyer moved on. "This paragraph gives the health care provider almost unlimited power to conduct medical tests on the patient. And this section here on page 24 is an assignment whereby your friend grants a proprietary ownership interest to the health care provider of any and all tissue or cultures removed from the patient."

Keith sighed. "In English, counselor."

"Right. Sorry. He's giving up ownership of any body parts, blood samples, tissue samples, stuff like that, that they take out of his body. They can do whatever they want with stuff they remove."

Keith nodded. "Mmm hmm. And what about tissue still in his body?"

The lawyer flipped through several pages and then paused to read. "Nope, that's his."

"What about compensation?" Keith asked.

"You mean money? Other than the—" the lawyer consulted his notes "—thousand dollars a week, that's it. They basically state in here that he's lucky he doesn't have to pay them for this treatment or whatever he's getting."

Keith sat back in his chair, thinking, his hands behind his head. "So what do you think, counselor. Would this contract stand up in court?

The lawyer rubbed his head and looked out the window behind Keith's desk. "Yeah. I think so. Unless your friend could prove he was under duress or something. You know, 'gun to the head' and all that." The lawyer watched Keith for a second but Keith didn't move, so the lawyer started gathering his things and straightening his tie, then he opened the briefcase and put the legal pad inside. "I'll have my notes typed up when I get back to the office and send you a copy."

Keith reached around the side of the open briefcase and grabbed the legal pad. "You know what?" he said. "Why don't you leave them here with me, and I'll take care of them."

"Uh, all right," the lawyer said, "no problem." He stood and picked up his briefcase. "Will there be anything else?"

Keith looked down at the legal pad and then up at the attorney. "Yeah, there is one more thing. Is this contract binding on the spouse?"

The lawyer squinted. "You mean the patient's spouse? California is a community property state, which means the husband owns half of what the wife owns and vice versa, but I think blood or tissue is probably separate property. So if the spouse doesn't sign, they're not bound by it."

"And you said that any tissue still in the patient's body would remain his, not the health care provider's, right?"

"Right."

"And that tissue is probably separate property, right?"

"Right."

"But what about money the patient makes with or from that separate property tissue. Would that be community property?"

The lawyer scratched his nose and smiled. "Sounds like a bar exam question." He thought for a moment, and then recited out loud, as if from memory, "Proceeds from separate property that accrue during the period of marriage acquire the characteristics of community property." He brightened and looked at Keith. "Yep. I'd say the spouse would have a half interest in that money."

Keith smiled. "Thanks, counselor. Send me your bill."

—

"Jason, it's Connor."

"Hi Connor. Did you get the stuff from Rockport? And the contract?"

"I did. This is some pretty bizarre stuff, Jason. I mean, you had TL, and now you don't, so they want to guinea pig you to see what makes you tick. Is that it?"

"In short, yep, that's it."

"And they're going to pay you $1,000 a week for the privilege."

"That's what they are telling me."

"This contract is pretty one-sided. You're giving them all the stuff they take out of your body, and you agree not to tell anybody about what they do to you or the terms of the contract. So basically, I can't recommend you sign this."

"But it's a thousand bucks a week, man. And they're not going to kill me or anything, are they?"

"It does not come right out and say they are going to kill you, no, but you are giving up an awful lot."

"For which they are paying me nicely."

Connor paused. "Yes," he said.

"Hey look, I appreciate your concern, but I've got no job, no insurance, no wife, and no money. All things considered, this doesn't seem like a bad gig."

Connor laughed. "The gig hasn't started yet, my friend. You may hate it."

"Maybe."

"So I take it you're going to disregard my advice and sign it. Listen, they will own you, Jason. This contract goes for two years."

Jason paused. "Can I terminate it before the end of the two years?"

"Nope."

Jason looked down at the line for his signature. "You're a good man, Connor," he said. "Thanks for your help." He picked up a pen and pulled off the cap with his teeth, scrawled his name at the bottom of the last page, and then starting laughing.

"What is it?" Connor said.

"The ink in this pen," Jason said. "It's red."

CHAPTER 14

"Good morning baby," Carmen Holloway said, her voice trembling. "How are you today?"

"Hi Mommy." The thin voice issued from the pale, balding little girl in the hospital bed, her once robust strawberry-blonde waves now reduced to isolated strands. "Where's Daddy?"

Carmen moved to the side of the bed and took Jenny's hand. "He's still sleeping, honey."

Jenny rubbed her eyes. "That's all he does anymore. He never comes to see me."

Carmen started to squeeze her daughter's hand, then looked down at the frail fingers and stopped herself, afraid the bones would break. "Daddy's tired. He needs to sleep."

"He just thinks I'm ugly because I don't have any hair," Jenny said, with all the brutal honesty an eight-year-old could muster. "He thinks I'm going to die."

Tears flooded Carmen's eyes as she knelt beside Jenny's bed. "Sweetheart, he loves you very much. It's just hard for him to see you when you're sick. He knows you're going to get better. In fact, he's been spending his time planning a big trip for all of us to Disneyland when you get out of here."

"Disneyland?" Jenny blinked and snuffled, the flow of tears stanched a bit by this news. "Really?"

Carmen smiled. "Yes! And Knott's Berry Farm."

Jenny tried heroically to smile back. "Can we go now?"

"No sweetheart, not now. You need to stay here and get better first."

The tears were gone now, replaced by a fretful pout. "But I hate it here. The nurses are mean, and I never get to go outside."

"The nurses are just doing their job, and—"

"Excuse me. I didn't mean to interrupt, but did I hear someone say the nurses were mean?"

Jenny and her mom turned in unison toward the door. A pretty nurse with a mop of curly brown hair and bright blue eyes stood in the doorway holding a syringe and a length of surgical tubing. "Oh, sorry," Carmen stammered, "she didn't mean it."

"No problem," the nurse said. "I'm new here. First day on the job, actually. But I'm sorry if the other nurses have been cranky. This place is in the middle of nowhere and people get a little cabin fever after a while."

Jenny smiled. "I like your hair," she said.

The nurse walked toward the bed, tousling the top of her head with her hand, warm brown ringlets bouncing. "Thanks. It sort of has a mind of its own, though. I like your hair, too."

Jenny touched her scalp. "The medicine is making it fall out, but it will grow back when I am better, right, Mom?" Jenny said.

"Right," Carmen said, mustering hope in her voice.

The nurse held up the syringe and tubing and said, "I think we can worry about this later." Jenny nodded with relief. The nurse took Jenny's hand in hers and smiled. "I'm Wendy Ross," she said. "No relation to Betsy."

Jenny giggled. "Hi Wendy. I'm Jenny and this is my mom."

Carmen's eyes met Wendy's, and Wendy winced from the pain and sorrow on Carmen's face. "Hello, Mrs. Holloway," Wendy said.

"Hey, you know my last name," Jenny said, tugging on Wendy's hand.

"I know a lot about you. I know you like chocolate ice cream and I know you like the Mighty Morphin' Power Rangers. In fact, . . ." Wendy let go of Jenny's hand and reached into a deep front pocket on her white lab coat. She pulled out a cellophane wrapped box and handed it to Jenny.

Jenny's eyes widened in delight and surprise. "A Power Rangers DVD!" She immediately turned to Carmen. "Can I watch it Mom?"

Carmen gave Wendy a look of deep gratitude. "Thank you," she said. "That was very nice."

Wendy nodded and took the video back from Jenny. "Tell you what," Wendy said, "I'll plug this in and then I want to talk to your mom for a second, O.K.?"

"Sure," Jenny said. Wendy started the movie, and as soon as Jenny's eyes had glazed over, Wendy motioned Carmen out into the hall and closed Jenny's door behind them.

"How's she doing?" Wendy asked.

Carmen's resolve crumbled at this and tears again filled her eyes. "The medicine is eating her up. It doesn't seem to be doing any good."

Wendy pulled a tissue from the pocket of her blue cardigan and handed it to Carmen, then placed her hand on Carmen's shoulder. "The medicine has to kill all the viruses, and to do that sometimes it has to kill some of the good cells, too."

Carmen rolled her eyes and pulled back away from Wendy. "I know that," she said. "But that's my point. The TL virus *has* stopped replicating, apparently, but it's not dying so they have to keep giving that stuff to her, so the good cells don't have a chance!"

Wendy remained silent for a moment, thinking. Then she said, "Have you talked to Dr. Marcus about this?"

"Dr. Marcus is hardly ever here. It's always just one of those staff physicians, and they're basically just orderlies as far as I can tell. I looked at her chart. I wasn't supposed to, but I took it from the nurses' station." Carmen took a deep breath, steeling herself. She looked Wendy in the eyes. "They only give her another three months to live—and that's *with* the medicine, this 919 stuff."

Wendy watched Carmen for a moment, then reached out and embraced her, holding her tight against her chest. "It's O.K.," she whispered. "It's going to be all right."

CHAPTER 15

Jason rubbed the inside of his left arm and looked up at the nurse hovering over him with an empty syringe. "You can't be serious," he said.

The nurse did not smile. "Serious as a crutch," she said, reaching for Jason's arm. "Let me have it."

Jason pulled his arm away and hid it under the covers. "No! You did that one last time. It's this one's turn," Jason said, holding out his right arm.

The nurse shook her head. "Wrong. We're having a hard time finding a good vein in that arm."

Jason pulled the covers up around his neck. "If you weren't poking it with a needle every two hours it might not be so difficult."

The nurse folded her arms and started tapping her foot. "Am I going to have to call Dr. Marcus?"

Jason stared her down. "Yeah, why don't you do that?"

With an exasperated sigh the nurse turned and walked out. Fifteen minutes later Marcus came into Jason's room carrying a folder and wearing khakis and a UCSF sweatshirt. His eyes were bloodshot disks buried in a puffy face that wore salt and pepper stubble, and his hair was unkempt. He shuffled over to Jason's bed. "I hear you're being difficult again," Marcus said.

"It's three a.m. and Nurse Ratched is in here like some damn vampire every ten minutes."

Marcus sat down on the edge of the bed and rubbed his eyes. "I know you're tired, Jason, but we've been through all this before."

"Yeah, well, it might help if somebody told me what was going on. I sit in here day after day eating hospital food, watching TV, wearing this stupid little gown, with so many needle tracks on my arm I look like a junkie and all anybody tells me is 'We're still doing tests' and 'We need more blood' or 'more urine' or 'more saliva.'" He took a deep breath and laid back into his pillow. "I think I'm ready to check out."

Marcus scratched the top of his head and sighed. He stared at the floor and began talking. "I'm sorry we haven't kept you more well informed," he said. "It's just that we're not really sure what's going on either. All we know is that you went into spontaneous remission from a case of TL that should have killed you, just like it's killing a lot of other people out there." Marcus motioned toward the news ticker crawling across the bottom of Jason's televised baseball game: "CDC fears TL mutation imminent. President calls for calm. Press conference tonight at 8 p.m. EDT."

"If it mutates before we can kill it, it might be game over. For everyone. Even for you. Remember, you might only be immune to the current viral strain. Even now more and more cases are being reported, and more and more deaths. CDC predicts an exponential growth in death rates worldwide if Trips Lite mutates like they think it will. Then it really *will* be life imitating art."

"What?" Jason said.

"Captain Trips will no longer just be a fictional character in *The Stand.*"

"Ah," Jason said, nodding.

Marcus watched the ball game for a moment and noticed how empty the stands were, and that the few people that were there in person appeared to be wearing surgical masks. He continued his earlier thought: "But, I mean, you got better fast! We've never seen anything like it."

Jason waited, but Marcus remained silent, still staring at the floor. "Is that it? I got better fast?" Jason asked.

Marcus looked up. "There *is* something else, something weird in your blood," he said.

"Weird?" Jason asked.

"We've isolated this protein that we've never seen before."

"And?"

"And we think there might be some connection between this unknown factor in your blood and your cure. But we're not sure. That's why we need to keep running tests."

Jason took a deep breath. "This stuff in my blood. You say you've isolated it. What does that mean?"

Marcus put his hand to his mouth and cleared his throat. "That's the bad news," he said. "We can find the stuff, but there's not much of it to work with. We've even been able to . . ."— Marcus searched for the right word— ". . . *strain* . . . some of it out of your blood."

"And you think it might be connected in some way with my remission?"

Marcus stood up and began to pace back and forth at the foot of Jason's bed. "We can't seem to find any other causative factor."

Jason smiled. "You mean it wasn't the carrot juice."

Marcus grinned back. "No."

"So if you can extract the stuff from my blood, can't you find out if it kills TL?"

Marcus stopped pacing and looked at Jason. "That's the bad news. We injected some of the, uh, X-factor into lab mice that had late-stage TL, congestion, soft bones, the whole bit."

Jason waited. "And?"

Marcus looked down. "It killed them."

"The viruses?"

Marcus shook his head. "The mice."

"Oh."

"And we only gave them a very small dose, partly because we weren't sure what would happen and partly because we could only extract such a limited amount. That's why we have to take so many blood samples. It takes a lot of blood to filter out a little of the factor."

"If it killed the mice, why doesn't it kill me?" Jason asked.

Marcus shook his head again. "Beats me."

Suddenly, Jason gasped and sat bolt upright in bed, his eyes wide open. He reached out and grabbed Marcus' sleeve. "The blood!"

Marcus jumped. "What?"

"The blood! I gave blood!" Jason yelled.

Marcus stared at Jason, not comprehending.

"Two months ago, at work," Jason said. "I was a blood donor."

Marcus continued staring, and then went pale. "The factor, . . ." he said, his voice barely audible. "Oh, crap. Which blood bank collected it?

"What? How am I supposed to remember that?"

Marcus shook Jason's hand off his sleeve and reached for the phone just as the door flew open and a nurse burst into the room, her face red.

"What's all the screaming about?" she shouted, looking first at Marcus, then at Jason, then back at Marcus. Jason opened his mouth to speak, but Marcus held up his hand. He turned to the nurse and held his index finger up to his lips. "Shhh," he said, "people are sleeping." He smiled a broad, ingratiating smile and waited. The nurse relaxed, then smiled herself.

"Mr. Kramer won't need any more blood drawn until further orders from me." Marcus said, still smiling.

The nurse nodded, looking at Jason, confusion evident on her face. Jason gave her a look of victorious defiance in return. The nurse turned and left the room.

Jason watched the door close then turned to Marcus. "What was that all about?"

The smile had vanished from Marcus' face. He grabbed his cell phone and punched a long series of numbers, then listened, waiting for the connection. Without looking at Jason he said, "We're taking a little trip. I hope you like the desert."

"The desert?" Jason asked.

"Yeah. Arizona," Marcus said. He opened his mouth to continue, but was interrupted by a voice on the other end of the phone. Marcus started and spun around, his back to Jason. "Yes, hello Mr. Porter," he said, whispering, his hand covering his mouth and the telephone mouthpiece. "I'm sorry to call you so late, but we need to arrange emergency transport to The Complex."

In the bedroom of his spacious Marin County home north of San Francisco, Phillip Porter sat up, suddenly wide awake. He lit a cigarette before responding. "What happened?" he said.

"Jason Kramer donated blood recently, and it may be best to sequester him until we can locate the recipient, given the effect of the factor on the, um, test subjects."

"I agree," Porter said, pulling on a silk robe and walking out onto his balcony. Sausalito and the Pacific Ocean stretched out beneath him in the darkness.

"I'm going to try to find out who received it," Marcus said, "but Jason doesn't remember which blood bank collected it."

"Start with Irwin Memorial," Porter said. "They're the biggest."

"Right," Marcus said.

"And if you have any problems gaining access to the information . . . ."

Marcus waited. "Yes?" he asked.

Porter inhaled and blew tobacco smoke into the cool Marin County night air. "Let Walter know," he said.

Marcus paused, considering Porter's words. "I understand," he said.

Porter flicked the still-glowing butt into the rose bushes beneath the balcony. "You haven't said anything about The Complex to Kramer have you?" he said.

Marcus shot a glance over his shoulder at Jason, who was lying in bed staring up at the ceiling. "No," Marcus said. "Of course not."

"Good," Porter said. A large gray tabby joined Porter on the balcony and rubbed against his legs. Porter reached down and stroked the cat. "Hello, Claudius," Porter said. Claudius purred and played in the hem of Porter's robe. "I'll have the car in front of the hospital in one hour," Porter continued, "and the jet will be waiting. And Dr. Marcus?"

"Yes?"

"Well done." The line went dead. Marcus turned back to Jason and hung up the phone.

"Who was that?" Jason asked.

"Your very generous benefactor. You need to get packed."

Jason shook his head. "I'm not leaving in the middle of the night to head off into the badlands of Arizona."

Marcus stared at Jason. "It's all in the agreement," he said. "You *will* go wherever we need you to go during the term of this contract, so get your butt out of bed."

Jason lay in bed another few seconds, then rolled out and landed on his feet. He pointed his finger at Marcus. "And you need to remember that *I'm* the one with the mystery blood. If I walk, contract or no contract, you'll never figure out what's going on."

Marcus watched Jason bounce on the balls of his feet. "Fair enough," Marcus said. "But in the short run, we do not want anyone to die, do we?"

Jason thought for a moment, and then shook his head.

"I'll be back in one hour," Marcus said. "Be ready."

"You're coming along, aren't you?" Jason asked.

"No," Marcus said, "but I'll join you there in a few days."

Jason nodded and Marcus left the room. Jason waited for a moment, listening, then dashed to the side of the bed, grabbed the phone, and dialed. He counted the rings out loud: ". . . six . . . seven . . . ."

"Hello?" The voice was thick and slurred with sleep.

"Scott, it's me," Jason said.

"Jason, where are you?"

"Where do you think? In the hospital."

"Oh. That's nice. So you just called to chat at three a.m.?"

"No, listen," Jason said. "They're moving me out of here. To some secret place in Arizona. I didn't know if I'd be able to contact you once I was there. I'm kind of freaked out."

"Have fun! Send me a postcard. And remember—it's a dry heat."

"Scott, I'm not joking. This is bizarre."

Jason could hear the tone of Scott's voice change. "Hey, it's all right, man, I was just kidding around. Wait while I grab a pen." There was a pause during which Jason heard a desk drawer being rifled, and then Scott came back on. "O.K., shoot," he said. "Tell me everything you know."

"I overheard Dr. Marcus talking to some guy named Porter. They're taking me to some place out in the desert called The Complex."

"Hmm. Never heard of it. When do you leave?" Scott asked.

"In an hour."

Scott whistled. "Wow. Total covert ops. Middle of the night and everything."

"If you haven't heard from me in a couple of weeks, I want you to come and find me. Can you still fly that plane of yours?" The phone was silent for a moment. "Scott?" Jason asked.

Jason could hear the emotion in Scott's voice. "Yeah," he said. "I'll be there, man. I'll fly out and get you." Then, laughing: "I should have never let you sign those papers."

Jason smiled. "Thanks, Scotty. Take care."

"You too. I'll be in touch."

"And Scott?"

"Yeah?"

"There's one more thing. I listed you as my next of kin on the paperwork I filled out, so if anything happens, you'll need to—"

"Stop it, man. Nothing's gonna happen," Scott said. "But thanks for listing me."

"Sure."

Jason hung up the phone and looked around the room. Get packed, he thought. Big deal. All I have is a toothbrush.

CHAPTER 16

"I appreciate your concerns, Dr. Marcus, but that information is confidential by law." The administrator looked over the top of her glasses at him. "You should know that."

Marcus took a deep breath and looked around the office, shifting in his seat. "Yes, of course I know that, Ms. Buxton, but that law was written to protect the identity of donors who might be infected with HIV. It was never meant to foreclose access to the names of individuals who may have received tainted blood."

Ms. Buxton reached forward and placed her hand on a file resting on the top of her desk. Both she and Marcus looked down at the folder. "Irwin Memorial's policy on these matters is clear. The names of both the donor and the recipient are protected."

"But in this case I have the name of the donor," Marcus said, leaning forward in his chair.

Ms. Buxton looked down at her notes. "Ah yes. Jason Kramer. Collected May 20 from a corporate donation at Anderson Kaplan."

Marcus reached into his inside jacket pocket and withdrew a piece of paper, then unfolded it and laid it on Ms. Buxton's desk, partially covering the sign that read "Gloria Buxton–Supervisor." Marcus pointed a finger at the paper. "That's a signed consent form from Jason authorizing you to release the information."

Ms. Buxton glanced down and gave the form a cursory inspection. "Doesn't matter," she said. "Without the donee's consent too, my hands are tied." She pushed the paper back across the desk. "Sorry," she said, smiling.

Marcus studied her face for a moment looking for some sign of compromise, but the smile remained fixed. Marcus put his head down and rubbed his forehead. "All right," he said, without looking up, "I'll come clean." He took off his glasses and rubbed his eyes. "That blood may kill whoever got it."

Ms. Buxton shook her head. "I already checked the file. That blood passed every screen with flying colors."

Marcus looked up and locked eyes with Ms. Buxton. "You didn't know what to look for."

Ms. Buxton's smile fell. "What do you mean?" she said

Marcus looked away. "Nothing," he said as he stood and extended his hand. "Thanks for your time."

Ms. Buxton remained seated, looking up at Marcus, eyes fixed. "If this situation is going to expose Irwin Memorial to some liability," she said, "I need to know about it. Right now."

Marcus withdrew his hand and moved to the door. "Have a nice day," he said over his shoulder. Ms. Buxton's mouth was still open when the door closed behind him.

Marcus returned to his car in the parking lot and sat, drumming his fingers on the steering wheel. He thought about walking back up to Buxton's office and quietly placing five one-hundred dollar bills on her desk. She can't make much money, he thought. Finally, with a sigh, he picked up his phone and called Phillip Porter.

"Mr. Porter? Craig Marcus. You were right about Irwin Memorial. They collected Jason's blood, but I can't get them to tell me who the recipient was."

"Don't worry about that," Porter said. "As long as we know it was Irwin, I can handle it from here."

"I almost had it," Marcus said. "There was a file on her desk with the name in it and—"

"Dr. Marcus," Porter interrupted, "I said that was the end of it. We'll call you with the information when we have it. Good bye."

Marcus put the phone back into the cradle and started his car. He glanced at the clock in the dashboard and shouted "Oh, hell!" as he slammed the BMW into gear and roared out south onto Masonic Drive back toward UCSF. He grabbed the phone again and speed dialed number. "Hi," he said. "I need you to get a message to Ruth Wilson and Vincent Samuels. I have a meeting with them scheduled at—" he glanced at the clock again "—right now, but I'm running a few minutes late. Let them know I'm on my way."

Doctors Wilson and Samuels looked up when Marcus burst into the room. "Glad you could make it," Vincent said.

Marcus moved to the conference table and opened his briefcase. "Sorry," he said. "I was double booked. So, now that we're all here, let's begin."

"Almost all here," Vincent corrected, frowning and tapping his pencil on the table.

"What do you mean?" Marcus looked to Ruth for support, but she kept her eyes down, locked on her hands folded on the table.

"All of us except the patient," Vincent said. "We're missing the patient." He glowered at Marcus and waited, and then Ruth looked up and watched him as well.

Marcus felt the hairs on the back of his neck stand up. He took a deep breath. "The patient," he said, "has been sequestered for security reasons."

"Security reasons!" Vincent jumped to his feet and started around the table toward Marcus, breathing hard. "What bull! You and I both know Phillip Porter smelled a profit and so decided to tuck our golden boy away somewhere safe." He stopped in front of Marcus' chair and panted down on him. Marcus smelled sweat and coffee and stress.

"CDC knew this research was being underwritten by Porter Pharmaceuticals," Marcus said. "As Porter's Director of Research, I am obligated—"

"Director of Research! What a joke!" Vincent said, his face in Marcus'. "Everybody knows you're nothing but a yes man for

Porter, smiling and making nice, publishing trumped up research about how wonderful your boss's company is."

Marcus opened his mouth to reply, but Ruth held up her hand. "There's no reason this project can't go forward even if Mr. Kramer is . . . sequestered . . . for a time," she said. "We still have enough blood and tissue samples to last us for the time being." She turned to Dr. Marcus. "Craig, do you expect we will be able to have access to Kramer again at some point in the future?"

Marcus' and Vincent's stare-down continued. "Yes, I'm sure you will," Marcus said.

"Very good then," Ruth continued. "I see no reason we can't proceed with our meeting." She looked at Vincent. "Can you, Dr. Samuels?"

Vincent started to puff up again, but resigned and settled back into his chair instead. "No," he said, "I guess I can't."

"Thank you, Ruth," Marcus said to Dr. Wilson. He pulled a folder from his briefcase and opened it. "So, where are we? Any new theories on the blood factor? Where it comes from, how he makes it, how it works, how we make more, you know, the usual stuff."

Ruth and Vincent exchanged glances. Marcus saw it, and his eyebrows popped up. "What?" he said.

"Since no one is going to say it, I'll say it. Is it possible this guy has some kind of immunity?" Vincent said.

Marcus jumped on him, firing objections. "That's ridiculous. TL is a totally new virus. His immune system had never been exposed to it before. You can't be immune to something your body has no defenses to. And so far, nobody else's immune system has fought this thing off."

"Exactly," Vincent said, "*if* you have no defenses. But the body does have one inherent and specialized line of defense against infections, in addition to plain old white blood cells. Interferon."

Marcus snorted, but Vincent pushed ahead. "I'm surprised by your reaction, Craig," Vincent said. "I thought you were the resident expert on interferon."

Marcus went red, but Ruth put her hand on his arm. Marcus took a deep breath before continuing. "Naturally occurring interferon is far too weak to explain results like this," he said. "Jason's remission was so total, so complete . . . the closest we've ever come is with the altered interferon I was using in my research as a grad student—"

"And we all know what a success that was," Vincent said, cutting in.

Ruth sucked air and winced, and the room went quiet. Marcus looked down at his hands and examined his nails, then stood and closed his briefcase with a loud pop. "I think we're done here," he said. Marcus looked at his watch. "I'll see you back in Marin." He removed his case from the table and left the room.

The two doctors sat in silence until Ruth finally broke the ice. "Nice," she said. "Our one shot at the Nobel Prize, and you just burned the bridge. Hell, you nuked it."

Vincent turned to Ruth and smiled. He reached into his pocket, pulled out a small vial full of clear, light yellow liquid, and held it up for Ruth to see, turning it over and over in his fingers. The liquid caught the sunlight and glowed with an amber iridescence. "You're wrong," he said. "We don't need the bridge anymore."

CHAPTER 17

The conference room at Porter Pharmaceuticals' Marin County headquarters was crowded. Marcus looked around. Porter was there, as well as Doctors Samuels and Wilson, both of whom carefully avoided looking his way. Two suits flanked Porter; one, a man in his late thirties, and the other a woman in her fifties. Probably attorneys, Marcus thought. The Driver lingered in the corner, cleaning his sunglasses. The low buzz of quiet conversation filled the room until Porter cleared his throat. All eyes turned to the head of the table.

"I think you all know one another," Porter said. "Let me introduce Mr. Quincy and Ms. Michaelson," Porter said, nodding to the suits. "They're attorneys with Porter Pharmaceuticals. And Doctors Vincent Samuels and Ruth Wilson, virologists from the CDC in Atlanta, are joining us as today as well. You all know Dr. Wilson, of course, TL's discoverer." Porter continued, "Would those of you wearing masks please remove them? It does little to instill confidence to see my top leaders cowering behind thin pieces of cotton."

Three men and one woman blushed and pulled off their surgical masks.

"The purpose of this meeting," Porter said, "is to evaluate the Jason Kramer situation. I want to thank my Director of Research, Dr. Craig Marcus, for the excellent summary—" Porter held up a typed report "—he submitted. I've shared copies with Mr. Quincy and Ms. Michaelson, so everyone now has the same information. Dr. Marcus, I'll turn the time over to you."

Marcus stood and moved to the back of the room. "Thank you, Mr. Porter," he said as he walked. He flipped a switch, and a slide containing four numbered items appeared on a screen on the rear wall. "As you can see," Marcus said, "we know four main facts. First, Jason Kramer's blood contains some type of factor, a protein, unlike anything we've ever seen before. Second, this factor can be isolated and extracted, but only in very small quantities. At present, it takes one-and-a-half pints of Kramer's blood to extract half a cc of the factor.

"Third, we know Jason formerly tested positive for *Triptovirus L,* confirmed with both redundant ELISA enzyme immunoassay testing and with electron microscopy, and now is in complete remission—a seemingly inexplicable remission. Fourth, this factor has been administered to laboratory animals symptomatic with late-stage TL, and the animals died from causes unrelated to the virus. The factor itself probably killed them. Unlike the mice, however, Jason has not been harmed by the presence of the factor in his system." Marcus looked around the room. "And that's about all we know," he said. "Questions?"

The room remained silent, all eyes focused on the screen. "Oh, come now," Porter said, "this is an intelligent group. Surely one of you has a comment or question."

"I'll be brave and ask a stupid question." Everyone turned and looked with relief at the lawyer, Mr. Quincy. "Why did it kill the mice and not the human?"

"That is not a dumb question, Mr. Quincy," Marcus said, "it's an excellent question. The answer? I don't know. But we have a few hypotheses. Dr. Samuels?"

Vincent stood and faced the group. He held a piece of paper, the ends of which shook vigorously as his hands trembled. "Um, the mouse autopsies indicate that the Kramer factor has a very potent cytotoxic—" he looked up at the lawyer "—er, cell-killing, effect. It did not discriminate between healthy cells and virus cells, and the mice died of massive organ failure in most cases. Now this may be a function of the differences between mouse physiology and Jason Kramer's physiology, or it may mean the factor is deadly to anyone but Jason Kramer, regardless of the species. Of course, without another human who has been exposed to the factor to study, we won't know the answer."

Marcus felt Porter watching him, gauging his reaction to Vincent's statement. Vincent was still standing, hands shaking, with nothing else to say, his eyes growing wide with anxiety. Marcus noticed his discomfort and jumped to his feet. "Thank you, Dr. Samuels. Are there other questions?"

The lawyer Quincy raised his hand again. "How can you think there's a connection between the factor and Jason's remission? If the factor is responsible, why would he have ever gotten TL at all?"

Dr. Wilson raised her hand. "Dr. Marcus? May I?" Marcus nodded. "That was very troubling to me too, at first, Mr. Quincy," she said. "But then it occurred to me that the factor could have been coursing through his bloodstream, not doing a thing, until he became exposed to the TL virus—at the store, at work, who knows? Then, suddenly, the factor had an enemy and went to battle, killing the viruses. It may be that the stuff has a TL-specific antiviral effect—at least in Jason, that is. Sort of like white blood cells. They are only activated by the presence of foreign bodies, invading organisms, in the system. Other than that, they're inert."

"So then," Porter piped up, "let's assume we can further isolate the stuff and refine it so it's not a killer. It will obviously have significant pharmacological value. I am sure you all saw the President's press conference last night. I have a clip." Porter nodded to the back of the room, and a video was projected on the screen behind him. The President of the United States, flanked by the First Lady, the Surgeon General and Dr. John Cornwall from the CDC, took the podium. An American flag stood behind him.

"My fellow Americans," the President said, "I come before you tonight to update you on what is arguably the greatest threat to our national security since nine-eleven. I speak, of course, about *Triptovirus L,* the virus that has reduced our once fearless citizenry to a group of timid, mask-wearing shut-ins. Since Dr. Cornwall at the CDC first identified the virus ten weeks ago—"

Vincent nudged Ruth at this. "Cornwall is taking credit?" he whispered.

"Shhh!" Ruth whispered back.

"—we have had teams working around the clock to find a vaccine for this scourge. I am told that great progress is being made, and that soon we will look back on TL the way we today think of chicken pox and malaria. But until then, we encourage you to live your lives as you normally would. We do, of course, recommend frequent hand washing, and good hygiene practices, but we see no benefit to your otherwise curtailing your normal activities. I'll now take a few questions. Ms. Walsh?"

"Thank you, Mr. President. I have a two-part question. First, can you tell us exactly how many people have died from TL, and second, can you please comment on the reports that it is mutating into a more virulent strain?"

The President glanced at Cornwall, who shook his head almost imperceptibly. "The figures," the President said, "are in flux because there were many deaths from TL before it was identified. But we believe that thus far there are approximately 1.2 million deaths in the U.S. attributable to TL. When you consider that on average about 36,000 Americans die per year from complications of the normal flu and that 600,000 Americans die annually from cancer, you can see that the risk is not to be underestimated, but that does not mean that you must curtail—"

Porter stopped the video at that point and took his place at the front of the room. "The lesson from all that political doublespeak? Everyone is afraid of TL, afraid of even the concept of a pandemic like TL. If the President doesn't fix this thing and people don't start going out and buying new cars and new houses and going out to dinner, he will certainly lose his upcoming reelection bid."

"Not to mention an entire generation of upcoming voters," Vincent whispered to Ruth.

"Thus," Porter continued, "it is certainly in this company's best financial interest—"

“And in the country’s best interest,” Ruth added, her voice over Porter’s.

“Yes, of course, the country’s best interest, if we can perfect this Kramer factor and turn it into a vaccine for TL. Assuming we can do that, refine and perfect the serum, could we patent it?"

Ms. Michaelson fielded this one. "Doubtful," she said. "There can be no patent protection for naturally occurring substances. Let's say you discover a new kind of oil-eating bacteria. They could be of tremendous benefit in cleaning up oil spills. But you can't get a patent on them because you didn’t invent them, they occurred naturally, meaning anybody else could find them and use the bacteria to clean up oil spills. In other words, they wouldn't have to buy them from you, which they would if you had the patent."

"So even if we succeed in isolating it and refining it, we can't keep others from getting their hands on it and selling it."

"Correct," said Michaelson, nodding, "assuming they can get their hands on it.”

"Hmmm," Porter said, nodding. "The patent problem aside, the other barrier to marketability is the quantity of the stuff that can be produced," Porter said.

Dr. Samuels raised his hand. "Excuse me," Vincent said. "Aren't we forgetting something? We don't know if the stuff works in *other* humans. Kramer may be some sort of freak. Plus we're still not sure it's the factor that caused his remission. For all we know, that factor could be doing nothing more than causing elevated cholesterol levels—"

"His cholesterol is 148," Marcus whispered in an aside to Ruth.

"—or keeping his hair from turning gray," Vincent said.

"All that just highlights the need for us to be able to begin human trials as soon as possible," Porter said.

"Human trials?" Vincent snorted. "We're months away from that. The Food and Drug Administration requires a complete battery of animal tests first before they'll approve human trials, and even then we have to test it for toxicity first in healthy people before we can try it on people with TL. But the way this stuff kills lab mice," Vincent laughed and shook his head. "Fat chance."

Vincent didn't notice Porter's frosty stare. "Thank you for that primer on the FDA, Dr. Samuels," Porter said, "but I suggest you leave the problem of human trials to us."

Marcus glanced up and looked around the room, certain all eyes were on him. They weren't.

"Now I'd like to return, if I may, to my original question," Porter said. "Quantity." He looked at Craig Marcus' graphic projected on the screen. "If it takes a pint and a half of blood to get half a cc, it's going to take a very long time to amass a workable volume of the factor." Porter pulled a stack of papers from his folio. "That's why I've been reading up on recombinant DNA technology. Dr. Marcus, you're our resident expert on that subject, so please give us your thoughts."

Marcus stood up. "I presume you're talking about using recombinant DNA to mass produce the Kramer factor."

Porter nodded, cigarette bobbing from his lips.

"I may have to give a little history here. I should also add that I'm only familiar with the subject as it relates to interferon." Vincent made a little noise deep in his throat, but didn't say anything. Marcus ignored him, and then continued. "Interferon is a protein, produced by the cells in the body. The cells only make a very small amount, though, and so it's tough to isolate a large quantity of the stuff. When interferon was first discovered, the research community was very excited because interferon is a natural anti-viral, anti-tumor agent and everybody thought this was the big breakthrough in fighting cancer. But they were hampered by two problems. Quantity and scope of efficacy. By the latter I mean that natural interferon was effective against only a fairly narrow range of cancers. Hairy cell leukemia, for example. But it was not much of a hammer against the big killers, like lung and colon cancer.

"Researchers figured out a way to address the first problem, quantity. Using recombinant DNA technology, they identified the human gene responsible for the production of interferon. They then figured out a way to clone that gene inside a very common type of bacteria, *E. coli,* the same bacteria that thrives in your intestinal tract—although *E. coli* does not naturally produce interferon. With that gene now inside the bacteria, the bacteria started to manufacture interferon, just like the interferon-producing cells in the human body, and with billions of *E. coli* cells doing nothing but producing interferon all day, it wasn't long before they had manufactured and refined sufficient quantities to begin larger scale testing and sales."

"What about the second problem, efficacy?" Vincent said.

Marcus smiled gamely and went ahead. "Although some experiments with genetically altered interferon were undertaken to try and increase naturally occurring interferon's efficacy against a broader range of cancers, this research was halted when the altered interferon proved to have some dangerous side effects." To Marcus' surprise, Vincent remained silent.

"So then," Marcus continued, "what about using this same technology to mass produce the factor?" He sighed and rubbed his forehead. "We would first have to identify which of Jason's genes is responsible for producing the factor. Human DNA is extraordinarily complex, and isolating that one gene could take years, despite the work done on the human genome, because Jason is apparently the only person in the world with that one specific gene."

"That assumes the factor's genetic makeup is different from that of normal interferon," Porter said.

"I'm sure it is," Marcus said. "I mean, the body produces a huge variety of substances, from blood to fingernails, and a different set of genes is responsible for producing each. The odds of the same set of genes producing both the factor and interferon are astronomical. Moreover, the stuff doesn't act like interferon. Both normal interferon and the altered interferon I mentioned earlier produce flu-like side effects, like fever, fatigue, joint pain and loss of appetite. None of the mice injected with the factor demonstrated any of these symptoms. Of course," Marcus said, looking down at the table and rubbing his eyes, "it might have killed the mice before they had time to develop any side effects." He smiled a wry smile. "No side effects to strychnine."

"So," Porter said, "it appears we should begin spending time trying to isolate the gene responsible for the factor inside Jason Kramer." The three researchers nodded.

"So then," Quincy said, "it looks like the stuff is a bust if we can't make enough of it to sell—even assuming it doesn't kill people."

The room was quiet until Porter spoke. "Not necessarily," he said. "Let me ask a question. How do jewelry stores make money?"

Silence descended again in reaction to Porter's seeming non sequitur.

"Margin!" Porter said. "They take advantage of the fact they deal in relatively scarce commodities—gold and diamonds—and charge incredible markups on their products. So instead of selling fifty pieces at an eight percent profit margin—volume selling—they sell ten pieces at forty percent profit. Margin is the key. Since we obviously have a limited and scarce supply of the factor—"

"Assuming it works," Ruth interrupted.

"—yes, yes, assuming it works, we'll simply have to recover our investment and realize a profit by tacking on an adequate profit margin and controlling distribution."

"Assuming we get approval for human use," Vincent said.

Porter leaned back in his chair and sighed. "Now I know why you people are in academics and not in business."

"One other problem," Quincy said. "Since we can't patent it, what's to stop Kramer from going next door to another pharmaceutical company? He is, after all, the 'factory' for this stuff."

"What about the consent forms he signed?" Marcus asked.

Quincy pulled a pile of papers from his portfolio. "Not broad enough."

Porter turned on him. "Not broad enough? You wrote those."

"We could not have anticipated a situation like this when these documents were prepared," Quincy said. "The problem is that we get ownership of all tissue and specimens removed—all the factor we can harvest. But those little cells inside Jason Kramer that churn out the stuff stay his."

"Then we'll simply have to think of some way to engender his continuing loyalty to Porter Pharmaceuticals." Porter said. His intonation made Marcus' skin crawl.

"And I noticed," Quincy said, "the contract is signed by Jason only. Is there a spouse?"

"They're separated," Marcus said.

"Not divorced?" Quincy asked.

Marcus thought for a minute. "I'm not sure. Why?"

"This is a community property state," Quincy said. "If they're not divorced, the wife can claim a one-half interest in the proceeds from the sale of the factor. Jason assigned his interest over to us, but without the wife's signature, she could become our partner in this venture."

Porter made a note on the pad in front of him. "If that's the case, I'd like to talk to her. What's her name?"

"Linda," Marcus said.

"Bring her in," Porter said, looking at the Driver while he jotted down her name. He finished writing and looked up at the group. "That should just about cover it. Anything else?"

The group remained silent.

"Very well then," Porter said. "I have just one more thing for you." He nodded to Michaelson, who removed a set of forms from her valise. She passed them around the table.

"What are these?" Vincent asked.

"Non-disclosure agreements," Porter said. "For obvious reasons, the subjects we discussed this afternoon must remain confidential. Please read them over, but I'll have to ask you to sign them before you leave the room."

Marcus noticed the Driver had interposed himself between the group and the door. Marcus signed the form and slid it back across the table toward the lawyers.

When all the forms had been signed, Porter stood. "Thank you all for coming," he said. The group began to file out, but Porter called after Marcus, "A moment of your time please, Doctor."

Marcus lagged behind and waited until the group was gone, then approached Porter. Porter straightened his tie and smoothed the collars of his shirt. "I think you can now see why it is imperative we locate the recipient of Mr. Kramer's donated blood," he said.

Marcus nodded.

"We'll let you know as soon as we've determined the identity of the donee," Porter said. He removed a cigarette from a gold case and tamped it on the back of his hand. "I trust Mr. Kramer has been sequestered successfully?"

"I put him on the plane myself," Marcus said.

"Excellent," Porter said, smiling. "There may be hope for you as a businessman yet."

CHAPTER 18

Jason sat looking out his window, staring at the flat expanse of desert stretching out under a sapphire sky and brilliant sun, thinking how perfect The Complex would be for a golf resort. Quiet, out of the way, discreet staff—all they need is a four-star chef, and they'll be set. He stood and walked to the bed where the supplies they had given him at check-in were piled in a heap. He took a quick inventory: shampoo, razor, shaving cream, toothpaste, comb—all the amenities of home, he thought. Jason picked up the pair of gray sweats he'd been issued and rubbed them on his cheek. Rough, he thought, but anything's better than one of those hospital gowns. He pulled off his shirt and pants and put the sweats on, then looked around his room. It was compact, like a Motel 6, with a bed, a nightstand, a small table, and two chairs. "Needs bigger rooms," he sighed, amending his earlier conclusion about this place being like a resort.

After a quick inspection of the drawers, which proved to be empty, Jason saw the TV remote control on the nightstand. He picked up the clicker and channel surfed for a while, stopping on ESPN and MTV. Thank heavens for satellite, he thought. The words to a Bruce Springsteen song popped into his head: "Fifty seven channels and nothin' on." Jason turned off the TV and lay back on the bed, whistling and staring at the ceiling. The phone was right next to him, but when he turned his head and examined it, he noticed no instructions or directory of any kind. Bummer, he thought. No pizza deliveries.

He looked at his watch. He'd been in the room exactly seven minutes, and he was bored stiff. I'm wearin' sweats, he thought. Guess I'll go for a run.

He had no trouble locating the exit to the outside grounds. No one asked him where he was going, and no one tried to stop him. The security seemed incredibly lax for what was supposed to be a top-secret facility. But then again, he thought, which of the patients was going to try to make a break for it? Tough to cross a hundred miles of desert to the airstrip in a wheelchair.

The grounds were well manicured and lush, an oasis carved out the harsh Arizona landscape. The grass looked like a putting green—Jason knelt down to feel it to make sure it was real—and all manner of trees and flowers decorated the area. The lawns were criss-crossed with asphalt paths about five feet wide—just wide enough for two wheelchairs, he noted. Jason was on one of these paths about a quarter mile from The Complex, about to enter a grove of trees, when he heard talking. He paused, listening.

"This is a palm tree," one voice said.

"It's big," said the other voice, a child's voice. Jason rounded the corner and peeked around the trunk of a huge palm. "They can even get bigger than this," he said. The couple looked around to see Jason's head sticking out from behind the tree. "Come on out," the child called.

Jason came out into a clearing. The child, a frail wisp of a little girl, sat in a wheelchair and wore a beret and a sweater, despite the heat of the July Arizona morning. Sitting on the ground next to her was a pretty young woman wearing a white lab coat, a tangled shock of brown curls on her head. The little girl held out her hand. "Hi," she said. "I'm Jenny."

Jason approached and took the girl's hand in his. "I'm Jason," he said. "Jason Kramer."

"Jason, this is my friend Wendy Ross," Jenny said. She looked at Wendy and grinned. "No relation to Betsy."

Jason studied Wendy's face. "Have we met before?" he said.

"Yeah, you do look familiar," Wendy said. They stared at each other until Wendy snapped her fingers. "Jason Kramer!" she said, "Now I remember. Dr. Montweiler!"

Jason continued staring, still not connecting.

"Remember," Wendy said, "the phlebotomist?"

Jason kept staring at her. Nothing. Wendy tried again: "The insurance physical?"

Jason blushed and slapped his forehead. "Oh yeah," he said. "I remember you now." They both nodded, enjoying their common bond. "So what are you doing out here?" Jason asked.

"I went to work for Porter Pharmaceuticals," Wendy said. "I left Montweiler about a month after your visit." She made a face. "He was a grabby old fart." Jenny giggled at Wendy's use of the vernacular. "Plus I wasn't happy with his rubber-stamping those Rockport insurance guys."

"Oh. So that's why you dissed me when you found I was getting a Rockport physical."

Wendy nodded.

"You've been here since then?" Jason asked.

"No, no. I started at Porter's Marin plant. This is my first rotation out here." She smirked. "I got promoted."

"So you know where we are," Jason said, kneeling next to Wendy.

"Somewhere in Arizona," she said. "They keep us in the dark. We had to sign confidentiality agreements before they let us travel out here, but I'm pretty sure we're west of Phoenix."

Jason nodded.

"So what are you in for, kid?" Jenny said to Jason. He grinned and looked at Wendy. "I taught her that," Wendy said. "Comes from watching too many old movies."

"Well?" Jenny said.

"Um," Jason said. "I'm not sure. They sent me out here for some tests."

"Tests, huh?" Jenny said. "You look pretty healthy to me." She nudged Wendy with her toe. "Pretty healthy." Wendy shot Jenny a glance, and Jenny unsuccessfully suppressed a giggle. Wendy tried to change the subject. "I thought you were going to go sell insurance for Rockport."

Jason rubbed his gut. "Didn't work out."

Wendy nodded. "Ain't havin' a conscience a drag?"

Jason opened his mouth to explain, but Jenny cut him off. "So, Jason," she said, "you married?"

Jason grinned at Jenny. "Why?" he said. "You lookin'?"

Jenny giggled again. "No," she said, "but I have a friend who is. Right, Wendy?" Wendy blushed and cleared her throat, and then stood and took her place behind Jenny's wheelchair.

"I think that's enough sun for today," Wendy said, bending down over the top of Jenny's head and going nose-to-nose with her. "I think your brain is getting cooked."

Wendy, still blushing, looked up at Jason. "Nice to see you again, Jason," she said.

"You too," Jason said. He looked at Jenny. "And goodbye to you, Miss Holloway."

"*Ms.* Holloway," Jenny corrected. Wendy wheeled her around and they started back toward The Complex. Jenny turned her head and craned her neck back around toward Jason. "Come and visit me," she hollered. "I'm in room 411."

"Will do," Jason yelled back. "See you." He continued watching the pair move back to The Complex. "Wait for it, . . ." he whispered. "Wait for it . . . ." "There!" he said, grinning, as he saw Wendy sneak a peek back in his direction. "Still got it," he said.

CHAPTER 19

Marcus was sipping a double tall skinny latte in his kitchen and listening to George Winston's "Winter Into Spring" CD when he saw the item buried on page C-4 of the San Francisco Chronicle.

He almost didn't see it because the headline was so small, overpowered by one of those garish electronics store ads. The headline read: "Irwin Burgled, Director Killed." His stomach twisted and the color drained from his face as he read the lead:

> Gloria Buxton, 32, was killed last night during a break-in at Irwin Memorial Blood Bank. Buxton, the facility's supervisor, was found dead by security guards responding to a silent alarm. Police report that nothing was apparently taken during the burglary and believe Buxton interrupted the crime in progress. Investigators will continue to examine bank records and inventory today looking for a possible motive. Police have no suspects in the slaying.

Marcus grabbed the edges of the kitchen table and steadied himself as the room began to spin. He stood and moved to the sink, his breathing rapid and heavy. "Oh, no," he said. "Oh, no." He turned on the faucet and splashed water on his face until he realized the phone was ringing. He turned off the water and picked up the handset, then placed his free hand on his stomach, hoping it would keep his voice from shaking. It didn't work. "Hello?" he said.

"Dr. Marcus?"

Marcus didn't recognize the voice at first. But its smooth iciness pricked his subconscious, and a face flashed into his mind. The Driver.

"Yes?" Marcus said.

"The woman who got Kramer's blood is named Carol Davis. She lives in Berkeley. Her number's in the book under James Davis." There was a click and then the dial tone.

Marcus let his arm drop, and the phone sank to the floor, the cord slipping through his fingers like water. He grabbed a pen and scribbled "Carol Davis—Berkeley" on a notepad by the toaster, then stood by the sink with his mouth half open as the handset hung next to him, buzzing with displeasure.

CHAPTER 20

"Thank you for coming in, Mrs. Kramer." Phillip Porter smiled effortlessly, his lips sliding back over perfect white teeth. He gestured toward a chair. "You're a hard woman to get a hold of."

"I know," Linda said. I've been staying with friends—"

"Keith and Mary Lawrence," Porter interrupted.

Linda nodded. "—since the separation," she continued, sitting. "Kind of laying low, trying to get myself back together, you know."

"Of course," Porter said, perfect smile persisting. "Can I get you something?" Porter picked up the crystal tumbler from his desk and shook it, ice cubes rattling among the vestiges of Porter's afternoon ration of Scotch.

Linda sat back in the chair and crossed her legs. She wore jeans and boots, with a white cotton Polo shirt. Her blond hair was loose around her shoulders. "No, thank you," she said. "But do you mind if I smoke?"

Porter extended his hand and pushed the ashtray to the edge of his desk. "No, no, go right ahead. As you can see, it's a habit we share." Linda took a cigarette from her purse and placed it in her lips. Porter watched her light it, watched as she inhaled and then removed the cigarette from her mouth, red lipstick on the white filter. She held the cigarette between two slender fingers capped with crimson nail polish. Porter watched her glance at her reflection in the mirror behind his desk.

"Filthy habit, though," Porter continued. "I can't seem to quit. Been smoking since I was twelve. I was up to three packs a day, but I've cut that back to two." Porter removed a cigarette from the gold case on his desk and lit it. "You?"

"I just started. After I moved out." She put the cigarette into the ashtray and watched the smoke curl up from the end. "Jason wouldn't let me smoke."

Porter placed his cigarette next to Linda's. "Ah yes, Jason," he said. "Non-smoker, I take it."

Linda rolled her eyes and looked at the ceiling. "He was a health freak. Always eating the right things, exercising, drinking protein shakes, all that stuff. I mean, that's great if you're into it and all, but it was like his religion."

Porter nodded. "Ironic, isn't it?"

Linda picked up her cigarette and stared at Porter over the glowing tip. "How's that?"

"He was so health-conscious and all and yet he's the one who ends up getting TL."

"Yeah, ironic," Linda said.

Porter let his eyes linger on Linda's legs for a moment—just long enough for her to notice. Then he looked up into her eyes. "Sorry to hear about your divorce," he said.

Linda studied the lighter she still held in her hand. "We're not divorced—yet," she said. "I had a hearing date set, but I postponed it." She watched Porter's face. "I thought I should wait for a while," she said.

"Oh? Why's that?"

She smiled. "Let's not fence, Mr. Porter. I know you've got Jason tucked away somewhere paying him a thousand dollars a week. He's obviously got something you want, and I want to make sure my community property interest is protected."

Porter laughed. "Whoa!" he said. "This was supposed to be a friendly little meeting."

"Please. Give me some credit. I know you didn't ask me here just to look at my legs."

The smile melted from Porter's face. "No, I didn't invite you here just for that." Porter stood and moved around to the other side of the desk, then sat down on the front edge, a foot away from Linda. He leaned forward. "The fact of the matter is," he said, "I have something very serious to discuss with you."

Linda swallowed, but she met Porter's gaze. She reached down and took a tissue from her purse, then blotted perspiration from her upper lip. "All right," she said. "What is it?"

Porter paused and took another long drag on his cigarette, then exhaled before speaking. "Jason's very sick. He's probably going to die."

Linda squinted, considering Porter's pronouncement. "But Keith said Jason told him he was cured."

"Keith had some bad information given to him by Jason, probably because he thought he could get the divorce put on hold that way."

Linda sat unmoving for a moment, staring at Porter. He got up and walked to the bar where he splashed some bourbon into the tumbler as Linda spoke up behind him. "What do you need from me?" she asked.

Porter turned around, sipping the whiskey. "Jason has been difficult to work with," he said. "He's very bitter about his condition. The TL he has appears to be a new strain and we want to study it after he's . . ." Porter paused, taking another drink, ". . . gone. But he's resisted our efforts at getting him to sign the consent forms." Porter looked at the floor, shaking his head. "He seems to have this irrational desire simply to be buried. Anyway, we felt that if he could see you and learn that you had relinquished your interests by signing the contract, we might have better luck convincing him to help us. This is a great research opportunity. No telling how many people might benefit from Jason's sacrifice."

Linda started to open her mouth, but Porter held up his index finger. "And of course we would compensate you for your consenting to the autopsy and our subsequent use of Jason's tissue."

"Of course," Linda said. She reached over and stubbed out her cigarette. "Look, Mr. Porter—"

"Phillip, please," he said.

"Phillip," she said, standing, "I appreciate your offer, but I'm going to have to think about it. Do you have the forms so I could look at them?"

Porter moved to his desk, took a thick file folder from a drawer, and handed it to Linda. "Do you have a lawyer?" he asked.

"No. Not really. I'll probably ask Keith to look them over."

Porter nodded. "I don't want to rush you, but for obvious reasons, time is of the essence. Jason is not getting any better."

Linda stood and extended her hand. "I understand."

Porter took her hand and shook it. "Next time we meet, let's not be so formal. Maybe I could take you to dinner. I know this great place up in Napa Valley. Auberge du Soleil."

Linda smiled and smoothed her shirt with her free hand. "I don't think so," she said. She paused, staring at Porter's forehead. "Um, I don't mean to be too personal, but do you use a bronzer?"

Porter touched his forehead, and then looked at his hand. "Bronzer?" he said. "No, but I do try to get in the sun when I can."

"Hmm. Must be the light in here." She turned to leave Porter's office. "I'll be in touch," she said.

Porter smiled and watched her walk away, admiring the fit of her jeans.

CHAPTER 21

Carol Davis lay on the examination table, her walker folded and resting against the far wall. The ultrasound operator stared at the screen. She reached out and twisted a dial on the console, then repositioned the probe on Carol Davis' pelvis, pressing the probe in deeper, turning it left and right and rotating it.

"Oww!" Carol said, as the technician pushed again. The operator continued to stare at the screen. "What's wrong?" Carol asked.

"Nothing," the operator said. "Don't move." Holding the probe in place with one hand, the operator grabbed the phone with the other and punched in an extension. "You better come and see this," the operator said. "I'm in exam room one."

Carol craned her head around, trying to see the screen. "What is it?" she asked.

Just then another technician came into the room and walked to the screen. He looked down his nose through bifocals and squinted, then grabbed the probe and started running it across Carol Davis' pelvis and thighs. Carol had been holding her head up trying to see the monitor, but the two technicians blocked her view. With a snort, she dropped her head back onto the pillow.

"Look at this," the second technician said, moving out of the way and pointing at the monitor. Smiling gamely, Carol lifted her head again and looked at the console. A ghostly green-black image danced on the screen, a diffuse group of whitish blobs. "That's your pelvis," the tech said. "You can see some scarring here . . ." the tech pointed ". . . and here, but . . . ." The techs looked at each other.

"But what?" Carol said.

The first technician looked at Carol. "Your bones are healing themselves."

—

Craig Marcus pulled up in front of a compact, neat house in Berkeley, California and saw three people—a woman, a man, and a teenage girl—standing in a tight circle, holding hands. Their heads were bent and their eyes were closed. The woman's mouth was moving.

Marcus got out of his car and moved toward the group. He could hear the woman speaking: "Heavenly Father," she said, "we thank thee for this miracle, and we thank thee for allowing me to stay with my husband and see my daughter grow. Amen."

Marcus cleared his throat. "Excuse me, Mrs. Davis?"

Carol Davis opened her eyes and looked at Marcus. "Yes?" she said.

Marcus extended his hand. "I'm Craig Marcus. I'm a doctor at UCSF. I apologize for interrupting, but there's something I need to talk to you about. It's rather urgent. Is there someplace we could talk in private?"

Carol reached out and shook Marcus' hand. "Oh, I don't think so," she said, smiling. "Anything you need to tell me you can say in front of my James and Julie. But I am surprised you heard so quickly. How did you get my name?"

Marcus shifted his weight from foot to foot. "Uh, well," he said, "I got over here as soon as I could. You see, Mrs. Davis, I have some bad news about the blood transfusion you received during your recent surgery."

"Bad news?" James said as he moved a step closer to Marcus. "Bad news?" James repeated, now eyeball to eyeball with him. "What is it? HIV? Hepatitis?" He turned to Carol and held his arms out to her. "Oh baby, there was something wrong with the blood."

Carol listened, stunned, then folded into James' arms, limp. She looked skyward, addressing the heavens. "Just can't leave well enough alone can you? First I get TL and my bones go soft. Then it's gone. Now this." She looked at Marcus. "Is it AIDS?"

Marcus did not answer her immediately. "Excuse me," he said. "Did you say your TL is gone?"

"Yeah," James said. "She had late-stage TL. They had gone in to try and put some pins in her femur 'cuz the TL was turning them to mush, but they said the bones were too far gone and they couldn't use pins. But she was just pronounced virus free—just this morning, in fact, they told us, after they did an ultrasound to see how her pelvis looked and then tested her blood. They called it a 'spontaneous remission' because they said they didn't know what else to call it. Her bones are already coming back. Apparently it's quite a miracle." He looked at the ground. "Or was," he said.

Marcus felt behind himself for his car and managed to sit down on the hood. "How long ago was the surgery for her femur?"

Carol looked at James and together they did some quick mental figuring. "About two weeks," she said.

Marcus began mumbling, thinking out loud. The Davises looked at each other, exchanging puzzled expressions. "Excuse me, Dr. Marcus, but the blood? You were saying?"

Marcus broke into a broad smile and jumped to his feet. "The blood was fine," he said, "just fine. No HIV or hepatitis or anything like that." He raced over to Carol and grabbed her wrist in a doctor's characteristic grip to check her pulse. "How do you feel?" he asked. "Any fever, joint stiffness, anything like that?"

"I feel great for the most part," Carol said. "Certainly better than if I was dead. What's going on here, scaring us like that?"

Marcus dropped her wrist, then hugged her. Carol's arms remained at her sides at first, but then, tentatively, she brought them up and patted Marcus on the back. Marcus grabbed her by the shoulders and held her at arms' length, examining her. "Would you mind coming in for a blood test?" he asked.

"Another blood test?" Carol said, wrinkling her upper lip. "I have been tested to death, and I am not anxious to head back to some hospital."

"I'll send someone to your home," Marcus said. "We just need a blood sample. That's it. I promise."

Carol looked at her husband and daughter, who nodded. "O.K., Dr. Marcus," she said, "you can have a little blood, but that's it."

Marcus smiled and shook her hand. "Deal. Do you have time for me to ask you a few more questions?"

Carol thought for a moment, then nodded. "Let's go in the house, though. The neighbors are watching." She pointed toward the front door. "Julie honey," she said, "bring Dr. Marcus a glass of lemonade."

—

"Eureka!" Marcus called out as he threw open the lab doors and descended on Vincent and Ruth. They stared at him with blank expressions. "The stuff is too strong!"

"Wait a minute, back up there, Archimedes," Ruth said. "What are you talking about?"

Marcus, panting, his face red, made a dash for the chalkboard, Ruth and Vincent on his heels. Marcus grabbed a piece of chalk and wrote "Jason" on the board, then tapped the chalk under the name. "The factor is in Jason's blood, right?" Ruth and Vincent nodded. "And in his bloodstream it apparently had a cytotoxic effect on the virus cells in his system, sort of like super white blood cells attacking an infection."

"That's the theory anyway," Vincent said. "So?"

Marcus wrote the word "mice" on the board and drew an arrow from Jason to the mice. "When we isolated the factor and injected it into the mice, it killed them, right?" More nodding. "But it's not *inherently* fatal outside the host, it's just too strong."

"Too strong? The amounts we're using are so miniscule, how is that possible? It's far more likely that the mice died because they were allergic or because of type incompatibility," Ruth said.

"No, no," Marcus said. "When we extracted it from Jason's blood and refined it, we also concentrated it. The mice O.D.'d on the cure!"

Vincent and Ruth looked at the board and looked at each other. "Maybe," Vincent said. "Still just a hypothesis at this point."

"Of course," Marcus said, "but what we should have done was keep the dosage the same, in the same ratio as it exists in Kramer's blood. For the mice, that would have been a very small amount—almost too little to inject. The lower dosage would have mitigated the adverse cytotoxic effects. We didn't account for the concentrating effect of the refining process. There's no way we could have known this without some real data from which we could extrapolate."

"How'd you figure this out, Craig?" Ruth asked.

Marcus put his hands on his knees and inhaled, trying to catch his breath. "We had no way of knowing until I found Carol Davis," he said.

"Who?" Vincent asked.

Marcus stood upright and drew another arrow from "Jason" down to the corner of the board and wrote "Carol Davis–Blood Recipient." "Several weeks ago," he said, "Jason donated blood at work. That blood went out into the world somewhere and Jason even forgot about it until I told him about the mice dying."

"And so Jason thought his blood would kill whoever received it, right?" Ruth asked.

"Right, and so did I," Marcus said. "We had to track down the recipients to warn them."

"How'd you find out who it was?" Vincent asked. "That information is confidential."

Marcus ran his tongue over his lips for a moment, then looked at Vincent and said, "The blood bank people understood our problem. I explained that it was a matter of life and death, and they worked with me." Vincent opened his mouth as if to ask another question, but Marcus cut him off. "Anyway, when we found the recipient, I was expecting to find that she was already dead or that I was going to have to tell her she had received some bad blood that would probably kill her very soon."

"And?" Ruth said.

"And instead, I found out she'd just come home from the hospital in complete remission from Stage IV TL."

Vincent and Ruth stared at Marcus, initially not comprehending. Finally, Ruth's eyebrows started moving up as her jaw began to drop. "The Kramer factor killed *Triptovirus L* outside the host!"

Marcus folded his arms and smiled a satisfied smile. "Spontaneously, and completely."

"Wait a minute," Vincent said, "that's pure conjecture at this point."

"Any side effects?" Ruth said.

Marcus' smile grew broader. "I asked her that. Only very minor ones. A bit of stiffness in her joints, a short-term low grade fever, a little fatigue."

"You have absolutely no data to back up this hypothesis," Vincent continued.

"She just happened to stumble on the right mixture," Marcus said. "A pint of that stuff coursing through her veins, and she's reborn. Who knows? *Two* pints of Jason's blood might have killed her."

"This is incredible!" Ruth said as she crossed the room, arms outstretched, and embraced Marcus.

Vincent watched them hug, then sneered. "If you go to Porter with this and you're wrong—"

Marcus suddenly turned and stepped toward Vincent, but Ruth held him fast. "I'm not wrong, Vincent," Marcus said.

"How do you know?" Vincent said. "There could be a dozen reasons for her remission."

"A dozen reasons for a complete, spontaneous remission of Stage IV TL," Marcus said, mocking him. "Yeah, right."

"Just because her side effects mirrored those of your altered interferon doesn't mean you've figured this out," Vincent said.

Marcus didn't look up, and Vincent pressed his advantage. "You're thinking that somehow Jason Kramer and his miracle blood are going to redeem your failed research on altered interferon, somehow maybe redeem *you.*" Vincent moved toward the door. "Funny, isn't it, Craig?" he said. "You almost lost your career looking for the cure for cancer—and now nature drops something just as good right in your lap." Vincent laughed and left the room.

Ruth and Marcus stood in silence for a moment, Ruth's hands still around Marcus' neck. "He's right you know," Marcus said. "That's what this is all about: Redemption."

Ruth put her hand on his cheek. "Craig, I don't think—"

Marcus brushed her hand away and stepped out of her grasp. "No, I mean it. When I heard that lady tell me she was cured, with her husband and daughter gathered around her, praying and laughing, all I could think about was how good this was for me, how maybe I could undo that black mark from years ago, maybe regain part of who I had been, before Porter. I wasn't happy for her at all."

Ruth reached out and took his hands. "I don't believe that, Craig, and besides, don't let Vincent get to you. He's just jealous that you were the one to discover this. Plus," she said with a wink, "you knew that he was in the bottom half of his class at Yale, right?"

Marcus' face remained clouded, but then the lines in his forehead softened and disappeared. "Thank you, Ruth," he said. "You're right. In fact, we should be celebrating!"

"You know what all good researchers keep in the fridge in the event of a huge breakthrough."

Marcus smiled. "Dom Perignon?"

Ruth clicked her tongue and moved toward the refrigerator. "Please," she said, "some of us are on a budget." She opened the refrigerator door and pulled out a bottle of Cook's champagne. "Domestic, but still quite good," she said.

They moved to a table in the back of the lab, and Marcus began extracting the cork. "What do we do about Vincent?" he said, wrestling with the wire cage on the end of the bottle.

"What do you mean?" Ruth asked.

"Even though Jason is safely sequestered, I'm uncomfortable with Vincent's knowing about these most recent findings. You saw his reaction, and you know his attitude. He's a little wacky, and this is pretty valuable information." The champagne popped open, and the cork whizzed across the room and crashed into a row of test tubes.

Ruth ducked and giggled. "Glasses," she said, sitting up and looking around for suitable containers. Marcus grabbed two Styrofoam coffee cups off the counter and filled them with bubbly. "I wouldn't worry about Vincent," Ruth said. "He talks a good game, but when all is said and done I think he'll honor the confidentiality agreement he signed."

Marcus handed one of the cups to Ruth and lifted the other in a toast. "To Jason Kramer," he said.

Ruth knocked her cup into Marcus'. "To the cure," she said.

—

The Steinhardt Aquarium in Golden Gate Park was, as usual, bustling with tourists. It was penguin feeding time, and the benches in the amphitheater with an underwater view of the penguin habitat were packed. For now, though, the penguins waited, marching around the top edge of the tank like dwarf tuxedoed soldiers.

Marcus glanced at his watch, and then looked around. He jumped when he felt a hand on his shoulder. "Sorry I'm late," Porter said from behind him.

"No worries," Marcus said, looking back. "The show's about to start." Marcus saw the Driver watching from several yards away in a dark corner of the aquarium.

Porter squeezed in beside Marcus, drawing an irate stare from the Japanese tourist sitting next to him. "Thanks for meeting me here," Porter said. "I always prefer the anonymity of a public place." He smiled. "And I like the penguins," he said.

"This is fine. It's certainly closer than driving up to Marin," Marcus said. He looked at the tourist, who was still glowering at

Porter. "Although," Marcus said, "the matters I have to discuss are somewhat, uh, sensitive."

"Oh, I'm sure the penguins are much more interesting to these folks than anything you and I have to discuss," Porter said.

Just then the water in the tank came alive with zipping and darting black and white torpedoes. A moment later, attendants standing on the rim above dumped in hundreds of pieces of fish. Porter and Marcus watched the penguins zoom after the mackerel chunks and gulp them down, then dive after more. The crowd in the amphitheater laughed and pointed at the birds' antics.

Marcus leaned over closer to Porter. "We've finished the tests on Carol Davis," he said.

"Oh?" Porter said. "What did you find out?" The tourist next to Porter was now busy snapping photographs of the penguins.

"The most important thing we learned is that the Kramer factor is nowhere to be found in her system."

"Meaning?"

"Meaning the body must treat it like any other pharmaceutical agent. The stuff circulates through the system, kills TL, and is flushed out by the excretory system. Like penicillin or Retrovir. We were hoping to find that the factor persisted in the recipient's body for a while so we could study its longer term effects on the organs. We were also hoping to see if it produced a mutagenic effect on the recipient's own interferon."

"Sorry. I don't follow," Porter said, staring straight ahead, watching the penguins.

"Like a virus," Marcus said. "When a virus invades a host's body, it genetically alters the host's own cells, turning them into little virus factories. We were hoping that Jason's blood factor would produce a similar effect in Carol Davis' interferon. If it did, two things would happen. First, we'd have another source of the factor to study, and second, it would mean Carol Davis would have immunity from another case of TL."

Porter raised an eyebrow, but still did not turn his head toward Marcus.

"For example," Marcus said, "once you have the chicken pox, and assuming you survive, you're immune to it for the rest of your life. Your body produces antibodies to the virus that protect you from ever being infected by chicken pox again. That's the way a vaccination works. The dead or weakened viruses produce an immune response, and antibodies are created that stay in your body the rest of your life. If Jason's factor had caused Carol Davis' system to create antibodies to TL, she'd effectively be immune. But because the Kramer factor is not a vaccine made from dead or weakened viruses, no antibodies are created."

Porter turned to Marcus. "So Jason Kramer is the only one with that immunity, correct?"

"Apparently."

"So if Carol Davis has a recurrence, or if TL mutates, she'll need another dose. Like with the common cold. No vaccine for that because the virus mutates so frequently, and that's why you catch a new cold every year—you have antibodies to the old virus, but not the new strain. Imagine what would happen if the chicken pox virus mutated dramatically enough to fool your antibodies—even if you had it before or had a shot, you could get it again. Same thing with TL, since it seems to like to mutate."

Marcus looked down, thinking. After a moment he looked up at Porter. "Yes, but that stuff of Jason's is pretty strong. I have to believe that it offers some kind of ongoing protection, that it *did* change Davis' immune system such that she would kill even a mutated form of TL if she were exposed again. It's like being reborn."

Porter nodded, then reached into his inside jacket pocket and pulled out a legal size envelope. He handed it to Marcus.

"What's this?" Marcus asked. Porter didn't respond. Marcus opened the envelope and pulled out the single sheet of paper inside. He unfolded it and read:

Due to irreconcilable personality conflicts with Dr. Craig Marcus, I hereby tender my resignation as a consultant for Porter Pharmaceuticals. I cannot work in an environment that fosters such hostility and professional animosity. Dr. Marcus has demonstrated a complete lack of professionalism in almost all aspects of his research into, and study of, the Jason Kramer phenomenon. This resignation shall be effective immediately.

Dr. Vincent Samuels

Marcus finished reading and put the letter in the envelope. He began to give it to Porter, but Porter held up his hand. "No, no, you keep it. I thought you'd like it for your little FDA scrapbook," Porter said.

Marcus' upper lip twitched, but he still managed a terse "Thanks," to Porter. He stuffed the letter into his pocket. "Doesn't this concern you?" Marcus asked.

"No. Why should it? Samuels signed the confidentiality agreement."

"Yeah, well, I know how angry he was. I doubt that a contract will have much effect on him at this stage."

Porter nodded. "If he chooses to disregard his contractual obligations, we'll have to enforce the agreement in some other way, that's all," he said.

"Like you did with Gloria Buxton," Marcus said.

Porter turned and locked eyes with Marcus. "Yes," he said, his voice low and measured, "like Gloria Buxton." Porter pressed his finger into Marcus' chest. "A name you will never mention again." Porter stared at him a moment longer, then stood and moved through the room, disappearing into the crowd.

Marcus watched him leave, then shivered, his hands and feet numb. He stared at the floor, until suddenly a Nikon camera was thrust into his field of vision. He looked up into the face of the tourist who had been sitting next to Porter. The tourist jabbed the camera at Marcus again and again, gesturing and speaking Japanese, then pointing at himself. Marcus smiled and took the camera. The tourist grinned and ran back to the penguin tank. He splayed himself up against the glass and beamed in Marcus' direction. Marcus looked through the viewfinder and twisted the focus ring.

The tourist's image jumped into sharp clarity, but all the penguins were gone. He was standing against a huge empty tank of water. Marcus released the shutter and saw the flash light up the tourist's eyes, turning them red. A moment later the tourist ran back and took the camera, still grinning and now apparently thanking Marcus. Marcus handed the camera back and nodded. He looked around to see if he could catch a parting glimpse of Porter or the Driver, but they were gone.

—

"Thanks for seeing me, Dr. Carnelli."

Paul Carnelli extended his hand and gestured toward a chair. "Anything for a former student, Vincent," he said. "Please, have a seat."

Dr. Samuels moved across the room and sat down. He drummed his fingers on the arms of the chair and worried the knot in his tie. He shuffled his feet back and forth on the carpet.

"For heaven's sake, Vincent, stop fidgeting. You act like this is the principal's office and you've just been caught shooting spitballs," Carnelli said.

Vincent tried to smile and grabbed the arms of the chair in defiance of his nerves. "Sorry," he said, taking a deep breath. "Perhaps you've heard that I recently left the CDC and my consulting position with Porter Pharmaceuticals to hang out a shingle."

Carnelli stuck out his lower lip and scratched his forehead, thinking, then shook his head. "No, I hadn't heard that. What happened?"

"Not to sound trite, but let's just say I had creative differences with Craig Marcus."

"Craig Marcus!" Carnelli said, leaning back in his chair and putting his hands behind his head. "I haven't heard much from old Marcus since that altered interferon debacle." Carnelli looked off into the corner of the room, his eyes glazed, remembering. "He came here first before Porter picked him up. Thank heavens we didn't hire him. All that baggage!" Carnelli's eyes refocused. He looked at Vincent. "Brilliant researcher, though."

Vincent cleared his throat. "Yes, uh, well anyway, I'm no longer with Porter and I wanted to visit with you about an opportunity that Amwell Pharmaceuticals may be interested in."

Immediately, Carnelli leaned forward. "Hold on, Vincent," he said. "We got scorched in court two years ago when we, according to the jury, 'participated in and contributed to the breach of a non-compete agreement.' Some little guy from Pfizer was in my office sitting right where you are, telling me he had the cure for cancer, and ten months later our insurance company was writing out a fifteen million dollar check." He lowered his voice a notch and continued. "For obvious reasons, I'm still a little gun shy."

Vincent did not respond. Instead, he reached into his pocket and pulled out a small insulated carrying case, which he sat on Carnelli's desk. Carnelli's left eyebrow arched up a bit as he leaned in and looked down at the package. Vincent opened the container and removed a vial of clear, light yellow, semi-viscous liquid. He held it up between thumb and index finger.

"It looks like plasma," Carnelli said, squinting.

Vincent smiled. "What this is," he said, "is the answer to your prayers."

CHAPTER 22

Marcus leaned over the cage and watched the little white mice scamper about. He looked with particular interest at one that was now walking to the corner of the cage, thoughtfully chewing on a food pellet. The mouse walked with a slight limp.

"How's Mickey?"

Marcus looked up at Ruth walking toward him, the lab door closing behind her. "Fine," Marcus said, "considering that he should be dead."

Ruth joined Marcus and looked down at the mice. She reached in and grabbed Mickey and lifted him out of the cage. She placed him on her open palm and held him up at eye level, scrutinizing him. Mickey had been holding on to his food pellet for dear life, and now resumed crunching, oblivious to Ruth's inspection. "Hmm," Ruth said. "Marked decrease respiratory distress."

"Yes. And he's almost walking and running normally."

Ruth nodded. "Injection site is healing nicely, too," she said. As if on cue, Mickey dropped his food pellet and began scratching the tiny puncture wound on his neck with his hind foot.

"Looks like we've got the dosage figured out. For mice, at least," Marcus said.

Ruth looked at the clock on the wall. "How long since the injection?"

"Forty-eight hours."

Ruth stroked the mouse's back. "Remarkable," she said, lowering him down into the cage. "Now we just have to extrapolate from Mickey's data and the Carol Davis data to arrive at a safe dosage for humans."

Marcus laughed, half snorting. "Right," he said. "But let's not forget about poor Minnie and Ben."

"Good point," Ruth said, scratching notes in a three-ring binder. "May they rest in peace."

"So I guess that now raises the question," Marcus said, "whom will the human corollaries to Minnie and Ben be? And what about the FDA? You know we need more extensive animal trials before they'll let us try this stuff on people."

Ruth snapped the binder shut and slammed it down on the table. "We have *these* animal trials," she protested, "and what about Carol Davis? We've got to talk to Porter about getting exigent circumstances approval from the FDA for expedited human trials. You know that's what they did with AZT."

"AZT retards replication of the HIV virus," Marcus said. "It doesn't kill people if you give them one-tenth of a cc too much."

Ruth sighed and put her hands on her hips. "Hell, Marcus," she said, "what's your problem? Do you want to do this or not?"

Marcus stiffened. "Believe it or not, Dr. Wilson, I'm trying to keep you out of jail. We're going to toe the line on this. Period."

"I understand that, Craig. Thank you. But I think we need to move ahead as quickly as possible." Ruth walked over to Marcus and put her hand on his shoulder. "After all," she said, "this is the cure for TL we're talking about here."

Marcus took a deep breath and exhaled. "I know that," he said. "But the other thing you've got to remember is that we don't have an unlimited supply of the factor. The testing phase alone could kill Jason. Plus imagine what happens if we get the dosage right and we *can* replicate the Carol Davis results in a human trial. Everybody's going to want the cure—but there's only so much of Jason's blood to go around, and we can't clone the factor in *E. coli* yet."

"One step at a time, Craig. I know Jason's limitations. I'm the last person who wants to kill the goose that laid the golden egg."

Marcus winced at the bad metaphor.

"Sorry," she said. "It's the only thing I could think of."

Marcus' frown persisted before he finally relented. "Tell you what," he said. "I'll talk to Porter—on one condition. We complete the primate trials first."

Ruth studied Marcus' face for several seconds, her smile gone. "That's fine," she said. "But I want you to remember one thing—thousands of people will die from TL between now and the time those trials are completed."

"And you're prepared to kill those same people *now* through premature dissemination of the factor?"

Ruth stood and moved to the door. "I'm surprised at your attitude, Craig. I heard you approved of the use of unproven serum—even if it did kill people."

The two fell silent, Marcus at the table pretending to look at his notes, and Ruth at the door, pretending to look at her shoes. She turned and left the room.

The pencil Marcus was holding snapped in two in his fingers. "Primate trials first," he said.

CHAPTER 23

The small, well-lit library at The Complex had four tables, each with four chairs, a selection of current magazines, and an assortment of hard cover and paperback books arranged in prim rows on the bookshelves that lined the room. Jason moved to one of the shelves and removed a worn checkerboard with bold red and black squares. He also grabbed a wooden box, then returned to his seat. He opened the box and dumped a set of plastic chessmen onto the table, sending the black and white pieces clattering across the surface. Jason began to set up the game, centering each piece in its square. The library door opened, and Jenny came into the room in a wheelchair pushed by Wendy. Jenny, her head wrapped in a colorful scarf with tufts of hair sticking out here and there, was grinning madly. "I'm gonna cream you today," she said.

Wendy pushed Jenny up to the table and sat down next to her then looked across at Jason. "How are you feeling?" she asked.

"Good, good," Jason said, still worrying over the chess pieces. "You?"

"Fine, thanks," Wendy said. She gave Jenny a little nod and smile, which Jenny acknowledged.

"No coaching from the sidelines today," Jason said without looking up.

Jenny and Wendy broke out into giggles. "No fair!" Jenny protested. "You always win unless Wendy helps me."

"You'll never improve if someone helps you all the time."

"Yeah, right, that's what you always say."

Jason picked up a black pawn and a white pawn and concealed one inside each fist. He held out his hands to Jenny. "Pick your color," he said.

Jenny tapped Jason's right hand and he opened his fist to reveal the black pawn. "Darn it!" she said. "I wanted to go first."

Jason spun the board around so the white pieces were in front of him. He pushed the pawn in front of his king forward two spaces, then smiled at Jenny. "Your move," he said. "Show me your stuff."

"I've been working on that Ruy Lopez stuff you showed me last Thursday," Jenny said as she mirrored Jason's first move with her king pawn, per the Spaniard's opening. She then sat back in her chair, arms folded, and stared at the board, her index finger worrying one scraggly forelock. As they played, Wendy stood and walked around the library, pausing to pick up a book, then turning back to study the game. Once, when Jenny put her hand on her queen, Wendy cleared her throat and coughed.

"Hey!" Jason said, turning to Wendy with a frown.

"Sorry," she said, grinning.

Jason turned back to the board, only lifting his eyes when Wendy would sigh and look at her watch. "I'm hurrying," Jason said as he moved his rook. Jenny stared at the board, glancing up occasionally at Wendy. Suddenly, a big smile appeared on Jenny's face and she reached out and pushed her one remaining bishop to a square adjacent to Jason's king. "Check," Jenny said. Jason stared at the board, then whistled slowly. "Nice move!" he said. Just then the door to the library opened and an orderly walked in. "Time to go, Jenny," the orderly said. "Physical therapy."

"Awww, just a few more minutes," Jenny pleaded. "Please. I've got him on the run."

The orderly shook his head. "Nope," he said. "Those bones of yours are getting no use sitting in that chair. We've got to keep them strong."

Jenny opened her mouth to protest again when Jason reached out and knocked over his king. "I resign," he said. He extended his hand to Jenny. "Good game," he said.

Jenny's jaw dropped. "I won?"

"You won," Jason said.

Jenny looked up at Wendy, grinning from ear to ear. "I won!" she said.

"I see that," Wendy said. "Now scoot!"

The orderly walked to the table and grabbed Jenny's wheelchair handles, pulling her backwards toward the door. "I'll get a *real* checkmate next time!" Jenny called out as she and the orderly vanished into the hall.

Wendy and Jason watched her go, and then Wendy moved to the table and sat down next to Jason. She began to put away the chess pieces. "That was nice of you," she said.

"Not really," Jason said. "That last move of hers was a killer. She had checkmate in five moves. I was just trying to save face."

The two worked in silence for a time, placing the pieces back into the box. "She's been doing so much better since you got here," Wendy said. "Her dad had just left when I first met her, and she was really depressed."

Jason looked at Wendy with surprise. "Her dad left?"

Wendy nodded. "Yeah, it happens all the time. The parents can't take it, you know, watching their kid die from cancer or TL or whatever, so they bail out." Jason could see Wendy's jaw clench. "Pisses me off when they're such wimps like that," she said. "Jenny needs him."

"What about her mom?" Jason said.

"She's still here, but she's pretty much a basket case. She starts crying every time she sees Jenny, and that's no good for a kid's morale. She convinced one of the staff docs here to give her some Valium, so she's out of it most of the time."

Jason shook his head. "She's such a great kid, too." Jason then looked at Wendy. "How's she doing?"

Wendy shook her head. "Who knows? I look at her charts whenever I can, and as far as I can tell she's on some experimental antiviral regimen—Batch Nine-something—last resort kind of stuff. But she doesn't seem to be improving."

"Who's her doctor?" Jason asked.

Wendy thought for a second. "Craig Marcus," she said.

Jason's eyes opened wide. "Hey, that's my doctor, too. I should say something to him next time I talk to him."

"That would be great," Wendy said. She blinked as her eyes filled with tears.

Jason reached across the table and put his hand on Wendy's. "Hey, hey, hey, I thought you nurses were supposed to be tough."

Wendy squeezed Jason's hand and laughed, then wiped away tears and tried to smile. "I know, I'm sorry," she said. "I usually just draw blood from Montweiler's insurance guys. This is the first patient I've ever had who's going to die."

Jason looked at Wendy's soft curls and brown eyes. He reached up and wiped her cheek with his thumb, then placed his hand under her chin. "She's going to be fine," he said.

Wendy sighed. "You're a pretty nice guy, you know that?" she said. "Jenny needed a friend, and you've been there for her."

Jason placed his hand on Wendy's shoulder and then hugged her, lingering in her grasp. They sat in silence until Jason finally grabbed the two remaining chessmen and put them back in the box. He started to walk back toward the shelf, but stopped halfway, wincing and holding the inside of his left arm.

Wendy got up and moved to Jason's side. "What's wrong?" she asked, taking the chess set from him and placing it on the shelf.

Jason flexed and straightened his arm, massaging it. "Nothing," he said. "It's just that this arm gets pretty sore sometimes."

Wendy grabbed the arm and turned it up, examining the area opposite the elbow. "Bruising," she said as she touched and probed the skin. "How long has it been this tender?" she asked.

"About a week. It hurts like mad every time you draw blood."

Wendy let go of Jason's arm. "Why didn't you say something?" she asked.

"We guinea pigs are supposed to be tough," Jason said. "Besides, I'm under contract."

Wendy frowned. "You didn't sign on to get abused though, did you?"

Jason shook his head.

"Maybe they can put a shunt in, since we're taking so much blood."

"What's that?"

"It's a tube inserted into a vein, creating an opening to the outside," Wendy said. "That way, we just extract the blood through the shunt instead of creating a new puncture wound every time. People who use dialysis machines have them."

Jason nodded. "So they can just open up the tap and let it flow, huh?" Jason thought for a moment. "Hmmm," he said. "For today anyway, it hurts."

Wendy smiled. "I'll be more careful next time."

Jason grinned back. "And maybe you can kiss it better, too?"

Wendy eyed Jason with a raised left brow. "I thought you were married," she said.

Jason sighed and put his arm around Wendy's shoulder. "That," he said, walking with her toward the door, "is a long story. What are you doing for dinner?"

—

"I've read your memo." Porter put down the piece of paper he was holding and looked at Marcus over the top of his glasses. "The answer is no."

Marcus sat across from Porter, his mouth half-open, his breath pulled away like he'd been gut-punched. "Excuse me?" he finally said.

"You heard me," Porter said. "You may not seek FDA approval to conduct expedited human trials with the Kramer blood factor."

"But Mr. Porter," Marcus said, "the animal trials were uniformly successful. We have developed an algorithm for determining correct dosages as a function of body weight. We are now routinely achieving complete cessation of TL viral activity in chimpanzees. Human trials are the obvious next step."

Porter shook his head. "Frankly, I don't understand your enthusiasm," he said. "In the past you have always been . . . reluctant . . . to involve the FDA—"

"Hence my willingness to tolerate your covert chemotherapy trials at The Complex," Marcus said, cutting Porter off, his voice louder than it should have been. Marcus glanced over at the Driver, who was seated on the couch in Porter's office reading a magazine. The Driver looked up when Marcus raised his voice, and their eyes met over the top of the Driver's *New Yorker*. Marcus continued undaunted. "You're correct," he said. "This does seem paradoxical, my anxiousness to involve the FDA, but we're talking about a possible cure for TL here."

"The operative word being 'possible,'" Porter said. "If we seek permission for expedited trials, our ability to control the dissemination of information about the Kramer factor will be greatly impaired. News reports will circulate about an experimental TL cure being tested by Porter Pharmaceuticals. Our stock price will fluctuate on a daily basis as the market reacts to that day's news reports, and the shareholders will be distressed. We'll be overwhelmed with requests from people desperate to become part of the trial. Remember that Super Bowl commercial that showed Christopher Reeve walking up to receive an award, how everyone with a spinal cord injury wanted in on his treatment, even though the whole thing was computer-generated? And remember when that researcher announced he'd cured cancer in mice with angiostatin and endostatin? People went crazy trying to get the stuff—even though it didn't work in people. Plus, even if the Kramer factor *does* work in people besides Jason Kramer, the key—and I've said this before—the key is to control distribution of the product so that we can maximize our return on investment."

Marcus sat and watched Porter in stunned silence. Even the Driver was listening, engrossed by Porter's exegesis on the economics of the cure.

"Can you imagine what would happen," Porter continued, "if we found ourselves in the same position as Burroughs-Wellcome when it introduced Retrovir?"

Marcus nodded, thinking. The Driver looked from Porter to Marcus and then back again. "What?" Walter said, apparently emboldened by his interest in the conversation. Porter gestured to Marcus, inviting him to answer.

"Retrovir," Marcus said. "You've probably heard of it as AZT. A strong antiviral agent."

"Oh. Mmm hmm," the Driver said, nodding.

"When Burroughs-Wellcome, the pharmaceutical company that developed the drug, announced that it had an AIDS treatment available," Marcus continued, "tremendous pressure was put on the company to get the drug to market. Once they got it to market, even more pressure was put on them to cut their profit margins and surrender their patents—despite their investment of millions of dollars in research and development costs—and make the drug more widely available. Burroughs did so," Marcus said, "because they probably recognized the tremendous good will they could generate by helping more people get AZT, especially since it was one of the only drugs shown to be able to slow down the HIV virus."

"But by now," Porter retorted, "AZT is at best a loss-leader for Burroughs when it should have been their chief money maker. Think of it—they're losing money on a drug that is a source of hope for millions of people, people that would pay any price to get it."

"Doesn't make any sense," the Driver said.

"No, it doesn't," Porter said. "That's why we are going to be very careful with the factor. Let's assume this does turn out to be the cure. Let's assume we make it widely available, even subsidize it in case insurance companies decide not to underwrite it because it is an 'experimental' protocol. Three things would happen: first, TL would be eradicated. Second, we'd generate tremendous good will. Third, we'd all be out of business and broke. All that good will and a dollar bill wouldn't even get us a cup of coffee."

"Not even a cappuccino," the Driver said.

Marcus studied Porter through narrowed eyes.

"Oh please, Doctor," Porter said, "don't play naive, and don't try to impress me with your moral high ground. You have fed from the trough of despair as much as anyone. The only reason we enjoy the perquisites we do is because we sell chemotherapeutic agents. Not drugs that cure cancer, mind you, but drugs that kill cancer cells along with most of the patient's good cells. Tremendous doses, *repeat* doses, are required, and with each administration you and I make money.

"As long as people contract new cases of cancer," Porter continued, "you and I make money. Imagine what would happen if that demand for chemotherapy suddenly vanished because you invented the cure. Bully for you and your Nobel Prize, but no cash flow. No summer home in Tahoe. No new Mercedes. It is *exactly* the same thing with Jason Kramer and TL. If I were an altruist, I could perhaps see our championing the cause of the 'Kramer Factor' and finding a way to bring it to the whole world, but I am not an altruist, I am a capitalist, and as a capitalist my motivation lies in controlling the source and dissemination of this substance to take advantage of supply and demand and thus maximize my company's profits. Period. Now I understand your need to tinker with this factor and maybe cure TL in a few mice and chimpanzees, but that's as far as it's going to go."

Marcus sat and stared at his shoes while the grandfather clock in the corner of Porter's office ticked and tocked, accentuating the silence. The Driver resumed his perusal of the magazine, and Porter turned his attention back to the paperwork on his desk. Marcus looked up and over at Porter. "I can appreciate your concerns," Marcus said. "What if," he continued, "I were to propose a compromise?" Porter kept working and did not look up. Marcus stood and began to walk toward Porter's desk. "Let me try the cure on three TL patients at The Complex," Marcus said.

Porter's eyes remained down, but he stopped writing, his pen poised over the creamy white bond paper that bore Porter Pharmaceuticals' letterhead. "We already have every safeguard in place to maintain confidentiality," Marcus continued. "We can conduct human trials without involving FDA, just like we always do. Then if the cure works on those three patients, we can formally approach FDA with our animal trial numbers, already knowing that the eventual official human trials will work. No market uncertainty." Marcus stopped in front of Porter's desk.

Porter looked up now and stared out across his office, thinking. "Hmm," he said. "On which three patients do you propose to conduct these trials?"

"I'll have to review some files, but one name springs immediately to mind. Jenny Holloway."

"No," Porter said instantly. "You'll have to think of someone else."

Marcus blinked and took a half-step back. "Why not Jenny?" he asked.

Porter reached out and took a cigarette from an ornate walnut box on his desk. He lit it with a red-tipped wooden match, a pile of which stood next to the cigarette box. Porter inhaled, and then spoke as he exhaled, the smoke punctuating his words. "Jennifer Holloway," he said, "is in the last stages of a very successful—and very expensive—trial with Batch 919. I don't want you corrupting our data with some unproven nostrum."

"The cure is hardly unproven," Marcus said. "It worked in Jason, it worked in Carol Davis, and I have every confidence an additional human subject—"

Porter held up his hand. "There will be no more discussion about Jenny Holloway," he said. "Besides, I thought we had already resolved all this when you first came to me and asked to start her on Batch 920 instead." Porter paused, studying Marcus' face. "Oh, I see," Porter said after a moment. "You've gone soft, haven't you?"

Marcus reaction was immediate. "No! I have maintained strict objectivity. For you to suggest that I might compromise a study based on some personal emotional attachment—"

"I can see it now," Porter said. "The compelling, heart-breaking story of a cute little girl, stricken down, crippled by *Triptovirus L*, abandoned by her parents, until the brave doctor with the checkered past miraculously saves her." Porter laughed, and Marcus could hear the Driver chuckling behind him. "I'll tell you what," Porter said. "I'll let you try the Kramer factor on the three most recent admittees to The Complex—three who are not in the last stages of a successful drug trial. When those patients are in complete remission, come and see me."

Porter looked back down at his paperwork. Marcus continued to stand in front of the desk, waiting, but Porter did not look up as he spoke: "And I don't think I need to remind you how important it is for you to remain optimistic about Batch 919—" Marcus jumped as a hand rested on his shoulder. He looked back into the Driver's icy gunmetal eyes. "—do I?" Porter said.

Marcus locked eyes with the Driver, and then looked away. "No," he said.

—

"Dr. Marcus! Thank goodness you're here. I want to talk to you about Jenny Holloway." Jason slid to the edge of his bed and started to stand.

"Whoa, Jason, slow down," Marcus said as he moved to the side of the bed and eased Jason back onto the mattress. He took Jason's wrist, checking his pulse. "Let's talk about you first. How are you feeling?"

"Fine. Look, you really need to do something about Jenny. She—"

Marcus held up his hand, stopping Jason, counting to himself. After a moment he let go of Jason's wrist. "A little fast," he said. "How are they treating you?"

Jason relaxed. "It's been better ever since they put this in." Jason held up his arm. A length of tubing protruded from a vein on his forearm, held in place with white tape. The tube was capped, but Marcus could see the red liquid inside. Jason's blood.

"Oh, a shunt," Marcus said. "Good idea."

"Wendy thought of it."

"Wendy?" Marcus asked.

"She's a nurse here. A phlebotomist actually," Jason said. "This way she doesn't have to make a new hole in me every time she has to take blood."

"Which is pretty frequently, I bet, huh?"

Jason nodded, and then looked up toward the door. "Hi," he said.

Marcus turned around just as Dr. Wilson entered the room. Marcus moved toward Ruth and ushered her toward the bed. "Jason, you remember Dr. Wilson," he said. "She's going to help me out here at The Complex for a few weeks."

Ruth extended her hand. "Nice to see you again," she said.

Jason shook her hand, but immediately turned his attention back to Marcus. "Now, about Jenny. You really need to do something. She only has three months left to live, and that's even though she's on some secret experimental drug."

Marcus frowned. "Who told you that?"

"It doesn't matter where I heard it, you just need to help her!"

Marcus shot Ruth a glance, and then sat down on the edge of the bed. "I'm listening," he said.

"They're killing her!" Jason said, his face flush. "They keep pumping her full of that nine-nineteen crap, and it's just making her worse."

Marcus felt Ruth looking at him. "She's getting the best possible treatment—at no charge, I might add," Marcus said.

"That's bull!" Jason yelled. He held up his arm again and pointed at the shunt. "This is the best possible treatment."

The room fell silent as Marcus and Ruth stared at Jason's arm. Ruth opened her mouth to speak, but Marcus held up his hand, cutting her off. "Jason," he said, "you know how difficult it is to extract and refine the factor in your blood. We're using all that we currently have in the testing phase. Besides, we don't know what it will do to a human."

Jason glowered at Marcus. "You know what it did to me."

"And *you* know what it did to the mice," Marcus snapped back.

"Look, all I ask is that you see her," he said. "Just come with me to her room right now and see her. If, after that, you can tell me we shouldn't try some of this stuff—" he held up his arm "—on her, then fine. I'll drop it. But you need to see her."

Marcus watched Jason for a moment, looked at his face and his eyes. Then he turned to Ruth. "Let's go see her," he said.

Jenny was asleep when they entered her room. Jason moved next to the bed, then motioned Ruth and Marcus closer. Ruth looked around as she walked toward the sleeping girl. There were no balloons or flowers decorating the room, no pictures on the walls, no get-well cards on the dresser—just a stuffed animal, an elephant, on the nightstand with a tag around its neck. Ruth turned her head sideways and read the tag: "Love, Jason and Wendy." Next to the stuffed elephant, Red Ranger maintained his vigil, watching over Jenny.

Marcus moved to the foot of the bed and grabbed the chart. He began to read while Ruth went to the head of the bed and looked down at Jenny. She was bald, her head resting on a stiff white pillowcase. Ruth noticed how pale the girl's skin was, almost the color of the white sheets pulled up under her chin. Her cheeks were translucent, as if one could see the capillaries and bones poking through from beneath. Her breathing was shallow and barely audible, and the ubiquitous IV bag hung next to her, dispensing a clear liquid into a tube hooked to her arm. The IV bag was clearly marked: Batch 919.

"She's dying," Jason whispered.

Marcus looked up from the chart. "She has TL, Jason," he said.

Ruth looked up at Jason. "Where are her parents?" she asked.

"Her dad's been gone for weeks," Jason said. "Her mom's here, but she stays down in the guest quarters most of the time, zoned out on tranquilizers."

Ruth nodded, and then looked back down at Jenny, studying her face. "What do you think, Craig?" she said.

Marcus put down the chart. "Batch 919 is still her only and best hope." As he said it, Marcus felt Ruth staring at him, her eyebrows raised and eyes wide.

Jason reached down and pulled the blanket at the foot of the bed up to Jenny's chin. He moved back away from the bed and took a step toward Marcus, his fists clenched. "I'm trying to understand your position, Craig," Jason said, trying to keep his voice level, "but it doesn't seem to make any sense. Whatever they're doing to her obviously isn't working and we've got to help."

Marcus turned on Jason with sudden venom. "It's not your job to understand *or* to help," he said. "You're just a patient here—a very well-paid patient—and, believe it or not, despite your new-found notoriety you don't hold the power over life and death."

Jason's jaw tensed visibly and a vein pulsed in his left temple. "Yeah, well neither do you, doctor," he said. Jason pushed past Marcus, bumping shoulders with him as he left the room.

Ruth and Marcus stood in silence for a moment, looking down at Jenny, until Ruth turned to Marcus. "What was all that crap about 919 being her only and best hope?" she said.

Marcus met her stare. "I know what you're thinking," he said. "But we can't use the factor on Jenny. Porter has made that very clear."

"What about Jason? If we don't help Jenny, he could refuse to cooperate, and where does that leave us?"

Marcus looked out the window. "We are in the middle of the Arizona desert in July," he said, "100 miles from the nearest airstrip. Where's he going to go?" Marcus turned to leave Jenny's room and Ruth began to follow him, but stopped and moved to the head of Jenny's bed. She reached out and straightened the stuffed elephant, then turned on her heel and ran after Marcus.

"So you're going to let her die," Ruth said when she caught up to him.

"Ruth, people who have TL *do* die. That's what TL does to people—it kills them. Apparently, more and more of them every day. But for today, I truly am doing everything I can for that little girl. If you disagree, *you* may wish to talk to Porter."

Ruth stared at Marcus for several seconds, and then relented. "O.K.," she said. "For today. But I won't take this lying down."

"I know that, believe me," Marcus said. "But right now we've got to find three guinea pigs. The quicker we can show Porter this stuff works in humans, the better. Meet me up in Admitting in an hour." Marcus glanced at his watch. "I've got a quick errand to run."

—

The lab was on the fifth floor, one flight up. Marcus ducked into the stairwell and climbed two steps at a time. The hall was deserted except for a security guard stationed outside the lab. The guard glanced up at Marcus' access badge and nodded. "Mornin' Doc."

"Good morning." Marcus punched his security code into the keypad on the wall and the door swung open. The room was bathed in bright white light from the overhead fluorescents, making the white-coated lab technicians emit an ethereal glow. Marcus took a breath and steeled himself. He noticed one of the techs looking at him, a pretty young woman with olive skin and black hair. She was loading test tubes filled with red liquid into a centrifuge. Marcus walked over to her. "Hi," he said, "I'm Dr. Marcus. I'd like to see some test results."

The tech smiled, flashing straight white teeth. "I know who you are. Over there." She pointed across the lab to a glassed-in room. Marcus could see computer terminals and file cabinets through the windows. "Who are you looking for?" she asked.

"Jennifer Holloway."

The tech smiled again. "Oh, that little girl in four-eleven. She's a cutey." The technician put down the tray of test tubes she was holding and started for the file room. "Come on," she said, over her shoulder. "I'll show you."

Marcus walked with her to the file room door. He looked through the thick glass at the rows of file cabinets inside. Marcus lifted his access badge to slide it through the scanner, but the tech stopped him. "Won't work," she said.

Marcus stared at her. "It's all-access."

"Not in here. We're the only ones who can get into the lab results." She grinned. "Top secret stuff, you know." She slid her access badge through the scanner. Marcus heard the sound of heavy bolts sliding followed by a loud click. The tech grabbed the door and pulled it open, then motioned Marcus ahead of her. "After you."

Marcus paused, studying the woman's face. She smiled, and Marcus stepped into the room. He heard the low hum of the air conditioner, but the heavy glass muted all other external noise. He turned around and looked at the tech, who was still standing by the door. For the first time, he glanced at her name badge. "Thank you, Denise. I think I can find it from here."

"No problem. Call me when you're done." She nodded toward a phone on the wall. "Can't get out without me." She held up her badge and wagged it at Marcus. "I'm surprised you've never been in here before," Denise said.

"Never needed to before. I've always just waited for the summaries."

"So what's the rush this time?"

Marcus smiled. "It seems like I always get the summaries just before the patient dies."

Denise studied Marcus' face. "And this time you want to try and actually *save* the patient, right?"

Marcus bristled at the barb. "Right," he said.

Denise stepped back from the door and held the handle in her fingertips, ready to let go. "Hey, don't blame us if you guys can't keep 'em alive long enough for the lab work to arrive." The handle slipped from her hand and the bolts clicked into place.

Marcus watched her walk back to the centrifuge. He looked around the room to orient himself and was amazed by the number of files the room contained, one file for each patient who had spent time at The Complex. Katrine Waters is in here, too, he thought. Someplace.

He started walking through the rows of cabinets, reading the labels on the front of each, looking for the H's. "Franklin . . .

Johnson," he mumbled, ". . . Harper." He knelt and pulled open the drawer. Jenny's folder was near the back.

Marcus sat cross-legged on the floor, the file open on his lap, and began to read. He turned through page after page of lab work and test results, scrutinizing the findings and snapping pictures with his cell phone until finally—"Bingo," Marcus whispered.

"All done?"

Marcus jumped, dumping Jenny's file and his cell phone onto the floor. He looked up. "You scared me," he said.

"Sorry, but you've been in here an hour and I was getting worried."

Marcus retrieved the folder and stuffed it back into the cabinet while surreptitiously pocketing his phone. "I am glad you checked on me." He nodded toward the wall phone. "You didn't give me your extension."

Denise laughed. "You could've been in here a month!" She extended her hand and Marcus took it. Denise pulled back, helping Marcus from the floor. "Did you find what you were looking for?"

Marcus straightened his tie. "Not really," he said. "Nothing I didn't already know."

They walked together to the file room exit. Denise punched in her code, and the heavy bolts clicked open. "So, are you headed back to San Francisco now?" Denise said.

"No. We just arrived."

"Me too. I just started this rotation, so I'm stuck out here in the middle of nowhere for the next two weeks."

"Do you live in Marin?"

"I wish! No, I commute over to Porter every day from the East Bay. Oakland, actually."

They walked to the lab exit and Marcus pushed the door open. "Thanks again," he said to Denise as he turned and went out into the hall. Marcus nodded at the guard and hurried toward the elevator, then stopped and looked over his shoulder. The guard was reading. Marcus dodged into the men's room and locked himself into a stall, then took a pen and legal pad from his briefcase and scrawled page after page of notes, referring to the cell phone photos and cursing their poor resolution.

Someone knocked on the stall door. Marcus dropped his pen, which clattered on the tile. "It's occupied," he said as he grabbed the pen and threw the pad and phone back into the briefcase. He closed the clasps, and cursed them when they clicked.

"Dr. Marcus?"

Marcus felt his hands and feet go cold. "Yes?"

"Everything all right in there?"

Marcus stood and took a breath, then opened the stall door, briefcase in hand. He smiled at the security guard.

"I saw you go in the restroom, but you didn't come out. I was getting worried," the guard said.

Marcus massaged his stomach. "Yeah, I thought I was going to be sick. The flight in was a little rough. False alarm, though." Marcus made his way to the bathroom door and left the guard standing by the open stall.

—

The two doctors stood in front of the admitting room desk until Marcus finally cleared his throat. The nurse looked up. "Can I help you?" she said, not smiling.

"Uh, yes . . ." Marcus said, glancing at her name tag, ". . . Doris, I need to see the files on our three most recent patients."

Doris continued to stare at Marcus, but did not move. "Do you have their names?" she said.

Ruth suppressed a grin. "No," Marcus said, "I was hoping you could tell us that."

Doris sighed and looked down at her computer console. Her fingers flew over the keyboard as she mumbled to herself, "Date of admission, date of admission. Ah, here they are," she said. "We had two check in day before yesterday and one just this morning. One pancreas and two TLs."

"Excuse me?" Ruth said.

The nurse smiled. "Sorry," she said. "That's our shorthand way of describing the illnesses the incoming patients have. Three months ago I would have said something like, 'two lungs and a pancreas,' but now almost everything we are seeing is TL."

"So that 'pancreas' is a case of pancreatic cancer?" Ruth said.

"Yep," said Doris.

"Uh, excuse me," Doris said. "But what can you tell me about that new strain of TL? I had an uncle die from it a couple of weeks ago, and I remember everybody always getting real quiet and crossing themselves whenever they found out it was the new TL."

"It's so bad because . . . well, because it's so fatal," Marcus said.

Ruth looked up. "And," she said, "the mutated strain seems to magnify the symptoms of the old TL—quicker lung failure, more aggressive bone loss—plus with the new TL we are seeing rapid liver failure as well. All you can do for treatment—typically—" she glanced at Marcus "—is prescribe pain meds until they die."

Doris swallowed hard.

"That," Marcus added, "plus when the liver goes, you get horrible jaundice," he said. "It's really painful."

"Oh," Doris said. She sat for a moment, and then crossed herself.

"So, do you mind if we look at those files?" Marcus said to Doris.

Doris removed three thick folders from a cabinet and handed them to Marcus. "Knock yourself out," she said.

Marcus took the folders and handed one of the "TLs" to Ruth. He opened the other one and began studying its contents. Ruth did the same with her folder, her brow furrowed in concentration as she examined the patient's medical history.

Marcus looked over at Ruth. "Let's get these files back to the office," he said. "I want to meet the patients and start them on the Kramer factor as soon as possible. If we're lucky, we'll have some results within a few days."

"Then," Ruth said, "we go to Porter." She paused, watching Marcus. "Right?" she asked.

Marcus put his finger to his lips and motioned Ruth out into the hall. He turned to the nurse. "Thanks for your help," he said.

Doris was once again staring at her computer screen. "No problem," she mumbled.

Marcus joined Ruth in the hall. "Right," he said. "Then we go to Porter."

"What kind of a chance do you think these two really have?"

"With the factor?" Marcus said. "You are reading the headlines, right? Because these two patients just got here, it's likely that they have the mutated strain. So their odds at The Complex have got to be better than the odds they have out there."

CHAPTER 24

Wendy carefully uncapped the shunt and inserted a needle into the rubber stopper that prevented Jason's blood from flowing unchecked out of his veins. She withdrew a vial of red liquid and placed the lid back on the shunt. Jason sat on the edge of his bed, staring absently off over Wendy's left shoulder during the procedure. Wendy looked up into Jason's vacant eyes. "Something wrong?" she said.

Jason sighed and shook his head, then rubbed his temples. "My head hurts is all," he said.

"You do look a little pale," Wendy said. "Maybe you should lie down."

"When I lie down I get the bed spins. It's better if I sit up," he said. They sat in silence while Wendy made a notation at the bottom of a list of entries in a log book. She then placed the vial of blood in a pouch and took a black grease pen out of her pocket. She wrote "Jason Kramer – 4:35 p.m." on the pouch, then laid it on top of the instrument cart she had wheeled into Jason's room.

Jason still didn't look at her. "What do you do with that stuff when you leave here?" he asked.

"I take it down to the lab and give it to one of the techs for extraction," she said. "I guess that's where they refine the factor out of your blood."

"Hmm," Jason said. "Then what?"

"I don't know," Wendy said. "I don't have security clearance for the lab. I guess they keep the factor down there somewhere."

Wendy studied Jason's face. "Why so curious all of a sudden? You normally don't seem to care about any of this, except that it hurts your arm—and that the food is bad."

Jason sat impassively and stared at the floor.

"Come on," Wendy said, "what's up?"

"I saw Dr. Marcus today," Jason relented. "I asked him about Jenny."

Wendy brightened. "Oh, great! What did he say?"

Jason scratched his head and sighed. "He said no." Jason rubbed his arm above and below the shunt, and picked absent-mindedly at the surgical tape holding the device in place.

Wendy's mouth dropped open, and she sat staring at Jason. "No?" she said finally. "How could he say no?"

"He just did. Boom. End of story."

"That's ridiculous!" Wendy said. "This is your blood, after all—"

"Apparently it's not," Jason said, interrupting. "I re-read my contract," he said. "Once the stuff leaves my body, they own it, free and clear."

Wendy shook her head. "Why did you ever sign a contract that said that?"

Jason shrugged. "At the time, it seemed like the only way out of a bad situation."

"I understand," Wendy said. "That still doesn't explain why Dr. Marcus won't give her the cure."

"Marcus says the stuff she's on now is still her best hope of getting better."

Wendy's upper lip curled. "So what you're telling me," she said, "is that Jenny stays on Batch 919 until it kills her, right?"

"Hey, I'm not defending Marcus!" Jason said. "I tried, and he said no."

Wendy's lip remained curled.

"Look, I care about Jenny, too, but we're a little limited in our options. I mean, we can't give her my blood directly, and I don't know how to refine the cure out of it. Do you?"

Wendy looked down and shook her head.

"Can you steal some?"

Wendy shook her head again. "I don't know how I'd get to it, with my limited clearance. They keep it wrapped up tight. And even if I got some, I wouldn't know how much to give her. They are super strict with the dosage amounts."

Jason shrugged. "So, I'm open to suggestions."

Wendy looked up at him. "We can't let her die."

Jason reached out to her, and she took his hand. "We won't," he said. He looked down at the shunt in his arm. "We won't."

CHAPTER 25

Linda Kramer looked around the restaurant. She signaled the waiter by holding up her empty highball glass and rattling the ice cubes. "Another," she mouthed when the waiter saw her. He nodded, smiling. Linda put the glass down on the table next to its predecessor and reached out to play with the salt shaker. She jumped when a hand rested on her shoulder.

"Sorry I'm late," Keith said as he sat down opposite Linda at the table. "Did you order yet?"

Linda pointed at the glasses. "Just a cocktail. Or two."

"I see," Keith said. "I'll have to catch up." He caught the waiter's eye and held up one of Linda's empties, then pointed toward himself. Keith placed his valise on the table and removed several pieces of paper.

"It's about time," Linda said. "You've had those forever. Porter's people call me every other day to find out when I'm going to sign them." Linda reached out for the papers, but Keith pulled them away. Linda looked at him. "What?" she said.

Keith paused. "I don't think you want to sign these," he said.

Linda waited, her lips pursed. Keith remained silent, still smiling. "I give up," Linda said. "Why not?"

Keith put the papers back into his valise and leaned forward, his elbows on the table. "I have a friend with TL. Nasty case. He was on oxygen, and his hip broke whenever he tried to stand up."

"That's too bad," Linda said. Just then the waiter returned with two drinks and placed the glasses on the table. Linda grabbed one and took a big swallow. "Not to sound rude," she said, setting the glass down, "but so what?"

Keith chuckled. "That's why I like you so much, Linda. You're so mercenary. The point is *not* that my friend has TL. The point is that he no longer *has* TL."

"Bully for him," Linda said, looking at her watch. "Look, Keith, I'm showing a home in Pacific Heights at 1:30."

"My friend," Keith continued, "was almost dead. But then he got enlisted into some type of super-secret clinic hosted by—you guessed it—Porter Pharmaceuticals."

Linda looked up and let her arm drop back to the table. "How'd you find this out?"

"His wife called to tell me the good news." Keith picked up his martini and took a sizable swallow. "Although quite frankly I think she was looking forward to collecting his life insurance."

"I can relate," Linda said. "That's fascinating, but we're back to my original point. So what?"

"Let's consider what we know. One. Jason had TL. Two. He is now cured. Three. He signs up with Porter for some top-secret research. Four. My dying friend goes away to some hospital nobody's ever heard of, a hospital run by Porter and where they are presumably doing this 'top-secret research,' and boom, a couple of weeks later my friend is also cured of TL. So I did some more checking. The buzz is that for a price you can buy the cure from Porter. There's got to be some connection."

Linda rolled her eyes. "What, you think Jason is the cure for TL? Mr. Carrot Juice? Porter says he's still dying."

Keith pushed back from the table. "Maybe," he said. "I don't know. But what I do know is that it's time to go see Mr. Porter for a little negotiation. If my hunch is right and we play it so Porter thinks we've got the goods on him, I bet we can strike a pretty good deal for you. After all, you *are* still Jason's wife." Keith paused, a brief look of panic crossing his eyes. "You didn't go to the hearing did you? You did like I told you, right?"

Linda sighed. "Yeah, we're still married." She thought for a minute. "You think this is worth a lot of money?"

Keith leaned forward even farther. "Are you kidding? You know how many people die from TL every year around the world and how much they would pay for the cure? The mutated strain is spreading like wildfire. This has got to be worth billions to Porter."

Linda grabbed her drink and tossed it back, finishing it. She picked up her phone and dialed a number. While she waited for the connection, she looked at Keith and said, "I'm canceling my 1:30. Why don't you go call Porter?"

Keith grinned. "That's my girl," he said.

CHAPTER 26

The intercom buzzed before the receptionist's voice boomed from the speaker, "Dr. Samuels? You have a call on line one."

Vincent smiled a quick apology to the patient seated across from his desk and grabbed the handset. "Who is it?" he asked. He listened for a moment, and then his face went pale. He placed his hand over the mouthpiece and looked up at the patient. "Will you excuse me for a moment?" he said.

The patient sat for a moment, not understanding, then stood and left Vincent's small office. Vincent spoke into the phone: "Put him through."

The voice in the earpiece was deep and resonant. "Thank you for taking my call Vincent," the voice said. "Sorry I haven't stayed in touch. It took us longer than expected to analyze the sample you left me."

Vincent grabbed a pen and a pad of paper. He scribbled "Amwell call" at the top of the page and noted the date and time. "No problem, Dr. Carnelli," he said. "It's good to hear from you."

"So, Vincent," Carnelli said, "what have you been up to since you were here? Gone back to consulting for Porter?"

"Oh, no, no," Vincent said as he loosened his tie and took a sip of water from a cup on his desk. "I hung out a shingle."

"No kidding," Carnelli chuckled. "I thought you guys in research were too risk-averse to ever consider entrepreneurship."

"Hey," Vincent said, "I had to pay the bills." There was a moment of silence while Vincent waited for Carnelli to speak. When he did not, Vincent ventured: "So what do you think?"

The silence on the other end of the line continued. "Vincent," Carnelli finally said, "where did you get this stuff?"

Vincent scribbled "asked about source" on the notepad, and then took another sip of water. "It's a new compound being tested by Porter," he said. "They haven't patented it yet, though."

Carnelli cleared his throat. "Don't lie to me, Vincent. I could always tell when you were lying to me in class. This is a biological, not a synthetic preparation. You know you can't patent a naturally occurring substance. Now if we're going to work together on this deal you need to come clean with me."

Vincent wrote the word "busted" on the paper. "You're right," he said. "It is a biological. But I can't tell you where I got it. Suffice it to say Porter owns it."

"Then Porter's a lucky man. You were right about this stuff being toxic to *Triptovirus L.* We tested it on every strain of the bug we could grow, including the new mutation, and it killed them all *in vitro*. I assume the results would be the same in an actual subject." There was a long pause. "Remarkable," Carnelli said. “But now we have run out of the substance."

Vincent sat forward in his chair. "Then let's make some more," he said. "I'll come to work for Amwell and we'll beat Porter to the punch. I kept all my research notes and—"

Carnelli cut him off. "Sorry," he said. "It's not that simple. We can't clone it."

Vincent stopped breathing. His eyes darted back and forth as he thought, scrambling for a reply. "I understand," he began, "there might be some problems in replicating the exact genetic sequence, but—"

Carnelli jumped in again. "You know as well as I do that we could determine the gene responsible for production of the material—*if* we had the host." Carnelli paused. "There is a host somewhere, right?"

Vincent swallowed. "Yes."

"But even with the host, reverse engineering the gene sequence could take a very long time," Carnelli continued. "Remember how long it took to figure out which gene was responsible for producing interferon so they could clone it in *E. coli*? Bottom line, by the time we figure out how to clone this stuff we'll be so far behind the curve in terms of Porter's market share that it probably wouldn't even be worthwhile for us to proceed. As long as Porter has the host, for all practical purposes he has the only supply of this stuff in the whole world."

Vincent tapped his pencil on his desk. "Perhaps you can synthesize it—" he began before Carnelli cut him off again.

"Nope," Carnelli said. "We've been trying to synthesize the stuff since you brought us the sample, but it's an extraordinarily complex molecule. The human body is an amazing thing, Vincent. It managed to create a protein that kills TL, and we can't even figure out how to replicate it."

There was a silence while Vincent tapped his temple, head bent. Carnelli finally broke the impasse. "Thank you for thinking of us, Vincent," he said. "It's too bad we weren't able to work together on this. Somebody's going to win a Nobel Prize when they decode the genome for this stuff." Another pause, then Carnelli continued. "You do still have the rest of the vial, don't you? You only left us a small sample."

Vincent glanced at the small locked refrigerator on his credenza. "Um, no," he said. "It's all gone. Other tests and all that."

"I see," Carnelli said. "Of course." There was a long pause while Vincent sat and listened to Carnelli breathe. Then Carnelli spoke: "My heavens, Vincent. The cure for Trips Lite."

The line went dead. Vincent sat, holding the handset for several seconds before returning it to the cradle. He tapped his pencil on the desk, bouncing it by the eraser. He stood, moved to the refrigerator on his credenza and opened the padlock securing it. He reached inside and removed a half-full vial of light-yellow, semi-viscous liquid. He held it up in the sunlight streaming in through the window and shook it, watching it tumble in the vial. "The cure for Trips Lite," he said.

CHAPTER 27

Phillip Porter turned his face toward the sky, closed his eyes and removed his sunglasses, and basked in the pure heat of the Arizona sun until his skin began to complain against the unfiltered rays. He opened his eyes and looked around, seeking shelter in the Driver's shadow. "Where are the tennis courts?" Porter said.

The Driver, carrying several suitcases, stood beside Porter. "They're not quite finished yet," Craig Marcus said. "The crews have been working around the clock, but we're still ironing out a few bugs."

"Good," Porter said. "We want people to get their money's worth."

"You'd think the cure for TL would be enough," Marcus said under his breath.

"Excuse me?" Porter said.

"Nothing," Marcus said. He offered a hand to the Driver to help with the baggage, but the Driver ignored him. "How long are you planning on staying here at The Complex, Mr. Porter?" he asked.

"A couple of weeks—maybe until the first of September if the food is passable," Porter said. "I haven't been out here in a long time, and with all these upgrades I might make a vacation of it." Porter coughed, and then rubbed his stomach. "Too much stress back at the office."

The three made their way toward The Complex's front entrance. Workers bustled around them, moving shrubbery, planting flowers, washing windows, scrubbing sidewalks. Porter turned to Marcus. "What about the brochures?" he asked.

Marcus watched the Driver place a cigarette in Porter's lips and light it. They stopped in front of the doors leading to the main lobby, and Marcus fished a four-color flyer out of his inside jacket pocket. "They just arrived from Phoenix this morning," he said.

Porter opened the brochure and motioned to the Driver. "Look at this, Walter. If you were dying of a terminal illness, would you want to come here?"

The Driver moved closer and looked over Porter's shoulder. Large letters at the top of the mailer spelled out, "The Complex at Bigwood Springs." The Driver raised one eyebrow and smirked. "Bigwood Springs?" he asked.

Porter's jaw tightened. "The marketing people spent a lot of time coming up with that, Walter. It's supposed to convey a certain healthy Western ruggedness."

The Driver's smile vanished. "Sounds good to me," he said. He continued reading out loud. "Hospice care for the acutely ill patient," the Driver said. "Revolutionary new treatment pioneered by Porter Pharmaceuticals has resulted in spontaneous remission of Trips Lite in 100 percent of test subjects." The Driver looked up at Porter. "Wow," he said. "That's impressive." He read to himself, then looked at Porter and said, "Pretty posh. Sounds like a resort instead of a hospital."

Porter beamed and slapped the Driver on the back. "Exactly, Walter. That's exactly right." He handed the brochure back to Marcus. "Come to the desert, play some tennis—if you're still able—and get the cure, all at the same place. And you'll notice," Porter said to Marcus, "there are no express references to Jason Kramer or his miracle blood. Some poor sap reading this could think we were talking about Vitamin C or garlic or echinacea. Or macrobiotic diets, for that matter. Got to keep the FDA at bay, right?"

Marcus cleared his throat. "Yes, that's true, but those are some pretty strong statements about remission rates."

Porter sighed, his shoulders slumping. "Your complete lack of marketing vision never ceases to amaze me, Dr. Marcus. For as many years as we've worked together on cancer, you've never understood one thing." He turned to Marcus. "Why do people buy chemotherapeutic agents and subject themselves to the abject horror of having the chemicals strip them of any quality of life? Because they enjoy the pain and nausea?"

Marcus studied Porter's face. "No," he said. "It's because the chemo will kill the cancer, I suppose."

"Wrong," Porter said. "They *know* the chemo won't cure them. They know that most of the time it only serves to prolong life, and it certainly doesn't enhance their quality of life." Porter turned and began to walk again toward the entrance. "It's *hope*, Dr. Marcus. The hope of being cured of cancer—and now the hope of being cured of TL—is what allows me to have homes in three countries and permits you to drive a new Mercedes every other year. People don't buy drugs. They buy hope. I mean, good grief, do you listen to those drug ads on TV? With all the warnings about side effects? And yet people still ask for, *demand*, those drugs despite those horrific warnings!"

"I don't disagree," Marcus said, "but what if the Kramer factor doesn't work against TL as promised, in all cases?"

Porter moved forward, his face just inches away from Marcus'. "Who cares?" he said. "If it doesn't work we'll just start them on Batch 920 or 921 or whatever until they die, and they'll pay us for the privilege." He moved back a step, softening. "Besides, it will work. It cured Carol Davis, didn't it?"

Marcus nodded.

"So nothing to worry about," Porter said. He looked back over his shoulder. "Get the door, Walter," he said.

The Driver moved around Porter and pulled open the front door. Marcus followed Porter into the lobby, the Driver bringing up the rear.

Porter looked around the lobby. "Where is Kramer?" he said.

"In his room," Marcus said.

"Make sure he's well sequestered. And we need to increase production quotas on the factor. We've already received reservations from fifty guests and we want to make sure there's plenty of the serum available."

Marcus cleared his throat. "Jason is still pretty weak from the testing phase," he said. "It may not be wise to push him too quickly. The factor takes about as long to regenerate after we extract it as it does when you donate blood, so we really shouldn't try to start refining more until—"

Porter stopped short, then turned on Marcus with disdain. "You still don't understand, do you? I don't care if Kramer lives or dies."

Marcus stared at Porter. "You're kidding, right? He's the blessed cure for Trips Lite, and we've got him. Nobody else is even close to finding a vaccine for this bug—it mutates too fast."

"Allow me to explain. You've already told me we can't synthesize more of the factor, right?"

"Not in the short run, no, because that requires isolating the gene responsible so we can clone the factor in *E. coli*."

"And that will take what, two years?"

"More or less," Marcus said.

"And for every person cured, that's one less TL patient who will be dependent on Porter Pharmaceuticals' existing antiviral agents, like Batch 919, right?"

"Right."

"So don't you see that my hands are tied?"

Marcus stared at him, and Porter sighed.

"Look. We cannot get enough of the factor out of Kramer to save an appreciable percentage of the population. We cannot mass produce the stuff for at least two years. We cannot patent it even if we could mass produce it. There are people out there who *are* going to die from TL, but if we can prolong the lives of *some* of them with Batch 919, or 920 or 921, why not?

"In the meantime, my intent is to try and profit from the situation that has been handed to me. We'll let the rich suckers come out here to Bigwood Springs and get the cure. At a million dollars a head, I figure we can make over 200 million before we run out of factor."

Marcus stared at Porter. "By that you mean before the extraction process kills Jason," he said.

Porter turned and started across the lobby, the Driver on his heels. "Potato, puh-tah-to," he said over his shoulder. "And if he does die, well, at least we'll know that our income from selling Batch 9-whatever will be secure. But let me be clear: if you *can* figure out a way to keep Kramer alive *and* make Porter Pharmaceuticals the only source of the cure for TL—come see me."

CHAPTER 28

"Hi Jason," the nurse said, a little too cheerfully. "We're going to be switching rooms today."

Jason opened one eye and stared out from under his pillow at the white starched figure standing in his room. "Oh goody," he said. "Does that mean you get my room and I get yours?"

The smile remained on the nurse's face, but with no humor behind it. "No," she said. "It means you're moving to a different room. We need this room for a new patient."

Jason closed his eye. "What is it with all these new patients? It's beginning to look like Club Med around here." Jason pulled the pillow tighter around his head as an orderly pushed a wheelchair into the room. The orderly stood behind the wheelchair, gripping the handles, the sinews in his forearms standing out like bands of hemp. He cleared his throat.

Jason opened his eye again and tried to focus on the six-foot four-inch, 245-pound object looming in the doorway. Jason smiled gamely. "The cavalry has arrived, I see," he said. He pulled the pillow off his head and sat up, his hair smashed flat in some places, sticking wildly out in others. Black stubble covered his chin and cheeks. Jason swung his feet out over the edge of the bed and tried to pull himself forward, stopping and wincing as he grabbed the inside of his left arm. "Ow," he said, rocking back and forth and holding his arm. He looked down and moved his hand. The area was blue and purple, with needle tracks from healed puncture wounds still obvious in several distended veins. The shunt protruded from his forearm, halfway between the elbow and wrist. Jason looked up at the orderly. "Looks like I need a hand here, sport."

The orderly pushed the wheelchair over to Jason and grabbed him under the arms, lifting him and placing him in the chair. Jason looked up at the nurse. "How'd you teach the gorilla to shave?"

Jason could hear the orderly chuckling behind him. "You only weigh 140 pounds," the orderly said.

"I was over 160 when I came in here," Jason said. "I really must speak to the chef."

The orderly wheeled Jason into the hallway and followed the nurse to the elevator. They got in and the nurse pushed a button. Jason watched the lights flash in descending order: 3, 2, 1, B1, B2. The doors slid open and Jason looked out into a long hallway, illuminated by a soft fluorescent glow. The nurse headed down the hall, and the orderly, pushing Jason, brought up the rear.

They came to a metal door recessed into one of the concrete walls. Jason looked for the handle, but there was none. The nurse slid a card through a scanner on the wall and the big door swooshed open. "Just like Star Trek," Jason said, over his shoulder. The orderly grinned.

They entered a bare room, adorned only with a hospital bed and a refrigerator. A television set hung from brackets bolted to the ceiling, and a nightstand with a reading lamp stood next to the bed. A door at the back of the room led to the bathroom where Jason could see a stainless steel sink and toilet and the gleaming white tile floor. The nurse moved to the bed, pulled back the covers, and patted the mattress with her hand. "Climb in," she said.

Jason looked back over his shoulder at the orderly. "Looks like I'm trading down," he said. The orderly placed his hands under Jason's arms and started to lift him out of the wheelchair, but Jason shrugged him off. "I'm not an invalid," he said. The orderly withdrew, and Jason stood, wobbling a bit. He took three halting steps toward the nurse, paused, then continued shuffling until he finally made it to the foot of the bed and sat down.

"Very good," the nurse said. "Why don't you get yourself all settled in, and we'll be back down later with your clothes and personal effects." The nurse eyed Jason up and down. "And it looks like you could use some supper."

Jason managed to climb into the bed and pull the covers over his legs. He looked at the nurse. "Man, this mattress is like concrete! Why did they move me down here?" he asked.

The nurse shrugged. "Sorry. I just know we received instructions to put you here for the time being."

"I don't think this was in my contract," Jason said. The orderly pushed the wheelchair through the door and into the hallway, and the nurse moved out beside him. She positioned the card into the scanner, holding it there. "That," she said, "is something you'll have to take up with Dr. Marcus." She swiped the card through the scanner, and the door slid shut.

—

"You look like you were ridden hard and put away wet," Wendy said as she came into Jason's room.

Jason looked up and tried to grin. "I'm surprised you could find me all the way down here," he said.

"They gave me a map," Wendy said. She pushed her cart next to Jason's bed and placed a framed picture on his nightstand. She then removed a syringe from the cart and grabbed Jason's wrist. She frowned as she probed the bruised flesh on Jason's inner arm.

Jason winced and tried to pull his arm away, but Wendy held fast. "I have some good news and some bad news," Wendy said as she tucked Jason's hand under her arm and clamped down on it. She held up the syringe and uncapped the needle.

"Give me the good news first," Jason said, closing his eyes and turning his head as Wendy slid the needle into the shunt.

"The good news is that I'm going to get to spend more time with you." She pulled back the plunger and watched the syringe fill with Jason's blood. When it was full, she capped the shunt and placed the syringe on the cart.

Jason opened his eyes and looked at Wendy. "That's great," he said. "What's the bad news?"

Wendy sighed and sat down on the edge of the bed. She reached out and put her hand on Jason's forehead. "You're cold," she said. She reached down to the foot of the bed and pulled the comforter up around Jason's arms. "The bad news," she said, grinning, "is that I get to spend more time with you." She watched Jason's face for a moment, and then her smile faded. "They've increased production quotas on your blood factor," she said.

Jason continued to stare at Wendy's face. "What does that mean?" he said.

"It means I have to take more blood so they can extract more of the cure," she said. Wendy watched Jason's eyes focus and then unfocus on her face. "I'm tired," he said. His eyelids closed and his head slumped to one side of the pillow, his breathing slow and labored. Wendy watched him for a moment and brushed the hair away from his face, then stood and pushed the cart toward the door. One of the wheels banged into the bed's metal edge with a loud clang, and Jason's eyes popped open, his head turning toward the noise. "Don't go," he said, his speech thick. He rubbed his eyes, then managed a smile. "Sorry," he said. "I must have nodded off." He tried to sit up and adjusted the pillow behind his head. "What did you say?"

"They need more blood."

"More?" Jason rubbed his arm above the shunt. "More? I'm lying here like a pincushion, getting sucked dry, and they want more blood?"

Wendy nodded. "Hey, I hear you. Porter has turned this place into a resort for rich people with TL. You should see it upstairs. Tennis courts, fresh flowers, a new exercise room—it's like a hotel. That's why they moved you down here. They needed your room for a paying guest. And business is booming. Every room is full. Word of mouth is that this is the place to come for the cure." Wendy stared at Jason. "And you're it."

Jason shook his head and opened his eyes wide, then yawned. "Damn, I'm tired," he said. He looked around the room, his gaze falling on the picture Wendy had placed on his nightstand. It was a photo of Jenny in her wheelchair with Wendy and Jason standing behind her. "How is she?" Jason asked.

Wendy moved back to the head of the bed. She took Jason's hand in hers and held it, stroking the back of his wrist. "Not good," she said.

"I haven't been able to see her much lately."

"I know Jason, I'm sorry. You've been too weak. I know it's not much comfort, but she probably wouldn't know you were there anyway. She sleeps most of the time now." Wendy sighed and squeezed Jason's hand. "She's so frail."

Jason nodded. "Tell her I miss her when you see her next," Jason said, his eyelids drooping.

"I will," she said.

Jason managed to open his eyes again and stared at Wendy. "Hey," he said, "this thing about needing more of my blood. How much more? I mean, I've only got so much."

Wendy met his stare for several seconds. "You know what?" she said. "You're right." She closed her eyes, thinking. "You're absolutely right." She took a deep breath. "The plan to take more is bad," she exhaled, her jaw tightening. "Very bad."

"Very bad," Jason echoed as his grip on her hand relaxed.

Wendy placed his arm back under the covers. "We'll have to see what we can do about that," she said. She maneuvered the cart toward the metal door, careful not to displace the vials of blood from their containers, and then passed her card through the scanner. She pushed the cart through into the hallway and the door was about to close when Wendy heard a noise from inside Jason's room. She turned and saw Jason lift his head from the pillow. "Hurry back," he called out as the heavy door slid shut.

CHAPTER 29

The four wheels on the gurney squeaked with each revolution as the two orderlies pushed the cart into the room. The squeaking synchronized with the rhythmic breaths that issued from the respirator affixed to Jenny's throat. Her lungs pulsed and inflated each time the black bag on the respirator filled with air, then deflated with a gasping sound as the air was sucked back out. It was an odd symphony: the percussion of the beeping electrocardiogram, the soft woodwind-like wheezing of Jenny's lungs, and the squeaking wheels.

The orderlies moved the gurney next to Jenny's bed and looked down at the emaciated frame lying under the sheets, her right hand curled tight, fetus-like, under her chin. Carmen Holloway stood at the door and watched, her hands clasped together on her chest, her knuckles white. Her eyes were red and swollen, her nose raw. An imitation leather purse hung limply from the crook of her arm, a white piece of paper protruding from the zippered pouch on the side. Large letters at the top of the paper read "Discharge Instructions." Carmen reached into the purse, pulled out a tissue, and dragged it under her nose.

One of the orderlies looked around the room, and then turned to Jenny's mother. "Do you have everything?" the orderly asked.

Carmen nodded and pointed toward a brown paper sack on the floor. The bag contained a folded pair of pajamas, a framed picture, and Jenny's Red Ranger doll. The stuffed elephant's trunk hung over the edge. The orderly picked up the bag and tucked it under the gurney.

"Are we all set?"

Carmen jumped, startled by the high, cheerful voice of the nurse who had entered the room behind her. "Yes. All set," she said.

"All righty then," the nurse said, moving briskly to the edge of the bed. She shooed the orderlies out of the way and stood, looking down at Jenny. "Sweet angel," she said, reaching down to stroke Jenny's cheek. She looked up at Carmen. "So sad," the nurse said. The nurse pulled back Jenny's covers, exposing her thin, vein-riddled arms. The nurse reached down and grabbed the needle still inserted into Jenny's arm. Her eyes followed the tube back up to the bottle that hung from a stand next to Jenny's bed. The nurse nodded. "Batch 919," she said, reading from the label. "We had high hopes for that one." The nurse slid the needle back and out of Jenny's vein, and residual drops of Batch 919 dribbled out onto Jenny's arm.

The nurse nodded to the orderlies, who pulled Jenny's blanket back up to her neck. With one easy, fluid motion, the orderlies lifted Jenny from the bed and laid her on the gurney. They began to push her toward the door, the wheels still squeaking, the nurse following behind. They reached the door when Dr. Marcus entered the room. He moved to Carmen and put his arm around her, smiling.

"How are you doing?" Marcus asked. Carmen remained silent, looking down at the floor. Marcus left his arm around her shoulder, waiting, but Carmen continued to stare at the floor. Marcus moved his arm, and then walked to the nurse, who handed him a clipboard and a pen. Marcus perused the form attached to the clipboard, then scrawled his signature at the bottom. "Discharge will be effective immediately," he said. The nurse nodded, and Marcus gestured to the orderlies, who moved ahead and out into the hall with the gurney. The nurse followed, Marcus on her heels, until Carmen reached out and grabbed Marcus' arm, pulling him back.

"Dr. Marcus," Carmen said. Marcus stopped and turned around. The nurse and the orderlies stopped, too, but Marcus waved them on. "I'll be right there," he said. Marcus studied Carmen's face while he waited for her to speak. He watched her lower lip tremble, watched a tear well up in the corner of her eye.

"You can't send her home," Carmen said.

Marcus' face softened, the earlier edge brought on by Carmen's silence fading. "There's nothing more we can do," he said. "Batch 919 stopped TL's growth and replication, but it didn't kill it. That's what happens sometimes with an experimental protocol. I'm sorry, but the trial's finished."

Carmen straightened, bringing her shoulders back and raising herself to her full five feet three. "I've heard the nurses talking," she said. "I know about the cure."

Marcus studied Carmen's face, then turned and began to walk down the hall. "I'm sorry, Carmen. I'm not sure what you think you heard, but there is no 'cure,'" he said. "We've done all we can." Marcus continued walking, listening for Carmen's footsteps behind him, but it was silent, except for the squeaking of the gurney.

"You son of a bitch!" Carmen screamed, running at Marcus and stumbling, then colliding with him and knocking him to the ground. Carmen stood over him, swaying back and forth, her finger in his face. "There is a cure! I know there is! And I want you to give some to Jenny. Now!"

The nurse stopped and the orderlies descended on Carmen, but Marcus held up his hand and they froze. Marcus remained on the floor, looking up at Carmen and holding his shoulder. "I'm sorry," he said. I know how you must feel—"

"You couldn't possibly know how I feel," Carmen said, backing away from Marcus and limping toward the gurney, her eyes on the orderlies. "You have the power to save her and you won't." She stopped and rubbed her thigh, wincing, her back to Marcus. "But I would give my life for her, if I could." Marcus stayed on the floor and watched Carmen hobble to the gurney and take Jenny's thin hand, lift it, and stroke it against her cheek. "Come on baby," she whispered. "We're going home."

CHAPTER 30

"I'm a little disappointed we couldn't meet in person. These Skype hookups are so . . ." Keith searched for the right word ". . . sterile. Especially for a subject this important."

A thousand miles away in the middle of the desert, Phillip Porter sat in front of a webcam, a tall glass of iced tea and a cigarette at the ready. He picked up the cigarette and inhaled, then blew smoke at the lens. "When I got your call, I had already planned to take this little vacation," Porter said. He smiled. "But I knew we needed to talk."

"You look tan," Keith said. "Where are you?"

Porter's smile widened. "At my private retreat. The air is very good here. Very dry." Porter finished the first cigarette and lit another off the still-glowing butt. "Is Mrs. Kramer with you?" he said. "It is still Mrs. Kramer, isn't it?"

Linda moved into frame and sat down next to Keith. "Yes, I'm here and yes, Jason and I are still married."

Porter's smile wavered a bit, then regained its normal radiance. "Ah yes. Good to see you again. Linda, isn't it?"

Linda nodded, and then leaned forward into the camera. "How is Jason, anyway?" she said. Keith put his hand on her leg under the table and squeezed her thigh, then patted her knee. Linda relaxed in response and let her shoulders drop. "What I mean is, I haven't seen him for a while."

"Of course," Porter said. "He's hanging on, but just barely. Oh, and by the way, Linda, we still haven't received those consent forms you and I spoke about."

"Look, Porter," Keith said, "Linda won't be signing any releases or consent forms or relinquishing her interest in Jason's tissue. We know what's going on."

Porter's left eyebrow arched upward. "Oh? Tell me, then, Mr. Lawrence. What is going on?"

"We know you're holding Jason hostage and we know you've got some sort of top secret TL cure that you and that quack Craig Marcus are selling to desperate patients."

Porter laughed and shook, ashes cascading from the end of his cigarette into a gray pile on the table. "Well, well, Mr. Lawrence. You've been reading the tabloids it seems." Porter turned his attention to Linda. "Perhaps I can explain," he said. Porter motioned off camera and the Driver moved stiffly into frame. He handed Porter a flier, then shuffled back into the shadows. Porter held up the brochure. "You must be referring to Bigwood Springs."

Keith grabbed something off the top of the desk and held up the identical brochure. "Yeah, we've seen the propaganda. But it doesn't take a rocket scientist to figure out what's going on." Keith threw the flier back down. "Jason is miraculously cured of TL, then signs up with you for research, then disappears. Then we see these ads." Keith smiled into the camera. "Looks like you've found your golden goose."

Porter laughed again, then took a sip of tea and leaned back in his chair. "If by that you mean my goose that laid the golden egg," he said, "yes, Jason's here, and while it is true that we have been experimenting with an unusual protein we found in his blood, thus far the results have been inconclusive and less than promising in terms of that protein's effect on TL. And contrary to what you may have read, we have not made a dime off Jason. He has proven to be a rather . . . *expensive* . . . addition to our staff, and not at all your 'golden goose.'" Porter paused to suck in a lungful of smoke, and then exhaled as he spoke. "He is, of course, free to leave whenever he wishes, but I doubt his failing health will permit that.

It thus appears you have fallen prey to the misinformation foisted upon the American public by the mass media. But you are in good company. We are getting literally thousands of inquiries from TL patients every day."

"Look, Mr. Porter," Linda said, leaning forward and removing Keith's restraining hand from her knee. "Jason is still my husband—"

"So you said," Porter interrupted.

"—and I have a . . ." she looked at Keith, who nodded ". . . a community property interest in anything you take out of him."

"Actually," Keith said, "what Linda means is that she is entitled to fair compensation for the revenues you derive from any money you make selling Jason's tissue." Keith reached down and grabbed a letter, holding it up for Porter to see. "Our attorney is quite certain of that."

"Oh, you've involved the lawyers now have you?" Porter asked. "I guess I'd better just write you out a check." Porter chuckled and looked down, then reached forward and emptied three sugar packets into his tea. He lifted the glass and drank, a dribble of brown liquid running down his chin. "Look," he said, wiping his face, "the bottom line is, I've got Jason and you don't. You can't prove that Jason is anything more than a willing—and well-paid—research subject. His contract says as much."

Keith smiled. "I guess we'll let the jury decide that." He paused for dramatic effect. "After you get out of jail."

Porter's face stiffened. "Oh, Mr. Lawrence. There is no need for such melodrama. Things have a tendency to get ugly when I'm threatened like that. Besides," he said, "I've done nothing illegal."

"According to the FDA," Keith said, "it *is* illegal to test or administer pharmacological agents to people before the drug has been through a rigorous screening process, including animal trials, which may take several months. Jason's only been in your employment for a few weeks, and that's not enough time to complete the animal trials, but here you are offering up the stuff at this Bigwood Springs." Keith folded his hands on the table in front of him. "Besides," he said, "I'll bet you a nickel Jason's mystery blood isn't the only untested drug you're administering out there at your 'retreat.'"

Porter looked out of frame, his eyes unfocused, thinking and smoking. After a moment he looked back into the camera. "It's of no consequence to me whether Jason stays or leaves," he said. "However, it would be unfortunate to have all our good work here at Porter Pharmaceuticals interfered with as a consequence of your baseless and defamatory allegations." Porter lit another cigarette. "What do you propose?" he said.

Keith smiled and threw a glance at Linda, who grinned back. Keith held up another piece of paper. "A partnership," he said. "A three-way partnership among you, Linda, and me for distribution of revenues from the sale of the cure you are extracting from Jason's blood."

Porter squinted at the screen, trying to read the document Keith held. "You'll need to fax that to my lawyer in San Francisco," he said.

"Of course," Keith said. "It's a standard general partnership agreement." Linda leaned forward and spoke into the computer monitor. "We're not being greedy, Mr. Porter. We only want what's fair. 50 percent for you, 25 each for me and Keith."

"That's absurd," Porter said. "We have borne all the development and research costs, not to mention marketing—"

"Uh, Mr. Porter," Linda interrupted, "one more word and it will go to 40, 30, 30." Keith smiled and patted Linda's knee under the table.

Porter glowered into the camera. "Very well," he said. "50, 25, 25."

"I thought you'd see it that way," Linda said.

"Great," Keith said. "I guess we're done. Except for one little detail. I've arranged for these materials to be delivered to the FDA regional office in Portland if anything should happen to us."

Porter nodded, still smoldering at them through a cloud of smoke. "You know," he said, "Jason's still a free agent. He could walk out of here tomorrow and you wouldn't see a penny from your blackmail."

Linda smiled. "Oh, I've thought of that," she said. "I'll take care of Jason." She waved at the camera. "Bye, bye," she said. Keith reached forward and tapped the computer keyboard and Porter's image winked off the screen.

In the conference room at The Complex, Porter pressed his fingers into his gut and rubbed, a low moan escaping his throat. "Walter," he said. "I'm sending you back home. I want somebody close to headquarters—in case Kramer and Lawrence try anything. And you'd better put Claudius in that kennel in Sausalito—the one with the free cat toys." The Driver nodded and started to move for the door, then turned and looked back at Porter. "What about you, Mr. Porter?" he said.

Porter squinted and shifted in his chair, his fingers now probing the small of his back. "I'll be staying here," he said.

CHAPTER 31

"She's gone, Jason! I was just in her room and she's gone!"

Jason opened his eyes and looked at Wendy running toward him, the metal door to his room sliding shut behind her. "Who's gone?" he asked, blinking and trying to focus.

"Jenny!" Wendy yelled, now right next to Jason's bed, her face in his. "They discharged her!"

Jason tried to lift his head from the pillow, but it fell back with a soft thud as Jason groaned from the effort. "Discharged her? Why? Is she all better? Dr. Marcus said they weren't going to give her any of the cure," Jason said, gesturing to the shunt plugged into his arm.

Wendy sighed and pulled Jason up by his shoulders, propping the pillow behind him. "They didn't give her the cure. I checked her records. They show that she completed her trial of Batch 919 and so was being discharged." Wendy's jaw tightened. "To go home and die," she said. Wendy continued to tug on Jason and adjust the pillows, her anger carrying over into the vigor with which she jostled Jason. His head flipped back and forth like a rag doll.

"Ow," he said, as Wendy shoved him to one side, tucking in his sheets. "You're hurting me."

Wendy stopped in mid-motion, holding one of Jason's legs in the air, the sheet in her other hand. "Sorry," she said, lowering his leg. "I just got so angry when I saw what he had done."

"What who had—" Jason said.

"Craig Marcus!" Wendy said, cutting him off. "It was Dr. Marcus who discharged her." Her face grew flush at the thought. "That bastard," she said. Wendy looked down at Jason and saw that his eyes had closed again and his head had slumped to one side of the pillow. "Jason!" Wendy yelled, "did you hear me?"

Jason's eyes popped open, the irises swimming lazily in a bloodshot sea of white. Wendy held his face in her hands and studied his eyes for comprehension, like a referee checking a boxer after a mandatory eight count. Jason looked at her. "I'm sorry," he said. "I'm just so tired."

Wendy held his face a moment longer and then lowered his head back onto the pillow. She looked down at the stainless steel cart she had wheeled into the room, her face reflected in its shiny surface. She stared at her image, listening to Jason's shallow breathing and the buzzing of the fluorescent lights. The TV was on, and a reporter was talking about the vaccine riots in Atlanta and DC. Behind the reporter, thousands of people, most of whom were wearing masks or respirators, marched, carrying placards and signs, one of which read: "Where's The Cure, CDC?" The reporter began her stand-up: "Brian, the scene here in Atlanta well reflects the mood of the country in general as the death toll from Trips Lite continues to climb. Fear and isolation are growing, as demands for a vaccine become more vocal. I spoke earlier today with Dr. John Cornwall of the CDC." Wendy looked up at the screen and saw Dr. Cornwall, his pate shiny with perspiration.

"Dr. Cornwall," the reporter said, "let me ask you what every American is wondering right now. Why is there no vaccine for Trips Lite?"

Dr. Cornwall cleared his throat. "Please know that we are working tirelessly, both here and with our international colleagues, to find a vaccine, and that all available government resources are being deployed in the fight. But to answer your question, Trips Lite mutates very rapidly, and each time we think we have a workable serum, the virus changes into something else—but equally deadly, equally virulent."

Wendy clicked off the television and, with a sudden movement, she pushed the cart around to the edge of Jason's bed and removed the cover, exposing syringes, surgical tubing and collection vials. She picked up a length of tubing and pulled on the ends, testing it, stretching it. Then, with a glance around the room and up at the TV, as if it could both play and watch like the telescreens in Orwell's *1984,* Wendy sat down on the edge of Jason's bed and tied the rubber tube around her own left arm, just above the elbow. Jason looked on, dreamily. "What are you doing?" he asked.

Wendy pulled the tourniquet tight and made a hard fist several times until a blue vein bulged from the inside of her arm.

"What are you doing?" Jason asked again.

Wendy uncapped a syringe and held the needle next to her skin. She looked up at Jason. "I'm saving your life," she said.

CHAPTER 32

The fist came down on top of the receptionist's desk with sudden violence, upsetting a stapler and a container of paper clips that sat near the phone. The clips scattered in every direction, clicking and bouncing on the hardwood floor of the foyer. The receptionist behind the desk looked up and primly adjusted her glasses. "I'm sorry, Mr. . . . Durrant, was it? Getting angry will not help matters. We have no records of a patient named Jason Kramer."

Scott leaned forward, neck muscles taut, his face now level with the receptionist's. "That's not true," he said. "I talked to Jason just three weeks ago, and he told me that Porter Pharmaceuticals was jetting him away somewhere as part of a secret experiment—" Scott raised his voice dramatically to emphasize "secret experiment," then glanced around the waiting room to see several pairs of eyes watching his exchange "—and now I want to know where he is."

The receptionist placed her hand on Scott's shoulder and smiled at the onlookers. "I'll tell you what," she said turning back to Scott, "if you'll have a seat right over there—" she pointed to a chair on the other side of the room "—I'll have someone come down and talk to you."

Scott stood his ground, staring her down. After a moment, his neck relaxed and he took a step back from the desk. "Sure," he said. "O.K."

The receptionist smiled and nodded, then looked around again, smiling and nodding more. Gradually, the spectators also relaxed and turned back to their waiting-room magazines and coffee as Scott ambled over to the chair and took a seat. He watched the receptionist speak into her headset, then reached down and grabbed a copy of *Popular Science*. He was engrossed in an article about Internet telephony when he felt someone standing close to him, leaning over and above him. Scott looked up into the unblinking steel gray eyes of the Driver.

"Hi," the Driver said. "I understand you're looking for Jason Kramer."

Scott swallowed and closed the magazine. "Yeah," he said. "I am."

The Driver motioned down a corridor leading off from the reception area. "If you'll come with me to a conference room," he said, "I'm sure I can help you."

Scott looked down the hallway and then up at the Driver. He stood and took a tentative step into the corridor. The Driver smiled and gestured again, and Scott began walking down the hallway, the Driver at his side. They walked in silence for several yards until they reached an open door leading into a conference room. The Driver pointed inside. "After you," he said.

Scott entered the room and sat down at a round table and the Driver sat next to him, his shoulder touching Scott. Scott edged away, but the Driver moved closer and reached to the center of the table to grab a pencil and a pad of paper. "Now then," he said, "I just need to get a little information from you before I can release anything on Jason." He leaned forward and whispered, "Industrial espionage and all."

Scott leaned back, away from the Driver's intrusion into his personal space. "What do you want to know?" he asked.

The Driver positioned the pencil over the pad. "Your name?" he said.

"Scott Durrant."

The Driver scribbled on the paper. "Relationship to Mr. Kramer?"

"I'm his friend."

The Driver made some more notes. "Uh-huh," he said. "And your address?"

"Why do you need my address?" Scott asked, now poised to push himself back away from the table. The Driver reached out and grabbed the edge of Scott's chair, impeding its movement. "Company policy," the Driver said. "In case we need to contact you."

Scott pushed hard and his chair flew back from the table, breaking free of the Driver's grasp. "I don't think so," he said. He stood and made a move for the exit, but the Driver was on his feet and running, ending up between Scott and the door. The top of the Driver's head was just level with Scott's nose. Scott looked down, and the Driver looked up, his eyes bright with intensity. "I really need your address," the Driver said, his voice low in his throat.

Scott's lanky arms flew out and shoved the Driver backward, hard. The Driver, surprised and off balance, bounced against the conference room wall and cracked his head against the corner of a picture frame. Scott made a grab for the door handle and yanked it open, then sprinted out into the hallway, the Driver staggering after him, his hand pressed to his head. "You son of a bitch!" he yelled as Scott sprinted down the hall toward the reception area. The Driver stumbled after him, careening off the hall's opposing walls. Scott was ten feet in front of him and gaining, his long legs pumping. He reached the entrance and straight-armed the glass doors leading to the parking lot, not even breaking stride.

"Call security!" the Driver screamed at the receptionist as he ran by, following Scott into the parking lot. Scott jumped into his red Karmann Ghia, started the engine, and jammed it into reverse, backing out with tires screeching. The rubber was still smoking when Scott pulled out into traffic on the boulevard in front of Porter Pharmaceuticals. The Driver stood in the parking lot, blood oozing from between the fingers clamped to his head. Two armed security guards ran up to the Driver, their eyes wide.

"What happened?" one of the guards asked. The Driver turned to him and stared into his eyes. Behind his back, the Driver curled his free hand into a tight fist, and then lashed out with a wicked right hook, connecting with the guard's chin. The guard dropped like a rock, twitching inside his blue uniform. The other guard knelt to attend to his unconscious co-worker. "I need the address of a guy named Scott Durrant," the Driver said to the guard as he ran toward Porter's black Mercedes. "Check the file, and check the security camera videos of the reception area and the parking lot and see if you can ID him off his plates. He's a friend of Jason's. Call me back on my cell phone when you have an address."

Scott looked in his rear-view mirror as he sped away, wildly dodging in and around cars on the boulevard, the speedometer on the little Karmann Ghia pegged to the top end. He zoomed toward an intersection, praying for the light to stay green. It did. He took a hard right at the light, his rear wheels trying to skid out from under him. Just as he rounded the corner, he saw the black Benz barrel out of the Porter Pharmaceuticals parking lot, tires smoking. Scott cranked the wheel and pulled down a side street, then whipped the car around into an alley. He shut off the engine and waited, listening. He looked at himself in the mirror. He was pale, his hair matted to his forehead with sweat. He could see his pulse pounding in a vein at his temple. "Idiot," he said to his reflection, "just march right in and demand to see Jason. Smooth, very smooth."

Just then Scott heard the engine of a car that had pulled onto the side street behind him. He froze, not breathing, barely mustering enough courage to sneak a peek in the rear view mirror. The engine sounds moved closer, and a battered Ford pickup motored by the entrance to the alley, an old man wearing a dirty baseball cap at the wheel. Scott laughed and slumped in his seat, then wiped his forehead and ran his fingers back through his hair. With another glance over his shoulder, Scott started the car and idled out to the boulevard. He looked around and up and down the street, but saw no black Mercedes.

It was dark when he reached the Oakland exit that led to his apartment. He pulled off the freeway and made his way toward the complex, stopping when he was a hundred yards away. He felt around in the glove compartment for the remote to the garage and was about to punch the button when he noticed the black Mercedes parked in the shadows across the street from his front door.

"Cripes and crud," Scott swore as he threw the remote back into the glove box and pulled to the curb. He shut off the lights and let the engine idle, watching the Mercedes for signs of life. The car remained dark and silent, so Scott put his car in gear and inched forward until he could see his apartment window. He watched for several seconds, and then felt his heart stop when the curtains fluttered and opened a crack. He could see the outline of a person standing inside.

Scott gulped, his hands wet on the steering wheel, then performed a very slow U-turn and idled up the street, away from the apartment complex. "Oh man," he stammered, looking around in near panic. "Now what?" He took a deep breath and exhaled. Get a grip, Scott, he thought, get a grip. Suddenly his eyes grew wide, a smile growing on his face. He stuffed the pedal to the floorboard and accelerated, heading toward the freeway entrance. "Of course," he said out loud, laughing. "Veronica, Archie and Gopher to the rescue!"

CHAPTER 33

A white-coated lab tech removed the vials of blood from a refrigerator and held them up. "Kramer," he said, reading Wendy's handwriting on the sides. "Time to go for a little spin." He walked the vials over to a counter, placed them inside a centrifuge, and turned on the machine. The tech looked down inside through the glass lid and watched the tubes whirl, watched the heavier red blood cells and platelets pulled by centrifugal force to the bottom of the vials, the lighter plasma and serum remaining on top. As the plasma separated and collected, the tech smiled. "White gold," he said.

He set the timer on the centrifuge for ten minutes, then turned his back on the machine and walked to his desk. He grabbed his coffee cup and took a swig, then picked up a novel, opened it to the bookmark, and started reading. The tech made a face and glanced up at the centrifuge when his reverie was interrupted by a loud ding. "Hey Sheryl," he called out, "put that batch in the separator, will you?"

The other tech looked up. "Do it yourself, Kyle," she said, pen in hand. "I'm in the middle of recording these test results."

Kyle's eyes didn't leave the page. "That's Kramer factor," he said. "You know how Dr. Marcus gets when that stuff isn't processed right away. Besides," he grinned, "it's your turn."

Sheryl's eyes narrowed and her jaw clenched. "You're such a jerk," she said as she opened the lid and reached in for the vials.

"Thank you," Kyle said. "Don't spill any."

Sheryl smirked, but didn't respond. She took the vials to a different machine, then suctioned off the plasma with a pipette and injected it into a hole on top of the device. "Let's get you on your way into some rich guy's veins," she said as she punched a series of buttons on the control console.

Sheryl returned to her desk and continued writing until the separator signaled that processing was complete. She got up and moved to the machine where drops of clear, light yellow liquid had gathered in the collection chamber. Sheryl bent down and peered at the substance, squinting. "This doesn't look right," she said.

Kyle didn't look up. "Hmm?" he said.

"This batch doesn't look right," Sheryl said. "It's a different color than normal."

"Did you get the dilution ratio correct for the dose?"

Sheryl bent over and peered at a digital display on the front of the separator. "Yeah, it's right."

"What can we do?" Kyle said, looking up, annoyed. "You know there's a lot of variation in that protein."

Sheryl thought for a moment, then stood up and looked at Kyle, squaring her shoulders. "Not *that* much," she said. "I'm calling Dr. Marcus." She moved toward her desk and reached for the phone.

Kyle's eyes opened wide and he dropped his book. "Wait a minute," he said. "Let me take a look." Kyle watched as Sheryl's fingers paused over the telephone keypad, then relaxed as she put down the handset. "No need to get upset," he said. Kyle walked to the separator and bent down, then tapped the digital display as he looked into the collection chamber. "Hmm, yeah, you're right. It is a little darker than normal." Kyle glanced up, judging Sheryl's reaction. "But I don't think we need to call Dr. Marcus."

"You sure?"

"Oh, yeah. I mean he'll come in here and accuse us of up screwing up the batch and then they'll have to run a lot of tests. One of us, . . ." Kyle paused, staring hard at Sheryl, ". . . could even get fired."

Sheryl returned the stare for a moment before looking down and nodding. "Yeah," she said. "Maybe you're right."

"Besides," Kyle said as he removed the collection chamber from the separator and siphoned off the contents into a vial, "who's to say what the right color for this stuff is, anyway? Nobody even knows how it really works."

Sheryl relaxed. "True," she said, laughing.

"I mean, that protein is just like everybody else's. It's just that in Kramer, it kills Trips Lite. Go figure."

Sheryl moved next to Kyle and watched him label the vial. He placed it into a short blue cylinder with the name "Adams" written on it. "There you go, Mr. Adams," he said, sealing the container. "No more TL for you." Kyle handed the cylinder to Sheryl, who ceremoniously placed it into a pneumatic delivery tube. She closed the door on the receptacle and pressed the send button, then listened for the gentle "whoosh" that signaled the package was on its way to the nurses' station upstairs.

"You just saved a man's life," Kyle said.

CHAPTER 34

Scott's office at Anderson Kaplan was dark, except for the phosphorescent glow from the computer screen. Scott sat huddled over the keyboard, typing aggressively, the keys clacking. He glanced up every few seconds, looking back at the door to his office. Suddenly, Scott lifted his hands from the keyboard and leaned closer, peering at the screen. The cursor flashed in the upper left hand corner, then the words "ENTER NEWSGROUP NAME" appeared on the screen. Scott smiled and typed "alt.talk.drugs" at the prompt, then pressed "Enter." He sat back in his chair, pulling distractedly on his ear lobe and chewing on his lower lip, watching the screen as lists of entries rolled by. "Veronica, Archie and Gopher," he muttered.

"Hello?"

Scott jumped out of his chair and spun around to face the intruder, grabbing his stapler and holding it like a weapon. Light from the hallway flooded the room, the stranger illuminated from behind, glowing with an aura. "What do you want?" Scott called, squinting at the backlit form. The figure moved out of the light and into the shadows, then walked toward Scott's desk and reached out. Scott yelped and ran behind the desk. "Don't do it, man," he said. "I haven't found anything yet."

The figure's hand stopped, then reached down and grabbed the trash can under the desk. "Found what, Mr. Durrant?"

Scott grabbed the pull chain on his desk lamp and tugged, illuminating the face of the janitor.

"Oh, man," Scott laughed, wiping his eyes and running the palm of his hand over his damp forehead, "you scared me."

"Sorry, Mr. Durrant. I didn't know you were in here. Who are Archie, Veronica and Gopher?"

Scott laughed, then moved back around the desk and sat down. "Those are the names of different tools that help you search the Internet," he said.

"I thought everybody just Googled these days," the janitor said.

Scott looked back down at the screen and watched a list appear and scroll down the page. "Google's for wimps," he said. "If you really want to search, you use Veronica, Archie, and Gopher, and you look in the Usenet newsgroups."

"I'll go Google that," the janitor said.

Scott squinted at the screen and ran his finger down the newsgroup list, stopping beside one and reading the name out loud. "Porter," he said, grinning.

"Find something?" the janitor asked, moving over to look at the screen.

"Yep. Looking for a friend."

"Cool. Who ya looking for?"

Scott tabbed the cursor down to the entry labeled "Porter" and pushed the "Enter" key. "Just an old friend. He's been sick and I want to make sure he's all right."

The janitor nodded as he emptied the trash. "Good luck," he said before replacing the can and leaving Scott's office.

Scott's eyes remained glued to the screen. "Thanks," he said. "I'll need it." He put his fingers back on the keys and typed, "Anybody know anything about where Porter Pharmaceuticals conducts its drug testing?" then pushed "Enter." He leaned back in his chair. "Cast your bread upon the waters," he said.

CHAPTER 35

The nurse reverently picked up the vial labeled "Adams" from the receiving box at the end of the pneumatic tube. She held it up and looked at it, watching the clear, light yellow liquid swish back and forth. She placed the vial next to a syringe on a stainless steel tray covered with a white cotton cloth, then lifted the tray and placed it on the counter of the nurses' station. "Gwen," she called out. "The Adams dose is ready."

Gwen looked up from her position at the counter, medical charts open in front of her, smiled, and picked up the tray. "Thanks," she said. "And Mr. Adams thanks you." Gwen moved down the hall toward Mr. Adams' room, carrying the tray like an open carton of eggs. She could hear the television blasting out a report about a beleaguered baseball team on the east coast. Gwen peeked in the room. "Everybody decent?"

"Who's that?" came the reply.

"Just the nurse."

The TV volume descended. "Yeah. Come on in."

Gwen walked into Mr. Adams' room and placed the tray on the bedside table. She paused for a moment, looking at him. His face was worn and thin, his head bald except for the places that tufts of gray hair clung tenuously to life. Gwen picked up his wrist and checked his pulse through ice-cold skin. "How're you doing?"

Calvin Adams looked up into Gwen's face. "Did you know," he said, "that tomorrow's my birthday? I'll be seventy-three."

Gwen smiled and looked back through Mr. Adams' thick glasses into warm brown eyes. "I heard," she said. "Happy birthday."

"Oh, there's more to it than that," Adams said. "The whole fam damily is flying out here to Bigwood for the party. You're invited." He gestured toward a picture on the dresser. In it, Calvin Adams was surrounded by a herd of young men and women, who in turn were surrounded by children of varying ages and sizes. "Kids, grandkids, the whole lot."

"That's great! And thanks for the invite. I'd love to come, if my schedule permits."

"Make it permit! It's not every day a man gets a second chance at life as a birthday present."

Gwen smiled and nodded. "True," she said. She looked at the vial. "It's a miracle."

Calvin extended his arm. "Let's get 'er in there."

Gwen picked up the vial and the syringe. She filled the barrel with the pale fluid and held the hypodermic upright while she swabbed Mr. Adams' arm with an alcohol prep. Adams looked at her, grinned, and took a deep breath. Gwen slid the needle in and shoved the plunger home, watching the liquid slide into his vein.

"Warm," Calvin mumbled. "Feels warm."

Gwen withdrew the needle and bandaged the puncture. "Strong stuff," she said. She turned her back on Calvin for a moment to cap the syringe and clean up the tray. When she turned around, Calvin was wiping a tear off his cheek.

"Sorry," he sniffed, wiping the back of his hand across his nose. "My family had to sacrifice a lot to be able to send me here."

Gwen rested her hand on his shoulder. "And now you'll have plenty more years to spend with them. To say thanks."

"If that damn stuff works. Oughta work, for how expensive it was."

"Don't you worry. We've had a 100 percent success rate. We'll check you in a day or two and I bet those viruses will be dead and gone." Gwen lifted the tray and moved toward the door.

Calvin nodded, rubbing the inside of his arm. "Let's hope so," he said. He grabbed the TV remote control and pointed it at the set in the wall, the volume suddenly growing louder and louder. Gwen winced and put her free hand over her ear. "Maybe I'll put a bet on the World Series this year after all," Calvin called after her.

Gwen left the room and moved back toward the nurses' station. She looked up at the figure approaching down the hallway and smiled in greeting. "Hi Wendy," she said. "Haven't seen you in weeks."

Wendy walked up next to Gwen at the counter. "Been busy," she said. "I haven't been up on this floor much. They kept me working with the remaining cancer patients downstairs, but now that they're almost all gone, they've reassigned me to this floor part time to help with all the new TL patients."

"Great!"

"Plus," Wendy said, "I've been working with Jason."

Gwen's eyes widened. "Jason Kramer?"

Wendy nodded, suppressing a smile.

"Wow! I've never even seen him. Is he here somewhere?"

Wendy thought about the cold metal door separating Jason from the rest of the world down in the basement. "Yeah. He's here."

Gwen waited. "Where?" she finally asked.

"You can't see him. He's sequestered to make sure the factor remains uncontaminated."

Gwen's face fell. "Oh," she said. "Sure. I understand."

"So anyway," Wendy said, brightening, "they keeping you busy?"

"Oh, my gosh, yes. Ever since they changed the name of this place to Bigwood Springs, I've been busier than the only lawyer at an ambulance convention."

Wendy smiled. "Lots of new patients?"

"Tons. And they all want four-star service. Except Mr. Adams, of course. He's so sweet."

"Mr. Adams?"

"Yeah, Calvin Adams. Room 314. Nice old guy with liver failure from TL. Had about three weeks to live when he got here, and that was a week ago. His family bought him the cure as a birthday present."

Wendy smiled. "That's great. When did he get it?"

Gwen looked back over her shoulder, indicating with her chin. "Just now. I just left his room."

Wendy looked down at the empty syringe on the counter. She felt her stomach twist and the blood drain from her face. "Is that batch date right?" she asked pointing at the numbers written on the barrel.

Gwen glanced at the syringe. "Yeah. Why?"

"You gave him the factor?"

"Yeah. The batch that just came up from the lab. What's wrong?"

Wendy felt around behind herself for a chair and sat down. "They weren't supposed to use that batch for a while. . . . It was supposed to be at least a week before they needed any new factor."

"Nope. Demand exceeded supply, I guess. Marcus ordered it used immediately."

Wendy put her hand on her forehead, breathing fast, hyperventilating. She felt nauseous and cold. Gwen looked down at her, worried. "You all right, honey? You look a little pale."

Wendy managed a smile and nodded. "Yeah. I'm fine. I ate in the cafeteria for lunch today. Must be the meatloaf."

"Do you want some Pepto?"

Wendy shook her head. "Do you know who else got the new batch?"

Gwen grabbed a clipboard from the wall of the nurses' station and flipped through the pages. "So far, just Calvin, and he's—" Gwen stopped, her mouth half-open. She put her hand on Wendy's forehead. "Are you sure you're all right? You feel warm."

Wendy tried to smile. "Fine. I'm fine."

Gwen watched her a moment longer. "You just sit there until you feel better. I'll just be right up the hall at the station if you need anything."

Wendy swallowed hard, trying not to faint. "I appreciate that," she said. "Thanks."

Gwen walked back to the station and disappeared inside. Wendy watched her go, and then covered her eyes with her hands as tears seeped through her fingers and slipped down her cheeks. "They weren't supposed to use it, they weren't supposed to use it," she whispered again and again as she stood, her knees weak. She wiped her face, and then looked up and down the empty hallway. "Adams, Adams," she mumbled as she moved down the corridor looking at all the nametags on the doors. "Adams," she said, stopping in front of a room. "Calvin Adams."

She looked inside and saw Calvin propped up in his bed, three large white pillows behind his head, the remote control in his hand. He was flipping through the channels and laughing, like a kid with a new toy. She saw the picture of his family on the nightstand. Then, while she watched, Calvin put down the remote, made a fist and curled his scrawny biceps, then prodded the muscle with the fingers of his left hand. He looked at the picture and flexed again, assuming a body builder pose. "Not bad," she heard him say. "Not bad at all."

Wendy moved back from the door and leaned against the wall, her heart pounding, sweat building in the hair around her temples. She stepped back and massaged the puncture mark on the inside of her arm. She remained in the hall for ten minutes, listening to Calvin and trying not to cry.

CHAPTER 36

Denise Dalton tapped on the door to Phillip Porter's suite on the third floor of The Complex. "Mr. Porter," she said, "I've got your dinner."

"Come!" Porter yelled from behind the door. Denise shifted the tray she was carrying and reached for the knob. Porter was talking to himself and swearing as she pushed her way into the room. Denise looked around. Porter was standing naked in front of a full-length lighted mirror, wearing only a short white towel around his waist.

"Damn fluorescents!" Porter shouted at his reflection. He turned to Denise. "Come over here!"

Denise placed the tray on the table and moved to stand beside Porter, their reflections side by side in the mirror. Under the harsh lighting, Porter's rib cage stood out like xylophone keys, a stark contrast to Denise's more rounded form. She averted her eyes and looked at Porter's face. "Mr. Porter," she said, "I'm Denise Dalton. I'm a lab tech here, down in the file room. It's nice to finally meet—"

"Hold out your arm!" Porter yelled. Denise jumped, then complied, her arm shooting out straight toward the mirror. Porter leaned forward, his arm similarly extended, and compared it with Denise's reflection. "Yellow," Porter said. He took a step back and turned to Denise. "Yellow as a banana." Denise stared uncomprehendingly at Porter. "These lights make my skin look yellow," Porter said. "But not yours."

Denise's forehead wrinkled and furrowed as she self-consciously rubbed her arms, olive skin glowing in the fluorescent light. "I've been in the sun a lot. I'm pretty tan," she said.

Porter sniffed and adjusted his towel. He moved to the table and lit a cigarette before examining the food on the tray. He lifted the silver domes covering each plate, made a face, and slammed each one back down. "Ridiculous," he said. "I own this place and I can't even get a decent meal." He moved away from the table and plopped down on the bed, puffing on the cigarette.

Denise shifted her weight back and forth on the balls of her feet. "You know, Mr. Porter, you really should eat something."

Porter glared at her. He stood suddenly and moved to the table, then grabbed one of the lids and lifted it, stabbing it in the air toward Denise. "You want this slop?"

Denise paled and moved back, toward the door. "No," she said.

"Then why should I eat it?" Porter continued glaring at her then threw the lid across the room, where it slammed into the wall with a loud bang. "Take it away."

Denise stood unmoving, trembling, while Porter made his way back to the bed. He stretched out and picked up his cigarette, puffing viciously and rubbing his abdomen just below his ribcage. Denise took a step toward the table, then another. "Mr. Porter," she said, her voice wavering, "are you O.K.?"

Porter stubbed out the butt he was smoking and lit another. "I'll be fine as soon as I get back to San Francisco. Get a real meal."

Denise stopped in front of the table and started to reassemble the trays. "About your skin, . . ." she said, hesitating, judging Porter's reaction before proceeding. He said nothing, but glanced at her out of the corner of his eye. "You might want to see a doctor," she said.

"Why?" he snorted. "So they can tell me to stop smoking and cut down on fatty foods? I've been smoking since I was twelve and eating red meat since I was three, and I'm not going to stop simply because some doctor thinks my skin looks a little yellow." Porter held out his hand in front of him and turned it over and over, studying it. "Probably just nerves."

Denise had finished stacking the plates and now lifted the tray to her shoulder. She stood, watching Porter examine his palm. Finally, she took a step toward the door, the dishes clattering. Porter looked at her, his hand frozen in mid-air. "What'd you say your name was?"

Denise stopped and looked back over her shoulder. "My name's Denise Dalton. If I can do anything for you, I'm at extension 2110, downstairs in the lab." She grinned. "I mean, I usually work down in the file room, but I'm filling in for somebody on this floor tonight. So anyway, if you need anything—"

Porter let his eyes run up and down Denise's body. "As a matter of fact," Porter said, "there is something."

Denise's smile retracted at Porter's leer. "Yes?" she said.

"I want you to contact my driver, Walter Heinz, back at the home office. Tell him I'm ready to leave."

Denise frowned, thinking. "Are you sure you don't want to see someone first, Dr. Marcus or somebody?"

Porter sat bolt upright. "No! Don't say anything to Marcus. I'm not supposed to be leaving yet and I don't want Dr. Marcus to . . . worry."

Denise thought for a moment, then nodded. "Will do," she said. "I'll take care of it."

Denise turned and left the room. Porter stared at the closed door for a moment, then looked back at his hand. He stood and moved again to the mirror, then leaned toward it, his face just inches away from the glass. He opened his eyes wide and pulled the lower lids down with his fingers, examining the sclera. "Damn," he said. "Just like summer squash."

Denise scurried down the hallway and placed the trays on a kitchen cart. She paused in thought, her hand on her forehead, then turned and marched to the elevator. She got in and punched the button for the fifth floor. "Not good," she muttered to herself, "not good at all." The doors opened and Denise started down the hallway, reading the name tags on the outside of each office. She paused when she got to the one labeled "Craig Marcus," then reached out and knocked.

"Come in," Marcus called from behind the door. Denise tentatively turned the knob and peeked inside. Marcus and Ruth were seated at a round table, computer printouts spilled all over the table in front of them. They looked up, waiting. "Yes?" Marcus said.

"Uh, hi, Dr. Marcus. You probably don't remember me—"

"Sure I do," Marcus interrupted, "you're the file clerk who helped me out that one time." The memory caused Marcus to think of the Jennifer Holloway file and the notes that remained in his safe at home.

"Uh, right, um lab tech actually." Ruth and Marcus smiled, still waiting. "Anyway," Denise said, "the reason I'm here, is Mr. Porter."

Marcus frowned. "Is something wrong? Did he do something?"

Denise blushed. "No, no, nothing like that, it's just that . . . ."

"Yes?" Marcus said.

"He doesn't look good. He's all yellow."

"What do you mean?"

"I mean his skin, his eyes, they look yellow. He said not to tell you, but—"

"No, no, you did the right thing." Marcus turned to Ruth. "Have you seen him lately?"

Ruth shook her head. "I haven't seen him since he got here last month. He stays in his room most of the time."

"Yeah, he's like a hermit. I've not seen him much either," Marcus said. He turned to Denise. "Don't worry, you did the right thing. We'll check on him."

"There's just one more thing," Denise said. "He says he's going to leave, go back to San Francisco, as soon as he can. He wants me to call his driver and tell him to fly out here right now and get him."

"Walter." Marcus shook his head. "Don't call the Driver yet. We need to make sure Porter stays here until we look at him. And don't worry. We won't say anything." Ruth nodded in agreement.

"Thanks," Denise smiled, relieved. She backed out of the room and shut the door.

Ruth turned to Marcus. "What do you think that's all about?" she said.

Marcus shrugged. "Beats me. But he can't go anywhere tonight without Walter and the car, so I'll stop by and see him in the morning."

—

Porter looked around his room and swore. He walked to the door and opened it a crack, then looked down the hallway toward the reception area. There was one person at the desk, a secretary, who was reading a magazine. Porter eased the door shut and moved to the bed where his luggage sat, packed and neatly stacked. He opened a carry-on and pulled out a hat and a pair of dark glasses. He put them on, then pulled his collar up around his neck and tugged his long-sleeve shirt down to cover his wrists. Porter glanced at himself in the mirror and made a face, then opened the door and started down the hall.

"Going someplace?"

Porter turned with a start and bumped into Marcus. "No," Porter said, trying to look away and avoid Marcus' stare. "Just going to get a magazine."

"Good," Marcus said. "Then you won't mind if we go back into your room for a little visit." Marcus opened the door and looked inside at the suitcases. "Packed pretty heavy for a guy just going to get a magazine," he said. Porter hesitated, then went back into the room with a sigh.

"Mind if I look at your eyes?" Marcus said, pointing at the sunglasses.

Porter waited, watching Marcus, and then turned and marched to the writing desk where he sat down. "That damn Denise! She's talked to you, hasn't she? That's why Walter hasn't arrived yet."

"Denise was concerned about you. She asked me to look in on you before you went back to San Francisco."

Porter stared at Marcus, not mollified.

Marcus gestured toward Porter's face. "May I take a look?"

Porter scowled, and then yanked the glasses from his face. Marcus walked over and bent down, looking into the whites of Porter's eyes. They were the color of scrambled eggs. Marcus swallowed hard. Liver failure, he thought. Maybe cirrhosis or hepatitis. Maybe pancreatic cancer. Or TL. "Lie down," he said.

Porter hesitated. "Why?"

Marcus frowned and Porter acquiesced. Marcus pressed his fingers deep into Porter's abdomen and probed the gut, causing Porter to inhale and wince. Marcus continued his exploration, unfazed by Porter's protests. He pressed deeper, and—.

"Ow!" Porter cried out, trying to pull away.

Marcus kept his fingers thrust into Porter's abdomen and gave another quick push. "Ow!" Porter yelled again, pulling Marcus' hand away.

"Sorry," Marcus said. "I didn't realize it was so sensitive."

"Liar," Porter said. "You'll get your revenge any way you can, won't you? What did you find?"

"Hard to tell. I'd like to run a few blood tests."

Porter stared at Marcus then rubbed his eyes before he put his glasses back on. Marcus picked up Porter's hand and examined the palm and the inside of his arm. Light yellow, just like the eyes, except fainter, and more orange.

"What do you think it is?"

Marcus shook his head. "Could be a skin condition, maybe a vitamin deficiency," he said. "We'll know more after the tests. I'll have a phlebotomist come in and collect some blood."

"Is it TL? I don't see how it could be, given that I have not been around anyone who is infected with the virus."

"Yeah, no one except all the sick people you have out here in Bigwood Springs paying you blood money," Marcus said.

"I know TL's incubation period, and the math on that does not pencil," Porter said. "If I've contracted it, it had to be before I left the Bay Area. Perhaps it was Walter! He does tend to frequent many public places."

"Look, it'll take a few hours to get the results back, so just stay here and take it easy," Marcus said.

"Stay here? I'd rather eat cactus." Marcus stared him down until Porter relented. "Oh, all right," he said. "But at least let me get some decent food flown in." Porter paused, then sat up onto the edge of the bed and looked at Marcus. "Why are you doing this?" he said.

Marcus paused, and then said, "Doing what?"

"Helping me. Being nice to me."

Marcus laughed. "Can't help it. I'm a doctor. Hippocratic oath and all that."

Porter smiled thinly. "Hippocrates must spin in his grave every time you pronounce yourself a healer. Remember the oath you took: 'first, do no harm?'"

Marcus took a step toward Porter and raised his hand, index finger extended, as if to poke Porter in the chest. "You should realize" he said, "that at some point blackmail stops working."

Porter's smile broadened. "But not yet, right?"

Marcus finger remained poised over Porter's sternum.

"Right?"

Marcus lowered his hand, turned and went out into the hallway.

"Oh, and hey Warden," Porter called out, his voice redolent with mocking condescension, "may I please make a phone call? I want to ask Walter to come back from San Francisco with some take-out Chinese."

Marcus didn't answer and slammed the door behind him. Porter laughed out loud, then again donned his costume and made his way to the reception desk. The secretary glanced up, her eyes growing wide when she realized who it was, then averted her gaze and looked back at her magazine. Porter cleared his throat and spoke to the young woman. "Excuse me," he said, handing her a piece of paper. "Can you place a call for me? It's to a cell phone in San Francisco, and I don't know how to get an outside line." The receptionist swallowed, and then dialed the number. She gestured to the courtesy phone on the other side of the lobby. "I'll put it there," she said.

Porter smiled, his sunglasses riding up ascending cheeks. "Thanks," he said before moving to the phone. He picked it up just in time to hear Walter answer.

"Hello?" Walter said. His voice was muffled and faint. "Look, I'll have to call you back, whoever this—"

"Shut up," Porter said, cutting him off. "I want you to fly back out to The Complex right away. I've got to get out of here."

"But wait," the Driver stammered, still whispering, "there's this guy here, a tall skinny guy, that's been asking about Kramer and—"

Porter interrupted again. "Why are you whispering?"

"We're watching his apartment, waiting for him to get home. He got away from me at the office."

Porter sighed. "Stop playing secret agent, Walter, and fly out here. Now. And bring some take-out from Yet Wah. General's Chicken and Happy Family. And Tsingtao to drink." Porter hung the phone up with authority, not waiting for Walter's response. He glanced at his watch. Two hours from now, he thought, I'll be getting a nice MSG buzz. He fished a cigarette and a red-tipped kitchen match out of his pocket, then ignited the match with his thumbnail. He watched it flare and glow, then lit his cigarette.

CHAPTER 37

Ruth stepped out of the elevator into the concrete hallway. "Why did you want to come down and see Jason?" she said.

Marcus rubbed his hand on the rough cement wall. "I don't know," he said. "I haven't been down here for a while—thought it might do me good to see him."

"Mmm. 'Out of sight, out of mind' can only appease a conscience for so long, huh?"

Marcus nodded.

"How's he doing?" Ruth said.

Marcus slid his key card through the scanner then stepped back from the door. "The cure keeps flowing, so I guess he's fine, but we'll both know for sure in a minute."

The steel door glided open, and Marcus and Ruth entered Jason's vault. Jason was flat on his back, eyes closed, his head propped up and tilted to the right. "He's asleep," Marcus whispered as Ruth made her way to the foot of the bed. She looked around the room and wrinkled her nose. "It's so sterile in here," she said. "What's with all the stainless steel and concrete?"

"This room was used to house patients who became, um, uncooperative," Marcus said. "No need for amenities." Marcus watched Ruth reading Jason's chart. "How is he?"

"Not good. BP is low and his weight is down, and he's pretty anemic."

Marcus sighed and hung his head. "Crap," he said.

Ruth dropped the chart on the foot of the bed. "This constant bloodletting can't be good for him," she said. "I thought you had worked out a withdrawal regimen that wasn't going to be harmful."

Marcus shook his head. "That was before Bigwood Springs."

Ruth moved to the head of the bed and picked up a worn paperback from the nightstand. She looked at the cover. "*The Catcher in the Rye*," she said. One page halfway through was dog-eared. Ruth opened to the page, scanned the lines for a minute, smiled, and then read out loud: "What I'd do, I'd walk down a few floors—holding onto my guts, blood leaking all over the place—and then I'd ring the elevator bell. As soon as old Maurice opened the doors, he'd see me with the automatic in my hand and he'd start screaming at me, in this very high-pitched, yellow-belly voice, to leave him alone. But I'd plug him anyway. Six shots right through his fat hairy belly." Ruth closed the book and put it back on the nightstand. "Great stuff," she said. "Hope Jason's not going to pull a Holden Caulfield on us."

"'No guns at The Complex,'" Marcus recited. "There's a reason for that rule."

Ruth placed her hand on Jason's forehead, and Jason coughed and tried to open his eyes. Ruth jumped and yanked her hand back. "Holy mother of pearl," she said. "That scared me."

"Jason?" Marcus said, leaning down next to his ear. "Jason?"

"Come on, Jason, wake up," Ruth said. She lifted one eyelid and peered into his eye. "Nothing," she said. She removed her hand and looked up at Marcus. "We're killing him, Craig."

Marcus sighed and took a step back from the bed. "Maybe I can readjust the dilution algorithm so we can preserve efficacy and yet not have to take so much blood," he said.

Ruth shook her head. "Maybe," she said. "But adjusting those algorithms takes time. People upstairs don't have the luxury of waiting." Ruth walked to the side of the room and sat down on a metal exam chair. "Not to mention all the people out there who are dying of TL. You've seen the news, Craig. It's easy to forget what's going on when we get shuttled around in private jets and chauffeured cars and have clean environments to live and work in so that everywhere we go we don't worry about contracting TL. I know you saw the new numbers from the CDC: if the current statistics keep up, we will exceed the global mortality rates for the 1918 flu pandemic within six months, and that flu ran for almost three *years*. The first Trips Lite was diagnosed less than one year ago. I've been keeping my mouth shut, Craig, because I thought you knew what you were doing. But then that thing with Jenny, and now this," she said, pointing at Jason. "It looks like you're in over your head."

Jason coughed again, then rolled over.

Marcus took a step toward Ruth. "You have no idea of all the variables in play right now, Ruth!" he said. "From your perspective, the solution is simple: we've got the cure for TL, and everything else falls into place. But I've got Porter to contend with!"

"Porter," Ruth snorted. "I think you've got to focus on priorities here, Craig."

"You don't think I know how important this is? You have to understand that I would intervene if I could!"

Ruth made a face. "You can't just keep posturing like a victim! I may not understand the dynamics of your relationship with Porter, but I do know that the cure for the worst pandemic in history is lying in bed in front of you, comatose, obviously near death and getting nearer, and you seem ambivalent about the right course!"

Marcus glared at her. "Ambivalent? Do you know how many people I've seen die from TL?"

Ruth stood. "Apparently not enough," she said. She moved to the door and slid her card through the scanner. The door opened and Ruth stepped through into the hall.

Marcus watched the door close and lock into place. He sat on the side of the bed, listening to Jason's shallow breathing. He pulled back the covers and looked at the shunt in Jason's arm, fingering the tissue around the implant. The flesh had begun to heal around the shunt's inserted tube, an attempted union of plastic and skin. Marcus made a "tsk" sound with his tongue. "I'm sorry, Jason," he said.

CHAPTER 38

Linda pulled the thick envelope from the mailbox and looked at it lovingly. She admired its bulk and ran her fingers along the seam as she carried it into the front room of Keith and Mary's home. "The partnership papers came," she called out to Keith who was in the kitchen talking on the phone.

Keith put his hand over the mouthpiece. "It's about time. Porter must've told his lawyers to drag their feet."

Linda placed the package on the coffee table and sat down on the couch. She listened to Keith conclude his conversation: "You tell her that she can keep the golf clubs, but I get the tennis racquets . . . uh-huh . . . oh come on! Those clubs are worth at least fifteen hundred—the racque*ts* are half that. . . . Well, then tell her I'll see her in court." Keith slammed the phone down and joined Linda on the couch.

"Mary's lawyer?"

Keith nodded. "This was supposed to be a nice little parting, but Mary had to get a lawyer, and he started asking questions, and the next thing you know we're fighting about the pots and pans."

Linda looked at Keith, noticing the frown lines around his brows and eyes. She reached out and started to knead the back of his neck. "I know," she said. "Divorce is hell."

Keith shrugged her hand away and turned to her. "How would you know? You're still married."

Linda recoiled like she'd been punched in the stomach and slid to the far end of the couch, arms folded. She didn't speak, instead looking out the large view window into Keith's landscaped front yard. "And where would we be if I weren't?" she finally said. "The only reason we have a shot at making this deal work is because I stayed married to Jason."

"You could have divorced him any time you wanted, even back before we knew about this TL thing. You'd still be able to make a claim against Porter's profits based on your community property interest."

"Yeah, and you could've divorced Mary. But you didn't, even though you told me you would back when we first started sleeping together. Remember? 'Oh Linda, I love you. I'm going to leave Mary.' Yeah, right. Nothing, nothing until now, now that you have a shot at making some big bucks off me." Linda jumped off the couch and ran into the kitchen. She was crying freely now and grabbed a handful of paper towels to wipe her face. She blew her nose and turned around, bumping into Keith. She tried to sidestep him, but he grabbed her. She resisted and squirmed to get out of his clasp, but he held fast. "Look, I'm sorry," he said. "It just bugs me that you're still married. I've never had to be second best or second place to anybody or anything, and I want you all to myself. Is that so terrible?"

Linda resisted a moment longer, then let herself be pulled into Keith's embrace. He kissed her, holding her face in his hands, then pulled back and looked at her. "Forgiven?" he said. She studied his face, trying to gauge what was going on behind that clever insurance-salesman facade he wore so well, then smiled and half nodded. "Yeah," she said. "This time. But remember, this partnership thing was *your* idea."

"I know. I'm sorry." Keith suddenly let go of her and took a step back, then clapped his hands and rubbed them together. "Now," he said, "let's look at those papers." Keith grabbed the package off the coffee table and plopped down on the couch. Linda watched as he tore open the envelope, the expression on his face intensifying as he pulled out the thick set of documents. He doesn't even know I'm here, Linda thought, as Keith started making margin notes on the sheets with a pen, eyes glued to the papers.

Linda wished he'd look at her with the same focus. She'd suspected all along that Keith's interest in her was financially motivated, particularly in light of the ease with which he had discarded Mary. Linda remembered it clearly. She and Keith had waited in the car, across the street from the house, watching as Mary arrived after her tennis lesson. The process server was waiting for her on the front porch. Mary had cried when she read the papers that were handed to her. Keith had laughed at that, and had called her a "dumb bitch."

"Wow, look at this!"

Linda looked up, startled from her daydream. Keith was holding up the agreement, pointing at a clause. "Porter got it right. Full partnership with a 50/25/25 split. I thought he'd try to sneak something in on us."

"Why should he?" Linda moved to the couch and sat down next to Keith. "He knows we've got him by the short hairs. One word from me and Jason walks." Linda looked over Keith's shoulder down at the pages full of legalese. "Can you understand that stuff?"

Keith didn't look up. "You can't be in the insurance business for twenty years and not learn how to read a contract."

They kept reading together until Keith suddenly closed the document and jumped up from the couch. "The rest is just boilerplate," he said. "I've seen it all before." He walked into the kitchen and came back with a pen. "Let's sign it and get this show on the road."

Linda still held the stack of papers in her hand. This was so like Keith, she thought. Impulsive and arrogant, always so sure of himself. That's why she was initially attracted to him; he was so unlike Jason and his careful, methodical, health-conscious plodding through life. At least Keith was exciting and would eat a medium-rare steak once in a while! She stared at the papers, then up at Keith, who was sticking the pen in her face. He grinned. "Come on," he said. "We're late for our tee time."

Linda took the pen and turned to the last page where she signed "Linda Kramer" in the space for her name. "Kramer," she said, the pen poised over the page. “It sounds funny now, to say it out loud.” She handed the pen and papers back to Keith and watched him sign his name. "There," he said. "Now all we have to do is decide whether we want to retire to Switzerland or Rio." He tossed the documents into his briefcase and grabbed his car keys off the counter. "I'll courier these back to Porter tomorrow," he said. Keith moved toward the door, but Linda remained on the couch, her face vacant. She had trusted Keith so far, and it had always worked out.

"Come on!"

Linda blinked and shook her head, smiling. "Sorry," she said, joining him at the door and walking out toward the garage. "I'm just not used to being rich."

CHAPTER 39

Wendy opened the refrigerator and peered inside. Bags of blood, sorted by type, lay in rows on shelves in front of her. She glanced over her shoulder, then reached inside and shifted the bags around, looking through them, examining the labels. "Come on," she said. "Where are you?" Her fingers moved through the bags until finally she found one labeled "B-Pos." "Ah," she said. "Gotcha."

She took the bag of blood out of the refrigerator and placed it inside a towel, then rolled the towel up and placed it under her arm. She made her way back to the storage closet where she had stashed her phlebotomy cart and pulled it out into the hallway. Wendy looked over both shoulders, then placed the rolled-up towel on top of the cart and pushed it toward the elevator.

She walked down the hallway under a sign that read "Welcome to Bigwood Springs" and looked from side to side into the rooms of the patients housed in this wing. The sounds around her beat their way into her head, sounds that echoed and resonated with hope: laughing, talking, kissing. Wendy took a deep breath, and then forced her gaze straight ahead, her eyes locked on the elevator at the end of the hall.

A little girl darted out of an open door and careened into Wendy's cart, nearly upsetting it. Wendy made a dive for the towel, barely catching it before it and its contents tumbled to the floor.

"Oops, sorry!" the little girl squealed before collapsing in a cascade of giggles. "McKenna!" her dad barked from the open doorway. "Come here!" McKenna's giggles subsided before she turned and marched back to the room. Wendy looked at the man standing in the doorway. He was tall and gaunt with striking features and brown eyes peering out from beneath a shock of salt and pepper hair. He wore a blue bathrobe, and an IV drip bag hung from a wheeled metal holder at his side. "Sorry," the man said. "She's excited."

"I can see that," Wendy said. She looked down at McKenna. "You're sure happy," she said.

McKenna beamed. "My daddy gets to come home," she said. "He's all better."

Wendy swallowed hard before looking up at the man. "Not yet," he said. "We've got to wait for this cure stuff to work." The man rubbed his side. "I got the shot almost a week ago, but there's still no appreciable reduction in viral replication, and my liver is still sick." McKenna came running over and clutched her dad's leg. "But they're running tests," he said. "They think everything will be fine. Dr. Marcus says it may be that TL may have mutated again, meaning it will take longer for the serum to kill the viruses."

Wendy smiled and nodded. Bull, she thought. Dr. Marcus doesn't know what's going on. He's playing C.Y.A.—and I'm killing people. "I'm sure everything will turn out just fine," she said. She turned to McKenna. "You take care of your daddy."

McKenna nodded and smiled. Wendy resumed her march toward the elevator, but then saw Gwen coming out of another room. She diverted her eyes, but Gwen descended on her anyway. "Hey, girlfriend," Gwen said. "Long time no see. Where've you been hiding?"

"Oh, I've been around."

"Hanging out with Jason, I bet. Lucky girl. He's the star of the show!"

Wendy looked past Gwen toward the elevator. "Right," she said. "Star of the show." She paused, deliberating, then gave in to temptation. She looked Gwen in the eye. "So, a lot of people getting the cure?"

"Oh sure, bunches. Like this new lady, Susan Gunderson? She's from Salt Lake—her hip has broken *five* times from TL, and she's got five kids! Can you imagine? And they're all under ten! She and her husband must've been busy. Susan couldn't be more than, say, 35. Cute as a button, though—"

"That's great!" Wendy said, cutting her off. "Look, I gotta run." She gestured toward the cart. "Jason awaits."

"Oh, sure," Gwen said. "I'll see you later."

Gwen moved off toward the nurses' station. Wendy waited until she was out of sight, then made her way down the hall until she found a nametag on a door that read "Gunderson, S." She peeked in and saw a pretty young woman with long, straight brown hair sitting up in bed. A tired-looking man stood beside her. Wendy listened to their quiet conversation. They spoke of husband and wife things: Kelly needed new shoes, and Sierra had lost a tooth. Wendy leaned on her cart, her head down. After a moment, she lifted her head and shoved the cart toward the elevator.

Wendy pushed the cart into Jason's room just as she'd done twice a day, every day, for the past six weeks and moved it next to Jason's bed. She bumped the cart into the metal bed frame with a loud clang and Jason's eyes popped open. "Hey," he said. "Can't a guy get any sleep around here?"

Wendy stood, dumbfounded, frozen in place, looking at Jason. A slow smile spread across her face, and then she raced to the head of the bed and grabbed Jason in a bear hug. "How do you feel?" she said.

"Except for the fact I can't breathe," Jason said, muffled, his face still smashed to Wendy's bosom, "I'm fine."

Wendy giggled, and then released her grip on Jason and he slid back down into bed. Wendy wiped her face with the back of her hand, her bright smile contrasted with her red-rimmed eyes. "Thank heavens you're all right," she said.

"I'm hungry," Jason said. "I must've slept through breakfast."

Wendy laughed out loud, then stood up, looking down at Jason's thin face. "One or two breakfasts, actually," she said. "I'll get you something."

Jason looked at the cart next to the bed and in a Pavlovian response held out his arm and pushed up his sleeve, exposing the shunt. Wendy stood, motionless. She fingered the rolled up towel on the cart, feeling the soft, squishy package it contained. They stood in silence while Jason waited, arm extended, while Wendy stared at his arm. "Well?" he said.

Wendy continued staring, and then looked at Jason. "We need to talk," she said.

Jason withdrew his arm. "Uh-oh. I hate it when a woman says that. It always means trouble."

Wendy smiled and sat down on the edge of the bed. "You've been out of it for quite a while."

"'Out of it?'"

"Unconscious. Almost dead. You haven't been completely lucid for several weeks."

Jason shook his head. "Can't be. I remember your coming in here, taking blood, visiting, the whole nine yards."

"I haven't taken any blood from you for five days."

Jason fingered the shunt in his arm, and then ran his hands across his face, feeling the long scratchy stubble on his chin. He eyed Wendy. "What have you been up to?"

Wendy stood, her eyes down, and moved to the foot of the bed before finally spinning on her heel to face Jason. "They were killing you!" she said. "Porter and Marcus were killing you! They were draining the life out of you with all the blood they were taking. I had to do something."

Jason studied her. "What exactly did you do?"

Wendy blanched, then removed the towel from around the bag of blood lying on top of her cart. Jason stared down at it, not comprehending. "So? It's a bag of my blood."

Wendy felt the sting of conscience. "No," she said. "It's not."

Jason reached out and picked up the bag, then looked at the label. Suddenly, his expression changed. Wendy watched the lines in Jason's forehead deepen and his eyes open wide as he realized her ruse.

"I remember!" he said. "Just before I passed out, I saw you with a tourniquet around your arm." Jason tried to lift his head from the pillow. "But you can't do that!" he said. "They'll know it's not my blood. You have a different blood type."

"Doesn't matter." Wendy said. "To the lab techs, it's just blood. They just know to extract out this one certain protein, and a machine does that. The factor is a protein everybody has—like plasma— except that in you, that protein is specialized somehow to kill TL. And since it's like plasma, blood type doesn't matter. But lately I've been, uh, borrowing B-pos just in case. And I haven't used my own blood since that first time."

"But if you're not using my blood, it won't cure anything."

Wendy stopped, her back to Jason, the muscles in her jaw and neck tensed. She thought of McKenna and Mr. Adams. And Susan Gunderson. "I know that," she said.

"But Marcus will know something's wrong when he sees I'm not comatose anymore."

Wendy took a deep breath before turning around to face Jason. "That's right," she said. "That's why we've got to get you out of here."

Jason stared at Wendy, eyes wide. "What?"

"Yeah. Back to San Francisco. Out of here. Away from the needles and the stainless steel bank vault two stories below ground."

Jason looked at the floor and rubbed his hand through his already disheveled hair. He took a deep breath and exhaled. "You got a plan?"

Wendy held up the bag of blood. "You're looking at it. So far."

"Look, I'm all in favor of getting me out of here, but what about all those people dying upstairs?"

Wendy sat down on the edge of the bed and took Jason's hand. It was cold, and his skin felt dead next to hers. "Don't you think I realize what I'm doing?" she said. "Can you imagine how I've been rationalizing my actions?—'Oh, those people have TL. They would have died anyway.'"

Jason touched Wendy's cheek. "Look, we'll talk to Dr. Marcus, work something out. I can't go right—"

"You have to go," Wendy interrupted. "*We* have to go. Peoples' lives—your life—depends on it. If Porter and Marcus kill you, that's it. No more cure—for anybody." Wendy looked down. "Including Jenny," she said.

Jason withdrew his hand, suddenly tensing. "But why should you be able to withhold the cure from those people upstairs? I don't want to be a party to murder."

Wendy folded her hands in her lap and looked at the floor. "And I won't be a party to *your* murder," she said.

Jason opened his mouth to respond, but stopped and looked up as the huge silver door separating him from the rest of the world slid open with a series of soft clicks. Wendy dropped the syringe she was holding and threw a towel over the bag of blood on Jason's bed just as Phillip Porter walked into the room. Her jaw dropped when she saw his emaciated form, a cigarette hanging precipitously from his lower lip.

"I don't mean to interrupt," Porter said. "Please continue."

"Uh, no, that's O.K." Wendy stammered, sliding the blanket over the syringe, "we just finished."

Porter's eyes glanced down at her movement, but shot back up to meet her stare. "You seem surprised to see me."

Wendy's mouth hung open, moving, but no words came out. Jason saw her plight and sat up in the bed. "No, not at all, Mr. Porter. It's just that we weren't expecting anyone. Nice to see you." He pointed to Wendy. "This is Wendy—"

"Wendy Ross, your phlebotomist; yes I know. I made certain inquiries before I came down to visit." Porter waited, watching them, gauging their reaction the way a snake watches a mouse.

Jason reached out and gave Wendy's hand a reassuring squeeze, a gesture hidden by the blankets. "Great," Jason said. "Always nice to have company. Especially you, Mr. Porter. I don't remember your coming down here before."

"Oh, I've looked in on you every once in a while. Protecting my investment, and all that. Seems that every time I stopped in you were asleep, however." Porter shot Wendy another glance, and Jason squeezed her hand harder. "Glad to see you're up and around today, though," Porter said.

Jason laughed. "Up, at least, but maybe not around. Not yet." Jason caught Wendy's eye, encouraging her to laugh along, which she did, halfheartedly. The laughter subsided, and Jason paused in the ensuing silence, looking at Porter's yellow skin and eyes. "So, how have you been, Mr. Porter?"

Porter held out a hand and turned it over and back in front of them. "Not too well, as you can see. Dr. Marcus is running tests now. I'm sure I'll be fine." He lowered his hand and moved a step closer to the bed, turning to Wendy. "I think the more relevant question is 'How are you?'"

Jason watched the color drain from Wendy's face. "I'm fine, I think," she said. "Why do you ask?"

Porter reached inside his jacket and withdrew a sheaf of papers. He unfolded them and held them up, scanning the rows of numbers they contained. "It seems," he said, "that there's a problem with the cure."

Wendy's nails dug hard into the back of Jason's hand. "Problem?" Jason said.

"A concern really. Some of the patients to whom your blood factor has been administered are not showing signs of improvement."

Silence. Jason's eyes met Wendy's, and Wendy took a breath then spoke. "Maybe those patients' viruses don't respond to the factor," she said. "I heard that TL is mutating."

"True enough," Porter said. "But we have tested it on all the most virulent mutations Trips Lite has yet to offer, and the Kramer protein—" he said it objectively and in the third person, like Jason wasn't in the room—"completely suspended viral replication. It killed everything." He smiled thinly. "But not recently," he said. "It's very odd."

Jason let go of Wendy's hand under the quilt and pushed himself to a full upright sitting position. "Look, Mr. Porter, maybe it's time we ended this experiment, if the cure's not working and—"

Porter exploded in laughter, cutting him off. "Your gall is quite remarkable, Mr. Kramer."

Jason and Wendy stared at Porter.

"You are an investment to me, nothing more. Dr. Marcus persuaded me to play this little game for a time, but perhaps you're right. Perhaps you have outlived your useful life to Porter Pharmaceuticals. I frankly don't care if the cure works or not—people will still come and pay because they so desperately want to live, want to believe that a cure exists. But I *am* concerned about the financial repercussions of patients paying millions of dollars for what is, at the end of the day, snake oil when we have advertised it and sold it as having a 100 percent success rate. Do you have any idea of the exposure to damages we would face in the lawsuits for fraud that would surely follow this little episode?" Porter shook his head and sighed. "Thank goodness most of them will die before they can sue."

Wendy opened her mouth to respond, but Porter held up his hand. "A word to the wise, then. We promised these people a cure for TL, and we're going to give it to them—" Porter smiled "—for as long as we can. Agreed?"

Wendy and Jason nodded numbly.

"I do not plan on mentioning our little visit to Dr. Marcus. I suggest you refrain as well. Dr. Marcus has a tendency to get jumpy when problems arise. Now you'll excuse me," Porter said. "I'm expecting a new batch of take-out Chinese food from San Francisco." They watched as Porter turned and left the room, the steel door closing behind him.

They stared at the door for several seconds before Jason spoke. "Uh-oh."

"Yeah," Wendy said. "Uh-oh."

CHAPTER 40

Scott pulled a thick file folder out of the middle of a stack of magazines that sat on the corner of the bookcase in his cubicle. The folder was labeled "PORTER," written in Scott's thick, childish hand. He glanced around behind him, then opened the folder and stuffed another piece of paper inside. The folder had grown fat since the night he had avoided the black Mercedes and inquired about Porter on the Internet. That search had drawn a blank—either nobody knew where Porter had his secret hideout, or they didn't want to talk about it. When he finally made his way home from his office that night, he had fully expected the Mercedes to still be parked in front of his apartment complex. But when he rounded the corner leading to his street, he saw the man with whom he had had the confrontation at Porter's offices run out of the building and jump into the Benz. Since then, Scott had been covertly gathering as much evidence on Porter Pharmaceuticals as possible in an effort to find out where Jason was. There was a tremendous amount of information out there if you knew where to look. Scott did.

He opened the folder and riffled through the pages inside. He had amassed a respectable portfolio on the company. He had learned how much money Porter had made last year from selling chemotherapeutic agents. The figures were staggering. He knew who most of Porter's customers were. It was clear Porter was the leader in providing most of the nation's hospitals and clinics with cancer drugs. He had even discovered that Phillip Porter kept a little summer home, a modest 12,000 square feet, in Sun Valley, Idaho. But he could not figure out where Jason was sequestered.

He glanced at the clock on the wall of his cubicle. Two o'clock—time to check in. He slid his chair to the other side of the cubicle and turned on his computer. It had been 24 hours since he last surfed the Usenet newsgroups and checked his e-mail looking for someone who might know about Jason, and 24 hours was long enough to see if he had any new responses to his inquiry. He clicked on his mailbox icon and turned away from the machine to take a drink of the warm Coke that had been sitting on his desk since 7:00 a.m., but before he could swallow he heard a friendly female voice announce: "You have new mail."

Scott clicked the mailbox. Probably something work related, Scott thought. How annoying. He scanned his in-box for the new item and found it, highlighted at the bottom of the list. Great Grandma's Ghost, he thought. The subject line read: "Drug Tests–Reply." He paused, reading the subject line again and again. "Oh, boy," he said out loud, hesitating, his finger on the mouse. He took a breath and clicked on the highlighted item, then watched the mail open on his screen:

You're either stupid or crazy. Meet me in Google Chat, username "Complex," 10:00 p.m. MST. D-Day.

Scott stared at the screen, not blinking for several seconds before coming back to his senses. His eyes jumped up to the "From" line in the e-mail, but the return address had been aliased, showing only a nonsensical jumble of letters and numbers. He looked at the clock on the wall, then at his wristwatch—five o'clock; five hours to wait before he could talk to D-Day. D-Day?, he thought. Who could that be? He pushed the "print screen" button on his keyboard and watched D-Day's missive roll off the printer. He smiled as he tucked it into the folder. Gettin' warmer, he thought.

—

Scott paced back and forth in front of his computer, looking at his watch and re-reading the e-mail from D-Day. He watched the sweep-second hand move past the six, then the nine, and creep up toward the twelve. "Finally!" Scott said. "Nine o'clock—ten o'clock D-Day time." He sat down at the terminal and began to instant message "Complex" as he had been instructed. "D-Day?" he typed.

Scott stared at the browser screen, watching the cursor blink steadily on and off, on and off. There was no response. Scott IM'd again: "D-Day? Hello?"

The cursor blinked several more times before the words crawled across the screen. "I'm here."

Scott paused before responding. He took a deep breath and typed, "Hi there. Wondered if you were going to make it."

"Got stuck in traffic."

Great, Scott thought. A comedian. He continued typing. "Didn't think I'd get any hits on my query about Porter Pharmaceuticals."

The cursor blinked for several seconds. Oops, Scott thought. Came on too strong. The cursor continued to blink. Finally D-Day typed back: "Porter keeps his people in line."

"I understand," Scott typed. "Thanks for responding." Scott rested his hands on the keyboard, composing his next thought. He realized suddenly how unprepared he was to conduct this interview. "So," he typed, "how do you know Phillip Porter?"

"I used to work for him."

"Used to?"

"Yeah. He kept hitting on me. Plus, I pissed him off and that was it."

"What happened?"

The cursor blinked. Silence. Scott drummed his fingers on the keyboard with increasing intensity, waiting. Then, finally, D-Day typed, "Who RU?"

Scott read the line over and over, formulating several responses in his mind. He thought about using a fake name, but if he got caught, D-Day would never trust him. If he told his real name, though, and D-Day turned out to be one of Porter's thugs, he might as well kiss his kneecaps goodbye. Or worse. He muttered under his breath "Big game, big stakes," then typed, "My name is Scott Durrant. I am looking for my friend Jason Kramer. Porter has him. I want him back."

D-Day's response was immediate: "Is he your lover? :-)" The beauty of the Internet, Scott thought. Anonymity brings abandonment of decorum. He grinned, realizing all the unintended double entendres in his last message. "No," he typed. "Just a good friend I promised I'd look after."

"I understand," D-Day typed. "You sound like a good guy. Do you work for Porter?"

"No. I went to their offices and asked about Jason and got chased out by a mean little guy with no neck."

"That was probably Walter, Porter's driver."

"We didn't do introductions. He even went to my apartment looking for me."

"No wonder. You're looking for Jason."

Scott sucked in his breath. Breakthrough, he thought. "You know him?"

"Everybody at Porter knows him. We sign papers saying we don't, but we do."

"Papers?"

"Very hush hush."

"Why is that?"

The blinking cursor again. Then: "If you're Jason's friend, you already know that."

Time to open the kimono, Scott thought. You show me yours, I'll show you mine. Scott put his fingers on the keyboard and typed: Jason can cure TL.

"That's not technically correct," D-Day typed back. "Jason has a protein in his blood that can kill *Triptovirus L.* Extract the protein and extract the cure."

Mother McGee, Scott thought. Who have I found here? "Wow!" he typed. "You seem to know a lot about it. What's the deal?"

"The deal," D-Day typed, "is that you're in way over your head." There was a long pause as Scott watched the cursor blink. Then: "You're making me nervous, Scott Durrant. CUL8R."

Scott swore under his breath as his fingers flew across the keyboard. "No! Wait!" he typed, "I need your help! Where's Jason? Where's Jason?" He hit the enter key so hard his keyboard flew into the air and did a one-eighty before crashing onto the floor of his cubicle. He bent to retrieve it, his eyes still on the monitor and on the cursor, blinking in the browser's open window. "Please!" he typed, hitting "Enter" more gently this time, then typing and entering "please" again, and again, and again, but the cursor just blinked silently at the top of the screen, on and off, like a sly eye winking. Scott sat there another ten minutes watching the cursor and staring at the screen, but D-Day was gone.

CHAPTER 41

"Mrs. Kramer," Phillip Porter said as he extended his hand, "Thank you for coming. How have you been? You received the partnership papers, I trust?"

"Call me Linda, please," she said as she got out of the car at the front entrance to The Complex, squinting in the bright sun and trying not to stare at Porter's yellow skin and eyes. She glanced at the Driver, flanking Porter to his left. "Fine, thank you, and yes, we got the papers."

Porter blanched as she said "we," but quickly regained his composure. "Ah yes," he said, "and how is Keith?"

Linda studied Porter's face before answering, marveling at the shallowness of the smile, a smile now made even more repellent by the sickly yellow flesh that surrounded it, skin drawn taut over pointed cheekbones. "Keith is well," she said, averting her eyes. "Although he wonders why he wasn't invited along as well." Linda smiled her brilliant smile, the one that cut two dimples deep into her cheeks, the one that let her get away with anything. "We *are* all partners."

Porter waved the Driver around to grab Linda's bags and gestured toward the front door of The Complex. "Let's get out of this heat," he said. "Stifling."

Linda waited, measuring Porter's obvious effort to avoid her question before relenting and moving into the air-conditioned lobby. She took a breath and looked around, watching the Driver wrangle her two large suitcases. "I have arranged a guest suite for you," Porter said, indicating toward the elevator. "I hope you find it satisfactory." He took two steps then stopped and doubled over, coughing explosively, his body racked by the spasms. The Driver dropped Linda's bags and ran to Porter's side. Porter fumbled inside his jacket and pulled out a cigarette, his hands trembling so fiercely that the Driver had to hold the cigarette steady for Porter to grasp it in his lips. A gold lighter appeared in Walter's hand and a blue flame jetted to the tip of Porter's cigarette, the end glowing bright orange as Porter inhaled. He held in the smoke for several seconds, and then blew a cloud toward the ceiling.

Linda watched the spectacle, a mixture of concern and bemusement on her face. After Porter had taken three puffs, she spoke. "Nasty cough," she said. "You should see a doctor."

Porter met her stare but did not smile back. He leaned forward, one arm supported by Walter, the other hand on his knee. He looked at the couches in the anteroom. "Perhaps," he said, "we can visit in the lobby for a moment, then Walter can escort you to your room. I may retire early this evening."

Linda shrugged. "Fine," she said. "The suspense has been killing me anyway."

They moved to the couch and sat while Walter gathered the bags by the elevator then stood several feet away, pretending not to listen. Porter inhaled one last time on his cigarette, then crushed the butt in an ashtray. He cleared his throat before speaking. "The partnership is threatened," he said, rubbing his abdomen.

Linda stared, half-smiling. "Is that a joke?"

Porter shook his head. "I wouldn't fly you into the middle of nowhere to joke with you. It's Jason."

Linda's bright blue irises rolled skyward, hidden beneath the perfectly matched hue of her eye shadow. "That idiot," she said. "What's he done now?" She sat up, straighter, with urgency. "He's not gone dry, has he?"

Porter coughed again, the spasm mixed with a laugh. "If by that lovely euphemism you mean he has stopped producing the factor, we don't know. There does seem to be a diminished potency." Linda frowned at this. "Frankly," Porter continued, trying to affect a reassuring tone, "I think the problem is one of motivation."

Linda waited, expecting more, a puzzled expression on her face, but Porter merely looked at her. She sat in silence, feeling Porter's eyes on her, feeling the Driver's cold stare running up and down her body. "That's it?" she said, standing and glaring down at Porter. "He's tired? You bring me all the way out here to tell me that?" Her voice was rising in pitch and volume, and the nurse at the reception desk looked over, alarmed. Porter reached out and took her hand, patting it. "Sit down," he said under his breath, watching the nurse out of the corner of his eye, "or I'll ask Walter to break your fingers." The color drained from her face as Porter smiled. He caught the nurse's eye and shook his head, his lips pursed. The nurse looked back down to her keyboard.

Linda's eyes darted from Porter to the Driver and back before she realized he was not bluffing. She felt her palms begin to moisten and sensed wetness at the small of her back. She stretched out a hand for support and resumed her position on the couch. Porter smiled. "I simply need you to do us—you, Keith, and me—a favor. Can you do that?"

Linda nodded, her breathing increasing in pace. She wobbled a bit in her seat.

"I don't want Porter Pharmaceuticals to go down in a flurry of lawsuits—lawsuits in which you and Keith would be equally liable with Porter Pharmaceuticals, by the way," Porter said. "I'm sure you can understand that—as my *partners*."

Linda nodded again.

Porter brightened and reached inside his coat, then pulled out a piece of paper. "Oh, and on that subject, here is the first installment of our partnership proceeds. I'm sure you'll see to it that Keith receives his proper portion." Porter handed her a check. She looked at it and felt her throat tighten and her vision blur. "One hundred thousand dollars," Linda said. "My goodness."

"Is something wrong?" Porter asked.

"No," Linda said, "no. Not at all." She folded the check and placed it in her purse, then took a handkerchief from her jacket pocket and daubed her forehead and cheeks. She took a breath and exhaled, then smiled at Porter. "Did you say something about a favor?"

—

Jason did not look up when he heard the steel door whoosh open. He kept his eyes on the TV screen and held out his arm, shunt up. "Time for more blood?" he said.

"Nope."

Jason felt the hairs on his arms stand erect at the sound of the voice. He turned his head toward the door. "Hi, Linda," he said.

She looked radiant in a summer green yoga outfit, her blond hair tied back in a thick ponytail, white teeth glowing against the warm tan of her cheeks. She'd lost weight, Jason noticed, and the sweats could not conceal the svelte figure packed onto Linda's toned frame. He swallowed hard. "You look great."

Linda smiled more broadly, creasing her dimples into little thimbles of flesh. "Thanks," she said. "You look like crap."

Jason self-consciously ran his fingers back through his hair to smooth the wayward curls, but they bounced back skyward, defiant. He scratched his stubbly chin and grinned. "I don't get out much."

"So I hear." Linda moved closer to the bed. "You're thin—too thin—even for a guy who lives on yogurt and wheat germ shakes."

"Sorry," he said. Jason noted she still had her knack for putting him on the defensive, even when he'd done nothing wrong. "I haven't had much appetite. I've been kind of out of it."

Linda nodded and continued moving toward the bed. Jason could smell the clean, not-quite-perfumey scent that Linda wore. She stopped when she reached the edge of the mattress. "Mind if I sit down?"

"Uh, no, not at all."

Linda sat on the crisp white sheets and edged nearer to Jason, then reached out, took his hand, and stroked it. "It's good to see you," she said.

Jason licked his lips and found them dry, his whole mouth like cotton. He reached for the cup of water on the nightstand with his free hand and drank it down. He looked back at Linda. "Why are you here?" It came out a croak, and Linda giggled. She poured him another glass.

"You're pretty flustered, aren't you?" she said. "I mean, I knew I had you whipped, but I didn't know it was this bad."

Jason sat the glass down and looked at her flawless airbrushed skin. He tried to focus. "Why are you here?" he said again.

Linda squeezed his hand, and then placed her open palm on his thigh. "I was worried about you," she said. "I *am* still your wife." She leaned forward and kissed him on the cheek. Jason felt his face grow hot. "Mr. Porter said you weren't doing too well. Thought maybe you were sick. He called me, and I flew right out."

Jason studied her bright blue eyes. "Really? That's hard to believe. Last time I saw you, you were suing me for divorce."

Linda slid closer to Jason. "Can't a girl have a change of heart? That's a woman's prerogative, you know," she said.

Jason grinned, relenting, then reached out and took Linda's shoulders in his hands and pulled her to him. "You smell so good," he breathed into her ear.

Linda stayed in his embrace for a moment, then disengaged herself. "This is our chance, Jason. Our chance to be happy. We won't ever have to work again. The money from the cure will guarantee that."

"Money?" Jason said, blinking. "I know it's nice and all, but I don't think it's enough to live on."

Linda's smile cracked. "What are you talking about?"

"The money from the contract I signed when I agreed to come here. I've been putting it in a savings account—in your name, of course. I guess I've got a little over ten thousand dollars in there now."

Linda stared for a moment, then began to laugh as her head rolled back and mouth dropped open. "You've got to be kidding!" she said, regaining her composure. "You're kidding, right?" She started laughing again.

Jason reached into the drawer on the nightstand and removed a piece of paper. He handed it to Linda. "Here's the account statement. See for yourself."

Linda threw the paper back at Jason and made a face. "They must have sucked out some brains with all that blood," she said. "You used to be a pretty smart guy. Financial analyst and all that? No, Jason, think about it. Your body produces the cure for TL. You do understand that, don't you?"

"I wasn't in this for the money, Linda."

"Exactly!" Linda shouted and jumped up from the bed. "That's exactly right, Jason! You never are. You're never in it for the money, and look where that got us! Porter and I have a deal. He's offering to pay us hundreds of thousands of dollars!"

"Us?"

Linda realized her gaff. "Uh, you know, you and me."

Jason nodded, listening.

"You've got to start looking out for Number One, Jason. You've got to start looking out . . ." Linda stopped herself and took a breath ". . . for me."

Jason folded his arms. "Why?" he said. "You're already gone."

Linda moved back to the bed and took Jason's hand. "Am I? As long as you're here, and the cure is coming, we'll get rich, and I'll be here for you."

Jason looked back at Linda. "It's not that simple," he said.

"What?"

"There's this problem with the cure."

Linda frowned. "Porter said something about that."

"There's a reason . . . ."

Linda's eyes grew wide, and she leaned toward Jason her face in front of his. "What have you done?"

Jason pulled back, his eyes wide. "They were killing me, Linda! If Wendy hadn't stopped extracting my blood when she did—"

"What? Who's Wendy? You mean they haven't been using your blood?" Linda went pale and reached out for the mattress to steady herself. "Oh my heavens, Jason. Do you realize what you've done?"

Jason stared at her. "I know what I've done," he said.

"Do you? You've breached your agreement with Porter, that's what!" Linda said. "Now he won't have to pay you, and he may not have to pay me!" Jason opened his mouth, but before he could respond, Linda was back in his face, her smile and pluck restored. "But it's all good," she said. "We can make it, if you help me. Can you help me, Jason? And we can't tell anybody about this, about what you've done. It has to be a secret. It's the only way we can be together."

Jason breathed in and smelled her again, then looked at her smooth cheeks and golden hair and reached out to stroke her face. "What do we do?" he said.

"We start making the cure again, honey, that's what we do. I'm going back to San Francisco in a little while, so you let me take care of the financial arrangements with Porter. You stay here and just keep churning out that potion. What you've got is priceless. We should be compensated for it, that's all. You've got to tell Cindy—"

"Wendy."

"—Wendy, right, you've got to tell Wendy to stop what she's doing. You've got to make sure they're using your blood. Can you do that, honey?"

Jason nodded. "I can," he said. "I love you, Linda."

Linda smiled back, showing too many teeth. "I know," she said. She leaned in and touched Jason's cheek with her lips, then made her way to the steel door. She opened it with a key card and stepped through. "I'll be back as soon as I can to check on you."

"Thanks, hon," Jason said, as the door slid shut and clicked into place. He waited a moment, and then called out, "She's gone."

The door to the bathroom in the back of Jason's room opened and Wendy's head poked out. "Beautiful," she said. "That ought to buy us some time with Porter. He knew something was wrong, and as long as he thinks Linda has turned things around, we should have some breathing room."

Jason nodded. "Man, I should get an Academy Award for that. Do you believe me now?"

Wendy came out of the bathroom and moved to the head of Jason's bed. "You mean about what a monster she is? Wow, yes, she's quite the piece of work. Thank heavens Gwen mentioned she was here," Wendy said. She took Jason's hand in hers. "My rotation ends tonight," she said. "I need to go to San Francisco. I'll be back as soon as I can."

Jason looked at her. "With the cavalry?"

Wendy's grin belied her churning stomach. "With the cavalry," she said.

CHAPTER 42

The cupboard in Craig Marcus' small office at The Complex hid a surprisingly well-stocked bar. Marcus was surveying the contents and had just selected a bottle of vodka when Dr. Wilson entered without knocking.

"Hi, Ruth," he said without looking up. "Cocktail?"

"Please. Double." Ruth kicked off her shoes and sat down at the table in the corner of the office. "So how long did you stay down in the dungeon with Jason?" she asked.

"About an hour. Did some soul searching."

"That's what I intended when I got in your face. So what's it going to be?"

Marcus filled two glasses with ice and poured in liquor to the rims, then took a swallow from one. "I'm going to take a stand with Porter," he said. "I just saw him, and he's not getting better. Might be an ideal time to negotiate." Marcus refilled his glass, then moved to join Ruth at the table.

"Good for you," Ruth said. "It's the right thing to do." Ruth took a glass from Marcus, and then said, "You've checked the jaundice thing out, I presume?"

Marcus nodded. "The blood's in the lab right now," he said. "But whatever it is, it hasn't affected Porter's temper. Made it worse in fact."

"What happened?"

"Oh, this lab tech, Denise Dalton—"

"I know her. Cute girl. D-Day," Ruth said.

"Excuse me?

"That's her nickname. I've heard the nurses use it."

"Yeah, well anyway, remember when Denise told me to look in on Porter because she was worried about him?"

Ruth nodded.

"When I went to his room, I couldn't believe how bad he looked. I made the mistake of using my best bedside manner, and he ate me for lunch. I heard he fired Denise after that," Marcus said.

Ruth recoiled. "Ouch. So much for the brother's keeper thing, huh?"

Marcus nodded and refilled his glass, then gestured toward Ruth's tumbler with the bottle. She put her hand over the mouth of the glass. "Thanks, but I'm on call tonight. But leave the bottle where I can find it." Marcus smiled and nodded, then screwed the lid back on. He looked up when the door to his office opened a crack.

"Dr. Marcus?"

Marcus looked up and recognized the lab tech, a young man who was carrying a computer printout. "Come in," Marcus said, his hand extended for the papers. "What have you got?"

The tech blushed and nodded toward Dr. Wilson, then handed the papers to Marcus. "Mr. Porter's blood test results," he said, and then added, "I'm sorry."

The tech turned and left the room as Marcus scanned the numbers on the page. "Look at this," he said to Ruth, pointing at one of the figures. Ruth squinted and followed his finger over to the number. She took off her glasses and rubbed her eyes. "Oh, boy," she said. "And it looks like the latest mutation."

Marcus put down the printout. "This confirms my physical exam. Thought it might just be cirrhosis, given the way he drinks, or pancreatic cancer, given the way he smokes and eats. But based on this, he'll be dead in three weeks."

"Without the cure," Ruth said.

Marcus sat in silence, nursing his drink.

“Right?” Ruth said again. “That’s without the cure.”

Still nothing.

Finally, Ruth grabbed Marcus’ arm and said, "He doesn't deserve it, you know. He may be a bastard, but we are still doctors."

Marcus studied her for several seconds, then sighed and nodded. He turned and reached into a nearby refrigerator, then pulled out a small vial of clear, light yellow liquid. He held it up to the light, shook it, and watched the fluid tumble around inside the glass container. "Yeah, but it's just not right. He lives, Jenny dies. Let's pour this down the drain."

Ruth raised her tumbler and finished her drink. "Do you know for sure that Jenny’s dead?"

"No, but she was in bad shape when we discharged her—"

"When *you* discharged her. Two wrongs don’t make a right. Now go deal with this," Ruth said.

—

The irony of the situation was not lost on Marcus as he, with printout in hand, knocked on the door to Phillip Porter's room.

"Come in!" Porter yelled from inside. Marcus opened the door and found Porter lying in bed, the white pillowcase and sheets in stark contrast against Porter's yellow skin. The Driver sat in a chair on the other side of the room. Porter, his head on the pillow, did not look up. His eyes were closed, and his hands were extended in front of him, his fingers moving, playing along with the Chopin piano sonata that issued from the speakers in the corners. The room was littered with open cartons of Chinese take-out, and the ripe smell of soy and garlic and ginger hung in the air. Porter opened his eyes and looked at Marcus. "What do you want?"

Marcus stepped forward and extended his hand and the printout. "We got your blood tests back," he said.

Porter sighed. "And?" he said.

Marcus glanced at the Driver and cleared his throat. "Do you want to ask Walter—" the Driver stared at him "—to step out?"

"Why? I have no secrets from Walter."

Marcus looked at the Driver, who glared back. "Very well," Marcus said. He moved to the bedside table and unfolded the papers. "I'm afraid our suspicions have been confirmed. You have the latest variant of *Triptovirus L.*"

Marcus imagined he could hear Walter sucking wind at the pronouncement and wondered if it was because he felt sorry for Porter or because he thought he'd be out of a job. Then he thought he heard Porter laughing.

Marcus shook his head to clear the sound, but indeed, Porter was laughing, his mouth wide open, his nicotine-stained teeth working up and down.

"Sorry, but what's so funny?" Marcus said.

Porter reached over to his nightstand and grabbed a cigarette, then motioned to Walter, who jumped to attention and lit it. Porter inhaled and blew smoke toward Marcus. "I always thought it would be cancer that got me, not some damn virus. I made it through the 70's and 80's disease-free, and now this."

"I'm sure the pain has been intense," Marcus said. He reached into his jacket pocket and pulled out a vial of light yellow liquid, then held it up in front of Porter and shook it. "Perhaps we can do something about that," he said. He reached into his other pocket and withdrew a syringe and an alcohol prep.

Porter watched, then said, "Your altruistic tendencies will be your undoing. You could just let me suffer."

Marcus filled the barrel of the syringe with the liquid. "I know," he said. "But then who'd get my file if you died?" Marcus sat the vial down on the nightstand and tore open the foil wrapper on the swab. He reached out for Porter's arm. "I understand it feels warm going in," Marcus said.

Porter pulled his arm back away from Marcus. "What does?" he said.

Marcus stopped, the syringe poised in mid-air, his mouth open. "The cure," he said.

Porter looked at the syringe, then at the vial on the nightstand. "The cure? The Kramer blood factor? Is that what that is?" He gestured toward the syringe.

Marcus nodded.

Porter stared for another half-second before beginning to laugh. His head fell back on the pillow and he held his stomach. "Oh, this is rich! This is good!" he said. "My stomach hurts!" Porter gasped for air between laughs and looked at the Driver. "He doesn't know, Walter. He doesn't know!"

Marcus shifted from foot to foot and retracted the syringe. He opened his mouth to speak, but Porter reached out and grabbed the hypodermic and shook it in Marcus' face. "This?" Porter said. "This is the cure? Where did you get this?"

"From storage in the nurses' station."

Porter threw the syringe hard against the wall, where it exploded in a shower of glass and yellow liquid. "It's plasma, you idiot! There's been no true cure from Kramer for two weeks now!"

Marcus took a step back from the bed, then looked first at the stain on the wall, then at Porter.

"His girlfriend has been switching the blood," Porter said. "Some misguided effort to save his life, I presume."

Marcus blinked several times. "You mean those patients, Mr. Adams, Mrs. Gunderson—"

"All of them," Porter interrupted. "They all got a placebo."

Marcus studied Porter for a moment. "You knew about this?" he said.

"Of course. I confronted Kramer and the girl when I saw the efficacy dropping off. Caught them in the act. Told them to reverse the trend—had his wife talk to him, too. But this, . . ." he said, gesturing to the mess on the floor, ". . . this is the old stuff."

"Do you know what this means? All the people that have come here for the cure . . . ."

Porter nodded. "Yep. Better call your lawyer."

Marcus stood and began to walk around the room, one palm resting on the crown of his head, his fingers moving through thinning blond hair. "At least we still have Jason. I mean, we can start producing factor again, at a more reasonable and controlled rate this time. Get some cure for the patients—some for you. It's not too late. We can refine some new factor for your use."

Porter considered for a moment. "I suppose that's better than the alternative," he said.

Marcus raised an eyebrow.

"Dying," Porter said. Marcus nodded.

The room remained silent for another minute, and then Porter spoke. "You say we need to get some new factor from Kramer. Walter and I would like to pay him a personal visit to ensure that Mr. Kramer understands the urgency of our need, in light of this new situation." He took another long drag on the cigarette and exhaled toward the fluorescent lighting. "Plus there's the issue of his and Ms. Ross's participation in this fake cure matter. We'll need to address that problem, too. Isn't that right, Walter?" The Driver nodded, a cold smile on his lips. Porter coughed spasmodically, then spat into a tissue that he handed to the Driver. "We'll go down to his room first thing in the morning," Porter said. "I'm not up to a messy confrontation tonight." He looked at Marcus and smiled. "You'll join us, of course."

Marcus glanced at the Driver and nodded. "Of course," he said.

"Oh, and by the way," Porter said. "I received an interesting e-mail from one of your former associates the other day."

Marcus raised an eyebrow. "Oh? Who?"

"Vincent Samuels."

"Samuels! What did he want? I haven't seen him since he threw that little tantrum when he resigned."

"Seems that he has chosen to disregard our nondisclosure agreement. I heard he visited Paul Carnelli at Amwell Pharmaceuticals trying to sell a vial of the cure."

"How did you find this out?" Marcus said.

"Carnelli called me. Didn't want to end up on the wrong end of another lawsuit."

"And Samuels stole some of the cure?"

"Apparently so. In any event, Carnelli turned him down, so Samuels e-mailed me to see if he could get his old job back. Told me he'd been doing some independent tests on the factor and was close to determining the gene sequence for cloning."

"He's full of crap. We're years away from nailing the genome on the Kramer factor. What did you tell him?"

"I told him no, of course. Although I did express my concern that he had kept some of the factor." Porter smiled and looked at Walter. The Driver rolled his head back and around in a circle, and his neck snapped and popped. Porter stretched and yawned. "Time for bed, then," he said. "And we'll see you in the morning?"

"I can't wait," Marcus said, under his breath.

CHAPTER 43

Scott had checked the Internet newsgroups and his mailbox every hour around the clock since D-Day had broken off their chat. Nothing. D-Day was a ghost.

Scott had just returned from lunch and sat down at his desk. He made a conscious effort not to look at the screen and started to open his afternoon mail. He was halfway through a software magazine when he turned just enough to catch a glimpse of the monitor with his peripheral vision—I'm not really looking, he thought. He imagined he could see a small red flag in the upper right hand corner of the screen and felt his pulse jump. Scott allowed himself an actual full-blown glance, and then jumped to his feet as he realized he had not imagined the flag at all. He grabbed the mouse and double clicked on his in-box. There it was! Mail from D-Day! It took him two tries to open the message because his hands were shaking, but the item finally popped open on his screen. Two words appeared on the screen: "Good luck." Scott didn't understand at first, but then he noticed that the mail had an attachment.

Scott wiped perspiration from his forehead and opened the attached file. It was a map, a road map of—Scott squinted at the screen—Arizona, that D-Day had scanned. There was a red "X" drawn on the map on a spot that seemed to be in the middle of nowhere, along with a series of numbers: 34.919719, -113.366776. "GPS coordinates," Scott said. "Nice work, D-Day."

He pressed the "Print" button and ran to watch the map materialize. Scott picked it up and looked at it, fingering the spot marked by the "X." He returned to his desk and had just called up Google Maps on his browser when the computer beeped. He looked at the screen—the red message flag was back. He grabbed the mouse and clicked on the message. It was from D-Day.

"You need to find Wendy Ross," it read. "She works at the place marked by the 'X.' She can take you to Jason. She lives in the Richmond District in San Francisco. Her contact info is in the attached Word doc. Be careful. D-Day."

Scott closed his eyes, moved his head forward and kissed the screen. "Thank you, D-Day," he whispered. He looked back at the screen and noticed a postscript in the email: "When this is over," it read, "let me know what happens and I'll send you my real name. You can friend me on Facebook :)."

CHAPTER 44

"How was your flight?" the cabbie said.

"Excuse me?"

"Your flight." The cabbie grinned into the rear view mirror. "How was it?"

Wendy let go of the button on her cardigan that she had been worrying since getting into the taxi. "Fine," she said. She glanced at a passing street sign. Second and Balboa. Almost home.

"Not much traffic tonight," the cabby droned through his surgical mask. "The cab stand at SFO was almost empty. Pretty weird. Nobody flyin' cuz of TL, I guess."

"I'm sorry," Wendy said, "but I have a lot to think about right now. Do you mind?"

The cabbie pulled down the brim of his baseball cap. "No," he said. "Not at all."

Wendy reached into her pocket and pulled out a pad of paper. The words "People to Call" were written at the top. The list was blank.

"Eighth and Balboa," the cabbie announced. Wendy got out of the taxi and made her way up the steep steps of the Victorian. The apartment door creaked open as she reached in to turn on the light. Suddenly, Wendy realized the door was still moving—but she wasn't pushing. She glanced back behind her and simultaneously reached into her purse. She grabbed a canister of pepper spray, then spun around and thrust her arm forward, unleashing a stream of the irritant directly into her attacker's face.

"Cheese and rice!" the assailant yelled as he backed away from Wendy and fell to the ground, his hands covering his eyes. "I was just holding the door for you!"

Wendy assumed a defensive posture, her feet shoulder-width apart and the spray still at the ready, aimed down at the tall blond man on the ground. "Who are you?"

The man remained inert, making little snuffling noises. "I'm Scott Durrant. Jason's friend. I got a message to meet you here."

Wendy's mouth opened as she dropped her packages and knelt to help Scott. "Oh, my gosh, I'm sorry!" she said as she pulled a tissue from her purse and tried to wipe his face. "Scott! Jason's told me all about you. I just didn't expect you. Let me help you in the house."

Wendy reached down and grabbed Scott under the arms and half-hoisted him to a standing position, his eyes still closed. "Man, that stuff burns," he said.

"It's supposed to," Wendy said as she moved Scott into the kitchen and began wiping his eyes with a cold wet washcloth. After several minutes Scott was able to open his eyes, but he still had groups of angry red welts on his cheeks. He stuck out his hand and smiled. "I'm Scott Durrant."

Wendy took his hand and pumped it up and down. "Again, sorry . . . ."

Scott grinned. "I'll be fine—" he paused, then grinned more broadly "—D-Day."

Wendy's head was in the refrigerator and her back was to Scott. "Excuse me?" she said over her shoulder.

"D-Day," Scott repeated. "That's you, isn't it? Your on-line name?" Scott gingerly touched his cheek. "Now I see why."

"I'm sorry, you've lost me," Wendy said. "The only D-Day I know is a technician at the place I work named Denise Dalton—except they just fired her."

"Ah," Scott said, nodding, "now it begins to make sense. See, I went surfing on the Internet looking for someone who knew about Jason, and I got this message from someone called D-Day. Told me to find you. That's how I got your address."

Wendy removed a can of Coke from the refrigerator and handed it to Scott. "Why were you asking about Jason?"

"Jason told me to come and find him if I hadn't heard from him after Marcus—"

"*Dr.* Marcus? Craig Marcus?"

"The same. Anyway, after Marcus took Jason away in the middle of the night. I assume you know the whole history, right?"

Wendy nodded.

"I hadn't heard, so I started looking." He opened the Coke and downed half the can, then held it against his cheek. "Looks like I found you."

"Why did D-Day—Denise—tell you to find me?"

Scott grinned his big horsey grin and belched. "You tell me," he said.

"Look," Wendy said, moving toward Scott and shaking a finger at him. "These are dangerous people we're dealing with, and I want to be careful."

"Tell me about it. You know a little gorilla that drives a black Mercedes?"

Wendy nodded. "The Driver. He's Phillip Porter's chauffeur. You had a run-in with him?"

Scott took another swallow of Coke. "Umm hmm."

"And you lived?"

Scott nodded. "Barely," he said.

"Look," Wendy said, "I don't have time right now to tell you what's happened since Dr. Marcus took Jason. I just know I need to get Jason out of The Complex immediately—and I need some help."

Scott's brows jumped up when Wendy mentioned The Complex. "The Complex," he said. "D-Day said something about that." Scott reached into his pocket and pulled out the map D-Day had e-mailed to him. He spread it out on the table and smoothed it with his palms. "I don't suppose you know what the big red 'X' is, do you?"

Wendy bent over the map and studied it for a moment. "The 'X'," she said, "is The Complex."

"Wow. D-Day did good," Scott said, tapping the latitude and longitude coordinates. "She must have GPS'd it on her phone the last time she was there. There's an app for that, you know. How do you get there?"

"They usually fly us in on a charter jet to an airstrip about a hundred miles away. Then we take a bus out to the site." Wendy sat on the kitchen counter and rubbed her eyes. "We need a plane," she said. "And we need to go tonight. I'm off for two weeks, but we can't wait. Plus we have to be there by 5:00 a.m. so we can take the bus in to The Complex with the new crew coming on." Wendy laughed. "Yeah right," she said. "I don't suppose you're a pilot."

Scott grinned. "As a matter of fact," he said, "I am."

Wendy stared at him. "You're kidding."

"Nope. I've got a Cessna 185 out at the Oakland Airport that's all fueled up that I use to fly over to Tahoe. Jason and I used to fly up there almost every weekend to play poker—" Scott's countenance clouded "—until he married Linda."

Wendy nodded. "I understand. She's a real prize." She folded the map and put it in her purse. "So, will your plane get us to Arizona in time?"

Scott choked on his Coke. "Wait a minute, sister," he said, spluttering. "You mean right now?"

Wendy widened her stance and folded her arms. "Right now," she said.

"Look, we've got to file flight plans, check the weather—this isn't like a weekend puddle jump up to Tahoe!"

Wendy nodded. "I see," she said. "So you can't do it."

"Oh, no," Scott said, backing away, "no you don't. You're not going to use that female reverse psychology on me!"

Wendy moved after him. "Scott, you need to understand what's going on. Jason is the cure for TL. The *cure*! Porter and Marcus are killing him. If we don't get him out of there, he'll be dead—and the rest of the world loses the cure. You understand that, don't you?"

Scott continued backing up until he bumped into Wendy's couch. "Look, I'm just a computer programmer. You didn't have Walter trying to kill you."

Wendy stopped approaching and closed her eyes. "You're his friend, Scott," she said. "You promised."

Scott sat on the edge of the couch without speaking for several seconds. "Now I know why I never got married," he said. He stood and hoisted his pants up around his skinny waist. "All right," he said. "Let's do it."

CHAPTER 45

Marcus looked at the clock on the nightstand. Seven a.m. He had been awake and ready to go since six, waiting for the Driver to come and get him to accompany Porter down to see Jason. He had not slept well last night, his mind roiling with the substance of his conversation with Porter. There was a knock on the door.

Before Marcus could cross the room and answer, the door opened and Walter's head appeared. "Let's go," he said. Marcus noted the Driver had his sunglasses on, those same impersonal shades he always wore when dirty deeds were afoot.

Marcus stood and moved to join Walter and Porter in the hallway. He nodded to Porter, who did not return the acknowledgment. Porter's long bathrobe, gloves, hat, and sunglasses reminded Marcus of Claude Raines in *The Invisible Man*. "How are you feeling?" Marcus asked.

"Yellow," Porter said, not smiling.

Walter gestured toward the elevator and ushered Marcus and Porter into a waiting car. Marcus pushed the button labeled "B2" on the console, and the doors slid shut. He heard a "ding," and they stepped out into a narrow hallway leading to Jason's room. Marcus pointed, and the Driver and Porter headed for the steel door.

As they got nearer, Marcus noticed the door was already open a crack, and light was streaming out into the dim hallway. He motioned for the Driver and Porter to stand still, and then moved toward the glow. He took two steps, then froze and threw himself up against the wall. The Driver did the same, reaching out and pulling Porter behind him. Just then, Jason moved out into the hallway with Wendy and Scott close behind. Marcus could see that Jason carried a small suitcase, Scott a larger one. Scott spoke; Marcus could hear him: "Kidnapping, I think they call it," he said.

Marcus lay pressed up against the wall, but his peripheral vision caught some movement beside and behind him: it was Porter, moving toward the threesome.

"You're wrong, my friend," Porter called out. "It cannot be kidnapping when the subject willingly sequesters himself."

The three froze, and Jason turned toward Porter, who continued to approach. "Mr. Porter," he said, as he gestured toward the tall man standing behind him. "Scott was just joking."

Scott turned, a huge grin on his face, and dropped the bag he was carrying. He thrust out his hand and took two long strides toward Porter. "So you're Phillip Porter," he said. "Heard a lot about you—bad mostly." Scott eyed him up and down. "And, I love that look—is that what all sick, rich recluses are wearing this fall?"

Porter looked down at Scott's hand but did not accept it. Instead he walked past Scott, ignoring him, and moved closer to Jason. The hem of Porter's silk robe touched the floor as he walked, hiding his feet and making him appear to float along the concrete floor. Jason took two steps backward, away from the jaundiced apparition.

Scott watched Porter glide by, and then looked down the hallway toward Marcus and the Driver standing in shadow. Scott squinted and pointed at Walter. "Hey, I know you!" he said. "How's your head?"

The Driver stiffened and moved forward, but Porter held up his hand. "Later, Walter," he said. "We first need to ensure ourselves that Jason will continue to accept our generous hospitality. Isn't that right, Jason?" Porter had stopped and now had Jason and Wendy backed up against the wall. "Jason?" he repeated.

Jason reached out and pulled Wendy close to him. "We're leaving," he said.

Porter laughed. "Leaving? I'm afraid not. You and your friend here—" Porter pointed at Wendy "—have created quite a mess for us with all the faux cure you've disseminated. We need to clean things up a bit." Porter now motioned for the Driver, who slid forward into place at Porter's flank.

"Mess?" Jason echoed. "*We've* created a mess?" Jason laughed and took a step forward, but looked past Porter at Marcus and pointed his finger. "I trusted you, Dr. Marcus. I trusted you because I thought I had something that you could use to help people." His eyes narrowed. "But you hurt them—and you hurt Jenny."

Marcus' mouth opened an inch, then his eyes fell and he lowered his head.

"You're quite right, Jason," Porter said. "Craig Marcus is an idiot. We'll take him out of the loop, and you and I will get things back on track. We'll help all those people upstairs, and we'll help little Jenny. Plus," he said, as he took off his sunglasses and removed his gloves, then held up his yellowish hand for inspection, "I obviously have a vested interest in seeing that production of the cure is, shall we say, restored."

Jason did not move for several seconds, his eyes down. Then he raised his left arm and pulled up his shirtsleeve, exposing the shunt. He reached up and uncapped the tube that opened his vein.

Wendy made a noise in her throat and moved forward, her arm outstretched, but Jason held her back. He turned his arm over, and everyone watched as the red liquid collected at the end of the shunt and dripped onto the cold concrete floor. "My blood," Jason said. "Your salvation."

Porter watched each drop as it coalesced at the end of the tube then fell to the floor, a crimson puddle growing at Jason's feet. "Yes," he said. "My salvation." He motioned again to the Driver, who moved from behind Porter and reached inside his jacket, then pulled out a sleek black pistol and leveled it at Jason's head. "That's why I can't let you leave," Porter said.

Jason stared down the barrel of the Driver's Glock, and then looked at Porter. "What are you going to do? Shoot me?" Jason pointed at the shunt and to the drops of blood falling down to the ground. "I die, you die," he said.

"If Walter puts a bullet through your brain, we'll just wheel you upstairs, drain your blood before it coagulates, and refine enough of the cure to make me well." Porter laughed. "Even in death you have the power to save," he said.

Jason didn't flinch. "That's a huge risk to take," he said. "You don't know if that will work. Maybe as soon as I stop breathing the protein dies. Maybe the stuff stops working if it doesn't get oxygen. Who knows? But as long as I stay alive, there's a chance you'll get some of the cure." Jason smiled, then said, "And I hear Trips Lite is a horrible way to go, especially when it attacks your liver like it is apparently doing to you. Very painful." Jason and Porter watched each other, neither moving, as the blood continued to drip from Jason's arm, Porter's face twisted with indecision and pain.

"Checkmate," Jason said. He gestured toward Scott and grabbed Wendy's shoulder. "Let's go," he said. Jason lowered his arm and placed the cap back on the shunt.

The flat-black pistol was rock solid in the Driver's hands as his finger tightened on the trigger, but Porter placed his hand on Walter's shoulder. "You're no better than I am," Porter said, "dispensing life and death capriciously. You're killing the people upstairs, you're killing all the people out there who have or who may contract TL, and you're killing me, it's all the same."

Jason swung around and stared Porter down, his face red. "No, it's not all the same!" he yelled. "Jenny Holloway had no other option but to rely on you and Marcus. She had no other resources. You have unlimited resources and access to a whole world of antiviral drugs that Jenny couldn't afford. So don't equate me with you. You and Marcus are murderers. I'm just a man exercising his free agency to leave here. After that, you go cure yourself." Jason turned and again walked away, Scott and Wendy at his side, the Driver's gun still fixed on the back of his head.

"Antivirals are a poor substitute for what you carry in your veins, Jason," Porter said. Jason continued walking. "Think of the people who believe they bought the cure!" Porter continued. "You have sentenced them to death!" The Driver widened his stance and took a breath, then held it as he squeezed the trigger. Porter's eyes darted between Jason and the Driver's pistol. "You are not God, Mr. Kramer!" Porter called out.

Jason didn't look back. "Neither are you," he said.

The pistol jumped in the Driver's hands, and a sharp report cracked up and down the basement's concrete hallways. Jason dropped to his knees, his hands over his head. Marcus held his breath and watched, the echo of the gunshot fading. Wendy made a move toward Jason, but stopped as he straightened and stood erect. He turned and looked at Porter, who was on his hands and knees in front of the Driver.

"Nice dive, Phillip," Scott called out. "Next time, try to actually knock the gun *out* of his hands."

Porter scowled at Scott, and then looked at Jason. "Maybe your life means nothing to you," Porter said, breathing heavily, his head down near the concrete, "but perhaps your friends' lives do." Porter pointed up at Wendy and Scott. "Kill them," Porter said.

The Driver smiled and again took his stance, then aimed at Scott. "This will be fun," he said.

Scott held up his left hand, index finger extended. "I don't think so," he said. Walter's finger tightened on the trigger as Scott turned to face Porter. "You see," Scott said, "there's a timer ticking away on my computer right now, and unless somebody enters the correct password in exactly—" Scott glanced at his watch "—five hours and six minutes, several hundred e-mails and Tweets will be sent to the FBI, the FDA, the local police, and all the major newspapers, networks, blogs and web sites outlining in great detail your whole sordid little operation—including the fact that you killed us." Scott smiled. "Oh, and plus a map to The Complex. Google Earth is a wonderful tool."

"And I hear the medical care you get in jail is pretty lousy," Wendy said.

The Driver paused and lowered the end of the barrel a quarter of an inch before pulling the pistol up again, his sights locked on Scott's forehead. The muscles in his forearms tensed. "I don't care," he said.

"No!" Porter yelled as he reached for the gun. The Driver ignored him and pushed Porter to the ground with his foot, pinning him. Walter closed one eye and continued to squeeze the trigger. "No!" Porter cried again, his arm upraised. The Driver hesitated and licked his upper lip. Then, with a disappointed grunt, he lowered the weapon and removed his foot from Porter's neck. Marcus dropped to his knees by Porter's side and lifted Porter's head from the concrete.

"Jason, . . ." Marcus called out as he cradled Porter's head, but Jason turned and walked away. He did not look back.

Porter watched the three get into the elevator, then looked up at the Driver and motioned for him to come closer. Walter knelt down and placed his ear next to Porter's mouth.

"Vincent Samuels," Porter whispered.

CHAPTER 46

The last existing vial of the cure for *Triptovirus L.* sat in a small brown refrigerator on a credenza in Vincent Samuels' seedy office just north of San Jose, California. Dr. Samuels sat at his desk across from the credenza, twiddling his thumbs. He glanced at the clock on the wall—it was 2:30. His calendar was open in front of him, and it showed he had no engagements—except for one entry at 2:45. He had not seen any other patients that day, nor the day before, and in fact would not have come in to the office today if not for the 2:45 appointment.

Vincent drummed his fingers on the arms of his chair, then, with a look on his face reminiscent of a child returning to play with a favorite toy, he pushed himself back away from his desk, the castors on the bottom of the chair humming, and maneuvered across the floor to the credenza. He pulled open the door to the refrigerator and looked inside. The half-full ampoule of clear, light yellow liquid rested on a shelf next to two cans of Dr. Pepper. He reached in to grab the container just as he heard his office door creak open.

"You're early," he called out as he fumbled with the vial and placed it back in the refrigerator. Vincent spun around and pushed himself over to his desk. "No problem, though. Please come in and sit down." The office door finished opening, then closed, and Vincent looked up into the Driver's gunmetal eyes.

Vincent stood and extended his hand. "Hi," he said. "Have we met? You look familiar."

The Driver moved across the room and took Vincent's hand. "No," he said. "I don't think so."

Vincent held onto the Driver's hand for a moment and studied his face, then released his grip and sat down. "Funny," he said. "I thought for a minute I knew you." Vincent grabbed a pad and a pen and sat up in his chair. Then, smiling, he said, "So, what can I do for you, Mr. . . . ." Vincent glanced down at his appointment book.

"Heinz. Walter Heinz." The Driver smiled and put his elbows on the arms of his chair, then put his palms together and interlocked his fingers. "I have a friend," he said, "who has TL."

"I'm sorry to hear that. How is he doing?"

"Not well. It's in his liver."

"I had read how the latest mutation was attacking the liver, almost like cirrhosis."

The Driver sat silently, watching.

Vincent cleared his throat and ran his finger around the inside of his collar, between skin and fabric. "So, how can I help you?" he said.

"It's not me you can help. It's my friend."

A sweat broke out on Vincent's face, and he stood and moved to the window, cracking it open. "Warm in here," he said. He returned to his desk and sat. "I'm sorry," he said, "but there's probably very little I can do for your friend. I'm sure he's under a physician's care already, and with Trips Lite it's likely not going to do him any good to get a second opinion."

"I don't want a second opinion. I want the cure," Walter said.

Vincent swallowed hard and the color drained from his face. "I remember who you are," he said. "You work for Phillip Porter."

The Driver nodded. "Not to be rude," he said, "but I really need the cure. Now."

Vincent's eyes darted toward the credenza, and the Driver followed his glance. Walter stood and moved toward the refrigerator, but Vincent was on his feet and ran in front of the Driver. "No," he said, his hands up, palms out, "please don't."

Walter grabbed Vincent's shoulders and threw him out of the way like a rag doll, sending Vincent sprawling across the top of the desk. The Driver grabbed the refrigerator handle and yanked it open, then bent down and peered inside. He had just reached in to remove the ampoule when Vincent broadsided him at a full sprint, knocking Walter face-first into the sharp edge of the credenza. Vincent grabbed the vial and held it in both hands against his chest, then made a dash for the door. The Driver stood up, one hand pressed against his cheek, blood oozing through his fingers. He sprinted after Vincent and grabbed him from behind, then, with a growl, lifted him from his feet and hurled him against the wall.

Vincent hit the wall hard, then sagged to the floor without a sound and came to rest on his stomach. Walter rushed forward and turned him over with his foot. Blood poured from Vincent's flattened nose, the tissue around his half-opened eyes already bruised and discolored. Walter swore under his breath and reached down, placing his fingers against the side of Vincent's neck. He felt only inanimate flesh, gradually growing cold. After a moment he stepped back and looked down at Vincent's chest. His hands were still clasped together, and a clear liquid seeped through his fingers. Walter reached down and pried the hands apart, finding only bloody shards of glass imbedded in Vincent's palms, the fragments mixed with all that was left of the cure.

Walter backed away from the body, then pulled a handkerchief from his jacket pocket and held it against his bleeding cheek. He moved back to the refrigerator and looked inside, finding only the two cans of soda. He walked around Vincent's office, opening drawers and pulling pictures off walls, looking for something that might contain more of the serum. After half an hour, Walter sat down in Vincent's chair and spun it around, then wheeled himself over to the refrigerator and grabbed a Dr. Pepper. He popped the top and took a long swallow, then placed the cold can against the side of his face. Mr. Porter, Walter thought, is not going to be happy.

CHAPTER 47

"Fraud, breach of contract, wrongful death. It's all in here." The lawyer closed the document and slid it back to Keith and Linda, who sat across from him at the desk. "Pretty good complaint," the lawyer said. "When did you get it?"

"This morning. The process server came to the house." Linda was pale and her hands trembled as she reached out and picked up the hefty document.

"Has Porter been served?" the lawyer said.

"I don't know," Keith said. "We've been trying to reach him, but he's still out in the middle of the Arizona desert."

The lawyer sat back in his chair and put his feet up on the desk. "Wow," he said. "A class action suit by the survivors of all the people who went to Bigwood Springs for the cure and who died instead. Nasty. Juries eat this stuff up." The lawyer scratched his head. "You charged those poor people a million bucks each?"

Linda nodded. "Porter did, actually."

"But you're his partners."

Linda nodded again.

The lawyer shook his head and whistled. "Police contacted you yet?"

Keith stared blankly at the lawyer. "The police? Why would the police be involved?"

"Think about it. You, Mr. Porter and Ms. Kramer took these poor dying people to the tune of fifty million dollars. That's against the law. Plus, the prosecution's going to try to make it look like you knew the cure was phony and caused these people to forego conventional therapies that might have saved their lives. Sounds like second degree murder to me—or at least manslaughter."

"That's ridiculous!" Linda was on her feet, pacing in front of the desk. "We had no way of knowing what that woman and Jason were doing!" Keith reached up and tried to grab her arm as she passed by, but she threw his hand back at him.

The lawyer shot Keith a sympathetic glance. "I understand that," the lawyer said, "but if you'll forgive my abruptness, that's not the point."

Linda wheeled around and planted herself in the lawyer's face. "What do you mean?"

"You were his partners, Ms. Kramer. Phillip Porter's *partners*."

"We've established that," she said.

The lawyer sighed. "Partners are presumed to share the knowledge of the other partners. The jury will be led to believe Phillip Porter knew what was going on. He owned the company, for heaven's sake! People were dying all around him, and he let it continue, then he invited more people to come, and took their money, too, and then they died. His knowledge will be imputed to you."

Keith rubbed his eyes. "At least Porter's got deep pockets."

"What?" Linda said.

"Deep pockets. You know, lots of money to pay any judgments against the partnership."

Linda turned back to the lawyer. "Is that right? Is Porter going to have to pay for all this? Keith and I won't be hit by all this, will we?"

The lawyer scratched his head. He reached out and grabbed another thick document that sat on his desk. He turned to the last page of the contract and pointed at a section labeled "Partnership Loss Sharing."

Keith leaned forward and read out loud: "In consideration of Porter having borne all research and development costs to date associated with production of the blood factor, Lawrence and

Kramer agree to the same pro rata sharing of any and all liability arising out of or associated with the factor in the same percentages as earlier recited regarding profit sharing." Keith paled, then frowned. "Hmmm," he said.

"You read the agreement," Linda said. "Didn't you see that?"

Keith shrugged. "Guess I missed it."

"That's a pretty big 'miss.' So we get stuck with 50 percent of any losses, just like we get 50 percent of the profits?" Linda said.

Keith nodded.

"So that means we're wiped out."

"Unless you've got a thirteen million dollar nest egg tucked away somewhere," Keith said.

"Smart ass," she said. "I don't need your sarcasm right now."

The lawyer cleared his throat. "Keith does bring up a good point. Do you have any plans for dealing with the various outcomes? I mean even if there's no civil liability and the grand jury doesn't indict you on criminal charges, there will probably be at least a quarter million in attorneys' fees before this is over. Plus, I think it's naive to think Porter Pharmaceuticals can survive this. Porter was heavily leveraged to support all its research and development. This much exposure will probably put it under—bankruptcy or receivership, I bet. So don't plan on staying in business and recovering your losses after the fact."

Linda and Keith fell silent.

"You'd better start coming up with some ways to raise cash for a war chest," the lawyer continued. "Second mortgage on the house, liquidating securities, things like that. And you'd better do it fast. You've got thirty days to answer this complaint or they'll get a default judgment against you." The lawyer paused and then said, "Let me see the complaint again for a second."

Linda handed him the papers, and the lawyer flipped to the last pages. "Just as I thought. They've also asked for punitive damages—extra money on top of the fifty million to punish you for your bad conduct. Punies could be another fifty million. Ouch."

Linda took a cigarette out of her purse and threw it between her lips, the end waggling as she spoke. "Screw 'em," she said. "I'll just file bankruptcy."

"That's fine," the lawyer said, "but bankruptcy won't wipe out liability for fraud. A judgment like that will just follow you around for years, mucking up your credit. No VISA, no MasterCard—hope you like paying cash and eating ramen."

Linda continued smoking, sucking in big lungfuls of smoke and blowing them at the lawyer. "So what do we do?" she said.

The lawyer looked at Keith, then at Linda, and then shrugged. "Hire an experienced criminal defense lawyer and a good civil litigator," he said. "Prayer is good, too."

Linda exhaled into the lawyer's face and stubbed out her cigarette on a legal pad on the desk. "Let's get out of here," she said to Keith.

Keith hopped up out of his chair and joined Linda, who was halfway to the door, then turned and held his thumb and pinkie finger up to his mouth and ear and mouthed, "I'll call you," to the lawyer, who smiled weakly. Linda was several steps ahead out in the hallway, and Keith ran to catch her. "Linda, wait up!" he called.

Linda kept striding for the elevator, but Keith caught her elbow and pulled her around to face him. "Linda," he said, "I'm sorry about this. But there's no reason to act this way. We can work through this."

Linda pulled away and spun around into the open elevator. "In your dreams, pal," she said. "I'll see you in court." She stuck out her arm just as the doors were closing and bumped them open. "Maybe Mary'll let you sleep on her couch."

Keith opened his mouth to speak, but the doors closed in his face.

CHAPTER 48

"How'd it go with Samuels?" Phillip Porter said.

Walter stared at the floor of Porter's room at The Complex. "Not good. Dr. Samuels was, um, uncooperative."

Porter looked at Walter's bandaged cheek. "I see," he said. "And the cure?"

Walter shook his head. "He'd already used it all. Probably gave it to Carnelli."

Porter's jaw tightened. "I'm very disappointed, Walter. I guess that makes it even more imperative that we find Kramer, doesn't it?" Porter waited and watched Walter, who did not speak. "So how's the search going?" Porter finally said.

Walter shrugged. "We checked his apartment, the skinny guy's apartment, everywhere. Nothing." Walter moved into the room and sat down on the edge of Porter's bed. "He's hiding out."

Porter coughed and wiped phlegm from the edge of his mouth. "Thank you, Walter. I presumed that. What about the wife?"

"She's ditched that Keith Lawrence fellow, but Jason's not hanging around her either."

Porter chuckled. "Hell hath no fury, right, Walter?" He reached over to his nightstand and lifted a bottle of pills. He popped the lid and dumped two white tablets into his palm. Walter raised an eyebrow. "Pain killers," Porter said. "Dr. Marcus insisted. He seems to think it's necessary, in light of recent events."

Porter tossed the pills into his mouth and dry swallowed them. He sat, rubbing his stomach, until he finally stood and held out his arm toward the Driver. "Walter," he said, "I feel like going for a walk. Give me a hand."

Walter paused for a moment, then moved forward and took Porter's arm. "Sure, Mr. Porter," he said. "It's awfully hot outside, though."

Porter shuffled toward the door with Walter at his side. "I don't want to go outside, Walter. Let's just walk up and down the hallways inside. It's nice and cool in here." Porter and Walter moved out into the hallway and began a slow stroll, Porter's slippers making a soft "whush, whush" on the polished tile while Walter's heels clicked with military precision. "Where are the remaining TL patients?" Porter asked. "I know we kept some here who were in the beginning stages of new drug trials."

"Right," Walter said. "Marcus told me they moved them all downstairs to make space for the Bigwood Springs patients." Walter looked around into the empty rooms. "Plenty of room now, though," he said.

Porter chuckled. "Thank you for that observation, Walter," he said. "It's true, though, isn't it? People fled pretty quickly after word of the fake cure got out. Running to their lawyers before they died, I expect."

Walter nodded and shifted his grip on Porter's skinny arm. "Here we go," he said as he pushed the button to summon the elevator. They stood in silence, waiting, before Walter spoke. "Mr. Porter," he said, "why do you want to go downstairs and see the patients? Why don't you let us fly you back to San Francisco and get out of this place?"

Porter stepped into the open elevator with Walter still at his arm. "There's nothing for me there, Walter," he said as he pushed the button for the next floor down. "I've no family, no real friends."

"But what about Claudius?"

Porter sighed. "He is an old cat, Walter."

Walter nodded.

"You'll take care of him for me, won't you?"

Walter paused, uncomfortable. "Sure," he said.

They rode in silence for a moment before Porter continued. "Besides," he said, "this place is state of the art for advanced TL treatment. Every antiviral therapy under the sun, legal and illegal, right here at our fingertips."

“Except the Kramer cure,” Walter said.

“How astute you are!” Porter retorted. Porter watched the lights on the display above the door as they blinked. "Just between you and me," he said, "I think Marcus is afraid I wouldn't survive the trip back to the City." Porter paused, and then smiled. "Or maybe he's afraid I would. Probably doesn't want me going out and getting a second opinion. Maybe I'm not dying after all. May be I don’t have TL. Maybe it’s just plain old cancer. Hell, I’ve got drugs here for *that.*"

The elevator doors slid open exposing an empty corridor. Only half the lights were on, and illumination from the few occupied rooms spilled out into the hallway. Walter and Porter moved down the hall, stopping outside one of the rooms that still contained a patient. The TV was on, and Porter glanced into the room. He could see a young woman in her late twenties lying in bed, the remote control in her hand. She pushed the buttons on the clicker randomly, aimlessly, her eyes glassy from staring at the screen. Porter noticed the words "Batch 920" stenciled in big black letters on the IV bag that hung next to her. Suddenly, the woman stood and began to run toward the bathroom, her hand clutched to her stomach, but her feet became tangled in the IV pump power cord and she stumbled and fell to her knees, tried to stand, then fell again as she lost the war she was waging with her stomach. Porter watched as the woman convulsed again and again until nothing else came out. She began to cry, a low, mournful wail, a mixture of physical pain and despair.

Porter turned away, his hand now pressed to his own stomach. "Help her, Walter," he said. "I'll be by the elevator." The Driver moved from Porter's side and went into the woman's room while Porter made his way back down the hallway. He could hear Walter and the woman talking, could see the light flashing over the woman's door as Walter pushed the nurse's call button, could hear Walter summoning the nurse over the intercom when she answered. Porter sat on a bench and rubbed his abdomen, trying to abate his own nausea. "Tee-Ell, warning bell, Tee-Ell, what's that smell, Tee-Ell go to hell," he said in a sing-song voice, parroting the irreverent playground rhyme that had gained recent popularity. He sat on the bench, waiting for Walter and watching. After a time, a nurse appeared and went into the woman's room, and then Walter emerged and joined Porter. "Let's go back to my room, Walter," he said. "I want to rest."

Porter and Walter made their way back to the room in silence, Walter holding Porter's arm. They stood for a moment in front of the door, neither speaking, until Walter said, "She was pretty sick."

Porter didn't look up. "She's going to die, Walter," he said. Porter shook off the Driver's arm and opened the door to his room.

"Mr. Porter," Walter said, sticking out his arm to block open the door, "I talked to the home office this morning." Walter cleared his throat and ran his hand across the top of his head, brown crew cut bristling. "There's been some guy hanging out there looking for you, something about some legal papers you need to see."

"Ah yes," Porter said. "Those would be the lawsuits." He made his way across the room and sat down on the bed. "Big ones, I expect." Porter laughed. "'The first thing we do, let's kill all the lawyers,'" he said.

"What?"

"Oh sorry," Porter said. "It's a line from Henry VI. Shakespeare. You should read it." Porter reached into the front pocket of his robe and pulled out a pack of cigarettes. He removed one of the white cylinders and held it at arm's length between thumb and forefinger, looking at it. "You've made me a lot of money," he said. He motioned to the Driver, who came over and lit the cigarette. Porter inhaled, then looked up at Walter. He stood and placed his hands on Walter's shoulders, then moved his hands down the front of Walter's jacket, palms against the fabric. He stopped when they reached the level of Walter's sternum. Porter smiled and patted the outside of Walter's coat. "Walter," Porter said. "I need a favor."

—

The sun was low in the Arizona sky when Craig Marcus and Ruth Wilson closed and locked the door to their lab at The Complex for the last time. Marcus carried a box of papers, Ruth a thick valise stuffed with documents. "I can't believe Jason just walked away like that," Ruth said. "Do you have any idea where he went? I mean, just because Porter's involvement is concluded doesn't mean we can walk away from this, too."

Marcus made a little groaning noise as he struggled with the box. "I understand that, Ruth. But Jason's pretty angry right now. He probably doesn't want to be found. Not after what happened to him—and Jenny."

Ruth nodded. "Is it too late to get Jenny back in and start her on some conventional antivirals? I hear that Novelos is making good progress against TL with a new version of NOV-205."

Marcus shrugged. "I don't know if she's still alive. Even if she is, the only thing that could save her at this stage is the Kramer factor."

Marcus and Ruth continued walking for a time without speaking. Then Ruth said, "Do you really think Porter will respond to Batch 920?"

Marcus shook his head. "You know the answer to that. Batch 920 and some good painkillers might prolong his life a few months."

Ruth nodded. "I guess it makes sense, then, to close up The Complex. I mean, this was Porter's baby, so to speak."

"He doesn't have the money to keep it afloat, that's the reason, baby or not," Marcus said. He stared straight ahead, his brows furrowed in thought. "Listen, Ruth," he said. "There are some things about my involvement with Porter Pharmaceuticals . . . some things I think you should know about if we're going to be, well, if we're going to work together."

Ruth grinned. "I'll bite."

Marcus shifted the box of papers he was carrying. "I had some problems as a graduate student. Porter bailed me out. He's been holding that over my head all the years I've worked for him."

"What kind of problems?"

Marcus cleared his throat. "You know about my research with genetically altered interferon."

"Sure. We all heard about the UCSF whiz kid that had cooked up some recombinant interferon that was killing tumors. Whatever happened to that stuff?"

"We had to pull it off the market—after making millions in foreign sales. Never did get FDA approval."

"What happened?"

Marcus stopped and put down the box, then pulled his handkerchief from his pocket and wiped his face. "It was a little too lethal. Killed some people."

Ruth pursed her lips. "Oh," she said. "What's that got to do with you?"

Marcus looked down at his feet. "I knew the stuff was toxic. It killed a couple of my test subjects."

"You mean those rumors are true? You went to market even though it killed people?"

"I had to! Porter knew about the deaths and threatened to expose me if I didn't help take it to market. It's been the same ever since. Porter sends people out here to The Complex where we run secret human trials of new chemotherapeutic agents. If the stuff works, we seek formal FDA approval to conduct human trials, after we already know what will happen to human subjects. We can't lose. Plus, Porter gets new products to market months, even years, ahead of the competition. We were doing the same thing with Kramer and TL. Or started to."

Ruth whistled, slow and long. "Wow," she said. "What about the animal data?"

"We do a little at first, but if the new drug seems at all promising, we start the human trials on people who think they are coming out here to get experimental regimens as a last resort. The rest of the animal data given to FDA is faked—extrapolated from the human data."

"So why didn't you walk?"

Marcus shook his head. "Porter's got this incriminating little file on me that he waves under my nose every time I get a streak of conscience. Porter'd spin it to make it look like I was solely responsible. Plus he's the only one who knew anything about the deaths, so there's no one else at the company who could deny Porter's version—or corroborate mine."

"But if The Complex is closing—"

"Porter is much too smart to give up such a great money-making scheme. I fully expect the Driver will show up at my door Monday morning to take me to headquarters in Marin and continue operations there, business as usual." Marcus thought for a minute, then said, "At least it wouldn't be so bloody hot in Marin."

Ruth turned to him, her face red. "This is absurd, Craig. There must be some way to get you out of this. I mean, you're certainly not going to continue to work for Porter Pharmaceuticals!"

Marcus shrugged. "You tell me," he said. He pushed open the front doors to The Complex's parking lot. People were milling about, talking, making their way onto a host of assembled buses and ambulances. Marcus looked out over the crowd and saw a few familiar faces, including John Cornwall from the CDC. He met Cornwall's eyes and knew that a "come-to-Jesus" meeting was in his immediate future. "I don't think I'll have much of a choice," he said.

"The playing field has changed, Craig. Porter's dying, his business is failing—you might be able to speak with him now, reach some kind of compromise, find a way to clear your name."

Marcus continued walking toward the buses, but his pace gradually slowed. He stopped, and then placed the box he was carrying on the ground. He looked out into the Arizona desert, squinting in the bright sun, then turned to Ruth and took her shoulders in his hands. "Go run interference with Cornwall for me. I'll be right back," he said.

Marcus turned and began to run back toward The Complex. He threw open the doors and ran down the hall to the stairs, climbing them two at a time until he reached Porter's floor. He bumped open the door with his hip and kept running, finally stopping outside Porter's suite. He knocked twice, and then opened the door a crack. "Mr. Porter?" he said. "Phillip?"

He pushed the door open wider and looked inside the room. He saw Porter seated at the desk. His chin was down against his chest, and his head was tilted to the left, oddly askew. The wall behind him was spattered with flecks of red and pink and gray. The Driver's black pistol rested in Porter's lap.

Marcus instinctively rushed toward him, but stopped halfway, transfixed by the scene. He moved forward and touched Porter's shoulder, cold and unyielding. Marcus looked down at the desk and saw an envelope with "Craig Marcus" written on it in Porter's elegant hand. It had somehow remained untouched by the surrounding carnage. Marcus picked up the envelope, tore it open, and removed a sheet of creamy white bond paper with the Porter Pharmaceuticals watermark. He held it up and read:

Dr. Marcus:

Walter thinks I borrowed his gun so I could kill you. Sorry to report he was quite pleased with that prospect. I'm sure he'll be disappointed when he learns the truth.

I've sent your file to the authorities in San Francisco.

Regards,
Phillip Porter

Marcus stared at the note and read it twice before placing it back into the envelope. He looked around and saw an unopened pack of Porter's cigarettes; a gold lighter rested on the package, with a bundle of red-tipped kitchen matches stacked in a neat pile next to it. "Like a little shrine," Marcus said.

Marcus picked up the lighter and lit the edge of the envelope. The crisp paper burned like tinder and with little smoke. Marcus held it until the flames licked his fingers, then dropped it into an ashtray next to Porter's bed. The tray brimmed with spent butts. No one will notice the extra ash, Marcus thought. He moved back to Porter's body and knelt down to look at his face. Porter's eyes were wide open, the sclera shockingly yellow. Marcus reached out to close the lids, but stopped instead and withdrew his hand, then stood and walked out of the room.

CHAPTER 49

The cool mountain air was tinged with wood smoke, the setting sun filtering blue-gray through the trees surrounding the cabin. Jason stood on the porch and looked out at the lake fifty yards away. He could hear Wendy and Scott in the kitchen, doing dishes.

"Hey," Scott said, "when I agreed to dry these, it was under the assumption you would wash them first. Look at this crud on here!"

Wendy laughed. "So next time you wash."

Jason smiled and sat down in a wooden chair that had been rough-hewn out of the same logs that made the cabin, then pulled off his boots and scratched his toes. He turned around to watch Wendy and Scott jostle out through the screen door, still giggling. "Brrr," Wendy said, buttoning her cardigan, "cold for September." She walked up behind Jason and began to rub his shoulders. Scott took a seat on the front steps.

"Mmm," Jason said to Wendy. "Nice. You learn that in phlebotomy school?"

"Nope," Wendy said. "They just teach us how to find veins." Wendy stopped rubbing and leaned over Jason's shoulder. "By the way," she said, "let's see that arm."

Jason obediently rolled up the sleeve of his plaid flannel shirt and lifted his arm for Wendy's inspection. The shunt was gone. All that remained was a purplish bruise and two hairless patches of skin where the tape had been. Jason rubbed the needle scar. "How does it look?"

Wendy grabbed Jason's wrist and prodded the flesh of his arm. After a moment of scrutiny, she said, "Good. Pretty soon that scar will be your only reminder of this."

Jason rolled down his sleeve. "That assumes that the bad dreams stop."

"You, too?" Scott said, moving closer and joining the conversation. "The other night I dreamed that this big monster with Porter's yellow face and the Driver's eyes was chasing me around with this huge syringe."

Jason and Wendy watched Scott and waited for the rest of the story.

"But then I woke up and there was this really big mosquito in my room."

Wendy and Jason cracked up, and Wendy swatted Scott on the shoulder. "Funny," Jason said, laughing, "but don't you have some work or something to do? Seems a shame you brought that fancy computer with satellite wi-fi, and you're out here instead enjoying all this fresh air and scenic beauty."

Scott looked at Jason and Wendy, and then stood up. "I can take a hint," he said. Scott moved for the door of the cabin. "Besides, I need to go check in with D-Day. We've struck up quite an online relationship. You two behave yourselves out here."

Wendy watched Scott go into the cabin and listened to the stairs creak as he made his way up to the loft. She turned back to Jason. "Bad dreams?"

Jason looked out at the lake. "I keep thinking about those people who didn't get the cure."

Wendy removed her hands from Jason's shoulders and folded her arms. "We saved your life. We saved the cure," she said.

Jason stood and moved to the railing. The sun was just beginning to dip below the horizon, a brilliant orange ball reflecting off the surface of the lake, and Jason could see the faint outline of the moon as it grew brighter in the sky. "I mean, it was so typical of me to just get up and leave. All my life I've just gone with the flow, not really thinking about the impact my decisions have on others—or letting others make my decisions for me."

Wendy joined Jason at the porch railing and took his hand in hers. "I was there, Jason. I watched you grow weaker and weaker, watched them increase quotas, watched them take more and more blood. Hell, I was the one taking it! You were unconscious most of the time, but I . . ." Wendy paused and bit her lip, ". . . I was watching you die. Porter made promises to those people that you simply could not keep."

Jason watched two ducks land on the lake, webbed feet outstretched, and skid across the surface of the water. They came to a rest and quacked a ducky duet. "I didn't ask to be God's gift to the world," Jason said.

"You're not listening to me," Wendy said. "This is not your fault!"

Jason looked down at his arm. "Funny, isn't it?" he said. "I've got this stuff in my veins and I can't do a thing with it. I mean, have you thought about the different scenarios? We could go to the government, but they'd botch it up, and we already know how the private sector is going to treat us." Jason slammed his fist down on the railing. "It's a genie in a bottle—all the power in the world, but powerless."

The quacking subsided as the ducks went bottoms-up, their heads under the surface. Wendy stroked Jason's hair and watched him until the ducks righted themselves and flew away. "Close your eyes," she said.

"What?"

"Close your eyes."

Jason gave Wendy a pained expression, and then closed his eyes.

"Think about Jenny," Wendy said.

Jason's countenance remained unchanged for a moment, the same stern expression on his face. Then, a smile began to grow, displacing the tension and pain.

Wendy leaned in and whispered in Jason's ear. "Tell me what you see."

Jason's smile grew broader. "She's in a yellow sundress," he said, his eyes still closed. "Barefoot. She's laughing—I can see her front teeth missing. Strawberry blonde curls all around her face. She's running, holding that stuffed elephant you gave her. Hoover's there too, barking." Jason opened his eyes and looked at Wendy. "She's happy," he said.

Wendy wiped at a tear that trailed down her cheek. "That's the power you have, Jason. You can give that to Jenny—to other kids like her. To everybody."

Jason's turned to Wendy and studied her face. "I don't have that power," he said. "It's locked in my blood, and the only people who can free it have no interest in helping Jenny or anybody else but themselves. Besides," Jason sighed, "we don't even know if she's alive."

"But if you could help her, would you?"

"Of course," Jason said, "but that's not poss—"

Wendy put her finger over Jason's lips. "We've got to try," she said. "It's the only way to stop those bad dreams."

CHAPTER 50

Market Street in San Francisco at noon. The sidewalks were alive with business people hurrying to grab lunch, shoppers looking for bargains, and Craig Marcus trying to hail a cab. They all wore surgical masks, the fashion trend mandated by TL. It had become vogue to decorate one's mask with a signature design, like lawyers with gavels and doctors with a caduceus. Children's masks all featured the latest cartoon characters. Marcus stood outside the Market Street Marriott, one hand holding his briefcase, the other waving at every taxi that drove by. The sign behind him outside the hotel's main entrance read, "Emerging Technologies: TL Therapies." Smaller letters beneath the banner read: "Guest Lecturer—Dr. Craig Marcus." Marcus had just stepped off the curb and yelled "Taxi!" when he felt a hand on his shoulder.

"Need a lift?"

Marcus turned around expecting to see an off-duty cabby ready to go back on shift. "Man, that'd be terrific. I've got to be at UCSF in 20 min—" Marcus stopped in mid-sentence, his mouth half open.

"I heard you've been looking for me."

Marcus dropped his briefcase and grabbed the man standing behind him in a bear hug. The man was not wearing a mask. "Jason! Where have you been?"

Jason grinned and extracted himself from Marcus' embrace. "Wendy's uncle has a cabin up near . . . well, up north. We've been up there."

Marcus took a step back and looked Jason up and down. "You look great. How do you feel?"

"Good. Strength's back, weight's up to normal. Wendy's a good nurse."

"Wendy, huh? What about Linda?" Marcus said.

"We're divorced."

"You're kidding! I thought—"

"*I* filed," Jason said. "She had no money to fight me, and I borrowed money from Scott. Apparently, all computer programmers do is work and save for retirement. Anyway, I got off clean."

Marcus laughed. "That's great!"

There was silence next as the two men surveyed each other, then Jason spoke. "How about you? Things were pretty messy when I left."

"Yeah, it was bad for a while," Marcus said. "You heard about Porter?"

Jason nodded. "I saw it in the papers. Can't say I'm sorry."

"Me either."

"And whatever happened to that guy with no neck, the Driver?" Jason said.

Marcus laughed. "I heard he's working as a bouncer in a club over in the Haight-Ashbury. Perfect job for him."

"How come he's not in prison?" Jason said.

"Good question. Guess he sold himself to the cops as Porter's low level flunky. Maybe he's smarter than I thought."

Jason smiled. "He ever bother you?"

"Not really. He called me a couple of times looking for a job, of all things. Told him I couldn't afford him."

"Not to be rude," Jason said, "but why aren't *you* in prison?"

"Almost was," Marcus said. "That was a nightmare."

Jason gestured toward the sign behind them. "Couldn't have been that bad. You're still '*Doctor*' Marcus."

Marcus smiled. "They wanted to prosecute me and the whole Porter Pharmaceuticals board of directors. But I had a file tucked away that the police were very interested in. We cut a deal."

"File?"

Marcus hesitated, then sighed and said, "A file on Jenny, Jason. A file from The Complex, and a flash drive from headquarters in Marin. I went state's evidence. I had proof that the board knew that Batch 919 was killing Jenny because of autopsy results from a woman named Katrine Waters. Batch 919 killed Katrine, too." Marcus looked down. "But Porter gave it to Jenny anyway."

Jason didn't flinch. "*You* gave it to her," he said.

Marcus looked up into Jason's eyes. "Yes," he said, "I did. I'm sorry. And I'm sorry for what I did to you."

A cab pulled up next to the curb and the driver rolled down his window. "I couldn't get over to you. Had to go around the block. Hop in."

"Change of plans," Marcus said. "But thanks anyway." The cab pulled away and Marcus gestured ahead of himself. "Let's walk," he said. They headed away from the Marriott, up Market Street.

They walked for a block, then Marcus spoke: "Why did you find me?"

Jason stopped under an awning and turned to face Marcus. "You know what's it's like to cut yourself shaving and have a guilt trip because the cure for a pandemic is going down the drain?"

"No," Marcus said, "I don't."

"It sucks." Jason stopped in front of a Vietnamese restaurant and looked at the menu on the door. "Have you eaten?" he said. "I'm starving."

Marcus shook his head. "No, I'm fine. You go ahead, though."

Jason moved away from the door. "I'll wait," he said. He continued down the sidewalk, sidestepping a homeless man asleep under a piece of cardboard. Jason reached into his pocket and pulled out some change, then dropped the coins into a tin can near the man's head. The man roused and looked up at Jason, flashing a toothless grin. Jason turned and looked at Marcus. "It wasn't easy coming here today. You tried to kill me."

Marcus blanched and took a step back. "It was a bad situation, Jason, I—"

Jason held up his hand, cutting him off. "That's all right," he said. "I'm way past trying to assign blame." Jason moved to a bench and sat. After a moment, he motioned to Marcus to join him. Marcus hesitated, and then took a seat next to Jason.

"I've spent a lot of time talking to Wendy, trying to work through this," Jason said. "She's helped me understand that I have a certain responsibility now. I can't let what you and Porter did blind me to that."

Marcus nodded.

"I remember reading this short story once called *'It's a Good Life'* about a kid who got whatever he wanted simply by thinking about it," Jason said. "He became a god. And a monster." Jason absentmindedly scratched his arm where the shunt had been. "Absolute power is an interesting thing, Dr. Marcus," he said. "It can corrupt or it can heal."

Marcus waited and watched Jason's face. A bus roared by, kicking pebbles up onto the sidewalk, and Marcus reached down to brush the dust off his trouser legs. He looked up when Jason placed his hand on his shoulder.

"I choose to heal," Jason said.

Marcus placed his hand on Jason's and squeezed it, a broad smile on his face. "Good," he said. "Good for you, Jason."

"But we can't go public with this. Not yet. Too many people with too many ulterior motives would love to get their hands on the cure—and that means getting their hands on me. We have to stay low key."

"Of course. You'll need to be in hiding for a while."

"I want to help people, Dr. Marcus, but I'm just one man. I can't save every single person who has TL."

Marcus smiled. "You don't have to," he said. "I've got my notes and formulas from The Complex, and Ruth Wilson has agreed to help me in case we ever got this opportunity. Maybe we can still put out a little bit of the factor while we study your genome and figure out how to clone it in *E. coli.*"

"Excuse me?"

"Sorry. Once we figure out which of your genes are responsible for producing the factor, we can alter those genes in bacteria called *E. coli* and make them produce the factor for us. Then you retire to the Bahamas."

Jason laughed. "That'll be nice. But how do we decide who gets the cure until we figure out how to mass produce it? Who lives and who dies?" Jason gestured expansively at the passing people. "I mean, look around. Everyone lives in fear that they'll get TL, more and more people die every day, and all the government can tell them is that they are working on a vaccine."

Marcus stretched out his legs and looked up into the sky, thinking. "Once we clone it," he said, "that won't matter. There will be enough for everyone. But until then . . ." Marcus looked down at the sidewalk and shook his head ". . . I don't know. Children, maybe. Or maybe people with high risk jobs where they are exposed to sick people."

"Like Porter?"

Marcus rubbed his eyes. "Good point," he said. "I guess there can't be any bright-line tests." The two sat for a time without speaking, watching the pigeons that danced about their feet squabbling for food. Then Marcus spoke. "At a minimum, I think I know where we should start." Jason stared at him. "People that didn't get the cure," Marcus said. "People at Bigwood Springs."

Jason kept staring, his eyes growing wide. "Jenny?" he asked.

"If we can find her."

"And the others? You know who they are? How can we find them? Are they still alive?"

Marcus held up his hand. "Wait a minute," he said. "I don't have all the answers. I said it would be a good place to start. We'll have to try to find them. I understand Scott is pretty good with a computer."

Jason laughed. "Yeah, he is." Jason stood up and invited Marcus to do the same. "I have an agenda here, Doctor," he said. "I suggest you get busy figuring out where everyone is and how to get this stuff out of my veins."

Marcus searched Jason's face and saw the urgency of his expression. "You're right, of course," he said. "I'll call Ruth Wilson. We'll get started right away."

Jason grabbed Marcus' shoulder and shoved him toward the street. "You do that," he said. Jason stuck out his arm and waved it. "Taxi!" he yelled.

Marcus dodged a bicycle messenger and spun around toward Jason just as a cab pulled up behind him. "What about you?" Marcus said. "How will I find you?"

"You won't," he said. "Not right away. I'll contact you in a few days. And when I do, I expect you to be ready to go." Jason opened the car door and helped Marcus into the cab. Marcus rolled down the window as the cab started to pull away. "Let's do it right this time!" Jason yelled at the departing taxi. Marcus waved.

Jason waved back and watched the cab pull off into traffic. He stood there, enjoying the sun as it filtered down between the tall buildings, warm on his face. He glanced at his watch. "Lunchtime," he said. He looked around and made his way toward a street vendor selling hamburgers.

"Medium rare with the works," Jason told the kid working the cart. The kid was not wearing a face mask. Jason reached into a cooler and grabbed a Coke while the vendor went to work. He popped open the soda and sipped it, admiring the vendor's skill in flipping the giant patty, and slipped a five into the tip jar. Jason noticed two men in their early twenties standing at a nearby bus stop watching as the kid handed him the burger. Both men's face masks were emblazoned with graphics of a computer monitor and keyboard. IT geeks, Jason thought.

"I can't believe somebody would eat one of those. That guy is working without a mask," one man said. The other added, "And they just passed a new city ordinance requiring masks on all street vendors!" Jason glanced up at the two young men, his big, greasy hamburger parked chin-high, a two-fisted monster loaded with cheese and grilled onions. The two men watched and waited as

Jason held the burger. Then Jason smiled and took a big bite, ketchup running down his chin.

CHAPTER 51

A music box, its lid up, stood on a white shelf next to an open window. Curtains danced in the breeze while a little ballerina inside the music box twirled to a tinkling *Dance of the Sugar Plum Fairy*. A stuffed elephant, its trunk discolored in an area the shape of a child's hand, sat next to the music box.

"You'll be a ballerina like that one day," a voice said. "Tall and straight and beautiful." Wind blew into the room and rustled the white canopy of a child's four-poster bed as the plastic dancer continued to spin, *en pointe*, never tiring. The figurine's hair was done up in a tight bun, and her eyes were sapphire blue. Eventually the music began to slow, and the little ballerina came to a gentle stop. Carmen Holloway stood and moved to the shelf, then picked up the music box and wound it. The dancer began to pirouette again, and Carmen returned to her seat beside the bed, taking care to smooth the canopy before sitting down. She reached out and took Jenny's hand in hers, then kissed the back of it. "Tall and straight and beautiful," Carmen said.

She looked at her daughter lying in the bed, and then looked at the picture on the nightstand. "One year ago," Carmen said, shaking her head. The little girl in the photograph had mounds of wavy strawberry blonde curls framing round pink cheeks. The little girl in the bed was a shrunken vestige of that image, her hair gone, her countenance skull-like. The respirator hooked to Jenny's throat sucked and wheezed, mechanically giving her life. "Please God," Carmen whispered, her eyes closed, "take her home soon."

Carmen kissed her daughter's hand once more and tucked her arm back under the thick comforter. "Maybe we'll get a letter from Daddy today," she said. "I'll read it to you." Carmen stood and walked into the kitchen. She could still hear the Tchaikovsky melody coming from Jenny's room as she poured a cup of coffee. She stood over the sink, cup in hand, and looked out the kitchen window at the dusky landscape: two kids on bikes, an old lady walking her dog, a young couple holding hands, everyone wearing the required surgical masks. Carmen smiled and waved at the mailman coming up the front walk. She sat the cup down and moved to the door to greet him.

"Hello, Pete," she said as she opened the door.

"Hi, Carmen," Pete said, adjusting the mask that bore an emblem of the U.S. flag as was customary of all government workers. He dug into his pouch, pulled out three envelopes, and handed them to Carmen. "How's Jenny today?"

Carmen took the envelopes and looked through them. "Same," she said. "Although she opened her eyes once for me this morning."

"That's great," Pete said. "Has she talked any more?"

Carmen shook her head. "Just that little bit when we first got home. Do you want to go in and see her?"

Pete coughed. "Um, no thanks, it's getting close to the curfew, but tell her I said hi." He stepped backward off the porch and started to turn toward the street, but then stopped and moved back toward Carmen. "Oh yeah," he said. "One more thing." Pete jammed his hand deep into the bag and pulled out a small box wrapped in brown paper. He handed it to Carmen. "Special delivery," he said. "You gotta sign."

Carmen took the box and scrawled her name on Pete's clipboard, then looked at the package. "Funny," she said. "No return address."

Pete eyed the parcel. "Think it's from Tom?"

Carmen brightened. "Maybe," she said. "Jenny's birthday's coming up." She turned and went back into the kitchen, Pete on her heels, then took a knife from a drawer and slit open the package. An insulated vial tumbled out of the wrapping paper and fell to the floor, along with a hand-written note. With a start, she grabbed the note and held it in front of her face, eyes wide, reading.

"What is it?" Pete said.

Without looking up, Carmen fell to her knees in the middle of the kitchen and began to cry.

THE END

Printed in the United States
by Baker & Taylor Publisher Services

Printed in the United States
by Baker & Taylor Publisher Services